WIT— for Chrissie Manby

...nd addictive read will make you laugh – a lot!'
Closer

'I've been a fan of Manby's writing for years and thoroughly
enjoyed this'
Daily Mail

'Perfect, unputdownable summer adventures'
Jenny Colgan

'Manby's novels are made for holidays'
Glamour

'Nothing short of brilliant'
Marie Claire

'Funny and inventive'
Company

'Destined to keep you up until the small hours'
Daily Mirror

'What a wonderfully lighthearted and uplifting novel'
Bloglovin

'Heartwarming . . . truly funny'
The Bookbag

'[This novel] was funny and emotional, it was heartwarming,
it was so genuine and realistic and it is a MUST READ this
autumn. Highly recommended!'
On My Bookshelf

Also by Chrissie Manby

Flatmates
Second Prize
Deep Heat
Lizzie Jordan's Secret Life
Running Away From Richard
Getting Personal
Seven Sunny Days
Girl Meets Ape
Ready Or Not?
The Matchbreaker
Marrying for Money
Spa Wars
Crazy in Love
Getting Over Mr Right
Kate's Wedding
What I Did On My Holidays
Writing for Love (ebook only)
A Proper Family Holiday
A Proper Family Christmas
A Proper Family Adventure
A Wedding at Christmas
A Fairy Tale for Christmas
The Worst Case Scenario Cookery Club

About the author

Chrissie Manby is the author of twenty-four romantic comedy novels and a guide for aspiring writers, *Writing for Love*. She was nominated for the Melissa Nathan Award for Comedy Romance in 2011 for *Getting Over Mr Right*. Raised in Gloucester, Chrissie now lives in London.

You can follow her on Twitter @chrissiemanby
or visit her website to find out more:
www.chrissiemanby.com

Once in a Lifetime

Chrissie Manby

HODDER

First published in Great Britain in 2018 by Hodder & Stoughton
An Hachette UK company

1

Copyright © Chrissie Manby 2018

A CIP catalogue record for this title is available from the British Library

Paperback ISBN 9781473682931
eBook ISBN 9781473682948

Typeset in Sabon MT by Palimpsest Book Production Ltd, Falkirk, Stirlingshire

Printed and bound in Great Britain by Clays Ltd, Elcograf S.p.A.

Hodder & Stoughton policy is to use papers that are natural, renewable and
recyclable products and made from wood grown in sustainable forests. The
logging and manufacturing processes are expected to conform to the
environmental regulations of the country of origin.

Hodder & Stoughton Ltd
Carmelite House
50 Victoria Embankment
London EC4Y 0DZ

www.hodder.co.uk

This one's for Jane Wright.

Chapter One

The kitchen of The Majestic Hotel, Newbay.
Saturday, 29 June 1996

'Where is he?' Dani asked.

'He's out the back having a fag,' said Julie.

'Great. Keep him out there for a couple more minutes, will you?'

'How am I supposed to do that?'

'I dunno. Try talking to him?'

Tutting like she'd been asked to do something really difficult, Julie the waitress headed for the kitchen's back door and the row of enormous metal dustbins that constituted The Majestic Hotel's staff outdoor 'rest area'. Meanwhile Dani stayed behind to put the finishing touches to the cake. It was the most ambitious she'd ever tried but it was Nat's eighteenth birthday and if an eighteenth birthday didn't merit a truly great cake, then what did?

Dani carefully lifted the Tupperware cake-box from the larder shelf, where Dave the chef had let her stash it for the duration of service. Now service was over. The last of the evening's punters, a bunch of noisy friends celebrating a fortieth, had moved from the restaurant into the hotel's bar, where they were shaking their impossibly aged booties to the strains of the 'Macarena'.

'Impressive.' Dave the chef nodded as Dani unveiled her creation.

'Took me three days,' said Dani, settling the cake on a stand borrowed from the hotel's tea service. 'I used twenty-four eggs. Mum was doing her nut.'

'It was worth it,' said Dave. 'You're very good at this, you know. You should think about doing it professionally.'

Dani grinned. Coming from Dave the chef, that was praise indeed. But there was only one person whose opinion really mattered tonight.

It may have taken Dani three days to make Nat's birthday cake but she'd been thinking about the design a whole lot longer. She'd gone with a chocolate base, of course. That was definitely Nat's favourite. She didn't have to worry about getting that right. But after that? She'd spent evening after evening flicking through her mother's old baking books for inspiration but could find nothing that was quite 'Nat' enough.

Nat wouldn't want sugar flowers or a golf course complete with bunkers fashioned from royal icing. He was eighteen. He was an indie music fan who delighted in discovering ever more obscure bands. He liked reading science fiction and spouting off on political ideologies he didn't really know much about. He would be off to Bristol University to study philosophy in September. When he wasn't wearing his Majestic Hotel waiter's uniform, he wore tattered T-shirts (one with a picture of Che Guevara on it was his favourite). His nickname among The Majestic's staff was Frank, as in Frankenstein's monster, on account of his impressive height and square jaw.

Nat didn't mind being called Frank. At least, that's what Dani hoped, since in the end she'd themed his cake around his nickname. Two layers of chocolate sponge, sandwiched together with a rich raspberry-flavoured ganache, were covered with a sheet of green fondant icing. Dani had made a tattered black skirt for the cake from crepe paper, to look like the monster's hair. Two enormous gob-stoppers formed the monster's bulging eyes. The green icing was decorated here and there with black icing 'scars' that oozed blood made from raspberry jam. Now Dani placed eighteen black candles around the edges and the cake was complete. Just as Julie ran back into the kitchen.

'He's finished his cigarette!' Julie yelled as though sounding a fire alarm.

Dave the chef handed Dani his own cigarette lighter – his precious Zippo from Las Vegas – with which to light the candles.

'Everybody ready?' asked Dani.

Julie quickly gathered the kitchen and waiting staff around the huge stainless-steel table in the middle of the room. Dave turned off the main lights.

Nat walked in, wiping his feet on the mat as he always did. He was a well brought-up boy.

'What's going on?' he asked, finding the kitchen in darkness.

'Ta-daa!' The last of the candles was lit.

'Happy birthday!' the Majestic crew shouted.

Dani led the singing.

Nat paused on the kitchen mat as though frozen. He looked at his watch. Two minutes past midnight. It really was his birthday at last.

The light from the eighteen candles made Dani look more beautiful than ever. And if he needed proof that she liked him, here it was. She really liked him. She had made him a cake. Never mind that the decoration was a mickey-take on a nickname he hated. She had made him a cake because she cared. Dani Parker cared for him. It was all Nat could do not to burst into tears.

'*Happy Birthday to yooooouuuuuu!*'

The song rose to its traditional crescendo. Dave the chef harmonised the baritone.

'Make a wish,' someone shouted as Nat blew out the candles.

Nat didn't need to wonder what to wish for. He knew exactly what he wanted right then. And someone somewhere must have been listening, because seconds later Dani Parker leaned over the unconventionally wonderful cake she'd made for his big day and gave him a kiss.

'Happy birthday,' she whispered as her soft lips touched his cheek.

For once, it really was.

Chapter Two

Dani's kitchen, 15 Schooner Crescent, Newbay. Saturday, 19 May 2018

'Mum!' Dani shouted. 'Have you seen my Wilton 48 basket weave?'

'Your what, love?'

'My Wilton 48 . . . Oh, never mind. I'll find it.'

Dani continued to rifle through the kitchen drawers for just the right icing nozzle. Her mother Jane appeared in the kitchen doorway and watched her throwing discarded cake-decoration tools onto the counter top.

'That looks really beautiful,' Jane said, nodding at the cake on the table. 'Flossie's going to love it.'

'I hope so,' said Dani, finding the Wilton 48 at last. She held it up triumphantly. 'This is the one.'

'I can't believe she's nearly sixteen,' Jane continued. 'Makes me feel quite old.'

'How do you think it makes me feel?' said Dani. 'Seems like I only just left school and in two years my daughter will be old enough to vote.'

'Heaven help us when she does,' said Jane.

'What time is it?' Dani asked.

'Ten to eleven.' Jane read from the delicate watch she'd had since she was first married, some forty-odd years before.

'Aaaagh,' said Dani. She was running out of time to

finish the cake. It was hard finding a moment when Flossie and her awful new boyfriend Jed weren't in the house. Specifically, when they weren't in the kitchen, going through the fridge, the bread-bin, the freezer and the cabinets like they hadn't eaten in months. Jed was six feet five and had hollow legs.

That morning, however, Flossie was at her best friend Xanthe's house (she'd stayed overnight so they could revise for French GCSE together) and Dani had foregone a lie-in to get to work on her daughter's sixteenth birthday surprise. Now she had to go to her day job.

'I'll finish it later.'

Dani covered the cake – a lemon sponge, Flossie's favourite – with its cloche and carefully placed it back in the pantry, which was adorned with a homemade 'Keep Out' sign. Dani was already dressed for work in the T-shirt and trousers she would swap for kitchen kit when she got there. She kissed her mother on the cheek and headed for the door.

'Do not let Flossie go anywhere near that cupboard!' was Dani's final instruction. 'Or Jed. Especially not Jed. We need something left to eat at the party.'

Jane gave her a mock salute.

'Nobody is getting near that cake!'

Minutes later, Dani was on her bicycle, heading towards the sea front. There weren't many consolations to never having quite managed to leave her hometown but living so close to the sea was one of them. Dani never tired of that moment when she was whizzing down the long hill towards the promenade with the tang of sea salt in the air. Going back *up* the hill after she'd finished her shift was another story but she'd learned to savour those precious minutes when she could stop pedalling and coast towards the waves.

At the bottom of the hill, Dani took a sharp right turn along the promenade and there was her place of work, looming like an enormous six-layer wedding cake. The Majestic Hotel.

Unchanging, enduring, eternal. The huge white stucco building was one of the little seaside town's most famous landmarks. It was as important a part of the landscape as the Victorian pier. During the nineteen twenties and thirties, it had played host to many scandalous parties. The Duchess of Windsor was said to have stayed there when she was still Wallis Simpson (a photograph in the hotel lobby purported to be the evidence, though Dani secretly thought the person dressed as Cleopatra for a fancy-dress party was just as likely to have been a man).

If only the walls of The Majestic could talk. They'd certainly know some stories. How many thousands of people had celebrated life's big moments there? How many engagements, weddings, birthday parties, even wakes, had taken place in the restaurant? For many years, 'they're having their do at The Majestic' was synonymous with 'posh' to anyone who knew Newbay.

One of Dani's own earliest memories was of being taken to the hotel's winter garden to share afternoon tea with her mother, father and grandparents. It seemed impossibly glamorous to be in that room, sitting on a gilt-covered dining chair, eating sandwiches with the crusts cut off. And as for the cakes! Oh, those cakes.

Dani could still remember the three-tiered stand the waiter had placed right in front of her. Three gold-rimmed white porcelain plates were slotted into an ornate gold frame. Sandwiches on the bottom. Scones with homemade jam and clotted cream in the middle. Cakes on the very top. Dani's mother and grandmother both claimed they'd eaten more than enough after the scones so Dani had the cake plate they were supposed to share all to herself.

There were six cakes on that plate. There was something about their miniature nature that made them extra-special. And each one was different. In the order in which Dani tasted them that long-ago day, they were: a chocolate éclair, a strawberry millefeuille, a lemon meringue tart, a Paris Brest, a slice of chocolate torte and a dome of wobbling raspberry mousse on a perfectly crisp shortbread biscuit. Heaven only knew how the three women would have divided the cakes up if Gran and Mum hadn't conceded.

When she arrived in the kitchen this May morning, nearly thirty-five years after that long-ago tea, the early shift was already hard at work on lunch. Dani nodded her 'hello's and headed for her workstation. From a wide-eyed child stuffing her face with miniature cakes, she was now the hotel's chief pastry chef. And she was always busy. The hotel had experienced a downturn in the noughties – as had many places on the English Riviera – but lately it was on the up again, thanks to a refurbishment of the fabulous 'winter garden' dining room. You had to book months in advance to get afternoon tea at a weekend.

'Morning, Dani,' said head chef Dave as Dani walked past. 'Rough night?' He always said that.

'Cheers, Dave.'

Dave the chef was the only member of staff who'd been in the kitchen as long as she had.

'How's it going?' Dani turned her attention to Joe, her assistant.

Joe stepped aside to show Dani a tray of perfectly piped meringues.

'Good work,' she said.

Joe beamed. He was excited by patisserie in a way that Dani had never been. It wasn't quite natural. Mind you, more than two decades after her first summer on the Majestic team, Dani wasn't quite so enthusiastic about anything any more.

She hadn't meant to still be here. She'd only ever intended to work at the hotel during weekends and holidays until she finished university. Then, with her degree in hand – French and Communications Studies – she should have been off to conquer the world.

But life's what happens when you make other plans, right?

She'd salvaged a pretty decent life from the wreckage of her teenage dreams, so now she felt that perhaps she was always supposed to stay in Newbay. She had a lovely family, a comfortable home, steady work, good friends and an outlet for her creativity. She was supposed to be at The Majestic. She was supposed to be right where she was.

Dani looked at the list of things she would be working on this shift: a full house for afternoon tea, two special birthday desserts for the evening's dinner service, an anniversary cake for a couple celebrating their silver wedding anniversary . . . Dani rolled up her sleeves and got cracking.

Chapter Three

Though, in general, The Majestic's staff got along quite happily, there was one member of the team who drove everyone bonkers. That was Cheryl the events manager. She was never seen without a clipboard (Dave wondered whether it was in fact part of her arm) and she was constantly poking her nose in where it wasn't wanted.

'With all due respect,' she would say if anyone challenged her judgement, 'I do have a *degree* in hospitality.' And thus her word was final. Even if she was pronouncing on someone else's area of expertise. Such as in the kitchen.

Dave the chef refused to have anything to do with Cheryl after an incident during which she came into the restaurant and tasted a delicate consommé he was preparing for an event. Specifically, she tasted it *without* his permission, using a *wooden* spoon, which she allowed to fall back into the pot. She then had the cheek to suggest that Dave added more seasoning.

After an altercation that almost ended in disciplinary action all round, Cheryl agreed that all future requests to the kitchen would go via Dani. Cheryl herself would venture no further than the serving hatch unless officially invited.

She was at the serving hatch now, clipboard in hand.

'Dani,' said Cheryl. 'I wonder if I could borrow you for a minute or two? There's a customer here thinking of planning a birthday party celebration event.' Cheryl never used two words when she could use four. 'I said you'd be the one to talk to about the menu and the celebratory birthday party cake?'

'My pleasure.'

Dani quickly wiped the flour off her hands and followed Cheryl out into the dining room. As they walked, Cheryl briefed her.

'I need you to understand that this is a very important VIP client and we hope to be doing much more business of this kind with him and his extended family in the future so it would be most expedient if you could . . .'

For once, Dani didn't even notice that Cheryl was doubling up on VIP and using 'expedient' in the wrong context again. She was staring at the man in the dining room.

Cheryl's 'very important VIP' customer had his back turned to the kitchen doors as he looked out of the restaurant's vast windows to the grey sea beyond. Twenty-two years may have passed since Dani last saw him, and he had certainly made some sartorial changes since then – probably a good thing – but she recognised him at once. Her heart made a bid for escape through her mouth.

'Nat?' she asked, hardly trusting herself to say his name. 'Nat Hayward?'

He turned around. It *was* him.

'Nat! No way!'

Cheryl looked from Dani to her customer and back again as Nat's face broke into a grin. Meanwhile, Dani felt as though she might be about to fall over. Her legs had turned to jelly. Ridiculous.

'Dani Parker! You're still in Newbay?'

'Yes,' she said, desperately trying to act casual. 'And, and . . . so are you?'

'Just come back,' he said. 'Well, a few months ago actually. My dad's . . . Oh, I'll tell you later.'

Cheryl was standing between them with her clipboard.

'You two know each other?' Cheryl asked.

'We worked here together,' said Nat. 'Can you believe it?'

'*You* worked *here*?'

It was clear that Cheryl was surprised.

'Just for a summer.'

Nat of the Che Guevara T-shirt was long gone. His floppy fringe was just a memory. As was quite a bit of his hair, Dani observed. He was wearing a perfectly fitted navy blue blazer over his pristine blue jeans. He wore a pale pink shirt with a collar (he'd sworn that once he left Newbay for university, he would never wear a shirt with a collar again, let alone a pink one). On his feet were brown leather deck shoes – footwear about which he had always been so scathing. 'Shoes for people who never go near a boat.'

Nat's family ran a fleet of pleasure boats out of Newbay harbour.

'When was it, Dani? 1997?' Nat asked.

''Ninety-six,' she said.

'I'd just finished school,' said Nat to Cheryl. 'I was waiting to go to university. You had another couple of years left to go, didn't you?'

Dani nodded. 'A-Levels.'

Nat continued. 'We were waiting staff in this very restaurant for the summer season. We did all the weddings. I was hopeless.'

'I'm sure you weren't,' said Cheryl politely.

'No, I was. Always dropping things. Getting orders mixed up. Luckily, I had Dani here to rescue me, unless she'd been seconded by the pastry chef and spirited off to the kitchen. Where . . .'

'I remain to this very day,' Dani finished the sentence for him.

'Gosh, it's good to see you. It's been a long time.'

'Certainly has,' said Dani.

For a moment, holding each other's gaze as though they were alone, they stood in silence. Yet there was so much to say. And most of it would be about the events of just one day.

'A-hem,' said Cheryl, who was clearly keen to get on with organising this very important VIP celebratory birthday party event. 'Well, isn't it lovely that you've met again? A good omen, I think. Shall we run through exactly what it is Mr Hayward wants from us here?'

'Of course,' said Dani.

'It's a thirtieth birthday celebration party,' said Cheryl, flicking through the pages on her clipboard.

'For my girlfriend,' said Nat.

'Oh.'

Dani did her best not to look disappointed by the fact Nat had a girlfriend – though, of course he wasn't single. Why would he be? – or surprised by the girlfriend's age.

'Her name is Lola.'

'L-O-L-A Lola . . .' Dani couldn't help herself. They'd sung The Kinks' song all the time that long-ago summer. Dave the chef had one of their CDs on repeat in the kitchen.

Nat nodded.

'Her dad loved the song. Which is supposedly about a transvestite, I know, but . . .'

'Moving swiftly on . . .' said Cheryl. 'Mr Hayward's celebratory birthday party event of eighteen invited guests and family members will be having dinner here in the restaurant, at the end of which they shall certainly be needing a celebratory birthday cake.' Cheryl rustled through the papers attached to her clipboard again. 'I have already shown Mr Hayward pictures of some of the cakes you have made in the past and he particularly likes the idea of a cake of the chocolate varietal.'

'I know you make a good one,' Nat said.

'I hope I make a better one now,' said Dani.

'So,' Cheryl continued. 'A chocolate celebration cake . . .'

'Three tiers with cream and ganache?' Dani suggested. 'Do you want a classic glossy covering, like a Viennese torte, or is there a theme you'd like me to try to represent in the decoration?'

'Just a glossy covering and thirty gold candles?' Nat suggested.

'Good choice,' said Dani. 'Simple. Classy.'

'Like your partner, I'm sure,' Cheryl sucked up to her potential client. 'Ms Parker will do her best to ensure that the aforementioned desired cake is exactly to your requirements.' She turned to Dani. 'The dimensions for a cake for eighteen people are . . .'

'I know what they are,' said Dani, suddenly needing to be somewhere else. Being in front of Nat like this, totally unprepared, was awkward to say the least. Being asked to make a cake for his girlfriend's birthday was just surreal.

'You've got the price in one of your spreadsheets I

think. I'd better get back to the kitchen. Those éclairs won't make themselves.'

'It's great to see you again,' said Nat, reaching out to shake her hand.

To *shake her hand*? Dani closed her eyes for just a second. If her sixteen-year-old self could have seen . . .

'I'm a bit sticky,' she said, snapping back from her reverie and waving her fingers at him.

'I hope we catch up properly soon,' Nat said.

'Yes,' Dani nodded. 'I'll see you around, I'm sure. Newbay's not exactly huge.'

'No,' said Nat.

'Mr Hayward, perhaps I can take you through the possibilities for celebratory floral arrangements now.'

Cheryl was already whisking Nat back into the hotel's cocktail bar, where she would run through the rest of the details over a pot of complimentary filter coffee and, possibly, if Nat's budget was looking big enough, one of the kitchen's delicious éclairs.

As Dani made her way back to the kitchen, she glanced over her shoulder to see Nat one more time. Cheryl was still yakking away. But Nat was looking back at Dani with that smile. Just like he used to when they were sharing a private joke on a busy shift. Twenty-two years fell away.

Chapter Four

Nat Hayward.

Dani knew who Nathan 'Nat' Hayward was long before they ended up on the same waiting team at The Majestic. He went to the boys' grammar that was the 'brother' school to the girls' High School Dani attended. From time to time, the two schools joined forces to put on musical extravaganzas that required players of both sexes. Starved of male attention, Dani signed up for every one.

In the winter of 1995, when GCSEs still seemed a hundred years away, Dani was in the chorus of a production of *HMS Pinafore*. Nat was in the joint school orchestra providing the music. She noticed him at once and kept on noticing him. He looked so cool despite his slightly too-small sixth-form blazer and prefect's tie. Dani missed her cue a couple of times because her attention wandered from the action on stage to the orchestra pit.

On the last night of the play's run, the cast and orchestra were all invited to a party hosted by 'Call Me Mike', the drama teacher from the boys' school who had brought the production together. Dani spent the evening planning how she would talk to the shy but gorgeous 'Nat the Oboe guy' but by the time she worked out her opening line, he was gone.

Then there he was again six months later: the only boy on The Majestic's summer weekend waiting team.

He sat at the back of the first training meeting, with his fringe hanging over his eyes. Still shy. Still gorgeous. As soon as she saw him, Dani knew she was going to love her new job.

She was right. Every working shift felt like playtime, with in-jokes and pranks a-plenty. The team worked together and socialised together, at weekends heading from the restaurant to the nearby Mariner's pub, where the landlord would serve anyone who looked older than twelve. The lock-ins at The Mariner's were legendary. Dani told her parents that her Saturday shifts at The Majestic didn't end until one in the morning and hoped they would already be asleep as she weaved her way upstairs when she got home.

Less than eight hours later, Dani might be back at the hotel for another shift but no hangover could dull the prospect of another day with Nat and the gang. She always bounded into work, as though she would have paid for the privilege of being there. Just being near him.

Over the years, she'd thought about him, of course. But after that summer when he was waiting to go to university and she had two years of A-levels ahead, she only occasionally heard actual news of him. He was a superstar at university, just as he had been at school. He was definitely on course for a first. He was playing oboe in a radical, experimental jazz band. He had a girlfriend. Seemed serious about her. They'd moved to London together. He got a great job . . .

Everything she knew about Nat had come to her second-hand. She wondered what he'd heard about her in return.

Dani had flunked her A-levels. She stayed behind in Newbay for another year for re-sits. Eventually went to her fifth-choice university. She changed course three times. She got mixed up with the wrong crowd. Got herself a boyfriend called Lloyd, who chipped away at her personality like he was trying to sculpt her into a mouse. Their relationship made it difficult for her to concentrate on her academic work. Then she got pregnant at twenty-one and didn't finish her degree anyway.

By the time Flossie was born, Lloyd was already off the scene. Dani had to move back in with her parents. Then Dani's dad died suddenly of a heart attack and it was just her and Flossie and her mum. Dani had no idea life could be so hard.

It was easier now, Dani admitted. Flossie was nearly launched. She *liked* her mum as well as loved her. That helped with all three of them living in such close quarters. The Majestic management treated her well. Most days, she thought she was lucky. Then . . .

Nat's visit to the restaurant was one of those moments when the life Dani might have had edged aside the lid on its battered coffin and peeped out like the ghost of summer past. A summer past that Nat had described merely in terms of their working together.

Getting ready for bed that night, Dani stood in front of the bathroom mirror and gave herself an instant face-lift by pulling the skin back from her jaw. She wondered what Nat had made of their strange reunion. Was she on his mind as he was on hers? Dani frowned. If she *was* on Nat's mind, he would be thinking 'dodged a bullet there'. He had a thirty-year-old girlfriend.

Thirty years old. Nat's girlfriend Lola – who was

most definitely not a transvestite – was ten years younger than he was. Eight years younger than Dani.

Of course, at thirty it wasn't as though Nat's girlfriend was really all *that* young at all but Dani was still a little surprised. Eighteen-year-old Nat would have claimed that he wanted a peer. A true partner in life.

Though being thirty didn't mean Lola wasn't Nat's intellectual peer. A thirty-year-old wasn't a child. It was the age at which loads of people were marrying, becoming parents, planning to be partners at big city law firms . . . There were thirty-year-old surgeons, CEOs and politicians. To have attracted Nat's attention, Lola must be one of that breed of thirty-year-old. A high achiever. Someone who was going places. A businesswoman. Where did he meet her? What did she do? What did she look like?

Nat Hayward's girlfriend was about to turn thirty. That meant that when Nat and Dani were working at The Majestic together back in 1996, Lola was just eight years old. While Dani and Nat were listening to obscure indie bands no one outside the band members' families had really heard of, Lola was probably prancing up and down in her parents' sitting room, pretending to be one of the Spice Girls. Which of the Spice Girls would Nat have been attracted to? It was hard to imagine that the Nat Dani once knew would have been attracted to any of them.

But time moves on and people change. Every cell in our bodies is renewed every seven years. Isn't that the theory? Nat wasn't the eighteen-year-old Dani had been in love with. Just as she was no longer Dani the sixteen-year-old who was going to conquer the world. She was Dani the thirty-eight-year-old, single *mother* to a sixteen-year-old. Who was just at that moment coming in. And trying hard not to make any noise as she did so. Flossie was late home.

'Flossie?' Dani poked her head around the bathroom door as Flossie tried to get upstairs without drawing her mother's or grandmother's attention.

'Mum,' Flossie put on a slightly manic smile. 'I thought you'd be in bed.'

'I'll bet you did. What time is it?' Dani asked.

'It's late, I know. But the bus was really slow tonight. It's high season. The town is full of pensioners who need help getting on and off. The driver kept having to put the ramp down. It took forever.'

As excuses went, that was a new one.

'What did you get up to tonight?' Dani asked.

'We were round at Xanthe's again? Revising?' Flossie's rising tone made the statements into questions.

'Were her parents there?'

'Later they were. They went to a party for a bit.'

'Was Jed with you?'

'For a little while. He met up with some of his mates.'

'At the pub?'

Flossie shrugged. 'I don't know?'

That rising tone again.

'You didn't go with him, did you?'

Flossie shook her head. 'No. I know I'm not allowed. Besides, too much revision . . .'

Dani was pretty sure Flossie was lying but she didn't press her on it.

'I'm going to bed,' she said instead. 'Don't stay up too late, will you, sweetheart? You can do too much cramming, you know.'

'I won't. I'm really tired,' said Flossie. Dani went to kiss her. Flossie quickly turned her face so that Dani caught her on the ear. Trying to make sure Dani didn't smell any fumes, she guessed.

'Drink a glass of water before you go to bed,' Dani suggested.

Flossie nodded. 'I will.' Then she smiled the smile that always melted Dani's heart. 'I only had two halves of lager,' she suddenly admitted. 'At Xanthe's house. And only because it's nearly my birthday.'

'At which point you will still be two years off being allowed to drink legally.'

'Not in France.'

Flossie had an answer for anything.

'*We're* not in France,' Dani reminded her.

'Perhaps we could pretend we are?' Flossie said in a terrible French accent.

Dani couldn't help laughing. Oh, her beautiful daughter. Her beautiful funny daughter. She could always find a way to make Dani smile. Sometimes Dani couldn't believe that after all the things she had got wrong in her life, she had managed to make something so right.

Chapter Five

The following day was Flossie's sixteenth birthday. As was the family tradition, the birthday girl got to have breakfast in bed. Flossie requested pancakes. She'd had pancakes every year since she was six. This year they had to be vegan. Fortunately, Dani was well versed in adapting just about any recipe in line with food allergies and preferences. Vegan pancakes were no trouble at all.

Jane and Dani sat on the end of Flossie's bed while she opened her cards. For the past twelve months, Dani had assumed Flossie would want a fancy new phone as her birthday gift but Flossie had changed her mind about wanting new tech. She'd changed her mind about a lot of things.

Up until the end of her pre-GCSE year – year ten – Flossie seemed to have pretty much the normal teenage concerns. She spent all her allowance in Top Shop and Primark. After school her best friends Xanthe and Camilla would come over to watch on-line make-up tutorials and give each other makeovers (and conjunctivitis, when they shared an old mascara). On Friday nights, they would go to the local youth drama group and try out their new looks on their male peers, who seemed mostly bewildered by the girls' emerging beauty.

But at some point during the second term of year

eleven, Flossie, Xanthe and Camilla declared they were no longer interested in drama. The lads from the youth group were far too immature. Especially when compared with the gang from the sixth form college that hung out in the Newbay Arts Centre café.

Though she didn't like the idea of these new, older pals at all, Dani knew she couldn't keep Flossie from the café. All Flossie's friends went there and Camilla's mother, who volunteered at the Arts Centre, assured Dani that none of them would ever be served an alcoholic drink. Still Dani could only listen with concern as one particular name cropped up in Flossie's conversation with increasing regularity.

'Jed says . . . Jed told me . . . Jed thinks . . .'

Until Dani dared to ask, 'Floss, is this Jed chap your *boyfriend*?'

Flossie's response was immediate and enthusiastic.

'Oh Mum! I really think he likes me!'

Overnight, Flossie changed her image to match that of her new paramour. She told Dani that Jed didn't like make-up because even if the end product hadn't been tested on animals, most of the ingredients had. He didn't like fast fashion. It was exploitative, expensive and polluting. He didn't like commercial music. Commercial music relied too heavily on old-fashioned, sexist social tropes. Of course Jed was a feminist.

'He's a bigger feminist than any woman I know!' Flossie exclaimed.

Dani had to admit she was glad when Flossie ditched the heavy make-up, which made her look old enough to get into trouble. She was also glad when Flossie stopped spending all her cash on clothes she'd only wear for one Insta-pic. And she was positively delighted when Flossie stopped listening to awful dance music that necessitated grinding like a pole dancer, swapping it for songs with actual tunes played on proper instruments.

All the same, Dani wasn't sure what she thought about the degree to which the opinions of Flossie's new boyfriend seemed to be infiltrating every part of Flossie's life. And he was eighteen. Just two years and a month older than Flossie, but at that age it might as well have been a decade. When she found out about the age gap, Dani said she would only allow Flossie to continue to see him on condition that she brought him home to be vetted.

On first impressions, Jed was pretty much what Dani had expected. He was what she would have called a 'crusty' back in the nineties. If Flossie looked as though she had jumped straight out of the laundry basket in her crumpled dingy 'eco' clothes, Jed looked as though he dressed exclusively from wheelie bins. The rips in his jeans were less artful than awful. His oversized sweater was shiny with grease at the cuffs and the collar. His hair was matted. He basically looked as though he could do with a good wash. Alas, detergents were one of the things Jed disagreed with.

Over tea and cake in Dani's kitchen, Jed held forth. He was passionate about animal welfare, human rights and living a green life. But while his ideologies were sound, the way he delivered them was a little self-important. Dani couldn't help but feel harangued. Especially when he tried to tell her – while stuffing himself with homemade Victoria sponge – that it was a crime against future generations to use anything except ancestral grains.

'What do you mean by ancestral?' Dani asked.

'Spelt. Quinoa.'

'Makes a terrible sponge, quinoa,' Dani said.

After their first meeting, Dani would have been quite happy to see the back of Jed right away. But could she veto him on the grounds of being pompous?

'He comes from a really nice family,' Flossie assured her. 'His dad is a lawyer and his mum's a doctor.'

Dani was ashamed to admit those facts helped to put her mind at rest. He had a lawyer for a dad? His mum was a doctor? How bad could he be?

However, the next time Jed came over, Dani insisted that Jane be in to meet him too, so she could get a second opinion. Jane called for back-up in the form of her best friend Sarah, Dani's godmother, who lived in the house next door. If anyone would get the measure of Jed, it was Sarah.

Dani laid out the minus points. 'For a start, he's too old.'

Sarah played devil's advocate. The age gap between Jed and Flossie wasn't all that big in the scheme of things, she said. And underneath the grime he looked young and fit and clear-eyed. He seemed sensible. Far from encouraging Flossie to drink underage, Jed had refused the small glass of wine that Dani offered him at Sunday lunch.

Jane added that she'd read in the *Telegraph* that young people were much more conservative these days and actually far less likely to drink, smoke or do drugs than their parents' generation.

And yet . . .

'He's changing Flossie,' Dani complained to her mother when they were alone.

'Isn't it good that he seems to be making her think more seriously about the world?' Jane asked.

'Well, yes,' Dani admitted. 'But she's always pros-elytising now. She seems to have lost her sense of humour.'

'There comes a moment in every parent's life when they find their child's sense of humour bewildering,' said Jane. 'She's doing well at school. She still seems to want to spend time with us. I think, considering she's a teenager, that's pretty much all we can hope for. And she's happy to bring Jed home. If he really were that bad, I don't suppose we'd have even heard about him.

'I think we need to give this young Jed chap a chance,' Jane concluded. 'If you make a fuss about him and try to tell Flossie she shouldn't be seeing him, the chances are you'll only make her more determined that he's the love of her life. Just as you had your heart set on a number of unsuitable chaps back in the day.'

Whose names she couldn't even recall. Apart from Nat Hayward.

'She's very much like you, is Flossie,' said Jane. 'She's stubborn as an ox. But she's not stupid. If Jed is a waste of space, she'll work it out in the end.'

So Jed, for now, got to stay.

Chapter Six

Flossie went straight to the Arts Centre café for coffee after her birthday breakfast so that Dani could finish making her 'secret' cake. When she returned, Flossie had in tow her two best girl friends, Xanthe and Camilla, who had also embraced the grunge aesthetic since swapping the youth drama group for the Arts Centre café. The three girls looked like extras from a *Pirates of the Caribbean* movie that afternoon, with their shabby clothes and multiple piercings.

Thank goodness Flossie was slightly wary of needles and had only managed to get two traditional lobe piercings and a single hoop high on the rim of her left ear. Camilla had a new piercing, though, Dani observed, a nose-ring of the kind seen mostly on bulls.

'All right, Mrs P,' Xanthe and Camilla chorused.

'Ms,' said Dani. 'It's Ms.'

'Mizz is really difficult to say,' said Xanthe.

'Perhaps it is with a tongue ring,' Dani replied.

Xanthe self-consciously fiddled with the stud that pierced her tongue. She'd already chipped one of her front teeth.

The girls were invited for lunch to celebrate Flossie's big day. They would be joined by grandmother Jane, godmother Sarah and, eventually, Jed, who was going to be a little late. Something to do with picking up Flossie's present, she told Dani excitedly.

Flossie led her friends straight into the kitchen, where she pulled a bottle of cava out of the fridge.

'Can we have this?' she asked her mum.

'You're sixteen, not eighteen,' Dani protested.

'Oh, come on,' said Flossie. 'You know you got this for me really. And you're allowed to have alcohol with a meal at home when you're four.'

'Five,' Dani corrected her.

'Well, I'm well over that.'

'Being under age never stopped you from having a drink, Dani,' Sarah observed as she let herself in through the back door. Sarah's garden was joined to the Parker house by a gate, which Dani's dad had fitted so that Dani could go back and forth as a child. Dani was long since grown up but the gate had stayed. It was as convenient for the adults as it had been for the children. Jane and Sarah were always in each other's kitchens. 'Oh, the times I saw you rolling home!'

'Sarah, you're supposed to be on my side,' Dani said.

All the same, Dani popped the top of the cava and poured out six very small glassfuls of the glittering liquid.

'Oooh! Cava! Don't mind if I do,' said Jane, joining the others at the table.

'Happy birthday, Flossie darling,' she raised a toast to her granddaughter.

'Happy birthday,' the others joined in.

'Sweet sixteen,' said Sarah. 'And don't you all look . . . unusual,' she added, taking a proper look at Flossie's pals. 'New piercing, Camilla?'

'Yes, Auntie Sarah.' All the girls called Sarah 'Auntie'. 'It's gone a bit septic.'

Sarah took a large swig from her glass as if to wash down the thought.

'What are we having for supper, Mrs P?' Xanthe asked.

'Flossie's favourite,' said Dani. 'A vegetable lasagne.'

'With vegan cheese, right?' Xanthe confirmed.

'Of course. Everything on the table is vegan tonight. No need to worry about any of it.'

Xanthe nodded approvingly. 'My mum doesn't bother,' she said. 'She tries to tell me she's giving me vegan cheddar but I can so tell it's not. I said to her, Mum, this cheese smells of death.'

'Hmmm,' said Dani.

'And that death smell seeps out through your pores when you eat it,' Camilla added.

'Really?' said Sarah. 'I eat a lot of cheese. Do I smell like death?'

Sarah lifted her wrist towards Flossie to be sniffed.

'You always smell of Fracas, Auntie Sarah,' Flossie said.

'Well, there will be no pore-seeping here,' said Dani, wondering what arch-vegan Jed was eating to make him smell like silage. 'This is all one hundred per cent vegetable matter.'

'That didn't used to be a good thing,' said Sarah.

The three girls and the two older women sat down at the table and started tucking into the vegan canapés Dani had prepared that morning. There were little vegan crackers topped with olive tapenade, smoked mushroom pâté, celery with cashew nut cheese (which was a very poor substitute for Philadelphia, thought Dani, but if it was what Flossie wanted).

Jane went for some celery. 'Oh,' she said, barely hiding her disappointment at the lack of cheesy taste. 'These are . . . er, different.'

'What is this supposed to be?' Sarah asked, holding a cracker topped with mushroom pâté aloft.

'Magic mushroom paste,' Dani joked.

'Oh good,' said Sarah. 'Haven't had that in a long while.'

'You took magic mushrooms?' Xanthe looked shocked.

'In the sixties. It was the only way to make any sense of the music,' Sarah replied.

'Auntie Sarah is pulling your leg,' said Jane. 'The sixties didn't happen in Newbay.'

'Speak for yourself,' Sarah said.

Dani carried on preparing the rest of the meal while Flossie and her guests chatted happily. Sarah handed over a birthday gift of a bottle of Chanel No. 5. 'As Coco Chanel said, a woman who doesn't wear perfume has no future.'

Dani was relieved that Flossie accepted the gift with grace rather than a lecture on parabens. In this room full of women – young and of a certain age – Dani felt very happy. Friends told her that their teenage daughters wanted nothing to do with them, so Dani was proud that Flossie felt she did want to bring her pals home. Dani hoped Flossie would always feel able to be as free in her presence as she seemed to be now.

'So, Mum,' Flossie announced through a mouthful of cracker and tapenade. 'Xanthe and Camilla have clubbed together to get me the best birthday present ever.'

Xanthe and Camilla shared a complicit glance and grinned.

'What's that?' Dani asked, walking over to the table

and placing a rainbow-coloured salad in the middle of the cloth.

'Guess,' said Flossie, immediately stealing a cherry tomato from the bowl. 'You too, Gran and Auntie Sarah. You have a guess as well. What would be the best birthday present ever?'

Sarah jumped straight in. 'For me, it would be a night of passion with Alfie Boe.'

'Ugh!' said Flossie. 'Too much information. Gran?'

'Well, the best present anyone could get *me* right now would be a pair of smart yet fashionable boots that can accommodate a bunion,' said Jane.

The three young women grimaced. Bunions were still happily well outside their frame of reference.

'Mum?'

'I'd like a new bicycle,' said Dani. 'One with two wheels in actual alignment. But what would be the best present for you, Flossie.' Dani tapped her bottom lip as she thought about it. 'Gift vouchers for Top Shop?'

'Mum, *no one* goes to Top Shop any more.' Flossie was outraged. 'Didn't you learn anything when we watched *The True Cost*? Fast fashion is like the worst thing for the environment and it's supported by deeply unethical working practices.'

Xanthe and Camilla both nodded.

'I suppose that rules out Primark vouchers too,' Dani quipped.

Flossie feigned despair. 'How can you even say the word?'

'Vouchers?'

'Primark.'

'You used to love Primark.'

'Before I was *woke*.'

'Don't you mean awake?' asked Jane.

'*Woke*,' said Flossie. 'Grandma, it's woke.'

'This is fun,' said Sarah.

'Oh go on then,' said Dani, also wondering whether Flossie was using 'woke' in the right context. She'd already had a lecture on the word from Jed. 'I give up. What have you two lovely girls bought Flossie for her birthday?'

Dani popped a cracker with tapenade into her mouth as she waited for the answer.

Flossie's eyes sparkled as she announced, 'They're paying for me to have a tattoo!'

'What? A tattoo? No they're bloody not,' Dani spat cracker crumbs all over the table. 'Not happening. Over my dead body.'

'It's my body actually,' said Flossie.

'And it's illegal. You have to be eighteen.'

Not that that had stopped Flossie's mates. Both Xanthe and Camilla were tattooed. Someone in the Newbay tattoo business wasn't very diligent about checking his customers' ID.

'You can't have a tattoo at school,' Dani protested.

'Mum, I'm going to be leaving school in a couple of weeks. You can have whatever you like at sixth form college. They don't check. Besides I'll have it somewhere I can hide it. Like Xanthe and Mills do.'

'Then what's the point of having a tattoo at all?' Dani asked.

'Because I want one?'

'Well, sometimes I want to smoke a great big spliff,' said Dani. 'But you can't always get what you want . . .'

'Oh, I know where you can get . . .' Camilla began, before Sarah gave her a look that said, 'Not now, dear.'

'Mum, it's really not that big a deal,' Flossie continued. 'In many aboriginal cultures, people get their first tattoos while they're still babies.'

'That's different. That's cultural. You're not talking about a historically based ritual. You're talking about going to one of those terrible shops near the pier. Dirty needles. Septicaemia . . .'

'We'd only let her go to the best place,' said Xanthe.

'Which place? If they're tattooing under eighteens, I'm going to report them to the police.'

'Flossie,' said Sarah, trying to bring the temperature of the debate down. 'Do you really think it's such a good idea to have a tattoo now? In a couple of years, when you're eighteen, it really will be your choice and you'll probably have a better idea of what you want the tattoo to be. It's a life-long commitment.'

'I already know what I'm getting,' said Flossie.

Dani and the others were all ears.

'I'm having a hammer and sickle.'

'What? Under a portrait of Jeremy Corbyn?' Dani asked.

'What's so funny about that?' Flossie asked.

'A hammer and sickle? For heaven's sake, Flossie. Do you even know what that stands for?'

'I'm not stupid, Mum.'

'I wish you'd prove it.'

Flossie's birthday party was fast turning into a disaster and the vegan lasagne wasn't even out of the oven.

'Dani,' said Jane. 'Flossie. Please. We've got guests. Let's talk about this tomorrow. This is a birthday party. Nobody wants to have a fight.'

'I'm enjoying it,' said Sarah.

Dani shot her daughter's godmother a look.

Thank goodness, the ringing of the doorbell interrupted the argument.

'That'll be Jed,' said Flossie, jumping up and rushing for the door.

'I wonder what he's got her as a gift,' Dani hissed. 'A clitoral piercing?'

Xanthe and Camilla were agog.

'I understand they're rather good,' said Sarah.

'Oh oh oh!' Jane covered her ears. 'Sarah, please!'

But Jed had not bought Flossie a clitoral piercing for her birthday. Oh no. It was far far worse than that.

Dani's blood pressure started to rise again as she heard her daughter's excited 'ohmygodding' from the hall.

'Oh my god, Jed. This is the best! This is the absolute best. This is the best best best best present on planet earth!'

By now, Dani was actually hoping Jed had just bought Flossie a couple of giant spliffs. Anything would be better than a hammer and sickle tattoo. For their part Xanthe and Camilla couldn't wait a moment longer to find out what Jed had really bought their dear friend. They headed into the hall. Jane, Sarah and Dani followed. And there was Jed's birthday gift. On the floor. In a cardboard box.

'Mum! Gran! Look at this! It's the best present ever!' Flossie cried. 'Jed has gone and bought me a puppy!'

Chapter Seven

Dani did not know what to do. She wanted to scream. She opened her mouth as though she might scream but no one was taking any notice. The girls, Jed, Sarah and Jane all crowded around Flossie, who was now holding the puppy in her arms. A little ball of thick brown curls, studded with two glossy chocolate-button eyes and a nose like a piece of wet liquorice.

'Isn't he beautiful? He's like a teddy bear come to life. He's the best best best best birthday present in the whole world. I'm so happy I think I might cry.'

'I'm definitely going to cry,' said Dani. 'For heaven's sake, Jed. A dog?'

Everyone continued to ignore her. The puppy was just too enticing. As Flossie cradled the bundle of fluff, Jed stood behind her with his hands on her shoulders, giving the scene the air of a strange nativity.

'You always said you wanted a puppy,' Jed reminded his girlfriend.

'I know,' said Flossie. 'But I didn't think in a million years I'd actually get one. You've made me the happiest girl in the world. Look at his little nose, Gran. Look at his perfect paws!'

Flossie's friends, her godmother and her grandmother all duly cooed at the puppy's little footpads, which were still soft and smooth from never having walked outside.

The puppy was wriggling and making a squeaking sound. Flossie held him round his tummy so that his legs bicycled in the air and he strained to get close enough to lick Flossie's nose with his curling pink tongue. He wagged his tiny tail. And widdled straight onto the wall.

'Squeee!' the girls chorused.

'He's adorable,' said Sarah.

'He is a sweetie,' Jane agreed, reaching out to feel that curly fur.

'Isn't anyone going to get a wet wipe?' Dani asked.

While Dani cleared the wee from the hallway wall, the others were taking it in turn to kiss the new puppy's nose.

'You know we can't keep him,' was all Dani said when Flossie tried to make her hold the little chap. 'I'm sorry, Flossie. He's got to go back to wherever it is Jed found him. Jed, please take this dog away. Now. You've got ten seconds.'

Whenever Dani was desperate, she resorted to counting. It had worked until Flossie was six.

But now Flossie gasped as though she'd been stuck with a knife and fled upstairs with the pup. Xanthe, Camilla and Jed were right behind her. From the safety of the landing, Flossie yelled back down the stairs.

'You're ruining my birthday! Eff you!'

'Didn't I tell you that Jed would turn out to be trouble?' Dani asked Jane and Sarah when they were back in the kitchen, where Dani swigged back the last of the cava straight from the bottle.

'Well, it's not the kind of trouble I expected,' said Jane.

'No. It's worse. What are we going to do, Mum? How could he buy her a dog without asking first?'

'He didn't think,' said Sarah.

'Damn right he didn't. And now *we* have to deal with the consequences.'

'Can't we deal with them tomorrow?' Jane asked.

The vegan lasagne was smoking. Dani pulled it out of the oven and slammed it down on the kitchen counter.

'I don't suppose that's got any weed in it?' Sarah asked.

As if he was having a Pavlovian reaction to the smell of food, Jed appeared at the kitchen door. He stood in the frame, almost filling it, in the dirty parka he rarely took off. He was like a gigantic smelly version of Kenny from *South Park* and right then Dani hated him.

'What do you want?' Dani asked.

'I wanted to say sorry, Mrs P.'

Jane and Sarah smiled at him, encouragingly.

'I probably should have asked you first.'

'Yes, you should.'

'Look, I understand you're not very happy right now, Mrs P, but my uncle has this theory, right, that you don't go out and get a pet. The animal finds you. And this animal was meant for Flossie. I knew it the moment I saw him. I had this feeling.'

'Where did you get him?' Dani asked Jed.

'I bought him from a bloke in town,' said Jed.

'Which bloke?'

'I don't know.'

'What did he tell you about that pup?'

'Nothing really. He just said his dog had some

puppies but he couldn't keep them himself. He was looking for suitable owners. He said he could tell from having seen Flossie and me around town that we were the right sort of people.'

'You mean he could see you were suckers?'

'He meant kind,' said Jed. 'Proper animal lovers.'

'So you don't know anything about this puppy at all? You don't know how old it is. What breed it is. Whether it's had its injections? You don't even know if it was stolen.'

'It wasn't stolen,' said Jed firmly. 'It was his dog's puppy. She had five. This was the only one left. He's nearly four months old.'

'And you saw this man's dog?'

Jed nodded.

'And what kind of dog was that?'

Jed looked up to the ceiling as though he was trying to remember. Or as though he was trying to make something up.

'What kind of dog was it, Jed?' Dani asked again.

'I, er, I think it was a Jack Russell.'

'It was a what?'

'A Jack Russell,' said Jed. 'It might not have been, though. It might have been a sheepdog or something.'

'Sheepdogs and Jack Russell terriers are not easily confused. Look, Jed, just tell me where you got the dog from so that first thing tomorrow morning I can sort this all out.'

'He told me not to tell you.'

'What?'

'Because he said you'd go mad and chase him down.'

'Jed, is this strange man someone I know?'

Jed shrugged.

'It's someone I know,' Dani translated.

It transpired that Jed had bought the dog from some-body they *all* knew. Eric was the driver for the local organic farm collective that supplied food to dozens of hotels and restaurants in the area. He delivered food to The Majestic Hotel three times a week.

Dani had come to know Eric pretty well over the years. They always made time to share a joke while Eric was bringing boxes of lovingly grown potatoes and turnips and beetroot to the kitchen door. Eric always asked after Flossie and Jane. Dani, in turn, knew all about Eric's family. His wife, who'd been unwell for a decade. His children, who were, in Eric's own words, both terrible wasters who would never amount to anything. His secret dream that one day he would be able to go sport fishing in Florida.

Dani thought of Eric as a friend. But now he'd done this to her. He knew Flossie was her daughter.

'Right, well tomorrow morning I will have a word with Eric about giving you your money back.'

'You mean giving him back the dog?' Jed asked. 'You can't just do that. Flossie is really attached to him already. You're acting like a dictator.'

'I'm acting like a parent,' Dani said.

Jed slunk back upstairs. If he'd had a tail, it would have been between his legs. From the hallway, Dani could hear a chorus of 'not fair' as Jed relayed the news to the girls. Well, let them complain. They wouldn't be the ones who inevitably ended up looking after that puppy if Dani didn't send it back. They wouldn't be the ones feeding the puppy, walking the puppy, paying for it to have all its injections. Dani wasn't being cruel. She was being bloody sensible. Something Jed clearly was not.

The girls and Jed stayed up in Flossie's room all evening. Meanwhile Dani tipped the left over canapés and the burned lasagne into the bin. And at ten thirty, Dani made it clear it was time Flossie's birthday party came to an end.

In the fuss about the tattoos and the puppy, even Dani's lovingly made birthday cake had been forgotten. Dani remembered just as Flossie's guests were leaving and brought it out quickly but Flossie refused to have them sing 'Happy Birthday'.

'Because it's not a happy birthday for me,' Flossie said.

With her friends all gone, Flossie retired to her bedroom, still clutching the puppy as though he were a live hot-water bottle. Dani followed her upstairs.

'Mum, why are you so bent out of shape about this?'

'Why do you think?' Dani asked her.

'It isn't my fault. I didn't actually ask for a dog. But now . . .'

Dani sat down on the end of the bed. 'We can't have this dog, Flossie. We really can't.'

Flossie covered the puppy's ears, as though he might have understood that Dani was deciding his fate.

'Who's going to look after him?' Dani fell back on reason. 'I work full time. You're at school.'

'Gran's at home all day.'

'It's not fair to impose on her.'

'She'd be up for it. I know she would. And Auntie

Sarah will help too. And when I'm not at school, he'll be one hundred per cent my responsibility.'

'Like your hamster was?'

'I was seven,' said Flossie, remembering Dora the hamster's unfortunate demise.

'Come on, Flossie. Be real. I'm not saying all this just to upset you on your birthday. Jed was simply wrong to bring that dog home. It's not just the responsibility. It's the expense.'

'I can use the money Xanthe and Camilla saved for my tattoo to pay for his injections.'

'Well, that's almost a silver lining. But no, you can put that tattoo money towards your uni fund.'

'If I get that far. All this upset is going to make it really hard for me to get through my GCSEs next week.'

'Unfair, Flossie. Unfair. Look, hand the puppy over. He can't stay in your bedroom whatever. He's not house-trained. He's got to go in the kitchen overnight then tomorrow I'll sort out giving him back to Eric.'

Flossie's eyes glittered with tears.

'But this dog chose us, Mum. It's like Jed said. He *chose* our family. I really believe that. You saw how much Grandma Jane and Auntie Sarah liked him. We can't give just him back.'

The puppy cried all night, of course, keeping Dani wide-awake into the early hours. She did her best to block out the mournful sound by arranging her pillows around her ears but eventually she crept downstairs and set herself up on the sofa, with the pup in his cardboard box on the floor by her side. However, that wasn't enough for him either. He kept crying. He wouldn't go to sleep until Dani picked him up and let him make a nest in the blanket she spread over her knees.

'Don't get used to this,' she warned him, as he settled his warm weight in her lap and she ran her fingers through his silky soft fur. 'You're going back tomorrow.'

But there was something irresistible about those brown eyes. And those little feet. The bright pink tongue and the wet button nose. Even that puppy smell, which Dani knew was only the scent of wee on warm fur. If things had been different . . .

They weren't different. Things were as they were.

'Don't cry,' Dani said to the pup. 'Somebody some-where will really love you.'

Chapter Eight

When Eric the organic fruit and veg man arrived to do the drop-off at The Majestic the following morning, Dani could tell at once that he'd rather not stop to chat. Normally, he unloaded his van as though he had all the time in the world. Sometimes, in fact, he took too long. Today, he was in a hurry.

'Can't hang around,' he shouted as he dumped three pallets of veg on the kitchen steps. 'Running late.'

'Oh no you don't.'

Dani elbowed Dave out of the way so she could get to the errant vegetable man. 'You're not going anywhere until you and I have had a little talk.'

'What about?' Eric asked, all innocence.

'Eric, you sold my daughter's boyfriend a *dog* for her birthday knowing full well that getting a pet is not a decision Flossie is currently qualified to make.'

'Jed told me you both always wanted one. You and Flossie.'

'And that's true,' Dani admitted. 'But I haven't ever *had* one because I know as well as you do that *wanting* a dog isn't enough. Dogs need attention and company. They need to be with someone who has time to take them for a walk. I'm a single mother. I work full-time. I work weekends. I work evenings. A dog simply wasn't in the plan. You'll have to take him back.'

43

'No can do,' said Eric. 'Money has changed hands. He's your responsibility now. I don't do refunds.'

'I'm not asking for a refund, Eric. You can keep the money. I'm just asking you to find that puppy a new home. Somewhere he's wanted.'

'I don't have time. You're not the only one round here with a job.' He waved in the direction of the van. 'I'm run off my feet. If that puppy comes back to me, I'll have to drop him off at the dogs' home. You could do that yourself if you really don't want to keep him.'

'What? Oh Eric. For heaven's sake. We've been friends for years, you and I. How could you do this to me?'

'Jed told me he'd cleared it with you.'

'And you didn't think to check?'

'He's an adult.'

'Barely.'

Eric had the grace to look ashamed. Dani sighed.

'Maybe,' said Eric after a moment. 'Maybe you ought to try to be a little bit more open-minded about how you can make owning a dog work. They bring joy to your life, dogs do.'

'Then why don't you take him back and have a little bit more joy for yourself?'

'We've already got six including his mum,' Eric said, a little sadly. 'I never get a place on the sofa as it is. Besides, I can't afford to get him vaccinated. That twenty quid Jed gave me doesn't even touch the sides. I'm sorry, Dani. I didn't mean to put you in a difficult position. I honestly didn't. Jed had me convinced you and Flossie wanted a dog. He said he would sort it out with you. I thought you'd be pleased in the end.'

Dani could tell that Eric wasn't going to budge. She would have liked to smack him round the chops with a

44

squeaky dog toy for putting her in such a quandary but she knew it wasn't worth it. Eric had done Dani plenty of favours over the years. He was kind. She couldn't avoid him. They had to meet pretty much every week.

'What kind of dog is he anyway?' Dani asked at last, defeated.

'Oh, he's a good mix,' said Eric.

'Mix of what?'

'He's half poodle, half . . .'

Eric coughed out the end of the sentence so that Dani didn't have the faintest clue what he'd said.

'Half poodle, half what?'

'Staffy,' said Eric, only a little more clearly this time.

'Half poodle, half Staffy!' Dani shrieked. 'Half *Staffy*! You mean Staffordshire bull terrier? Eric, you are effing kidding me.'

But Eric was already getting back into his cab.

Dani grabbed a potato out of one of the pallets and threw it after him. It left a dent in the van's side panel.

Dani was furious. However, when Dave the chef heard what had happened, he was unsympathetic.

'It's not the end of the world,' he said.

Dave had a Dobermann called Sparkle. Never had a dog been so inappropriately named. Satan was more like it. Likewise, Joe the sous-chef had two dogs. Lurchers, named Beavis and Butthead.

'I love them more than anything in the world,' he said.

'Including your wife?' Dani asked.

'They're joint first with my wife,' said Joe, who'd been married for less than a year. 'But then they did bring her into my life.'

Shortly after getting his dogs, Joe had taken them for a walk on Pier Beach (it was during the winter when dogs were allowed on the sand). Joe's future missus was a Goth, who had a vintage Victorian fur muff. The lurchers mistakenly thought she might be carrying a rabbit and took her down in their eagerness to investigate. Joe helped the poor woman to her feet and the rest was history.

'Eric's right,' Joe said. 'Dogs can change your life. And your life does need changing if you ask me.'

'I didn't ask you,' said Dani.

'But when did you last go on a date?' asked Dave.

'You can't ask me that!'

'But we always talk about your love life.'

Dave and Joe were united on that front.

'Not in 2018 we don't,' said Dani. 'Now it's hashtag *inappropriate* so you can both sod right off.'

Dani turned to see Cheryl the events manager smirking by the serving hatch.

'What?' Dani spat at her.

'I just came to see how preparations for Mr Hayward's birthday party celebration event are getting on,' she said.

'Fine,' said Dani. 'We've got it all under control, haven't we, gentlemen?'

Dave and Joe nodded.

'And the cake?'

'Will be perfect.'

'Good.' Cheryl turned to go but hesitated. She turned back to Dani. 'You know a dog brought love into my life too,' she said suddenly.

'What kind was it?' Dave interrupted. 'Someone's guide dog?'

Cheryl pursed her lips. She carried on, 'I was just out of university and I was house-sitting for my parents' neighbours. They had this little Westie called Ellen, after Ellen Degeneres. They were big fans. Anyway I had to take Ellen out every day. It was while I was walking her in the park that I met my husband.' She paused. 'Of course, he's my ex-husband now.'

'Better stick to cats then,' said Dave.

Joe doubled over with laughter. Cheryl and Dani both ignored the men.

'If I didn't have such a busy life,' said Cheryl to Dani. 'I'd get a dog myself. I really would.'

'I know one that's available,' said Dani.

'He's not available,' said Dave, suddenly strangely firm on the matter. 'He's your daughter's birthday present, Dani. Flossie will be moving out before you know it and you'll be glad she's got a dog with her then to protect her and such. What's a bit of pooper-scooping in the meantime?'

Joe agreed. And so did Cheryl.

'It will teach her responsibility,' Cheryl added. Optimistically, Dani thought. Cheryl had never met Flossie.

'It will teach her about love,' said Joe.

'Oh yes.' Dave and Cheryl nodded at the profundity.

'Love? Balls. If none of you will have him, he's going to the shelter,' Dani said.

Dave, Joe and Cheryl all glared at her.

'Well, he is,' said Dani. 'And it's not my fault.'

All the same, for the rest of the day, Dave and Joe would barely speak to her. When Dani was carrying a bag of rubbish out to the wheelie bins, Dave said loudly, 'Some people think that anything can be thrown away.'

'That isn't fair!' Dani responded.

'Just saying it like it is,' said Dave.

'Word,' said Joe, as the two men shared a fist bump.

Later, Cheryl layered on the guilt when they met in the car park as Dani was getting onto her bicycle.

'After hearing about your dog,' she said, 'I spent half the afternoon on the local shelter's website. There are so many puppies looking for a home! Their little faces! Unbearable . . . All cold and lonely in those concrete-bottomed cages.'

'It's terrible,' Dani agreed. 'But what can you do?'

'I think you know what *you* can do,' said Cheryl brusquely as she got into her car.

'I can't have a dog!' Dani howled at Cheryl's taillights.

It was so unfair. None of Dani's colleagues were being reasonable. They knew she didn't have a partner to share the responsibility. They knew what kind of hours she had to work. They surely must have known that The Majestic didn't pay well enough to keep anyone in dog biscuits . . .

Yet they had all ganged up on her.

And so had the weather. Dani had to cycle back up the hill from the sea into a headwind.

When Dani finally got home, Flossie was in the living room with Jane and Sarah from next door. The three of them were sitting on the rug in front of the fireplace with the puppy in the middle. When Dani came in, the puppy bounded in her direction, with his candy-pink tongue lolling out of a big wide grin. It was completely obvious that he had Staffy in him now Dani knew for sure.

Dani tried to look underwhelmed by the puppy's greeting but the truth was that her heart leapt towards him even as he seemed intent on putting holes in her calves with his sharp puppy teeth.

'Did you talk to Eric?' Flossie asked. Her voice quivered ever so slightly.

'Yes.'

Flossie bit her lip.

'He won't have him back,' Dani said. 'He said if we can't keep him, I should take him to the dog shelter.'

Flossie snatched the puppy up and held him so tightly he squeaked.

'You can't!' said Jane and Sarah, quite spontaneously.

Dani sighed.

The truth was she couldn't bear the thought any more than Dave, Joe, Cheryl, Jane, Sarah or Flossie could. The people at the animal shelter were nice enough. Dani had often stopped to chat with them when they were collecting funds outside Tesco. But the idea of this puppy being taken from her warm home and put into a cage with a concrete floor, with who knew what sort of future ahead was just awful.

'But I don't have time to walk him,' Dani said.

'We're going to do that,' said Flossie. 'Me and Jed. And Gran sometimes as well.'

'I'll help,' said Sarah.

'I don't have time to train him.'

'We're going to do that too.'

'He'd have to be entirely your responsibility,' Dani reminded her daughter.

'I can take it.' Flossie gave her mum the Brownie salute. 'I need the practice.'

'I can't believe I'm saying this.'

'Saying what?' Flossie asked eagerly.

'We're keeping the puppy,' said Dani. 'So he'd better have a name.'

'Oh, I've already given him a name,' said Flossie.

'What is it?' Dani asked, fearing the worst.

'Jeremy Corbyn,' Flossie told her.

'Jeremy Corbyn? What kind of name for a dog is that?'

'It's the name of a hero,' said Flossie. She picked the puppy up and planted a kiss on his nose. 'Isn't that right, Jeremy Corbyn? Jezza for short.'

'Jezza? That's even worse.'

'It suits him,' Flossie insisted. 'It's masculine. It's playful. It's . . .'

'It's OK, I suppose.'

Dani got down onto the rug next to her daughter. The puppy rolled straight onto his back for a tummy tickle. Flossie and Sarah immediately obliged.

Meanwhile, Jane squeezed Dani's hand. 'It's going to be fine. In fact, I'm rather looking forward to having some male energy around the house.'

As if he'd heard Jane speaking, the newly named Jeremy Corbyn chose that moment to jump up and attempt a bit of beginner's leg-lifting by the sofa.

'Your dog,' Dani reminded Flossie.

'GCSE maths day after tomorrow,' said Flossie as she disappeared upstairs.

Chapter Nine

Fortunately for Dani, even if she didn't know the first thing about dog care, she knew a man who did. Her great friend Liz, whom she'd met when they were in the same antenatal group at Newbay General, had recently remarried. Her first husband was an unfaithful dental sales rep. Her second husband, who seemed altogether more suitable, was an extremely devoted vet.

When Dani told Liz about Jed's ill-considered gift, Liz was quick to leap to the thoughtless young man's defence.

'You're always saying you'd like to have a dog,' Liz reminded Dani. 'And,' she echoed Eric and Dave and Joe and Cheryl and just about everybody else, 'dogs are a great way to get more joy into your life.'

It was thanks to Liz's own dog Ted, a portly Norfolk terrier, that she had met Doctor Evan Thomas, of Thomas and Thomas Vets, when he insisted she sign Ted up for a Waggy Weight Loss course.

'Maybe I don't need more joy in my life,' Dani said.

'You need this dog. Evan will sort you out,' Liz promised.

Two days later, while Flossie was at school taking her maths exam, Dani took Jeremy Corbyn – Jezza for short – to Evan's surgery to be added to his register of pets. When Jezza met Evan, the warm feelings were obvious and mutual.

'Isn't he a little poppet?' said Evan. 'Just look at that doggy smile.'

'That doggy smile is typical of his heritage, isn't it?' asked Dani.

'Ah yes. What was it you said? Half poodle, half Staffy. A proper Frankendog. Great hair *and* teeth,' Evan quipped. 'But I like the look of him. Flossie's boyfriend chose a good one. He's been well cared for. He's in excellent shape. Strong paws. Nice legs. Excellently shaped head. Healthy nose. And intelligent,' he nodded, as Jezza made a playful lunge for his fingers. 'You'll have your work cut out keeping him amused. He'll need lots of toys for a start.'

'But he's half Staffy, Evan. Is it even safe for me to have him around the house?'

'Staffies have a bad reputation,' said Evan. 'But it's unfounded. Trained in the right way, they make exceptionally loyal and kind pets. There are no bad dogs, Dani, only bad owners. Isn't that right, Jezza?'

Evan nuzzled the puppy's nose with his knuckle.

Evan Thomas was a real Dr Doolittle. The animals under his care seemed to understand that he only had good intentions towards them. Jezza was already on his back, looking for another tummy tickle.

'Just make sure you get him properly trained from the very beginning and everything will go smoothly. He'll reward you with a lifetime of love and devotion. Owning a dog will bring you a whole new world of connections,' he said. 'You can start with Nurse Van Niekerk's puppy boot camp. Saturday mornings between nine and ten. Before Waggy Weight Loss.

Hopefully, Jeremy will never be a member of *that* club.'

'Nurse Van Niekerk's puppy boot camp?' Dani echoed.

'Where all the good dogs go. That's the motto.'

Dani had heard all about Nurse Van Niekerk, Evan's strict South African practice nurse from Liz. She had a reputation for being somewhat brusque.

'It's called Best Behaviour Boot Camp. Nurse Van Niekerk teaches general life skills and agility. Ah, here she is now,' Evan said.

Nurse Van Niekerk came into the room with her clipboard. She was a strong-looking woman with the air of an elite rugby coach about her.

'Jeremy Corbyn?'

'This is he,' said Evan, indicating Jezza.

'So you must be Mrs Jeremy Corbyn,' Nurse Van Niekerk said to Dani.

'You can call me Dani,' she suggested.

'No need,' said Nurse Van Niekerk. 'Just gets things confused . . . Now, puppy training. I thought we'd sign you up straight away.'

There was no getting out of it. And Jezza had greeted Nurse Van Niekerk with quite some enthusiasm. Now he tried to attract her attention again with his cutest whimper.

'Hello, little fella.' Nurse Van Niekerk tickled him under the chin, her stern face suddenly transformed by a huge and genuine smile. 'You're a clever little chap, I can tell. Look at those intelligent eyes. You're going to love Nurse Van Niekerk's Best Behaviour Boot Camp, aren't you?'

Jezza wagged his tail so hard that he wagged his whole bottom.

'Remember,' said Evan to Dani in an aside. 'Dogs never lie about how they feel.'

Nurse Van Niekerk and Jezza were certainly having a love-in.

'When do we start?' Dani asked.

'Saturday mornings. Nine o'clock sharp. A new term starts in two weeks. Don't be late,' said Nurse Van Niekerk.

'We wouldn't dare,' Dani assured her.

Leaving the clinic with Jezza in her arms again, Dani couldn't help remembering the last time she'd been entrusted with the care of something so young and small and vulnerable.

'You'll be fine,' the nurses said as they waved her and Flossie off from the Maternity Unit.

Back then, Dani hadn't been the least bit confident she was capable either. But if the nurses thought she could cope on her own, she'd decided, then perhaps she could. Likewise, if Evan thought Jezza was a good puppy who could be trained to become a great dog.

'Confidence,' Dani muttered to herself. 'Fake it till you make it.'

She straightened up. She was a dog owner now. She nodded to a woman who was trying to persuade a small French bulldog to get out of a car.

'Come along, Coco. It's hardly raining at all.'

While Dani loaded Jeremy into the basket of her bicycle, the French bulldog owner tied what appeared to be a genuine Hermès scarf around her little dog's head to protect it from the drizzle. Once the scarf was in place, the dog finally deigned to slide down from the car seat to the pavement and walked towards the surgery with her owner holding an umbrella like the Queen's equerry.

'Hello!' the woman said, as she passed Dani and Jezza. 'A new puppy! Oh, how lovely. What's his name?'

'Jezza. Jeremy Corbyn.'

'Oh, perfect. This is Coco Chanel,' said the woman, indicating the dog in the scarf. 'And I'm Mrs Coco.

'You've brought your boy to the right vet here,' she continued. 'There's nothing Dr Thomas and Nurse Van Niekerk don't know about dogs. We wouldn't be without them, would we, Coco?'

Coco made a snuffling sound that may or may not have signified agreement.

'Well, lovely to meet you Jezza and Mrs Jezza. Welcome to the Newbay canine community.'

With that, Mrs Coco continued on her way, managing three steps before Coco the dog sat down and refused to move until she was picked up. And given a treat.

'Don't get any ideas,' Dani told Jezza.

Chapter Ten

Everyone at The Majestic was very happy to hear that Jezza the Staffy-poo had found his forever home. Meanwhile, Dani was relieved to be back in everybody's good books. It was certainly helpful that everyone was talking to her again since there was a lot to do that week.

The day of Nat Hayward's 'celebratory birthday party event' for his girlfriend Lola was suddenly upon them. Cheryl could hardly contain herself as she bustled as far as she was allowed into the kitchen on the morning of the do.

'Is everything ready?' she asked.

'Of course.'

Dani had put an extra special effort into Lola's birthday cake. Though she had made hundreds of chocolate gateaux over the years, she treated this one as though it was her first. She threw away the initial attempt, which wasn't moist enough. A second attempt cracked as it cooled. It would have tasted OK but Dani refused to cover the fault lines with icing. She was a professional. A third attempt was, thankfully, pretty much perfect.

'Are the Michelin inspectors coming?' Joe the sous-chef asked, as he watched Dani smoothing on the chocolate mirror icing, which shone as though it was still warm.

'Just the great Nat "Frank" Hayward,' said head chef Dave. 'Even more reason to be nervous. If you're Dani . . .'

Dani scowled.

'I'm just taking pride in my work,' she said. 'It doesn't matter who the customer is.'

'Not much.' Dave elbowed Dani in the ribs. 'It's all right, Dani. Your secret is safe with me.'

'What secret?' Joe shouted.

'My lips are sealed,' said Dave. 'I'll tell you on our next fag break.'

'Whatever he says is absolute rubbish!' Dani countered. 'Nat Hayward's just another customer.'

If he was honest Dave was also interested in seeing how Nat, the scruffy, clumsy kid from all those years ago, had grown and changed. He was particularly impressed that Nat had a younger girlfriend. Though Dani reminded him he shouldn't go expressing that kind of opinion.

'Stinging a bit, is it? Thinking of him with someone else?' Dave prodded.

'Not a bit,' said Dani. 'After twenty-two years, I think I'm just about over him.'

'Yeah right. Keep saying it until you believe it.'

'I am! And if you do talk to him, Dave, for goodness' sake don't call him Frank.'

'But that's his nickname.'

'That *was* his nickname. Nat's a client now. Not one of us.'

'He'll always be one of us. Once you've worked in Dave's kitchen . . .'

'He got out,' Dani reminded him.

The cake was finished. Dani stood back and

admired her handiwork. Of course, she hoped Nat liked it, but only in the same way she hoped any of her customers appreciated what she'd made. Really, that was all.

Nat arrived at seven thirty in the evening, bringing the first of his guests with him. With nothing to do in the kitchen for a while, Dani watched from behind the screen that occluded the swinging kitchen door.

Nat was wearing a suit. It was the first time she'd seen him dressed like that – unless you counted the sort-of-matching blazer and trousers he wore for school. He was with three other adults. Dani recognised Nat's mother. The other man, she thought, must be Nat's father, but if it was, he looked frail. That must have been what Nat was about to tell her the other day. Nat helped his father into a chair.

Other guests arrived soon afterwards. Mostly younger people. They stood around and sipped champagne cocktails and nibbled at Dave the chef's excellent canapés (which were especially delicious if you hadn't watched Dave make them). Meanwhile Cheryl the events manager buzzed around them like a particularly officious wasp, clipboard still in hand.

Apart from Nat's family, Dani didn't recognise any of the other people at the party. Nat's big sister, Kate, wasn't among them. It was strange to see his parents again, though. She wondered if Nat had told them she was still working in the restaurant.

There were three women who might have been contenders for the role of Lola but while Dani was watching from behind the screen, Nat didn't seem to pay any one of them particularly close attention. In any case, surely the other guests would have been pressing gifts into Lola's hands?

'Is she there yet?' Dave asked, joining Dani in her lookout.

'Who?'

'Frank's younger woman?'

'I don't think so,' said Dani. 'And you've got to stop calling him Frank.'

As she said that, another small group of people arrived. A couple in their fifties and a younger woman. By the way the others reacted, this group definitely contained the birthday girl.

Lola. L-O-L-A Lola.

She did not look anything like Dani had expected. Dani had convinced herself over the past week that the Nat she once knew would have gone for a serious young woman with a slightly dowdy style. But this Lola, the real Lola, was something else. She was slim and pretty in a very polished way. Her blonde hair was piled high on her head in an intricate but chic up-do. She wore the sort of complicated make-up that Flossie was always trying to perfect before she met Jed and went grunge.

Nat took Lola's perfectly classic trench coat from her shoulders, revealing her to be wearing a short white sequinned dress, sixties-style, over bare brown legs and a pair of high gold stilettoes. Once out of her coat, she greeted her guests enthusiastically, squealing with delight as each one came up for a birthday kiss.

'What's she like?' Dave asked.

'Look for yourself,' said Dani, ceding her place at the gap between the screen panels.

'Wow.' Dave gave a low whistle. 'L-O-L-A Lola. Good work, Frank. Who'd have thought he'd get a girl like that? She is smokin'.'

'I hope she's got a personality to match,' said Dani primly.

'Who cares about her personality?'

'You did not just say that,' Dani complained.

'I don't rate your chances of winning him back now,' Dave continued.

'I don't want to *win* him back. But if you don't shut up, I will stick Lola's effing birthday cake in your face.'

As Dave and Dani watched, Cheryl the events manager ushered Nat's party to their places. If there was one thing she was good it, it was making sure that events at The Majestic always ran on time. As soon as the last bum was on a seat, Cheryl scuttled across to the screen behind which Dani and Dave were still hiding.

'Canapés are done. Main courses at the ready.'

Dave responded with a heel click and soon the waiting staff started streaming out of the kitchen, placing main courses on the table and filling glasses.

When Dani wasn't needed, she slipped out of the kitchen to find her spot by the wheelie bins. Dave came to join her with a cigarette.

'So what do you really think?' Dani asked him.

'I think our friend Frank has done all right for himself.'

'She's not his type, though, is she?'

'She's every man's type. Those legs.'

Dani shook her head.

'You've got great legs too,' said Dave. 'I mean, not that I've been looking at them or anything. Ever.'

'I didn't need you to say that,' Dani said.

'Only trying to cheer you up.'

'I don't need cheering up.'

'Really?'

'Really.'

Dani plucked the cigarette from Dave's hand and took a cheeky drag.

'You never smoke any more,' Dave commented.

'I know.'

Dani exhaled a long grey plume.

'It's weird seeing Frank back here as a customer,' said Dave.

'It certainly is.'

'But you're all right about it, aren't you? I mean, after everything . . .'

'Everything that happened *twenty-two* years ago? Of course I am. I've lived more than half my life since then.'

'Good. Because I know it can be tough. Seeing an ex.'

Dave's ex-wife Julie, who had also worked at The Majestic in the summer of 1996, still made a hobby of making Dave jealous.

'It's different. You and Julie were married. You shared a dog.'

'Don't know what I would have done if she got custody of Sparkle,' Dave said. 'Do you want to take the cake out when they're ready?' Dave asked then. 'You made it, so you should.'

'No,' said Dani. The very last thing she wanted was to stand next to the real Lola for even a second. She could imagine the picture they would make only too well. Her kitchen whites were no competition for Lola's mini-flapper dress. Her comfortable clogs would look like ancient coracles next to Lola's expensive shoes. And as for her hair. When she was in the kitchen, Dani had no choice but to stick her shoulder-length brown hair into a bun that could be covered by her white chef's hat. Health and safety demanded it. Still, she did not want to go up against Lola's bright blonde waves.

Go up against?

Hang on. This was ridiculous. There was no question of 'going up against' Lola. There was no competition between them. Full stop. Lola was Nat's girlfriend. Meanwhile Dani had let go of Nat more than two decades ago. She no longer even knew him well enough to call him a friend. It didn't matter that he was in love with someone else. Someone younger and slimmer with much better shoes. Lola was scrubbed up for her birthday. Dani was at work.

'I'll take the cake out,' Dani told Dave.

She wanted to claim her achievement. The cake looked bloody beautiful. It was well worth being proud of her efforts. She was a professional.

'But first I need to go and check my face,' she admitted.

Chapter Eleven

Before Dani left the kitchen, Dave lit the candles with the Zippo lighter he'd had for almost twenty-five years. The same one he'd used for Nat's eighteenth birthday Frankenstein cake.

As Dani walked in with the cake already ablaze, the birthday guests started singing. Meanwhile Lola started primping. In anticipation, presumably, of the obligatory photographs. While Dani was still halfway across the room, Lola whipped out her phone and checked her make-up with the selfie function.

As Dani drew closer, Lola's mother quickly cleared a spot where the cake could land. Dani placed it there carefully and stood back, with the other guests, to sing 'Happy Birthday' one more time.

When the singing was done, Lola didn't blow the candles out right away. She wanted some photographs first. And photo approval. So that by the time she actually got round to blowing the candles out, they were dripping wax onto the icing with which Dani had achieved a rare perfect mirror shine. To say that Dani wasn't pleased was an understatement, but she kept a lid on the urge to say, 'Please blow out the bloody candles before they melt the cake,' and instead smiled and agreed to stand behind Lola for one more photograph.

'Make a wish,' someone shouted.

'I know exactly what I'm wishing for,' said Lola, with a wink at Nat.

The man standing next to Nat gave him a friendly dig that almost knocked him over. Lola blew out the candles and the guests gave her a round of applause. Dani sank back into the shadows.

'Now, Lola,' said a man Dani took to be Lola's father. 'Before we cut the cake, there's something we've got to give you. It's been pretty difficult thinking of the perfect birthday present for a girl like you. What do you get the girl who has everything? I'm assuming you don't need another BMW just yet.'

The birthday guests chuckled politely.

'Your mother and I ruled out jewellery too, since that's the domain of another person in this room now.'

Nat gave a comic grimace and tugged at his collar.

'You go on far too many holidays and you've already got a beautiful home. So what could we get you, our darling girl? When you were little, you wanted a rabbit and we got you two of them. Though they didn't last long.'

Lola gave an embarrassed shrug.

'Then you asked for a pony and we got you one of those.'

'Awww, lovely Missy,' Lola remembered her horse. 'Mischief was her proper name,' she explained for Nat's benefit.

'Yes. Of course, you forgot all about Missy as soon as you got into boys,' Lola's father sighed. 'But there was something else you asked for that we never gave in on.'

Lola tipped her head to one side, as though racking

her brain for a single whim that had not been indulged during her clearly privileged childhood.

'We always said that you couldn't have one until we knew you'd be responsible,' her father continued. 'Well, now that you're thirty, we hope that's a given.'

'Oh, I'm very responsible now!' Lola promised.

'In that case.'

Lola's father dialled someone on his mobile.

'You can bring her in,' he said.

'Her?'

All eyes were on the doors to the restaurant as one of the hotel's porters used a luggage trolley to wheel in a large box that was covered in gold wrapping paper and finished with a huge pink ribbon.

'Don't get too excited. It isn't another pony,' said Lola's dad.

'Then what is it?'

Lola leapt up from her seat with unseemly haste. Dani was reminded of Roald Dahl's Veruca Salt as Lola scrabbled to get the ribbon undone. Then Lola pushed aside the flaps that kept the box closed and her eyes widened as she saw what it contained.

'Oh my god! Oh my god! Oh my god! Thank you, Daddy. Thank you, Mummy. This is the best best birthday present ever!'

Perhaps Dani should have guessed what was inside from the look on Lola's face. So similar to the look on her daughter's face just a few nights earlier.

Lola reached into the box and lifted out . . . a dog!

Lola's reaction was the exact opposite of Dani's upon seeing Flossie's surprise gift from Jed. Lola was delighted. She jumped up and down, looking much younger than her thirty years as she did so. She cradled the puppy – a pure black cocker spaniel – in her arms and kissed it all over its velvety head.

'Oh my god, this is wonderful,' she said.

'And cheaper than a BMW,' her father quipped. 'Though still bloody expensive. It's a pedigree puppy is this one. Years of breeding. Grandmother won something at Crufts. Nothing but the best for my girl.'

'Thanks, Ian,' said Nat, addressing Lola's father.

'Yeah,' said Ian. 'Sorry, mate. I guess it's you that's going to be doing the poop-scooping and wotnot.'

'No, he won't. I will look after *my* dog myself,' Lola insisted.

'I'll believe that when I see it,' said Ian, giving Nat another hefty nudge in the ribs.

'Well,' said Lola's mother. 'What are you going to call her, sweetie?'

Lola held the puppy at arm's length to get a better look at her. The puppy wriggled in the air.

'Princess,' said Lola after just a moment's thought. 'I don't know why. It just came into my head. But she does look like a princess, doesn't she?'

'Just like her new owner. It's perfect,' Lola's mother agreed.

While everyone was fussing over the puppy, Dani caught Nat's eye, just for a second. She did her best to keep her face pretty neutral, but she could tell that the puppy had taken Nat by surprise as much as Lola, and that he didn't have a clue how he was supposed to react.

He wasn't the only one. Cheryl the events manager didn't know what to do with herself or her clipboard. Dogs weren't allowed into the hotel dining room unless they were assistance dogs – guide dogs and the like. But these people were important customers and Cheryl had her eye on future bookings. She didn't want to upset anyone. On the other hand rules were rules. Lola's shrieks of delight had drawn the attention of everyone else in the restaurant and not all of them looked impressed.

'May I suggest you take your coffee through to the lounge,' Cheryl said, using her clipboard to waft Lola, Nat and Princess in that general direction. 'Yes. Just through there. The lounge.'

Strictly speaking, dogs weren't allowed in the lounge either but a new Majestic Hotel rule was being written.

As the birthday guests left the restaurant, Dani cut the cake into slices, ready to be served with the coffee. She secretly helped herself to a forkful. It was delicious. Magnificent. The best she had ever made.

Once the whole cake was cut, Dani carried it into the lounge and left it on a low table so that Lola's party could help themselves. Nobody noticed. They were all too busy fawning over the puppy. Nobody, that is, except Nat. He saw Dani come in and he watched her leave. In the low light of the bar, she looked to him exactly as she had always done. Exactly as he remembered.

'Nat! You have a go!'

Lola thrust the puppy into his arms.

'Perfect practice for a baby!' said Lola's dad.

Chapter Twelve

Since she'd worked an extra shift to be there for Nat and Lola's party, Dani had the next day off in lieu. She got up early, determined to get stuff done for once. Alas, the first thing she had to do was pick up some puppy mess.

'I would have done that,' Flossie insisted when she came downstairs. 'If you hadn't got up first.'

All the same, Flossie let her mother finish the clearing up with a quick squirt of Vanish and some elbow grease.

'Can I make you a coffee, Mum?' Flossie asked while Dani was washing her hands.

'Why?' Dani asked.

'Is that a yes?'

'Yes. But . . .'

Flossie had a way with the coffee machine. Dani could only get it to make espressos, but Flossie could get a veritable Starbucks-worthy array of drinks out of the thing. Fortunately, she seemed to think the coffee machine with its little plastic capsules was exempt from her – or rather Jed's – eco-diktats.

'What kind of coffee do you want?'

'I'll have a cappuccino,' Dani said.

'Coming right up!'

'But I want one *without* strings attached.'

'Mum, why do you always think I've got an ulterior motive if I do anything nice for you?' Flossie asked.

'Because you usually have.'

'That's not true. Sometimes I'm just a really lovely daughter.'

Dani had to laugh at that.

'And you let me keep Jezza,' said Flossie. 'I owe you a lot of coffee for that.'

'Three small poos' worth so far today. Is Jed coming over for lunch?'

Flossie nodded. 'If it's OK with you.'

It wasn't. Dani wasn't in the mood for another lecture. But she remembered what her mother had said. The more they welcomed Jed into the family, the better. With a bit of luck, if they let him become so welcome he started to seem like part of the furniture, Flossie might go off him altogether.

'So,' said Flossie, as she set the cappuccino down on the table. It was perfect. She'd even sprinkled chocolate on top. At least she could always get a job as a barista. 'There's something I've been meaning to ask you.'

'Hmmmm,' said Dani.

'It's about the summer.'

'Yes?'

'You know how you said last year that once I finished my exams, I could have a special treat. Well, given how hard I've worked, a holiday in Greece seems reasonable, doesn't it?'

'What? A holiday in Greece? I was thinking more like fifty quid to spend in Top Shop. Who's going to Greece? Has Xanthe's mum invited you?'

Xanthe's mum, Angeliki, had family near Halkidiki.

'Sort of.'

Dani tilted her head in a questioning way.

'She's said we can drop in.'

'We? Drop in?'

'If we get that far?'

'Hang on. I'm confused. Who's we? And why wouldn't you get that far?'

'Because me and Jed were thinking of backpacking down there?'

Dani was grateful that she had yet to take a mouthful of the coffee because she would certainly have spat it out.

'What? You can't backpack to Greece with Jed, Flossie. I'm sorry.'

'It'll be really cheap.'

'I'm not thinking about the cost. You're sixteen.'

'Exactly, I'm *sixteen*. I'm not a baby. Everyone I know is allowed to go travelling. They're allowed to drink. They're allowed to have their boyfriends sleeping over. They're allowed to live like the adults they are.'

'*Nearly* are. Who are you talking about anyway? I don't know any of your friends' mothers who think any differently from me.'

'They do. Loads of the girls at school have more freedom than me. You're like some nineteenth-century dad compared to everyone else's parents!'

'Because you're not an adult.'

'I'm old enough to go to work.'

'But you don't,' Dani pointed out. 'And you don't always act like the grown-up you seem to think you are. You promised me, for example, that you would look after Jezza. I have not seen you clean up after him once.'

'That's because you're always on it before I get a chance! He's usually not even finished cocking his leg before you're there with the Febreze and a wet rag.'

'It's unhygienic to leave the mess around.'

'Mum, a bit of dirt never hurt anyone. Just like a little bit of risk never hurt anyone. You have to put yourself out there in the world to get anywhere. Backpacking to Greece could be the experience that makes me.'

'Or gets you into a lot of trouble. Flossie, this discussion is finished. There's no way . . . What do you want for dinner?' She tried to change the subject.

'I told you. I'm staying over at Xanthe's tonight, like I always do. Then tomorrow, everyone from GCSE media studies is going to meet up at Xanthe's to work. You know that's what I'm doing, Mum. I do it every week.'

It was true. Flossie had been staying over at Xanthe's house every Friday night since the beginning of the school year.

'Isn't it Xanthe's turn to stay over here?' Dani suggested. 'Then you could both take Jezza to boot camp before you work on your project.'

'It's easier at her house,' said Flossie.

'Look, I'm glad you're taking your GSCEs so seriously,' said Dani then. 'I have to admit I was worried when you first brought Jed home that he might be something of a distraction. Promise me you'll keep your focus. It's only two more years of school then you can do whatever you like.'

'I promise,' said Flossie. 'If you promise you'll think about letting me go to a festival this summer at least. If I can't go to Greece then you've got to let me go to Reading.'

'After we've seen your GCSE results,' Dani attempted a compromise. 'And you'll have to find the money yourself. You'll maybe even have to get a job.'

Dani thought that would probably be the end of it. Flossie had shown no inclination to find weekend employment so far. But she was about to surprise her mother.

'I'll look for something after my exams. Jed's going to be so pissed off about Greece,' Flossie sighed. 'But I'll tell him we can go to a festival if we can get the cash.'

'That's not quite what I said,' Dani tried but Flossie was already on her way out of the kitchen, sending a message to someone as she went.

Suddenly, Dani didn't want her coffee after all.

Sixteen. It was a strange sort of age. A limbo. At sixteen, Flossie wasn't old enough to vote. She wasn't old enough to drink, or to get married without parental consent. But she was old enough to join the Territorial Army, with that same consent. That was messed up, Dani thought. How could you be allowed to sign up to die for your country if you weren't old enough to have a say in how it was run?

Sometimes Flossie seemed so much younger than her years. She could talk the talk. She seemed worldly wise when it came to politics and the machinations of the media. But she still had no idea how to do a load of washing without shrinking something important. Or how to feed herself properly.

And yet, were you ever more yourself than you were at that age, Dani wondered. When you were full of optimism and idealistic. Before the responsibilities of adult life started to grind you down. When you still thought you could do whatever you liked with no compromises?

The job of being a parent seemed to be to constantly knock the edges off your child, to help them to fit in by becoming less themselves year on year.

At sixteen, Dani would have wanted to go travelling. She would have loved to go to a festival. The difference was, she would never have dared to ask. It was progress, wasn't it, that Flossie felt she could even broach the subject? And that she'd not gone into a complete melt-down when Dani told her that backpacking through Europe was out of the question? Dani wouldn't have guessed that Flossie would be so sanguine about that.

Half an hour later, Flossie came back downstairs with her overnight bag, ready to go to Xanthe's.

'Is Xanthe's mum picking you up?' Dani asked.

Dani didn't have a car. Not since the last one had failed its MOT and had to be scrapped.

'No.' As usual, Flossie said she would walk. It wasn't far.

'Say hi to Xanthe's mum for me, won't you?'

'I always do,' said Flossie. 'I'm sure she'll send her love back.'

At least Dani could relax while she knew Flossie was round at Xanthe's house. Xanthe's mum, Angeliki, was an old friend. They'd met when their daughters first started primary school. When the girls were small, Ange and Dani were always bumping into each other at the school gates or at each other's houses when dropping their daughters off for play-dates and sleepovers.

Dani decided she should give Ange a call sometime

soon. Catch up properly, rather than through messages sent via their children. See if she fancied a girls' night out at some point. Yes, she really ought to get in touch with Ange again, if only to thank her for letting Flossie stay over so often. She was about to send a text when Jezza distracted her.

He was squatting on the mat by the back door.

'Oh no you don't!' Dani scooped him up with the intention of carrying him outside before he had an accident. But the backdoor was still locked and it took Dani a while to locate the key, and Jezza was really desperate and before she could get him out into the garden, he'd made a mess down the front of her jumper.

'No one must feed the dog titbits!' she shouted to no one in particular. 'He's got an upset stomach.'

By the time she'd changed into something clean again, Dani had forgotten all about calling her friend.

Chapter Thirteen

The next day somebody had to take Jezza to his first puppy training session and, predictably, that somebody was going to have to be Dani. Flossie was revising at Xanthe's and Jane was at her Third Age computing class with Sarah.

The vet surgery car park was full of puppies and their owners when Dani and Jezza arrived on foot. As they trooped out to the field behind the surgery building, Dani was strangely reminded of the first NCT get-together she attended after Flossie was born. The assembled dog owners looked just as frazzled as the new mums had been all those years ago. Dazed. Not getting much sleep. And not actually at all sure whether the furry bundles of joy they'd allowed into their lives were the best thing that had ever happened to them or the worst. Certainly, Jezza had been keeping the Parker household awake. Until, that is, Dani had secretly allowed Jezza to start sleeping at the bottom of her bed. And then on her bed. And then under the duvet. She told herself she would sort it out later, when Jezza had settled into family life. For now, everyone just needed some sleep. It really was like having a newborn all over again.

Nurse Van Niekerk was already on the field. She stood in the middle of a circle of foldable chairs and yoga mats. On each chair was a packet of dog treats. The hapless owner of a Labrador puppy didn't notice the treats until his dog had eaten most of them. Paper wrapper and all.

'You with the Labrador! Keep an eye on your dog at all times!' Nurse Van Niekerk barked.

Dani scooped the packet of treats that had been left on her chair out of the way before Jezza had time to spot them.

'Humans on the chairs. Dogs on the mats,' Nurse Van Niekerk continued with her instructions. 'Hurry up, please. We don't have all day.'

Dani sat on her chair and tried to persuade Jezza to likewise sit still for a moment. But he was too excited. He actually pulled Dani off her seat in his effort to get at the nearest dog. A chihuahua.

Nurse Van Niekerk tutted as she made a circle of her new pupils.

'I can see I'm going to have my work cut out with you,' she said to Jezza. 'Ladies and gentlemen, and owners . . .'

A polite titter from the crowd.

'Welcome to a new term of Best Behaviour Boot Camp. My name is Nurse Van Niekerk. I'm the senior nurse here at the practice and my speciality is puppy training. Now, a lot of people think puppy training is a waste of time but I guarantee that if you follow my instructions to the letter. To. The. Letter,' she said again, looking at each of the owners in turn. 'Then in six weeks' time, you will have a young dog you can be proud of. One that you can take into any situation, knowing that he or she will remain calm, safe and under control. Isn't that what we all want?'

There was a murmur of agreement.

'Good. Now I hear all sorts of excuses for badly behaved dogs. Believe me, they are *all* excuses. Before you even start, let me tell you I simply don't believe that there are dogs that are too stupid to learn. Neither are there dogs too intelligent or too wilful to be taught. Personality doesn't come into it. Every single dog has the potential to become a well-trained dog because, more than anything, they want to please us, their pack leaders.'

'Am I your pack leader?' Dani asked Jezza.

He wagged his tail at her.

'Attention over here!' Nurse Van Niekerk shouted, clicking her fingers so that both Dani and Jezza looked up. 'As I was saying, there are no bad dogs. There are only lazy owners. So I hope you people will prove to me that you're not lazy owners. If you skip a class for any reason – and remember there are no excuses, I have even had people do this class on crutches – you will be required to re-sit the session you miss before I can issue you with a certificate. At the end of the course, there will be prizes for the dogs and owners who have made the most progress.

'Right, let's introduce ourselves. We'll start with you.' Nurse Van Niekerk pointed at Dani.

'My name is Dani . . .'

'I don't need *your* name,' Nurse Van Niekerk assured her. 'I've got enough to remember. Remind me what your charming young companion is called.'

'His name is . . . His name is Jeremy Corbyn,' Dani muttered. 'But we call him Jezza.'

'Right. Mrs Jezza,' Nurse Van Niekerk went on to the next dog in line. A lurcher–collie crossbreed, all legs and long majestic nose.

'Vultar,' said his owner.

'Mr Vultar.'

Mr Vultar opened his mouth to protest and was duly ignored.

'Terry,' said the owner of a small but feisty chihuahua.

Roxanne was a bichon frise who looked like nothing so much as a snowball with teeth. Bluebell was the greedy Labrador. Messrs Roxanne and Bluebell did not seem terribly pleased with their new names but they were about to be given reason to feel a little better.

'OK. We're missing someone.' Nurse Van Niekerk consulted her clipboard. 'We've got Jezza, Vultar, Roxanne, Terry and Bluebell. There should be one more. Where's Mr Princess?'

'Mr Princess?' Mr Bluebell wondered out loud.

Just as 'Mr Princess' arrived.

It was Nat. He had with him Lola's new dog. Of course. Dani immediately wished she'd worn something different that morning. Something less like a dog-walking outfit.

'Hello, stranger!' Seeing Dani, Nat made a beeline for the empty space next to her. 'Good to see you.'

'You too,' she said, feeling oddly shy.

'Ah, Mr Princess,' said Nurse Van Niekerk, interrupting the moment.

Nat looked completely confused.

'You're talking to me? I'm Mr Hayward,' he said.

'You're Mr Princess to me,' said the nurse. 'And you're almost fifteen minutes late. You've missed my introduction to Best Behaviour Boot Camp and you've missed the opportunity to get to know your fellow students.'

'Sorry,' said Nat. 'I didn't know you had a dog,' he said to Dani.

'Mr Princess!' Nurse Van Niekerk said in her very best sergeant major's voice. 'Had you been here on time with everybody else, you would know that obedience is our watchword for dogs *and* for owners. While boot camp is in session, nobody speaks unless they are spoken to. By me.'

'That told you, Mr Princess.'

Nurse Van Niekerk fixed Dani with a glare. Clearly, she had the hearing of a dog as well as a formidable bark.

'OK. If everybody is ready, we'll begin. Let's start by getting rid of some of that excess puppy energy so everyone can concentrate more effectively. Everybody follow me!'

She set off at a jog.

'What?' said Nat.

'I guess we're running,' said Dani.

After a circuit of the playing field – Dani hadn't run so far since her last year at school and neither, it seemed, had the rest of the humans – the first class commenced in earnest. It was basically a lesson in bribery, so far as Dani could tell. Every time the puppies got something right, they were rewarded.

Jezza already had a couple of tricks up his sleeve. Jane and Sarah had spent a few jolly hours in the garden that week, attempting to teach Jezza to sit. He knew what the word meant and he would do it. For a fee.

It was fun, thought Dani. Unexpectedly. And she was very glad that Jezza seemed to be slightly ahead of his peers. Meanwhile, Princess wasn't biddable at all. She spent most of the class rolling onto her back every time Nat got near her.

'Not very Princess-like behaviour,' Nat observed, as his puppy flashed her best bits at everyone.

'So how come you ended up here this morning?' Dani asked, while Nurse Van Niekerk was concentrating on Bluebell the Lab.

'Lola doesn't do mornings,' Nat said.

'Neither do I,' Dani said as Nurse Van Niekerk announced they were off for a run again. 'Neither do I.'

Eventually the treats ran out and that morning's class came to an end.

'Excellent work, puppies! And owners,' said Nurse Van Niekerk. 'Now all you have to do is keep up that training during the week. Do not backtrack. Do not be soft. Remember everything I've told you and practice, practice, practice.'

'Yes, Nurse Van Niekerk,' said Mr Terry, the chihuahua owner.

'That's "yes, ma'am," to you.'

'Is she joking?' Nat asked.

'I think she's joking,' said Dani. Though she wasn't at all sure.

Chapter Fourteen

With Nurse Van Niekerk's words ringing in their ears, the puppies and their owners dispersed in the direction of home. Dani and Nat fell into step as they walked from the playing field towards the car park, where the overweight dogs that'd been signed up for Waggy Weight Loss were waiting for their turn on the field.

After all the running about they'd done, Dani was pretty sure she wasn't looking too elegant but then neither was Nat. Halfway through the class he had stripped off his jumper to reveal a blue shirt beneath. As he did so, it rode up so that Dani could see a little strip of hairy stomach. It was a flash of vulnerability that made her relax. As had seeing him act so goofy on the playing field. Running left when Nurse Van Niekerk said right. Nat may have been top of his A-level classes at school, but he'd never been an athlete.

Dani felt suddenly tender towards the Nat of her memories, who was prone to getting the tables mixed up on his waiting shifts and tripping over his own big feet.

'I reckon your Jezza's going to be a star pupil,' Nat commented. 'He's very clever. What breed did you say he was again?'

'He's a cross-breed,' said Dani. 'Half poodle. Half Staffordshire bull terrier.'

'A Staffy-poo!' Nat laughed.

'I really don't like that term,' said Dani. 'It sounds a bit undignified. The poo bit.'

'He's very good looking, though,' Nat said.

'He is, isn't he?' Dani was proud to admit. 'Though I have no idea what he'll look like when he's fully grown.'

Right then, he looked not unlike Dennis the Menace's dog Gnasher, with his sharp eyes and halo of sticky-out hair.

'Princess certainly seems to be taken with him.'

The two puppies were bouncing ahead of Nat and Dani. Now they stopped to run around each other, so that Nat and Dani both got tangled up in their leads, causing them to bump together.

'Sorry!' Nat held Dani upright so she didn't topple over while she untied their legs. It wasn't until she'd finished doing so that she realised this was the first time she had touched Nat Hayward since 1996. Perhaps he realised the same thing at the same moment. They gently moved apart.

With the puppies on slightly shorter leads and a bigger gap between them, they continued on their way.

'Did Lola enjoy her birthday party?' Dani asked.

'I think so. She was certainly happy to get a dog.'

'I could tell. And how about you, though? You looked a bit surprised to see a puppy in that box.'

'I was.'

'Lola's parents didn't ask you before they bought Princess?'

'I don't think Lola's father is the kind of man who asks before he does anything,' said Nat.

On what little she had seen of Lola's father, Dani thought that seemed a fair assessment.

'It's OK,' Nat continued. 'It wasn't in the immediate plan but I've always loved animals and getting a dog is one of the signs that you're a real adult, isn't it?'

'I hope so,' said Dani. 'Look at us. A*dulting*.'

'About time, I suppose.'

'Are you forty now?' Dani asked. A little disingenuously. She knew he would be soon.

'Almost. Thanks for reminding me.'

'I'm not far behind.'

'But you'll always be younger than me.'

'Twenty-one months and sixteen days.'

'No need to rub it in, Parker!' Nat joked.

No one had called Dani 'Parker' in a long time.

'Thanks for the cake, by the way,' said Nat.

'Did you taste it?'

'Of course. We took some home. It was great. I'm sorry I didn't have time to thank you in person on the night but I guess you were on duty and so was I.'

'It's hard work being the host.'

'It is when you've got such a demanding birthday girl,' said Nat.

Dani was all ears.

'Lola likes things done the way she wants.'

He didn't elaborate.

'Have you got time for a coffee?' he asked then.

'When?'

'Well. How about now?'

Dani glanced at her watch. Then she laughed. 'I don't know why I just checked the time,' she said. 'Today is my day off.'

'But you might have a hot lunch date.'

'The only hot thing I have planned for lunch is a jacket potato,' said Dani.

Nat grinned. 'Sounds good to me. Where should we go? I don't know of any places round here that take dogs. Never had to think about it before.'

'Me neither,' said Dani. 'There is one place I can think of but it's a pub.'

'Bit early for a pub.'

'Not if we're only drinking coffee.'

'You're absolutely right,' said Nat.

They went to The Sailor's Trousers. Dani wasn't entirely sure that dogs were allowed but it was a pub so grubby that the average dog could only raise the standard of general cleanliness by catching up some muck on its tail. The bar was empty, apart from two old chaps watching racing on the telly and a younger guy feeding a slot machine.

The landlord looked half thrilled and half shocked to see two more customers. He was less happy when Dani ordered two coffees, which were made with powder from a crusty-looking jar and UHT milk from a carton. The landlord was still trying to discourage his punters from drinking anything other than beer, long after all his competitors were making a fortune from frothy cappuccinos.

'The only way you're going to get froth on your coffee in this place is if the landlord spits in it,' Dani observed while he walked to the other end of the bar to get some change.

'I will never ever ask for a cappuccino,' Nat confirmed.

Dani and Nat sat outside in the garden. Such as it was. The landlord of The Sailor's Trousers didn't hold with outside spaces either. He'd only bowed to pressure to put out a picnic table because the smokers were threatening to go elsewhere. There were no plants in the little walled area, unless you counted the weeds.

Nat spread his handkerchief – a proper cotton one – over the dirty bench so that Dani could sit down.

'I think your hanky is possibly worth more than my jeans,' Dani said. 'But thank you. You were always very chivalrous.'

'You'll make me blush.'

Nat sat down opposite. They were silent for a minute or two before they both went to talk at once.

'You first,' said Dani. 'I was just going to say something silly.'

'Me too.'

'What was your silly thing?' Dani asked.

'I was just going to say I can't believe you're still here,' said Nat.

'Neither can I,' said Dani. 'I mean, it isn't what I planned.'

'I meant it in a good way. Newbay isn't so bad.'

'Ninety thousand pensioners can't be wrong,' Dani quipped, referring to the town's demographic. 'But what are you doing back here, Nathan Hayward? The last I heard, you were in London, making a fortune.'

'Not a fortune, exactly. And miserable with it,' said Nat. 'I wanted to get back to the sea. I was always going to come back to Newbay at some point.'

'Nuts,' said Dani, making a 'cuckoo' swirl next to her temple.

'OK. So maybe I came back here a little earlier than I expected. Dad's not been well.'

'I thought perhaps that was the case when I saw him at The Majestic. What happened?'

'He had a stroke. Last November. He's made a lot of progress since then, but he's never going to be well enough to run the business again.'

'So you're here to do it for him?'

'Yes. In short. And I know I said I never would . . .'

When he was eighteen, Nat decided that the family pleasure boat business was destroying the local environment. That was why he'd taken a job at The Majestic rather than in the family firm.

'I'm saying nothing. You're allowed to change your mind,' Dani said. 'Looking out for your family matters.'

Nat nodded. 'That's the conclusion I came to. I've actually been back since January'

'And you didn't look me up?' Dani tutted.

'I really didn't think you'd still be here. The last I heard, you were in Paris on your year abroad. You had a French boyfriend.'

'I wonder who that was supposed to be,' Dani said. 'Chinese whispers, I think.'

'No French boyfriend?'

'Not that I noticed.'

'Oh. Is there someone now?'

'A man in my life? No.'

Nat looked as though he might be about to ask the next obvious question. Dani pre-empted him.

'No woman in my life either.'

'You never know.'

'Though I have a daughter.'

'You've got a daughter?' Nat did a double take.

'Just turned sixteen.'

'No way.'

'Yes way. Her name is Florence. Flossie for short. Just doing her GCSEs.'

'I can't believe I didn't know.'

'You've been away for a long time. And I guess we stopped moving in the same circles after school.'

It wasn't just that they'd left school and gone away to university, and they both knew it, but for the moment it was a good enough explanation.

'Is she like you?' Nat asked.

'Looks-wise, people seem to think so. But I don't remember being quite so self-assured. She's very into saving the world. Equality. Animal rights. She's got all the answers.'

'She is like you then,' Nat teased.

'She's also got this awful boyfriend, which is how I've ended up with a dog.'

Dani explained the situation. 'Though I have to admit Jezza is growing on me.' She looked down to where Jezza was chewing on her shoelace. Princess was working on the other foot.

'Sorry,' Nat persuaded Princess to let Dani's shoelace go.

'Maybe Jed's right,' said Nat as he considered Dani's story. 'Jezza chose you. Princess seems to have chosen me. And seeing you at Best Behaviour Boot Camp is a bonus. I wondered when we'd have the chance to catch up.'

'Do you think we're going to survive the whole term?' Dani asked.

'If we can have an after-class support group every week?'

'We'll have to find some better coffee.'

Nat agreed.

'So how did you meet your Lola?' Dani asked then. 'Is she local to here?'

'Born and bred. I met her at the hospital. Dad was on the same ward as her grandfather. We got talking when she came in to see him and, well, the rest is history.'

'So you haven't been together long?'

'I suppose not. Five months.'

'But when you know, you know, eh?'

'She's got a boutique,' said Nat. 'Perhaps you know it. Lola's?'

'Do I look like the kind of woman who shops in boutiques?' said Dani, indicating the rip in one knee of her jeans. It definitely wasn't a designer rip.

'You always dressed pretty well, as I remember. Or rather you always looked lovely.'

'I was sixteen when you last saw me. You can wear a sack when you're sixteen and look like a goddess. Look at you, though? What happened to—'

'My hair?'

Dani blushed. 'I was going to ask what happened to the Che Guevara T-shirt? You've really changed your style.'

'I guess I got old.'

'We weren't ever going to grow old. Remember?'

Nat laughed. 'No, we weren't. But it's better than the alternative.'

'Where are you living now?' Dani asked.

Nat named a fancy part of town. 'But just while we do up a place I bought a while back.'

He named an even fancier part of town.

'And you?'

'The same place I always lived.'

'What? With your parents?'

'Just Mum now. Dad passed away fifteen years ago.'

'I'm sorry. He was a great bloke.'

'Thank you. We miss him still.'

'I'll bet. Let me see if I can remember your address. Fifteen Schooner Crescent?'

'You remember.'

'I could probably remember your phone number too.' He could. 'Weird, isn't it? I've got a head full of numbers from the nineties but I can barely remember my own mobile number now.'

'The world has changed.'

'Well, most of it has. Not Newbay.'

'Not Newbay,' Dani agreed.

'All the best bits remain. The Pier. The Majestic . . .'

'Talking of which, Dave the chef would love to see you, I'm sure, Frank . . .'

Nat groaned. 'Only if he doesn't call me Frank. I hated that nickname. I was self-conscious enough about my height as it was.'

'You've grown into it.'

'Got fat, you mean?'

'That is not what I meant at all,' Dani insisted.

'Lola's got me on a pretty strict regime,' Nat admitted. 'She's a yoga bunny.'

Of course, Dani thought. Of course she was.

'Always trying to get me to do it too.'

'I tried it a couple of times,' Dani said. 'Not really my thing.'

'Mine neither.'

This was weird. This conversation. So banal. So odd. If Dani had known that this is what they'd talk about? Yoga? Old phone numbers? She would never have believed it. Inside she just wanted to grab his face in her hands and say 'Nat Hayward! Nat Hayward! Nat Hayward! Is it *really* you?' again and again and again. Instead they were acting like this was all perfectly normal. Drinking bad coffee. Swapping news of family members and fitness regimes. Polite. Bloodless.

'This coffee really is terrible,' was as controversial as the conversation was going to get. As controversial as it should get, perhaps.

'It's the worst cup of coffee I've had in years,' Nat agreed.

After half an hour of small talk, during which neither Nat nor Dani finished their coffee, Nat suddenly said, 'Well, I suppose I should be going. Lola will start to wonder what's happened to me. Or to Princess, more to the point. I've definitely slipped down the pecking order since madam here came along. Give my love to your mum, won't you?'

'Of course, I'm sure she'll send hers in return.'

'And I'll see you next week. Same time, same place.'

'Definitely.'

Nat got up and started to walk towards the pub door. Princess seemed reluctant to follow him. She and Jezza had to be lifted apart.

'Dani Parker.' Nat paused on the threshold and breathed her name with the kind of wonder she'd been feeling since she saw him on the playing field. Since she saw him in the restaurant.

'Nat Hayward,' she said in response. And that was when it happened.

'Hang on,' he said then. 'I think I recognise this place. Didn't we once . . .'

He stopped mid-sentence then nodded to himself. 'Yeah. Of course.'

Dani nodded too as the horrible realisation hit her. It was . . .

Neither of them was going to say it.

Nat's smile wavered before it returned double-strength, as though he was trying to squash something down. A memory. A feeling.

'I'll see you next week,' he said. 'It's been really nice to catch up. I mean that. Dani Parker. Who would have thought . . .'

Dani lagged behind Nat on the pretence that she needed the loo but as soon as he was out of sight, she went back to the bar and ordered herself another drink. A real one this time. It felt wicked, though it was only half a pint of lager and it was nearly midday. It was a silly way to deal with the weirdness of the past half hour and she already knew it wouldn't make a difference.

'Nice dog,' said the landlord, spotting Jezza. 'What breed is he?'

'Half poodle, half Staffordshire bull terrier.'

'A Staffy-poo?' the landlord suggested.

'Yeah. I suppose he is.'

Dani had a feeling she was going to have to get used to it.

She sat back down at the table where she and Nat had spent the last half hour swapping stories. Of all the pubs she might have chosen, why had she decided on this one? Why hadn't Nat said anything when he realised where they were headed? Perhaps it really had only struck him as he left.

They'd both forgotten. That was a good thing, Dani told herself. They'd both forgotten, which meant that perhaps it hadn't mattered that much after all.

It was so weird. If she could have gone back in time and told her sixteen-year-old self that one day she and Nat Hayward would be making small talk in the place that had once seemed so significant? That they would part with a wave rather than a passionate kiss? It would not have seemed possible. How could you go from having a certain someone fill your every waking thought to not knowing what was going on in their life at all?

She couldn't believe Nat didn't know anything about Flossie. Sure, they didn't exactly have friends in common but at least one of his friends must have seen Dani around town, pushing her daughter in her pram. Had they stopped telling him what was going on in her life to save his feelings? Had he stopped asking?

It didn't really matter. Twenty-two years had passed. The time when they were everything to each other was more than half her lifetime ago. In any case, if Nat had tried to forget Dani deliberately, she could hardly blame him. She could hardly blame him at all.

Chapter Fifteen

Sarah and Jane were walking back from their class at the local university of the Third Age, held in the Newbay Arts Centre. Sarah, who had recently turned seventy, was very much taken by the possibilities of modern technology in all its guises. That morning, while the rest of the class was working through a project designed to highlight best security practice while on-line shopping, Sarah had asked one of the 'delightful young people' who ran the course to help her download some apps onto her phone.

The two women stopped at the bus stop and Sarah got her phone out.

'I've been thinking about trying this for weeks,' she said, showing Jane the screen, which was open to Tinder.

'Sarah!' Jane exclaimed. 'That's not that sex app, is it?'

'It is. I read all about it in the *Daily Mail*. It's not just for young people. Hundreds of seventy-somethings have signed up too.'

'You are joking,' Jane laughed.

'Not at all. Apparently it's fuelling a huge boom in STDs for people of our generation.'

'That's hardly a good thing, is it?'

'Well, no. But it does prove people our age are actually out there doing it.'

'All with the same unsavoury person, by the sound of things.'

'Oh, don't be such a spoilsport. There's no harm in looking, is there?'

'I suppose not,' Jane admitted. 'Show me how it works.'

'So,' Sarah explained, 'you turn the app on and then it shows you who's in the area and available.'

'At eleven o'clock in the morning?'

'Cupid never sleeps.'

'What's happening now?'

'It's loading up the possible matches. Then all I have to do is pick out the ones I'm interested in by swiping right and get rid of the ones I don't like by swiping left. Like so.'

Sarah swiped left on the first picture that came up.

'Bum,' she said. 'I don't think I meant to swipe him. Can you un-swipe?'

'How would I know?' Jane asked.

'Left or right?' asked the young man who was also waiting at the bus stop.

'Left, I think,' said Sarah, waggling her phone in that direction. She'd never been very good at knowing her left from right.

'That means you said you *weren't* interested. You can undo that if you want to.'

'Show me,' Sarah handed the young man her phone. Jane's jaw dropped. 'He's not going to steal my phone,' Sarah read Jane's mind.

'No,' said the young man. 'I've got a newer model. There you go, I've restored that match for you.'

Sarah and Jane had a look at the restored profile.

'No.' Sarah shook her head. 'I was right the first time. Look at his teeth.'

'But he might have a nice personality,' Jane tried.

'Does that matter if that's what you have to see first thing in the morning? Next.'

'I like your style,' said the young man.

'Thank you,' said Sarah, glancing up at him from beneath her lashes. Jane recognised that her friend was turning on her famous 'twinkle'. Irresistible to most men and dogs.

Three minutes later, the young man was leaning in over Sarah's shoulder to help with the elimination process. It was surprising to Jane just how many men in the Newbay area had signed up to this app thing. It was inevitable that at some point they would see someone they knew.

'Isn't that the mayor?' Jane asked as Maurice Lindley popped up. He looked quite different out of his robes.

'I think it is,' said Sarah. 'I didn't know he was single.'

'I didn't know he was fifty-five,' said Jane.

'He bloody isn't.'

'Ugh, next,' said the young man, swiping left on Sarah's behalf. 'I hate it when people lie about their age. What's the point of pretending you're fifty-five if when you turn up it's obvious you're sixty?'

'Or seventy, in this chap's case,' said Sarah. 'I wonder if we ought to tell the *Newbay Observer* that the mayor is lying about his age on Tinder? After all, he is in public office.'

'That would be cruel,' said Jane. 'He's always seemed very nice to me. Probably very lonely after losing his wife.'

'Didn't pay her much attention when she was alive,' Sarah observed. 'Ooooh. Look at this one. Nice eyes. Smart shirt.'

'Almost certainly ironed by his wife,' said Jane.

'Yes,' said the young man. 'I wouldn't bother with that one. See down there? That's the edge of a woman's hand at his waist. He's cropped her out of the picture.'

'So he has,' said Sarah. 'It's a good job you're here. I'd have swiped right on him for sure.'

'You get used to sorting the wheat from the chaff,' the young man said. 'There are a lot of people pretending to be something they're not out there in cyberspace. Always ask yourself if someone's been cropped out of the frame. I mean, it may be the other person in the picture was just a mate but when there's so much choice out there, why bother risking it?'

'Quite,' said Jane.

'How about this one?' Sarah asked their new friend.

'See that calendar hanging on the wall behind him?' The two women peered more closely.

'What's the date on it?'

'2009!' Jane exclaimed.

'Exactly. And he didn't look good for sixty even then.'

'You should do this for a living,' said Sarah. 'Dating consultant.'

'What happens after you've done all this swiping?' Jane asked, as Sarah swiped right on three men in quick succession.

'You wait for them to swipe back,' the young man said. 'If they like you and you like them, you're matched and then the rest is up to you. You arrange to meet in a pub or something.'

'Just like that?'

'Why not?'

'Isn't it dangerous?'

'No more dangerous than meeting in a club,' the young man assured Jane. He turned to Sarah now. 'Always make sure someone – like your friend here – knows where you're going. Perhaps even arrange for your friend to be there until the date arrives, so she can check him out. And then there's the nine o'clock emergency call, which is when you ring and pretend to be having an emergency which requires her to leave her date right away.'

'That sounds like a good idea,' said Jane.

'Are you on Tinder?' Sarah asked the young man then. He did his best not to look terrified.

'I'm on Grindr.'

'Is that where I should be?' Sarah asked.

'Not if you're looking for a straight man.'

Fortunately, the bus arrived.

Sarah had been married twice. Jane had never met Sarah's first husband, Toby. He was her childhood sweetheart. Sarah had married him just as soon as she was able – at eighteen – to get out of the parental home. Unfortunately, Toby turned out to be almost as restrictive as Sarah's parents had been. Sarah was hoping for escape. Toby wanted a traditional missus, who would have the dinner on the table every night. She left him two years later.

Sarah's second husband – whom she met at thirty – was a proper love match. They met at a concert, when Sarah asked him to stop sniffing during a performance of Bach's piano concertos. Mortified, Adam had asked if he could make it up to Sarah by taking her to see some Beethoven the following week. Sarah turned up to their first date with a packet of pure white cotton handkerchiefs. That evening they discovered that it was Sarah's perfume – Fracas – that caused Adam's nose to run. She promised to wear less of it. He promised to always carry a hanky and they were married within a year. They were divorced the year they should have celebrated their tenth. And Sarah started to wear Fracas all the time.

Sarah claimed she was bored of marriage and was much happier out of it. Jane thought she might have made a mistake. Adam was a lovely man. Still was. All these years later, Jane sometimes saw him in Waitrose. He hadn't remarried and he always asked after Sarah's health with a wistful look in his eyes. But Sarah wanted adventure. Novelty. She hadn't given up on the idea of having one more roll of the dice.

She'd started looking in the conventional way. She joined the local amateur dramatics society – the NEWTS – in the hope of finding a new leading man there. Alas, the demographics at the society were strongly in favour of the men. There were at least four women for every male member. When she was asked if she would consider playing Lord Capulet in the society's production of *Romeo and Juliet*, Sarah decided she was wasting her time. Tinder was a better idea.

'This gives me a much bigger pond to fish in. We could install it on your phone too,' Sarah suggested.

'I don't think my phone could cope,' said Jane.

Jane loved her dear friend Sarah very much but their approaches to life and love were very different. Sarah had been divorced for fifteen years by the time Jane was widowed. Having her next door helped Jane to get through the hardest moments. She could tell Sarah things that Dani didn't need to hear. Sarah understood what it was like to roll over to face an empty space in the bed where a loved one used to sleep.

But unlike Sarah, Jane was not keen to fill that space in the bed again. Though Tom was gone, he was not forgotten. Never would be. No matter how much time passed. Jane didn't feel the need to replace him because her head and heart were still so full of their love for one another.

Though from time to time Sarah joked that Jane should look for husband number two, she didn't press Jane on the matter. Jane was grateful that her old friend sometimes knew when she was about to push a joke too far. Sarah never tried to get Jane to justify the way she had lived her life since losing her husband.

'You had what I always wanted,' Sarah had said on more than one occasion. 'The pair of you were my romantic ideal. Always there for one another. Like two peas in a pod.'

You couldn't find that sort of love on Tinder. Jane was sure of that.

Chapter Sixteen

Sunday, 3 June 2018

Just as Dani expected, Flossie had not given up on her campaign to be allowed to go backpacking for the summer. When she got home from Xanthe's that afternoon, she was full of stories of how much Xanthe's big sister Zara had benefitted from her own happy travels.

'How can you be a proper citizen of the world if you don't know anything about it?' Flossie asked.

'Zara was not sixteen when she went backpacking. Perhaps we can go on a holiday to the Lakes or something?' Dani suggested.

'Not the same.'

'Well, now that we've got a dog,' Dani countered, 'we're rather limited when it comes to jetting off abroad for weeks at a time. If we weren't already severely limited by money. You didn't think about that, did you? Remember you're responsible for Jezza now?'

'Of course. How was his training class?' Flossie asked.

'He did well.'

'I knew he would. He's such a clever puppy.'

Flossie ruffled Jezza's ears. He was delighted.

'And he needs walking. As do you.'

Flossie rolled her eyes so Dani piled on the pressure.

'If you remember, my dear, one of the conditions of our keeping Jezza was that you would walk him every single day. So far, I haven't seen you take this puppy out once.'

'Mum!' Flossie protested. 'GCSEs.'

'Funny how much more diligent a student you've become since Jezza came on the scene.'

'I've still got two exams to go,' Flossie reminded her. 'As soon as they're over, I promise you I will take Jezza out every day. Twice a day. Three times a day. But until then . . .'

Flossie took out her phone.

Which Dani gently prised from her hand.

'I don't care. We're going for a walk right now. It's Sunday. The weather is beautiful. You need some fresh air. Even star students deserve a break once a week.'

'Going for a walk isn't a break,' said Flossie.

Using the tone of voice Nurse Van Niekerk insisted upon, Dani commanded, 'Flossie. Walk. Now.'

Since Flossie was small, Dani found that the best way to talk to her about anything important was to get her out of the house. There was no point sitting her down at the kitchen table in an attempt to get her to spill the beans. That was too confrontational and even the slightest hint of confrontation made Flossie, who was stubborn as an ox having a bad day, determined to take her secrets to the grave. Even if they were really quite innocuous.

There was a lot to talk about now. Flossie's determination to be allowed to go travelling or at least to a festival with Jed was worrying. Dani uttered a silent prayer every time Jed left the house that she was seeing the last of him. But three months after he'd first appeared in their lives, Jed was still there. Still cluttering Dani's kitchen and eating her out of house and home while telling her she was living all wrong. He was still the main topic of Flossie's conversation even when he wasn't there. Still the centre of Flossie's universe. Dani couldn't help but be worried that fate would deal Flossie a hand that meant she could never get rid of Jed even if she wanted to.

Dani was horribly sure that Jed and Flossie probably got up to more than she wanted to think about when they were alone. When Dani was a teen, her parents had insisted that if she had a male visitor, she was not allowed to shut her bedroom door. Times had changed but Dani half wished she could enforce her parents' old rules. Would it be too patronising for her to initiate a conversation about 'not getting pregnant'? She didn't think Flossie was secretly on the pill (Dani had done a search of Flossie's bedroom while she was at Xanthe's one night) and she'd found no sign of condoms. But was that a good sign? She hoped it meant that Flossie wasn't having sex at all, rather than that she wasn't being careful.

Dani knew what it was like to be left holding the baby. It wasn't much fun.

Five minutes after Dani insisted on the walk, Flossie came downstairs in her 'walking gear'. It looked pretty much the same as her pyjamas with the addition of a pair of combat boots. Jed had found them for her at a local second-hand shop.

'Are those shoes comfortable?' Dani asked.

'Mum, they were made for soldiers to walk thousands of miles.'

'OK,' said Dani. 'It is twenty-five degrees out there today, you know.'

Flossie just rolled her eyes.

It didn't take long for Jed to come into the conversation. Just that morning, he'd sent Flossie a link to a website where people could arrange to share lifts from the UK to the continent.

'Which would be useful if you were allowed to go,' said Dani. 'Which you're not.'

'Mum, Jed would look after me,' Flossie insisted.

'You're too young. You *and* him. I don't think he's anywhere near as capable as you seem to think he is. What about the other day, when he came round on his bike? He hadn't even noticed he had a flat tyre.'

Dani had fixed it for him.

'He's artistic, Mum. He's about philosophy, not practicality. He doesn't always notice the obvious because his mind is on a higher plane.'

Dani shook her head. 'How can I let my baby girl go all the way to Greece in the company of a young man who can't change a bicycle tyre?'

'He'd know how to ask someone else to do it in Greek though?'

'Does he speak Greek?'

'He's downloaded Duolingo.'

'You won't persuade me, Flossie. Not about travelling or about Jed. The fact is, I don't think you're really old enough to be in such a "committed" relationship at all. You should be spending time with a big group of friends, not putting all your energy into one boy.'

'He's not a boy.'

'He is to me. I think we need to change the subject.'

'Mum, just because Jed and I seem young to you doesn't mean our feelings aren't fully-grown. In some cultures, I would probably be onto my third child right now. There are places in the States where you're allowed to get married at fourteen.'

'If you belong to one of those churches where everyone marries their brothers.'

'That's really judgmental, Mum. Just because people have a different way of doing things, doesn't mean they're incestuous.'

'You're sixteen. You've got so many years ahead of you. There's no rush to spend all your time with one person.'

'Didn't Gran meet Granddad when she was my age?' Dani shrugged.

'She did, didn't she?' Flossie persisted. 'And they worked out, didn't they? They were together right up until Granddad died. They'd have stayed married for eighty years if they could.'

'Yes,' Dani agreed with a sigh. 'I'm sure they would have. But things were different then. Life was simpler. People didn't move around so much. They didn't have so many choices. There wasn't the Internet. People didn't know what they were missing so it was easier to be happy with the decisions they'd made. It was easier to settle.'

'I've got the Internet, I know what I'm missing and I still love Jed. He's everything I want in a man. I'm sure he always will be.'

'People change,' said Dani. 'Even people you think will be the same forever. Almost everyone starts out full of idealism and optimism, like you and Jed have now. But life knocks you. Sends you in different directions. If I'd married the man I was with at your age, I'd have ended up very disappointed.'

'Who was that, Mum? Did you even have a boyfriend when you were sixteen?'

'Don't look so surprised. Of course I did. His name was Nat and he wasn't that different from your Jed, only perhaps not quite so . . . pungent.'

'Mum!'

'I know. Jed doesn't believe in polluting the earth with detergents . . . Anyway, Nat was a lot like Jed. He was open-minded, he had a great heart. I had never met anyone quite like him and I was sure I never would. But I met him again a couple of weeks ago – he was throwing a party for his girlfriend at The Majestic – and he had completely changed. He was barely recognisable as the boy I fell in love with. It was clear he'd completely sold out. He was wearing a blazer and chinos.'

Dani knew that would make Flossie want to puke.

'Chinos!'

'I know. Exactly. The Nat I knew would have laughed at the idea he would ever wear clothes like that, but there he was, looking like he'd just stepped off the set of *Dragon's Den*. Talk about selling out. We've got nothing in common any more. If I'd married him, I'd have ended up living in a new-build semi in Newbay View. Which is where he is now.'

A fate worse than death according to Jed (and therefore according to Flossie). Dani didn't explain that it was a temporary move for Nat, while he and Lola did up a much nicer place. That didn't fit the narrative she needed to make her point.

'So, all I'm saying is, you never know how things

will turn out. Give this big love of yours some time to find out if it's really going to go the distance.'

'I get what you're trying to say, Mum, but it really doesn't apply to Jed and me. I mean, the clues were there from the start if you look. Your boyfriend didn't smell "pungent" as you like to put it, so he was obviously always a suit in disguise. Nothing matters more than the planet. If you know that, then you do what you have to do.'

Dani had to laugh.

'And I will make sure that Jed and I don't end up in a semi in Newbay View. There's no way. I'd rather live in a tent. In any case, that's probably all we'll be able to afford, thanks to Grandma's generation stealing all the cash in the boom years . . .'

And then she was off on another Jed-influenced rant about the selfishness of the older generation. Who still paid the younger generation's mobile bills, Dani observed.

Dani felt a little bad for having used Nat as an example of someone who'd grown up and abandoned all his ideals when the truth was that Nat had only done what so many people do. He'd embraced his responsibilities. He'd come back to Newbay to take over the family business so his mum could concentrate on improving his father's health.

In fact, in complete contrast with what she'd tried to make Flossie believe, Nat was exactly the kind of man Dani and most of her friends were looking for now. Sensible, solvent, still had his own teeth. (It was surprising how many didn't. Dani had heard a lot of horror stories from Liz, who was a dental hygienist.)

He was also funny, kind, and sexy in a self-deprecating way. Nat was the kind of bloke any straight woman would be happy to have as a partner in life.

Ah well. Nat would never know that she had used him as an example of the corrupting influence of capitalism and a poster boy for why you can't possibly know you've found 'the one' when you're still not old enough to drive.

Dani had recently read a newspaper article that said scientists had proved the human brain didn't mature until twenty-five. Perhaps that explained why Dani had chosen so badly when she hooked up with Flossie's dad.

That Flossie's father wasn't on the scene was a great cause of sadness for Dani. Less so now, after sixteen years of coping without him. But still, there were moments when Dani wished she could turn to Flossie's father – Lloyd – for back-up or just for a second opinion on the way Flossie approached life.

But Lloyd had never wanted to be a father. Oh, he talked the talk when Dani first told him she was pregnant, but he soon changed his tune. He tried to persuade her she should get an abortion, telling her that a boozy weekend they'd had soon after Flossie was conceived might have left her somehow damaged. When Dani decided to ignore that, Lloyd still continued to find ways in which they could both duck out of parenthood. Adoption was an option.

In the end, it was Dani's father who told Lloyd that he could go. He could walk away and never think again about the baby Dani was carrying. Jane and Tom would look after their daughter and their grandchild. Better an absent father than a resentful one, said Tom.

Was that right? Or had being raised by a single mother in a house that was always full of women left Flossie vulnerable to hero-worshipping the first man she met?

Big thoughts for a Sunday afternoon.

Soon Dani and Flossie were almost at Duckpool Bay. Flossie seemed to have forgotten that she didn't want to go for a walk because she had 'so much' studying to do and was now happily chatting away about Donald Trump and his latest insults to humanity.

Dani loved that her daughter was so passionate about the greater good. She really did. If only she could have been passionate about the greater good without the essential accessory of a pompous pungent boyfriend.

Jezza was also enjoying the walk. From time to time, Dani remembered to acknowledge how well he was doing, just as Nurse Van Niekerk had told the class they should. When Dani did that, Jezza looked up at her with something approaching adoration. Though he was Flossie's dog by name, his heart was all Dani's.

'Shall we have an ice cream at the beach café?' Dani suggested.

'Yes!' said Flossie, with almost as much enthusiasm as when she was five.

Ice cream had always been Flossie's kryptonite. When she was little, just about anything could be solved with the promise of a cone topped with a ball of vanilla the size of a baby's head, studded with chocolate buttons. Fortunately, the beach café did a great vegan version of Flossie's life-long fave. Dani preferred mint choc chip studded with miniature Matchmakers. The hedgehog effect made it impossible to eat without getting in a mess but it was worth it.

Dani and Flossie bought their ice creams and a little tub of special dog ice cream for Jezza, which he practically inhaled, so fast did he get it down. After that, Jezza sat between Dani and Flossie and tried his best 'starving' look on each of them in turn. It was difficult to stay resolute and not slip Jezza the end of a cone. Especially when he fixed you with those big brown eyes of his.

'Aw! Look at that little face. Do you think Jed did the right thing, yet? Getting us a dog?' Flossie dared to ask.

'The jury is still out,' said Dani, primly, though it was plain to see that she was falling deeply in love with the puppy. The little ball of fluff was impossible to resist.

Chapter Seventeen

The beach was busy. It was Jezza's first time on the sand and he was very excited. So many new things to see. So many new smells to smell. With so much distraction, Jezza soon forgot his training and Flossie, who hadn't been at the class, was not equipped to remind him.

'You've got to keep the lead shorter,' said Dani, as they walked towards the sea. 'And talk to him. Keep getting him to look up at you and reward him for his attention. Like this.' Dani reached across to take the lead from Flossie. At the same time, Jezza abruptly changed direction. Flossie stumbled over his lead. Thinking that Dani had hold of it, she let go. Dani felt the end of the lead whip through her fingers as Jezza made his dash for freedom.

He may have been half poodle and half Staffy but his spirit animal as he headed for the waves was pure greyhound. By the time the two women had righted themselves again, Jezza was nowhere to be seen.

Flossie went straight into a panic. Dani, thinking quickly, said they should split up to search.

'Back here in ten minutes,' she said. 'He'll probably come running back anyway.'

'Jezza!' Dani called as she walked towards the rocks, while Flossie headed back towards the car park. 'Jeremy! Jeremy Corbyn!'

His full name turned a few heads but didn't have any more success when it came to persuading the little sod to come back.

'Jezza!'

The beach was so crowded. It seemed that everyone in Newbay was making the most of this genuinely hot summer's day. As were all their dogs. There were dogs everywhere, running up and down the sand and in and out of the ocean, having a fabulous time. Never had Dani seen so many in one place. From the corner of her eye, Dani thought she saw Jezza making a dash for the waves, only to find that the dog in question was a completely different breed.

It didn't help that Jezza was pretty much the same colour as the rocks that studded the sand.

'Jezza!' Dani yelled. Still no response. So she muttered under her breath, 'When I find you, you stupid dog, I am turning you into a footstool.'

Dani was cycling through all the emotions as she walked the beach. Irritation, anger, embarrassment. Even fear. What if someone had stolen their Jezza? She knew it happened. There had been a report in the local paper about the problem. And there were two kinds of thieves who took a puppy. The first just fancied the idea of owning a particularly cute-looking mutt, who might just be a pedigree. The second . . . Dani tried to block the dog-fighters from her mind.

'Jezza!' she called more urgently. 'Where are you?'

Dani was almost at the rock pools now. Would Jezza know how to swim if he fell into one? Was swimming instinctive for dogs? Jezza had never been in the water on her watch or on anyone's watch so far as Dani knew. Assuming he hadn't already been washed out to sea,

Dani was going to have to make sure he knew how to get out of trouble in the water too. Oh, how she regretted letting Eric persuade her she shouldn't just march round to his house and drop Jezza off on the driveway.

But this moment was also teaching Dani something about how she really felt. She just wanted Jezza to be back in her arms. Even back on the sofa. If she could just find him, she would never think about getting rid of him again.

'Jezza!'

Sometimes you have to lose something to make you realise just how much you really love it.

'Jezza!'

Suddenly, Dani's cries were met with equally anguished cries from behind the rocks.

It was a woman.

'Get off! Get him off! Get him offffff me!!!!'

Assuming the very worst, Dani picked up her pace and ran to the screaming woman's aid. But she wasn't being ravaged by a gang of pirates fresh from the sea. She wasn't fending off any men at all. Rather, she was batting away the attentions of a young and enthusiastic dog. Jeremy 'Jezza' Corbyn.

'Get him off me!'

With a mixture of relief and embarrassment, Dani leapt into action and took hold of Jezza's harness, dragging him off the blonde woman whom she only now recognised. At the same time she recognised the woman's companion. Nat Hayward. Nat and Lola. And their dog. Little Miss Princess.

'I am so sorry,' said Dani, helping Lola up from the sand. 'Hi Nat. I'm sorry. I really am. Flossie was holding Jezza's lead but he somehow managed to get away and . . .'

Hanging on to Jezza's harness with one hand, Dani tried to brush the sand off Lola's dress, a broderie anglaise number that had been pure white until just a few moments ago.

'He must have got a whiff of Princess and come rushing to find her.' Dani tried to make light of the chaos. 'Not that Princess is whiffy, of course. But, dogs, you know, they've got that crazily good sense of smell thing going on. I'm sorry. I'm sorry. I'm sorry.'

Nat was checking Lola for bumps and bruises. The dress, though marked with paw prints, was otherwise in good shape. Not ripped, thank goodness.

'Is it machine washable?' Dani asked.

'Does it look machine washable?' Lola responded.

Dani stepped back, not knowing quite what to say, though feeling that she ought at least to hang around until Lola confirmed that she was still in one piece. She seemed to be quite upset about her hair.

'I had it done yesterday.'

'I'm just so, so sorry,' said Dani again, unaware that even as she was apologising, Jezza was working on giving her something even more serious to apologise for. He'd finished sniffing Princess's bottom and was now busy investigating Nat and Lola's picnic. By the time the three humans noticed that Jezza had managed to get into the Fortnum & Mason hamper, it was too late.

'Oh Jeremy!' Dani wailed in despair. 'I can't take you anywhere.'

'What did he just eat?' Nat asked. There was a strange hint of panic in his voice. 'What did he just have? Dani? Tell me?'

'I don't know,' said Dani. 'What did you pack? What was in there? Nothing with chocolate, I hope? Was there chocolate?'

Nat was on his knees now, gently shoving Jezza out of the way so that he could inspect what was left in the basket. He pulled out three empty paper cupcake cases and stared.

'Oh no, oh no, oh no.'

Nat sat back on his heels and grabbed at handfuls of his own hair as he stared into the basket as though it were the *abyss*.

'Oh no!'

'I'll go to the café and buy you some sandwiches,' Dani suggested. 'And cakes, if that's what he's eaten. They have really good cakes there. Their lemon meringue tart is to die for. Shall I get you one of those and maybe a slice of their chocolate cake too? Or ice cream? Maybe an ice cream would be better given how hot it is this afternoon. I'm sure you already know, Lola, but the Duckpool Bay ice-cream stall was voted best in the country last year. People come from miles away.'

Nat was still oddly inconsolable.

'It's not that bad, is it?' Dani said at last.

Nat turned to look at her.

'It is absolutely that bad,' he said. 'Your dog has eaten three cupcakes . . .'

And very nice Jezza had found them too. He was busy trying to clean the last of the icing off his whiskers. However, Dani was soon to understand just how serious the situation was.

'He's eaten three cakes and one engagement ring.'

Chapter Eighteen

While Dani just stared at the empty cupcake wrappers, Nat explained that he had taken an engagement ring – a whole carat's worth of flawless diamond set in platinum – to the Newbay Bakery where they baked it into a lemon-flavoured cupcake – Lola's favourite flavour. The plan was that Nat would propose with the cake at the picnic they were just laying out, when Jezza the Staffy-poo came charging over the rocks, trailing havoc in his wake.

And now Jezza had eaten the ring.

'I don't know what to say,' said Dani. 'Or *do*! He wouldn't have eaten a ring. Surely? He'd have felt it, wouldn't he? Are you sure he didn't spit it out?'

Nat and Dani checked the sand around the picnic basket while Lola sat on a rock, contemplating the magnitude of Nat's admission about the true ingredients of their lunch.

'Your dog ruined my big moment,' was all she seemed able to say while Nat and Dani were on their knees conducting a fingertip search.

'It's not here,' Nat said after a couple of minutes of digging around the picnic blanket. 'He must have swallowed it. There's no other explanation.'

'Then I suppose it's a good thing. At least we know where it is. We'll get the ring back,' Dani promised Lola. 'I swear to you. I will monitor every move Jezza makes – especially those – until the ring is found. I'll take him to the vet and get an X-ray.'

'You don't want to put Jezza through an unnecessary X-ray,' said Nat, who was sitting on the sand, looking wild-eyed and slightly desperate. 'We know he's eaten it. We've just got to wait for it to show up.'

'I don't want to wait!' said Lola. 'That's *my* ring he's eaten! Can't we take him straight to the vet now? They must be able to give him something to make the ring come out more quickly.'

'He's only a puppy,' Nat reminded his would-be fiancée. 'Dani really doesn't want to go giving him any unnecessary medication while he's still so young.'

Lola disagreed. 'But it wouldn't be unnecessary. That dog contains thousands of pounds worth of my jewellery.'

Technically not hers yet, thought Dani, unless Nat had already made the proposal. That didn't seem to be the case.

'Darling, I promise we will have the ring back before you know it,' Nat said.

'Covered in poo,' Lola muttered.

'Poo washes off,' said Dani. 'Diamonds are indestructible. Aren't they?'

Nat carried on trying to calm Lola down. 'We will have the ring back and I will propose to you in style and then this will just be a funny anecdote that we tell people on our wedding day.'

Nat looked to Dani for reassurance. She nodded. That seemed like the right thing to do. Though inside she wanted to scream.

'It will make a great story,' she forced herself to say. 'It can't have happened to many people, can it?'

'No,' said Lola. 'It can't.' She was not to be persuaded that it could ever be seen as a good thing.

'Perhaps it's lucky? Like when a bird poos on your head.'

Lola looked as though she was about to cry.

'Dani will let us know just as soon as the ring's come out again. You've got my number, haven't you?' Nat said.

'Has she?' Lola asked.

'No,' said Dani quickly. 'At least, not unless it's the same number you had when you were eighteen.'

'I've changed it a couple of times since then.'

Nat gave her the digits. 'Call me as soon as there's any news,' he said. Then he wrapped his arm around Lola and kissed her troubled forehead. And with that, Dani took it that she was dismissed.

She picked Jezza up and exited as gracefully as she could. Which wasn't that gracefully at all as it happened. On her second step, she ended up knee-deep in a rock pool.

Chapter Nineteen

Ten minutes later, Flossie caught up with Dani in the middle of the beach.

'You found him!' Flossie shrieked.

She at least was happy to see them both.

'Where was he, Mum?'

'He was eating somebody's picnic,' Dani said. While Flossie took Jezza, Dani tried to unstick the wet leg of her jeans from her skin.

'Oh no. You naughty boy.' Flossie wagged her finger at the dog. He wagged his tail back at her, giving her his best big Staffy grin. 'Were they OK about it, Mum? How much did he eat? A lot?'

'Only about five thousand pounds' worth,' Dani deadpanned.

'Eh?'

'Your dog has expensive tastes.'

As far as Dani was concerned, Jezza was definitely her daughter's dog now.

Flossie couldn't understand why there had been a ring in the cupcake anyway. She had Dani tell her the story several times as they walked back home.

'So, let me run through that again. It was your ex-boyfriend?'

'Yes.'

'About to propose to his new girlfriend? The one who's much younger than you?'

'Yes,' said Dani. 'Thank you for reminding me.'

'And he was doing it with a ring in a cupcake?'

'Yes,' said Dani. Again.

'That is the naffest thing I have ever heard,' Flossie announced at the end of the telling. 'I can't quite believe it.'

Later, when she heard the news, Jane was similarly surprised.

'Jezza interrupted your ex-boyfriend proposing to his new girlfriend?'

'Yes.'

'That's a heck of a coincidence. Will he think you did it deliberately?'

'How on earth would I have done that? I didn't know he was going to be there, did I?'

'He didn't tell you he was going to propose?'

'No. Why would he? I'm just someone he knew twenty-two years ago.'

'Bloody stupid idea putting a ring in something you're going to eat, if you ask me,' said Jane. 'Poor girl could have cracked one of her teeth. Or what if she'd gulped it down without noticing?'

'I think she'd have noticed she was swallowing a one carat diamond,' said Dani.

'Not if she's got a very big mouth,' said Jane.

Flossie couldn't help sniggering at that.

Then Sarah came round and Dani had to go through the whole story again.

'That Lola's going to think you let Jezza eat the cupcake deliberately,' Sarah echoed Jane's view.

'She is not!' Dani insisted. 'Anyway, ladies, the fact is that Jezza has eaten Lola's ring so he is not to be allowed out of this house or the patio area until further notice.'

'He's not allowed into the garden proper?' asked Jane.

'No. What if he buries a poo in one of the flower beds?'

'Do dogs do that?' Flossie asked.

'Knowing Jezza, he would,' said Dani. 'No, it's best that we know exactly where he is and where he's pooing at all times. If either of you see him doing it, you're to get out there and rescue the results at once.'

'What?' Jane and Flossie chorused.

'I thought we agreed that Jezza was going to be the responsibility of the whole family.'

Jane and Flossie shared a glance.

'Look, all I ask is that you gather the poo up and put it in a bag. Just like if you were pooper-scooping on a walk. I'll do the nasty bit when I get home from work, OK? God knows I've dealt with enough shit in my time.'

'Language!' Jane and Flossie chorused.

'I think it's justified right now.'

'I'm sorry, Mum,' Flossie said then. 'If I'd been hanging onto Jezza like you asked me to then none of this would have happened.'

'Oh Floss. It's not your fault. Having a picnic on the beach is just asking for a dog to come along and eat your cakes, if you ask me.'

'Besides,' said Sarah, 'if Nat Hayward wanted Jezza to notice he was eating a diamond, he should have bought a bigger one.'

Flossie and Jane both whooped at that.

* * *

'Now, ladies,' said Sarah, changing the subject, 'I need your opinions on something. I want you to help me choose between these.'

She pulled two dresses out of a carrier bag. Both were the kind of bodycon numbers most women would have swerved. Let alone most women in their seventies. But Sarah was very confident about the way she looked and with good reason. 'Tomorrow night I have a date,' she said.

The other three were all ears.

'How did you get a date?' Flossie asked.

'Tinder,' said Sarah. She showed them the profile of the man in question. His name was Malcolm. He purported to be seventy. Divorced with two grown children. He had hair. He had teeth. If they weren't his, they looked pretty expensive, which was almost as good.

'Of course, he might turn out to have a terrible personality but he's taking me to the Merry Widow, so at least I'll get a good meal.'

'Auntie Sarah,' said Flossie. 'That's so mercenary.'

Sarah cackled. 'Which dress?'

'The red one,' said Flossie without hesitation. 'You'll knock his eyes out.'

'Assuming he can see,' said Jane, taking a closer look at the profile. 'Are you sure he's really seventy?'

'I don't actually care. Dani, you should try this Tinder thing,' said Sarah. 'This time next year someone could be giving you a diamond-filled cake.'

'I can make my own cake,' said Dani.

Though she wouldn't have said no to a single carat.

She looked ruefully at Jezza, who was beneath the kitchen table, stomach gurgling.

Chapter Twenty

The next morning, Dani didn't remember straight away what had happened the day before. When she came down into the kitchen and discovered that Jezza had left her three small but perfectly spherical poos near the back door, Dani scooped them up and was just about to flush them down the cloakroom toilet when she remembered.

'Oh shit!'

Literally.

She carried the poos back through the kitchen and sat on the back step while she set about the unpleasant but important work of dissecting them over a sheet of newspaper in search of Lola's missing engagement ring. Jezza joined her and seemed to think it was great fun, putting his paws and his nose where they most certainly weren't wanted.

'Jezza! Keep your nose out of it! No Jezza! No!'

When he made a playful grab for a poo that was yet to be dissected, Dani shrieked her annoyance. But there was nothing to be found. Not this time. The poos were just and only that. No platinum or diamonds. No joy.

Having washed her hands and thoroughly disinfected them, Dani made herself a much-needed coffee. While she drank it she googled 'dog digestive system' and 'how long does it take for something to travel through a puppy's gut'. The answers were most illuminating.

When Dani typed in 'dog ate engagement ring' there were over three *million* results. The link at the top of the page showed an X-ray of a Labrador puppy from Tulsa who had eaten both his mistress's engagement ring *and* her wedding ring. Twenty-three thousand dollars worth! It made her own dilemma seem just a little less dramatic.

Dani was quickly learning that dogs really will eat anything but there was no consensus as to how to deal with the problem. The poor Tulsa pup had to have surgery. Dani definitely didn't want that for Jezza. But she was beginning to worry that it might be the only way.

As soon as it was open, she phoned the Thomas veterinary surgery and asked to talk to Evan. Nurse Van Niekerk would not put her straight through.

'I can answer most dog-related questions,' she said.

'OK,' said Dani. 'How long will it take my puppy to poo out a one carat diamond and platinum engagement ring?'

'Mrs Jeremy Corbyn, what on earth were you thinking, letting him eat an engagement ring?'

'Of course I didn't *let* him eat an engagement ring,' said Dani. 'He stole it. It was baked into a cupcake.'

'What? Who bakes an engagement ring into a cupcake?' Nurse Van Niekerk asked the question everybody seemed to ask. 'Did they do it by accident?'

'Ask Mr Princess,' said Dani.

'Well,' said Nurse Van Niekerk, once Dani had told her the whole story. 'What a pickle. You could be looking at a couple of days. After which time, if nothing has passed, I would recommend you bring Jeremy Corbyn into the surgery. Bring him in immediately if he seems in any kind of distress beforehand. For example, if he starts to seem constipated. The ring may cause a blockage. Actually, scratch that, I think you should bring him in at once. We can't be too careful. Was the ring in a claw or rub-over setting?'

'I don't know.'

'A claw setting raises the chance of it snagging in his bowels and then causing a tear and possible infection . . .'

Jezza's eating the engagement ring was still a very long way from becoming a hilarious anecdote.

Nurse Van Niekerk consulted with Evan the vet.

'Evan thinks you should bring Jeremy Corbyn in and perhaps have an ultrasound, just in case. That way we'll know exactly where it is. Or whether he actually ate it at all. There's no point you going through his stools if he didn't really eat the ring in the first place.'

'No,' said Dani. 'I suppose there isn't.'

Fortunately, as yet, a visit to the vet held no fear for Jezza. He jumped onto the examination table so he could better lick Nurse Van Niekerk's face. While Jezza was distracted, Evan gently palpated the little dog's stomach.

'I can't feel anything too worrying,' he said. 'Which is good. He's not a small dog so I say give him another day or two.'

'And keep going through the poo?'

'And keep going through the poo. No one said dog ownership was glamorous.'

That was an understatement.

Chapter Twenty-One

That afternoon, however, someone else would have to keep an eye on Jezza's bowel movements. Jane, to be precise. Flossie was 'revising'. Dani had to go into work.

She told Dave the chef what had happened over the weekend while they sat outside for a break.

'Oooh,' he said. 'That's not good. Frank's new woman is going to think you did it deliberately.'

'How could I have done it deliberately?' Dani was getting fed up with having to ask. 'How? I didn't know she and Nat were going to be there. I certainly didn't know he was going to propose.'

'He wants to get the deal sorted before she finds out what he's really like. When you get hold of a woman like that, you don't let her slip through your fingers.'

Somehow Dave had a knack for always saying the wrong thing.

'So, now he's got to wait until Jezza poos the ring out. I'll bet he's bricking himself.'

'Which is apt,' said Dani.

'Oh yeah,' Dave the chef chuckled. 'I wonder if she'll say yes.'

'Why wouldn't she?' Dani asked.

Cheryl, who had dared to cross the kitchen, interrupted them.

'Hey!' Dave protested. 'You're not meant to be in here. Or out here. This space is for kitchen staff only.'

'I have been standing at the kitchen hatch for the past ten minutes, trying to catch someone's attention. It's not my fault if you're both out here having an overly long cigarette break when I need to talk to someone about a golden wedding anniversary celebration.'

'Just get her out of my kitchen,' said Dave.

'I'm going,' said Cheryl, turning on her heel with a dramatic flounce. Dani followed her.

A fiftieth wedding anniversary. The couple were waiting in the lounge. Dani carried out a plate of éclairs to go with their coffee, chosing two that were decorated with tiny slivers of gold leaf.

While the couple ate their cakes, she asked them about their wedding day and whether they would like their golden anniversary party to echo anything about that earlier occasion.

'I don't think so, dear,' said the wife. 'We had corned-beef sandwiches at our reception.'

'I like corned beef,' said the husband.

Dani suggested a menu that was altogether more twenty-first century. The couple were delighted with all her ideas. Once she'd made a few notes, Dani left Cheryl to deal with the rest of the paperwork and went back to the kitchen.

To make it to fifty years of marriage was no mean achievement but it was something that Dani no longer felt she had any chance of doing. Maybe Nat would get to his golden wedding anniversary, though. He would be ninety but that wasn't impossible.

Gosh, Nat wanted to get married. He was *going* to get married. There was no way that Lola would say no, if the way she reacted on the beach was anything to go by.

What was Dani feeling right now? Envy? Of the fact that Lola was getting a proposal and a one-carat diamond ring? Or of the fact that Lola was getting Nat?

Dani phoned Nat that evening to assure him that she had the ring situation – or more specifically the poo situation – under control.

'There's nowhere to run and nowhere to hide,' she joked. 'If that dog poos, I'm on it. And in it.'

'Ugh,' Nat groaned. 'I'm really sorry you're having to do this, Dani.'

'No, I'm the one who's sorry. I should have had my dog under control.'

'But I was really short with you, when we were on the beach.'

'It's understandable.'

'No. I shouldn't have snapped. It's just that . . . well, I was pretty nervous.'

'About proposing?'

'Yes. It took everything I had to pluck up the courage and then . . .'

'At least now you know she would have said yes.'

'Do you think so?'

'Of course. You heard her, Nat. Once she knew what was going on, that ring was hers in her mind.'

'Well, hopefully it will be again soon.'

'And next time you won't propose on a beach full of marauding hounds.'

'No. It wasn't the best place to do it. I thought it would be romantic but . . . Duckpool Bay. It's not exactly the Caribbean, is it?'

No, thought Dani. 'But it's special in its own way,' she said out loud.

'Perhaps not special enough. Perhaps the picnic ending up in disaster was a good thing. I get another go at it. I'll have to put my thinking cap on when I'm planning the second attempt. Got any ideas?'

Was he really asking her? Dani didn't know what to say. Was he *seriously* asking her to help him plan a proposal? Eventually, she said, 'Oh! Sorry, Nat. I hate to cut you off but I've got to go. Jezza just went out through the dog flap. He might be off to do his business. This could be the one! Wish me luck.'

Dani put the phone down in haste.

But Jezza was not on his way out through the dog flap. He was in his basket, chewing on one of Flossie's old shoes. Or maybe it was one of Flossie's new shoes. From the general state of her footwear, it was hard to tell. It certainly looked ready for the bin.

Dani had just wanted to get off the phone. She didn't want to be a sounding board for Nat's proposal plans even if she had inadvertently wrecked his first attempt. What was he thinking? He either wasn't thinking. Or he didn't think it was a big deal.

That thought made Dani draw breath.

She crouched down beside Jezza's basket and engaged him in a playful tug of war over the filthy red ballet flat. Jezza had a poodle's cunning when it came to getting hold of things he shouldn't have and a Staffy's tenacity when it came to hanging on. Dani tugged the ballet flat away from him. Jezza tugged it back, twice as hard, putting his whole little body into the effort.

'Drop it,' Dani suggested. She used the tone and the

body language Nurse Van Niekerk had taught her. She was pleased when he responded as he ought.

'Good boy. Now fetch.'

Dani skidded the shoe across the kitchen floor. Jezza skidded after it, paws slipping as though on ice. He brought the shoe back to her. His eyes seemed to twinkle with excitement at the prospect of another round. He let her take the shoe from his mouth then adopted the play position. Front paws down, bum up, Staffy grin wide and enthusiastic. When Dani pretended to throw the shoe but didn't, sending Jezza on an empty errand, he gave a little yip. Those people who thought that dogs didn't have a sense of humour were definitely wrong.

'Did you eat that ring deliberately?' Dani asked the dog as he returned with the shoe for a third round of tug. 'Did you do it because you think Lola's wrong for him too?'

Jezza dropped the shoe and gave an insistent 'yip'.

'I agree,' said Dani. 'Totally wrong.'

'Mum!' Flossie shrieked, when she walked in and saw Dani and Jezza playing. 'Those are my best shoes.'

Chapter Twenty-Two

Poo duty took Jane back to being the mother of a newborn. It had been a long time since she'd been so interested in anyone's (or anything's) bowel movements. Thirty-eight years since Dani. Sixteen for Flossie. In the meantime, she found she'd grown horribly squeamish.

Two days after the ring debacle, with still no sign of diamonds in the dirt, Jane decided she needed some kind of gadget so she could help at arm's length.

The pet shop near the Newbay train station had been in the same place for decades. When Dani was small, Jane would take her in there to see the hamsters, guinea pigs and rabbits, which were the only animals the shop ever stocked. They had a policy of not selling anything larger. The only dogs and cats advertised in the window were mixed-breed mistakes and moggies, to discourage anyone from buying farmed pets.

The shop had a warm, yeasty smell to it, which Jane guessed was probably the scent of hamster widdle on straw, but Dani loved going in there all the same. Dani had asked for a hamster for her seventh birthday. She called it Noel, after Noel Edmonds. Of course, she didn't look after it and hamster care became another fixture on the ever-growing list of things Jane did around the house. Noel lived for three years, which was pretty ancient in hamster terms.

Years later, Jane found herself back in the shop with Flossie. Flossie also had a hamster as her first pet. Her hamster was called Dora the Explorer, after the children's cartoon. Dora the hamster lived up to her namesake. She was an escapologist. Always off on an adventure. Until the day she got stuck down the back of the sofa. That was unfortunate to say the least.

Jane pushed open the door to the shop. The smell took her right back. Straw. Animal feed. Damp guinea pig. It was like stepping back in time. Particularly since the man behind the counter was the same man who'd owned the shop when Flossie and Dani were small.

'Good morning,' he said, welcoming Jane with a genuinely friendly smile.

'Hello,' said Jane.

'What can I do for you today?' he asked.

'We've just got a puppy,' said Jane. 'Well, we've had him for a couple of months now.'

'Lovely. What kind?'

'Staffy-poo. Half Staffy, half poodle.'

'Unusual mix.'

'A mistake, I think. But he's very intelligent,' Jane said. 'Except . . . I need something to pick up his movements.'

'Is he unwell? Off his food? Have you spoken to the vet?'

'Well, yes but . . .' Jane described the predicament.

'The dog ate a diamond!' the pet shop owner exclaimed.

'Quite a big one by all accounts.'

'Then you really don't want to miss a single poo,' the pet shop owner agreed. He took Jane to the dog section of the shop and showed her the options for cleaning up without needing to bend down.

'This one is very popular,' he said, demonstrating a pooper-scooper with an end like the grabber in the 'win a cuddly toy' machines on the pier. 'Only really good for a firm movement, though.'

'If it's not firm,' said Jane. 'I shan't be picking it up.'

The pet shop owner laughed.

'Oh, the conversations you must have in here,' Jane said.

'I do hear some funny things. But a dog eating a diamond is a first for me. Though some dogs really will eat anything. I'm lucky my own's quite a fuss-pot.'

'What kind of dog have you got?'

'Greyhound. Called Sapphire. She's a rescue dog but has the refined taste of a born duchess. I had a Labrador once. She would eat anything. Including my son's home-work book.'

'Really?'

'Yes. All that was left was the torn cover with his name on it. It was fun explaining that to his teacher.'

The pet shop owner carried the pooper-scooper to the till and rang it up.

'Would you like to join our members' club?' he asked.

'I don't know,' said Jane.

'I hate to ask. It's my son's idea for boosting loyalty to the shop. He's more or less in charge now so I have to bow to his greater knowledge. He says when people can get everything they need in the supermarkets or on-line, we have to work a little harder to persuade them to come here instead. You get a ten per-cent discount on everything. Including this if you start right now.'

'In that case.'

Jane filled out the card.

'Mrs Parker. That name sounds familiar. In fact, I was thinking that your face is familiar too. You used to come in here with a little girl, didn't you?'

'Two little girls,' said Jane. 'My daughter Dani and then my granddaughter Flossie. But they're both very much grown-up now.'

'Time flies,' the pet shop owner observed.

'Doesn't it just.'

'But I never forget a face. And your husband, he used to come in here too. A nice man. Always very friendly. How is he?'

'Oh.' Jane hated that question. More than a decade and a half had passed since she'd first had to give the difficult answer but it still didn't get any easier.

'I'm afraid Tom passed away,' she said quickly.

'I'm sorry.' The pet shop owner bowed his head for a moment.

'Don't worry. You weren't to know. And it was quite a while ago now. Fifteen years.'

'Sometimes it feels like it was just yesterday, though, doesn't it? I lost my wife in 2009. Nearly a decade and I still miss her every day.'

Jane nodded. 'It's hard.'

'But life carries on, eh?'

'That's what they say.'

'Yes,' said the pet shop owner. 'I find keeping busy helps. My son has been very good to me. And my daughter-in-law invites me over all the time.'

'I'm lucky with my daughter too,' said Jane.

'So I'm never on my own if I don't want to be.'

'Me neither.'

'It's just those times when you see something you

want to talk about and you turn around to tell your special someone and . . .'

'They're not there.' Jane sighed. 'I know exactly what you mean.'

They stood in silence for a moment, both deep in their own memories.

'Oh. I'm sorry,' said the pet shop owner. 'You only came in here for this and I've made you listen to my complaining.'

'Hardly complaining,' said Jane. 'And sometimes it helps to say these things out loud. Especially to someone who's also been through it.'

'Thank you.'

He handed the pooper-scooper over. It was wrapped as carefully as a present in a curl of thick brown paper.

'I'll see you again, I hope. I want to know what happens to that diamond!'

As Jane was leaving the shop, her phone rang. It was Sarah.

'Jane, I've just been matched with a retired dentist from Paignton. He's in Newbay this afternoon, watching a sing-along matinee of *Seven Brides for Seven Brothers* at the Odeon. He wants to know if I can meet him for tea afterwards.'

'Well?' said Jane.

'Are you available for back-up?' Sarah asked. 'After last time . . .'

Sarah's date at the Merry Widow had turned out to be something of a disaster. Her date was not seventy. He hadn't been seventy since 2003. And those weren't his own teeth. He took them out to eat his soup. At least that's what Sarah claimed.

'I'll be there,' said Jane, promising to walk Sarah as far as the teashop where this new prospect wanted to meet when his film was finished.

'Heaven only knows whether it's worth it but there have to be some nice single men over sixty out there who aren't just looking for someone to help them remember their medication,' said Sarah.

'I'm sure there are,' said Jane. She'd just met one, hadn't she? She thought about telling Sarah about the man in the pet shop. He was a widower. He seemed very nice. His teeth looked original. But for some reason Jane decided to keep it to herself.

Chapter Twenty-Three

The diamond ring made its reappearance that evening, while Dani, Jane, Flossie and Jed were eating supper. Jed was holding forth about the evils of capitalism. As usual. Flossie was gazing up at him like a disciple. Dani and Jane were glazing over. Suddenly, Jezza made a bolt for the dog flap but didn't quite get there. Instead he squatted on the doormat and his doggy eyes bulged as he finally passed the precious gem.

'I feel sick,' said Jed, dashing for the bathroom. Flossie went with him, ever attentive.

'Wimp. I don't know how he expects to foment a revolution when he can't hack a bit of dog poo,' Dani muttered as she took the doormat outside to begin the real dirty work.

And there it was! No wonder Jezza had looked so uncomfortable, poor thing. The ring was bigger than Dani had imagined.

'Wow. Boil the kettle!' she called to Jane.

A little rinse in a bowl full of boiling water and washing-up liquid later – outside on the step, of course – and the ring looked absolutely perfect.

'Gosh, that is lovely,' said Jane, when she saw it.

'I think it's Tiffany,' said Dani, holding the ring between her fingers and tilting it back and forth so that the diamond caught the light.

'Can I have a go?' asked Jane, slipping it onto the ring finger of her right hand. 'Very classy. Nat's got good taste.'

'Yes,' said Dani, resisting the urge to say something about that taste not extending to his future wife.

Jane handed it back to Dani. 'Do you want to try it?'

'No,' Dani said. 'That's a bit weird, isn't it?'

'It's supposed to be lucky, trying on another woman's engagement ring. You have to twist it three times.'

'I think I'd need to twist it three hundred times,' Dani sighed.

Flossie and Jed returned now that the coast was clear of dog mess.

Unlike her mother, Flossie wasn't squeamish about trying the ring on. But Dani was disturbed to see that Jed wasn't squeamish about Flossie trying the ring on either. Despite it being the ultimate symbol of capitalism, surely?

'What do you think, *bae*?' Flossie asked him.

'You know what I think about blood diamonds,' he said. 'But it does look good on you.'

'Put a ring on it . . .' Flossie did her best Beyoncé impression, waggling her fingers in Jed's direction. Dani sincerely hoped he wasn't planning to. Of course he wasn't. He'd only just finished his A-levels. But . . .

'Right,' she said. 'That's enough of that.' She asked Flossie to give her the ring back. 'I'm going to put that ring somewhere safe until I see Nat at boot camp. Somewhere out of Jezza's reach. I'm not going through that again.'

Jed slid the ring off Flossie's finger while making goo-goo eyes at her.

Dani felt a little unwell at the sight.

* * *

Jed seemed reluctant to leave that night. He was still there at almost ten o'clock and Flossie had one more exam to sit.

'Time for this one to be in bed,' Dani said.

'Mum,' Flossie complained. 'I do know. I'm not a child.'

Flossie walked Jed to the door and watched him lovingly as he laced up the filthy old combat boots that made Dani's heart sink whenever she saw them in her hallway. Then she and Jed engaged in their usual ten-minute goodnight ritual.

'I'm shutting the door,' said Flossie. 'You've got to go. No way! I can't shut the door until you're halfway up the path. Jed! Please! You be the one to say goodbye.'

'No you,' said Jed.

'No, it's your turn.'

'It's yours.'

And on and on.

And on and on until Dani poked her head into the hall and said, 'Jed. It's twenty past ten. Please sling it.'

'Mum,' Flossie complained, when Jed was finally gone. 'I don't know why you have to be so rude to him.'

'You were letting all the heat out.'

'It's June, Mum. It's the middle of summer. Talking of which, it's the solstice in a fortnight and me and Jed . . .'

'No.'

'You didn't even let me finish. That's so not polite.'

Neither was spraying the seat where Jed had been sitting with Febreze, which was what Dani did next.

'Mum!' Flossie was outraged. 'Jed does not smell.'

'Love is nose-blind,' Dani referenced a freshener ad.

'Anyway, we've worked out how we're going to pay to go to a festival. We're going to make organic cupcakes and sell them at the beach.'

'No, you're not,' said Dani.

'Yes, we are. Mum, you said I should think about earning some money this summer and now me and Jed have come up with a plan, you're just pooh-poohing it.'

'Because unless it's some charity bake sale, you can't just make cakes and sell them at the beach like that. They've got to be made in a proper commercial kitchen. There's health and safety to think of. And then you'll need a trading licence.'

'You're just trying to stop me and Jed from raising the money to go away.'

'Well,' said Dani. 'I did tell you that I'd make my mind up after you got your exam results. And I never said you could go anywhere with Jed on your own.'

'I told Jed that you would help us,' said Flossie. 'I might have known I was wrong. Honestly, Mum, why can't you just be happy that Jed's being entrepreneurial?'

'Flossie,' Dani tried. 'I'm just telling you how it is.'

Flossie was already on her way to bed.

Up in her bedroom at last, Dani could take a closer look at the ring without interruption. Away from the eyes of anyone who might have taken the gesture the wrong way, she slipped it onto her ring finger and was surprised to discover that it was exactly her size. Not only was the band right for the width of her finger, the stone was perfect too. Not too small but not too big. Classy. Elegant. It was the sort of ring that whispered rather than shouted.

Dani sat at her dressing table and imagined for a moment that the ring was hers. She imagined herself sitting across the table from her fiancé. She leaned her cheek in her left hand. The diamond caught the light and sent little shards of flattering, glittering rainbow colour across Dani's face. It was beautiful and it made her feel somehow more beautiful too. She'd never really 'got' why so many women she knew went gaga for jewellery. But with this ring, she thought finally she understood. How could anyone not want to own something so exquisite?

She held her left hand out in front of her and admired the diamond's brilliance as she moved her fingers.

But she was not Cinderella and this was not her shoe, or her ring. No point getting attached.

Dani picked up her phone and texted Nat.

'Ring found at last.'

'You are a star!' he texted back. 'Can I pick it up tomorrow?'

'Catch me on my break at The Majestic?' Dani suggested. 'Three o'clock?'

Nat agreed.

Reluctantly, Dani took the ring off.

Chapter Twenty-Four

At three the next day, Dani met Nat in The Majestic's car park. She saw him before he saw her. As she watched him walk across the tarmac with his familiar loping stride, he could have been a teenager again.

'Hello.' He kissed her on both cheeks.

'Continental,' Dani commented.

'You taste of sugar,' he said.

'Oh. I was just dusting something with icing sugar,' Dani explained. 'It gets everywhere.' Which was the truth. All the same, she blushed.

'So . . .' Nat bounced on the balls of his feet, expectantly.

'Of course. The ring.'

Dani retrieved it from her pocket. She'd wrapped it in a tissue, which she now unfolded. She placed the ring in the palm of Nat's hand. His long fingers closed around it. He had beautiful hands.

'Thanks for this,' he said, shaking the ring in his fist.

'I'm sorry it took so long.'

'It must have felt longer for you,' Nat said.

'At least now I have in-depth knowledge of my puppy's digestive system.'

'Which is always useful,' Nat agreed.

'How is Princess?' Dani grasped for small talk.

'She chewed one of Lola's Manolos,' Nat admitted. 'Lola was not happy.'

'You mean a Manolo Blahnik shoe?' Dani said. 'Not much danger of that happening in my house, at least.'

'Lola was always complaining that those particular shoes hurt anyway. Too pointed . . .'

Meanwhile, Nat was putting the glittering ring back into its dark blue velvet box. It was like a reverse proposal, Dani suddenly thought, as he tucked the box into his breast pocket.

'I should go back in,' she said. 'See you at boot camp?'

'Actually,' said Nat. 'You won't. Not this week anyway.'

'Oh?'

'Mini-break,' Nat said.

'That's nice. You found somewhere dog-friendly?'

'Er no. Princess is actually still going to be at the training session. With one of Lola's friends.'

'I'll be sure to look out for her.'

'Him,' Nat corrected.

'Great. I'm sorry about the ring,' she said again.

'All's well that ends well,' said Nat. He kissed her cheek again.

'Better than a doughnut,' he said.

Back in the kitchen, everyone had heard about the ring and knew that Nat had come to collect it. Dave and Joe paused in what they were doing as Dani came in and watched her face for some sort of sign. Joe knew all about Dani's past connection with Nat now.

'Never mind, Dani. It'll be your turn one day,' said Dave.

'Eff off, Dave,' said Dani.

Chapter Twenty-Five

On Friday, Jane noticed that they were running low on kibble for Jezza's meals. She decided she would sort the situation out before it slipped her mind. She shrugged on her new beige trench coat and accessorised with the pretty scarf Dani had bought her for her last birthday. As an afterthought, she slicked on some of the lipstick she hardly ever wore. Then wiped most of it off again. It was still way too bright.

'You're only going to the pet shop,' she reminded her reflection.

The Newbay pet shop was busy that morning. There were three dogs tied to the special rings outside, regarding each other warily as they waited for their owners to come out with treats. Or flea spray.

Jane looked up at the shop's façade before she walked in. She'd never really noticed it before but now it struck her as silly that she had been coming to this shop on and off for the best part of three decades without knowing the name of the proprietor. It was there, in small lettering, underneath the name: 'Newbay Pets. W. T. Hunter and son.'

'Good morning, Mr Hunter,' said Jane, when the other customers had gone and she had his full attention at last.

'Mrs Parker,' he nodded in response. 'Sorry to keep you waiting. What happened with the diamond?'

'Safely recovered and possibly even more sparkly than when it went in.'

'Wonderful. And no ill effects for your puppy, I hope.'

'I don't think so. He seems just as lively as ever. He's back to eating shoes. But I've come to get him something more suitable.'

'Is he on a dry diet?' Mr Hunter asked.

Jane handed Mr Hunter the shopping list Dani had given her.

'You're in luck. We just got some more of that in.'

Mr Hunter disappeared into the back of the shop. While he was gone, Jane busied herself looking at the flyers and postcards that were tacked to the shop's noticeboard. Puppies, kittens and guinea pigs were all seeking homes. There were flyers for training classes, dog-walkers, dog-sitters, and dog yoga.

'Dog yoga!' Jane exclaimed.

'I hear it's rather good,' said Mr Hunter. 'Not that you would catch Sapphire on a yoga mat. Unless she was allowed to sleep on it.'

'I think Jezza could use a bit of Zen,' said Jane.

'How are you getting used to having a dog around?'

'Well, when he's not eating expensive jewellery . . . I rather like it. He's always so happy and it's nice to know that someone will be there when I get in.'

'That's how I feel,' said Mr Hunter. 'You should always come home to someone who's pleased to see you.'

'Even if it's only cupboard love,' said Jane.

Mr Hunter rang up the price of the kibble. 'With your members' club discount, of course. And an extra ten per cent for being . . . erm, our . . . tenth customer today.'

'Why, thank you. That's very kind.'

'My pleasure. Now, this is a heavy bag,' said Mr Hunter. 'How are you going to get it home? Where's your car? I'll carry it out to your boot for you.'

'Don't have a car. I came on the bus.'

'You can't carry this on the bus.'

'Of course I can. The stop is right outside our house.'

'But the stop where you get on is quite a walk away, isn't it? Let me deliver it for you later.'

'No. I couldn't possibly let you do that.'

'Then at least let me walk you to the bus stop.'

'But the shop?'

'Is closing for lunch,' said Mr Hunter as he put a cover over the cash register.

'I can't ask you to . . .'

'But I can insist. Come on.'

Mr Hunter turned the notice on the door of the shop to 'closed' and locked it shut. Jane continued to protest that it really was a favour too far but Mr Hunter wouldn't hear of it.

'This is the difference between buying your kibble at the supermarket and buying from us,' he said.

'Waitrose need to watch out,' said Jane.

And when she saw Mr Hunter hoist the bag onto his shoulder as though it were a little bag of sugar, Jane admitted, at least to herself, that she was glad he'd offered to help her. She was wearing the wrong coat and the wrong shoes for that kind of heavy labour. She was already worrying about how she'd cope at the other end. Flossie – who was at home on study leave – would have to come out to meet her.

Jane and Mr Hunter walked towards the train station. Jane's bus stop was just opposite.

'Isn't it a beautiful day,' said Mr Hunter as they crossed the road. 'I think we're going to have a proper summer this year.'

'About time,' said Jane.

'Good for all those events in the park. Remember how they got completely rained off a couple of years ago. The one year I managed to get my act together early enough to get tickets for the outdoor opera and it was washed out. Every show cancelled. Have you ever been? I hear they put on a very good show.'

'I haven't,' said Jane.

'It's *Così Fan Tutte* this year.'

'Oh. I don't know that one very well.'

'You should see it. I saw it years ago on holiday in Italy. I was with my son and his wife. She got tickets to see the opera in an old amphitheatre. It was magical, I tell you. I fell in love with the music at once. As a matter of fact, I've got tickets for the Newbay performance. Obviously, it won't be the same as watching an open-air performance in the Italian sun but . . . I wonder . . .'

Jane felt a weird prickling sensation under her arms as though she was suddenly nervous.

Mr Hunter cleared his throat then began again, 'They're pretty good seats . . .'

A bus pulled in to the stop.

'Oh that's mine,' said Jane, wrestling the bag of kibble from Mr Hunter's arms. 'Thank you so much. I'll see you again soon.'

She climbed onto the bus. Almost falling straight off again in her haste to get on board. The driver nodded her through when it became obvious that she was going to have a job hanging on to the kibble and fishing out her senior citizen's bus pass.

Mr Hunter still had his arms out, as though holding the dog food, when Jane got to her seat and waved goodbye.

That was a close shave, Jane said to herself. Was he going to ask her out? When he started to talk about the opera? It sounded as though that was his plan. And in order to head off the potential awkwardness, Jane had jumped onto a bus. A bus that she now realised was not going her way. Rather, it was going in the very opposite direction to the one she wanted.

'Bugger.'

She got off at the first stop – struggling with the ridiculous bag of dog food – and crossed the road to catch a bus going in the right direction. As she waited, Jane saw Mr Hunter walking back to his shop on the other side of the street. She pressed herself up against the bus shelter and closed her eyes as though not being able to see him meant he wouldn't be able to see her. Jane was still blushing by the time she got home.

Chapter Twenty-Six

For Dani, the rest of the week had passed quickly. The season was in full flow and the restaurant at The Majestic was packed every lunchtime, afternoon and evening. She and Joe were at their very busiest, piping out meringues and éclairs as though they were machines. Newbay's visitors had an insatiable need for cake.

Busy was good, thought Dani. Busy didn't give her time to think about what was missing from her life. The incident with Lola's engagement ring had left her feeling oddly reflective. She found herself ambushed by memories of that moment in the car park, when she'd handed the ring back to Nat, far more often than she liked. That moment and another moment from more than two decades before.

But then it was Saturday morning. Time for Best Behaviour Boot Camp again.

Of course, Dani recognised Princess at once. But Lola's friend . . .

Woah.

Dani gawped. She suddenly wished she'd made a tiny bit more effort with that morning's dog-walking outfit. She was still wearing the T-shirt she'd worn for the entire previous day and overnight (she always felt chilly in bed even in the summer). Lola's friend was incredibly good looking. He was not unlike Aidan

Turner around the face, Dani thought, with possibly an even better body.

'Hi,' Dani said as he stepped into the space beside her. This far into the course, everyone had their place and they stuck to it. 'You must be Lola's pal.'

'You know Lola?'

His eyes lit up at the mention of her name.

'We've met a couple of times. I know her boyfriend better. Nat. We were . . . well, I suppose you could say we were childhood friends. This is Jezza and I'm Dani Parker.' She held out her hand.

'Will,' said Lola's friend. 'Will Hamilton. I'm actually Lola's ex.'

'Oh.'

'But that was ages ago. We're just really good mates now. Nat sprung this mini-break on her but Lola didn't want Princess to miss out on her training so she called on me. I suppose you could say I'm Princess's godfather of sorts.'

'Or *dog*father,' Dani joked.

'Ha! That's a good one,' said Will. He laughed to show his perfect teeth. They were beautiful. Like a toothpaste ad. 'Now, tell me. What do we do here?'

'We do whatever we're told,' said Dani.

Nurse Van Niekerk was striding across the field to join them.

'Puppies, ready! Owners, ready! Your full attention, please!'

'She's fierce,' said Will. 'But I kind of like her.'

'Mr Princess,' Nurse Van Niekerk turned both barrels in Will's direction. 'I appreciate that you are new to Best Behaviour Boot Camp, but I would hope that you have already observed that Best Behaviour applies not only to the puppies on this field today. We lead by example, Mr Princess. How can Princess look up to you if she can't respect you? If she sees you giggling away like you're a twelve-year-old schoolboy, she is getting the wrong message. No talking unless I have told you that you must talk directly to your dog. You are not here to waste your time, your dog's time or my time.'

'That told you,' said Dani.

'I'm Mr Princess?'

'Mrs Jezza . . .'

Dani got the warning stare.

'Eyes front!'

For the rest of the class, Dani and Will spoke only when they were spoken to, but their joint humiliation at the beginning of the session had already fostered a closer bond between the two new friends. Every now and then they caught each other's eye and had to work hard to hold in the giggles. It was the most fun Dani had had in a very long time.

At ten o'clock precisely, the class came to an end. Nurse Van Niekerk blew the final whistle and puppies and their owners were dismissed with stern instructions to practise everything they'd learned that day over and over before the next session.

'Sir, yes, sir!' Will dared a mock salute.

Nurse Van Niekerk pursed her lips at him.

'You are bad,' said Dani as she and Will left the playing field. 'No one gets to take the mick out of Nurse Van Niekerk without consequences.'

'Good job I'm only here for a week, then.'

'You're just in Newbay for a break?'

'No,' said Will. 'I meant I'll only be at this doggy class for a week. Until Nat comes back. I'm in Newbay forever.'

'Forever?'

'Perhaps. I moved here last month. It was an out there kind of decision but every so often you have to shake it up.'

'The only shaking that goes on here is due to the high incidence of Parkinson's.'

'It's not that bad. I already knew it a bit because of going out with Lola. We were both in London at the time but we used to come and visit her parents here. I always liked it. The sea and the beach and all that fresh air . . . And I wanted a change of lifestyle so I just thought I'd go for it.'

'Honestly? I've spent my entire life trying to move out.'

'Why? It's really lovely here. You've got the sea. The beach.'

'The mobility scooter racetrack that is the prom . . . You're not old enough to move here, Will.'

'Then you're not old enough to live here. Come on, Dani. Let's go and get a coffee. There must be somewhere you can get a decent flat white around here.'

'You want to go for a coffee?' Dani was unduly surprised. 'With me?'

'Yes, you, Dani Parker. Lead the way.'

Chapter Twenty-Seven

Dani took Will to Daffodil's. It wasn't the best place to get coffee in Newbay but it was the nearest to boot camp and definitely better than The Sailor's Trousers. Dani had done her research on dog-friendly venues since then. Daffodil's did a proper latte and sometimes the girl behind the counter tore her attention away from her iPhone long enough to actually get your order right.

Will insisted on paying for their coffees. Dani had a flat white. He had a skinny latte.

'Payment in advance,' he said. 'Because I'm going to pick your brain about this town. What there is to see and do and which gym I should join . . .'

'I don't think I can help you there,' said Dani.

Will leaned an elbow on the table. He was wearing one of those T-shirts with the tightly rolled-up sleeves designed to show off muscles to best effect. Will had some impressive muscles. Dani glanced up to see that the girl behind the counter was taking a surreptitious pic of her new friend. He was probably the most interesting customer to ever grace the benches of this caff. He was twenty years younger than the average age of the clientele and twenty times more buff.

He smiled a little questioningly. Dani panicked that he'd actually asked her something while she was gawping at his biceps.

'You've got a tattoo,' she blurted, immediately regretting it.

'Ah, yes.' He rolled his sleeve up a little further so that she could see.

'What does it say? LAW?'

'That's right,' said Will. 'It's not finished. When it's completely done, it will say "Law unto myself".'

'Interesting,' said Dani.

Odd, was what she thought.

'How long were you and Lola together? If it's not too personal a question.'

'Oh, I don't mind answering questions,' said Will. 'Like I said, I'm totally over it. After all, we went out for eighteen months but we've been broken up for nearly five years now. That's almost three times as long as we were together. So as far as I'm concerned, that means our friendship is more significant than our relationship ever was, right?'

'I suppose so,' said Dani. 'And it's great that you've been able to stay friends. Not a lot of people truly manage it. There's usually one member of the former couple who secretly wants to get back together, isn't there? Who accepts the friendship but really is just waiting for something more?'

'That's not me,' said Will, quickly. 'Lola was right to end things. We weren't really that well suited. We'd have fallen apart eventually. I could see the first time I met Nat that he was a much, much better match for her.'

'Yes,' said Dani. 'They do seem very well suited.'

She had the sense that both she and Will weren't being entirely honest.

'And I hope they'll be really happy together for a very long time.'

Will raised his coffee cup in a toast. Dani reciprocated with her mug.

'Dani,' he said. 'I hope this doesn't come out wrong but I'm wondering if you'd like to go somewhere for a proper drink?'

'What? Like a pub?'

'Yes. A pub.'

Flossie was supposed to be at Xanthe's all day and Jane would be at her computer class with Sarah. For once, Dani didn't have to be anywhere particular. She had a day off. So why shouldn't she be in a pub with a gorgeous-looking man? It didn't have to mean anything. It was just nice to be in the company of someone other than work colleagues or well-meaning girlfriends. It was different.

'I'm up for that,' she said.

Will and Dani settled on The Pirate Ship, a pub that overlooked Duckpool Bay. It was extremely popular with the local dog owners, who raised money there each Christmas for the Guide Dogs for the Blind Association. The walls of the pub were dotted with photographs of the dogs they had sponsored over the years.

'I always thought I'd like to be a puppy walker,' said Dani. 'But now I've had this one for a couple of months, I know I'd never have had the right stuff to make sure a guide dog puppy was properly trained.'

'I don't know,' said Will. 'I was pretty impressed by Jezza's response to your calls today.'

'If only he'd been a bit more responsive last week.'

Dani recounted the story of Jezza and the engagement ring. Nat and Lola clearly hadn't told him.

'You mean Nat was going to propose to Lola?'

Will seemed surprised.

'Yes. But Jezza and I scuppered that.'

'Oh well,' said Will. 'I suppose fate sometimes takes things in hand. Look, Dani, shall we get a bottle instead of two glasses? We'll drink more than a glass each, won't we?'

'I guess so,' said Dani.

'I know I will now,' said Will.

Will carried the two dogs' bowls and the bottle of wine out into the pub's garden, where Dani found them a table in the shade.

'So, how did you meet Lola?'

'I was working as a model,' said Will.

Of course he was.

'And so was she.'

Of course she was.

'We were both booked onto the same job. A website shoot for a sportswear company specialising in tennis wear.'

'Do you play tennis?'

'Do I look like I play tennis?'

'Well, you must do, otherwise they wouldn't have booked you.'

'Fair point. Anyway, I don't really play tennis and neither does Lola, but they booked us for the shoot and they flew us down to South Africa to do the pictures. It was the middle of winter in Europe at the time and they wanted the pictures to look summery. So, we flew to Cape Town for a week and Lola and I had to spend the week pretending to be in love, and able to play tennis, for the cameras. Until, it started to feel like something was happening for real.'

'That's romantic,' said Dani.

'I didn't expect it to outlast the job. These things normally don't. It's easy to be all loved-up when you're in a beautiful location wearing clothes and getting your hair done every day. You get to see the best side of each other. It's a case of what happens on the shoot stays on the shoot. But when we got back to London, we started seeing each other officially. And one thing led to another and within two months we'd moved in together. Bish, bash, bosh.'

'So, why did you break up?'

'Lola met someone else on another shoot. At least that's the official line. It was pretty clear to me that her family didn't approve of our relationship. A male model for a son-in-law? Lola's father was more ambitious for her than that.'

'So you think he influenced her?'

Will nodded. 'He's a very persuasive man. It doesn't matter, though. If that's what's important to Lola, then she was the wrong woman for me, right?'

'Yeah,' said Dani. 'You can't choose who you fall in love with and you certainly shouldn't try to choose who your children fall in love with.'

Though as she said that, Dani knew that if Flossie decided to fall in love with someone even more 'unsuitable' than Jed, Dani would not hesitate for a moment to lock her in a high tower accessible only by fireman's ladder.

'So, Dani. Tell me some more about you. What do you do?'

'Oh, nothing so interesting as being a model.'

'Trust me, there is nothing interesting about being a model. Unless you enjoy standing around all day while a photographer faffs about and people smother you in make-up and paint definition on your pecs.'

'They do that? If I'd known that was an actual job, I would have signed up for it years ago.'

Will laughed.

'Maybe it's not too late for me to retrain. But for now, I'm a patisserie chef. I make cakes and desserts for a living. At The Majestic Hotel.'

'That's where Lola had her birthday party.'

'Were you there? I made her birthday cake.'

'NFI.'

Dani squinted.

'Not Effing Invited,' Will clarified.

'It was quite a small party,' said Dani. 'Anyway, on a day-to-day basis, I'm in charge of the team that makes the cakes for the afternoon teas and the desserts the restaurant serves in the evening. And then, as and when it's required, I'll make special cakes according to guests' requirements. Birthday cakes, wedding cakes. I even made a divorce cake once.'

'What did that look like?'

'It was a chocolate sponge with black icing. Three tiers. For the top I made two little figures in wedding dress, but instead of standing side by side, I made it look as though the bride was pushing the groom off the edge of the cake into oblivion. I think I may have a photo on my phone.'

Dani scrolled through until she found it.

'I like it,' said Will. 'Though remind me never to get on the wrong side of you.'

'So, that's what I do,' said Dani. 'It's what I've done since university.'

'You went to uni? I'm in awe of people who go to

uni,' said Will. 'It must be so great to have a brain. I've had to get by on my looks. And when they go . . .'

'I think you've got a little while before that happens,' Dani said. 'At least another fortnight.'

'Then I had better make the most of it.' He gave her a playful wink.

Was Will flirting with her? It was so long since Dani had flirted with anybody, she wasn't sure she would recognise it when it happened. But Dani eventually decided that he was. That wink. That 'make the most of it'. He was referring to the attraction she obviously felt for him, wasn't he? And implying that the feeling was mutual? Perhaps? Blimey, she hoped so.

When Will came back with the second bottle of pinot grigio, he was also carrying a bowl of chips. Instead of sitting opposite as he had been before, he sat down beside her.

'I took a risk. You do like chips, I hope.'

'You are a psychic!' Dani exclaimed.

'Ketchup?'

'Always.'

They shared the bowl and argued over who should have the last chip.

'It's yours,' said Will.

'No, it's yours.'

Will patted his stomach. 'I've got a job on Tuesday. Got to keep in shape.'

'Ah well,' said Dani. 'No one trusts a skinny chef.'

'But you've got a great figure,' said Will. 'Sorry. That was very personal of me.'

'Oh no, it's fine,' said Dani. 'Really.'

They were both blushing now. Or maybe it was just the wine and the sunshine.

Will looked for a distraction.

'Ah look,' he said. 'I think Princess and your Jezza are in love.'

'I think they are,' Dani agreed.

'Watch out, Jezza. She'll break your heart. Shall I get another bottle of wine?' Will asked suddenly.

'A third?' Dani asked.

'Three's a charm.'

Chapter Twenty-Eight

Three was certainly something . . .

It was almost four o'clock and Will and Dani were still at the pub. On the table in front of them, two empty bottles of wine and one that was more than half finished were testament to how good a time the pair of them had been having. Princess and Jezza were both asleep beneath the table now, curled up in a ball on Dani's windbreaker, which had been sacrificed for a dog bed. Dani didn't need a coat. It was a lovely sunny afternoon and she was glowing from all the booze.

'Will you look after Jezza while I go for a wee?' Dani asked her new best friend.

In the ladies' bathroom, she looked at her reflection critically. They'd had another snack – a couple of burgers – to try to soak up some of the alcohol, and she had a piece of lettuce between her teeth. That was the problem with salad-based garnishes. She wondered if Will had noticed. She checked her grin again and splashed water on her red cheeks.

As Dani walked back to the table, Will was transfixed by his phone. He didn't put it down when he saw Dani was on her way back. She sat down next to him and waited for him to put the phone away. He didn't. Instead he said, 'He's done it.'

'Who's done what?'

'Guess.'

Will handed Dani his iPhone. It was opened to Instagram. Lola's account. There were three new photos. The view from the top of the Eiffel Tower. A photograph of Nat and Lola grinning in each other's arms. And a close-up of an engagement ring. Which wasn't the ring that Dani had sifted out of Jezza's poo.

'Did you know he was going to do this?' Will asked.

'Well, no,' said Dani. 'I mean, he didn't tell me but I suppose it's obvious when you think about it. A mini-break in Paris after that aborted proposal the other week.'

'Nice, eh?' said Will.

'Yes. Good for them,' said Dani. 'I can't think of anything nicer than getting a marriage proposal on top of the Eiffel Tower.'

'Or anything more original,' Will added in a bitchy aside, which Dani found hilarious. The wine helped, of course. 'Top of the Eiffel *effing* Tower. I bet they weren't even the first couple that lunchtime.'

'Oh god,' said Dani. 'I bet Nat would be mortified if he knew we were looking at him on Instagram. We shouldn't look.'

'The whole point of Instagram is that people look.'

'Good point,' said Dani. 'Do you mind if I scroll back through Lola's account?'

'Be my guest,' said Will.

Dani tapped to turn Lola's feed into a patchwork of mini-pictures.

'Oh, I can't believe she hasn't taken that one down!' said Will, clicking on a shot that showed him by a pool somewhere sunny. There were several shots of Will in Lola's feed. Will talked Dani through each one.

But while Will and Dani looked at Lola's old

photographs, she was busy posting new ones. The newly engaged couple moved from the Eiffel Tower viewing platform to its restaurant, where they celebrated with a champagne lunch. Lola took half a dozen photographs of her hand, draped artfully across an Eiffel Tower menu. Her friends and followers were busy posting their congratulations and admiring her newest piece of bling.

'All that mashing up of poo I had to do and in the end Nat proposed with a different ring!' Dani observed again.

'That is just bloody rude,' Will agreed. 'But still, we wish them all the best. Right?'

'We do,' Dani chimed in. 'To Lola and Nat. How should we toast them?'

They toasted the engagement with another bottle of pinot grigio. The pub's landlord ensured that Princess and Jeremy were attended to before he even thought about the wine. He placed two bowls of water on the counter, along with two dog treats.

'Is Princess allowed to have these?' Will mused.

'Probably not,' said Dani. 'But it is a Saturday.'

'It is. And her parents are getting married.'

'Indeed.'

'Let's take an Instagram pic of our own?' Will suggested after bottle number four had gone down.

'We've got to get the dogs in it,' said Dani.

'Princess and Jezza send their very best wishes to the future Mr and Mrs Hayward?' Will suggested.

Click.

'We need another,' Will said. 'Put your chin down. Look up at the lens. Pout like this. No. Like this! Oh yes, baby! You're good.'

'Post it!' Dani giggled.

The next day, Dani would wish they hadn't posted that photograph. You always think you look better than you really do when drunk.

That afternoon, however, she was only too pleased to pose with Will and Jezza and Princess in the garden of The Pirate Ship. Lola had Paris. Nat had Lola. Dani had . . . well, at the very least she had a great big new crush.

Chapter Twenty-Nine

A big new crush and a horrible hangover . . .

Dani slept through her alarm the following morning. She was woken by the sound of Jezza objecting loudly to the fact that a neighbour's cat was in the garden, while Jane tried to persuade him, equally loudly but ineffectively, to calm down.

'Jeremy!' He was always Jeremy when he was in trouble. 'Jeremy, will you please be quiet!'

The more Jane shouted, the more Jezza barked. Dani took it as a message that it was time to get up.

'Are you OK?' Jane asked her daughter, when Dani staggered into the kitchen.

'I think I've got a bug,' said Dani.

'Or *delirium tremens*,' Jane said. 'What were you up to yesterday afternoon? You came in and went straight to bed. Reminded me of when you used to go out with your friends from school and try to get into the house without your father or me noticing you'd been drinking.'

'I just went for a drink with some of the puppy-training people.'

'Dogs really do seem to improve people's social lives,' said Jane.

'Something like that,' said Dani.

At last Jezza had stopped barking, satisfied that he'd seen the cat off, even though in reality the cat had taken its own sweet time to get through the garden and couldn't have given a rat's arse whether or not Jezza had anything to say about it.

Full of pride at having defended the household so vociferously, Jezza swaggered back into the kitchen and gave Dani the full morning greeting.

'Ugh, Jezza. No tongues!'

'How's he doing with his training?' Jane asked.

'He's an A student,' Dani responded. 'If A stands for absolutely unbiddable when the teacher's watching. Sit!' She attempted a command.

Jezza lay down and rolled over.

'See?'

'I'll take him out this afternoon,' said Jane. 'I could do with some fresh air. You look like you could do with some fresh air too.'

'I'll get some on the way to the hotel. Right now, what I need is coffee.'

Unfortunately, Dani couldn't get out of going to work. In her twenty-two years at The Majestic (on and off) she was proud to be able to say that she had never called in sick when she really had a hangover. The Majestic kitchen team were exactly that – a team. 'All for one and one for all,' as Dave the chef liked to say. Anyone who didn't understand that wouldn't last long on Dave's watch.

All the same, when Dani got into the kitchen, she wanted to walk straight out again. The smell of the food being prepared for lunch was more than she could bear.

'I'm not well,' she moaned.

Dave was unsympathetic.

'How many bottles?'

Four bottles shared over the course of a whole afternoon seemed pretty reasonable to him.

'You've got to be professional,' he said. 'Or build your tolerance before you go out on a binge,' he added.

'Thanks, Dave,' said Dani. 'I'll bear that in mind.'

Dani worked quietly in her corner of the kitchen and after a couple of strong espressos and a bacon sandwich, she started to feel a little better. If only a little.

She wondered how Will felt this morning. And whether she would ever see him again. Dani didn't think she had spent a whole afternoon drinking since Fresher's Week at university. Maybe Will made a habit of it. She'd probably never find out. He hadn't asked for her number and she hadn't asked for his. She knew he was on Instagram and could probably work out who he was if she looked up Lola's profile and went through her followers but . . . that was stalking, wasn't it?

'There's someone in the dining room wants to see the chef,' said Harrison, one of the waiting staff.

'I can't go out there,' Dave said, indicating the front of his apron, which was covered in something that looked like blood. Possibly was blood. 'Dani, you'll have to go.'

'I've got a hangover,' she tried.

'I'm pulling rank.'

So it was Dani who had to go out into the dining room, feeling and looking like death warmed up. She sincerely hoped that whoever it was that wanted to talk to the chef wasn't about to complain.

'By the middle window,' Harrison guided her.

A horribly familiar couple sat at the best table in the restaurant.

Dani's heart sank.

'We're here celebrating our daughter's engagement,' said Ian, Lola's father, when Dani got to them.

'What lovely news,' said Dani as though she hadn't already heard.

'She's got herself a very nice young man. Well, you've met him, of course. He's not that young but these days people take a while to grow into their responsibilities, don't they?'

'I suppose so,' said Dani.

'Anyway maybe we'll be back here for the wedding. We were very impressed by what your team did for Lola's birthday. It's still the best place in Newbay to have a wedding reception, this is, isn't it, Sheena?'

Lola's mother agreed.

'Though, of course, it's what Lola wants, dear,' she said. 'She might want to get married abroad.'

'She's not getting married abroad,' said Ian. 'Why would she want to get married abroad? She'll have a proper wedding reception here. If I'm paying for it . . .' He turned back to Dani. 'We wanted to know how much it would cost.'

'That's not really my area,' said Dani. 'But if you like, I could take your details and pass them on to Cheryl the events manager. She'll be in tomorrow.'

'Yes, please,' said Ian, handing Dani his card.

Ian Taylor. Waste disposal was his game. Well, there was obviously brass where the muck he dealt with was concerned.

'Maybe they should have their engagement party

here first,' said Ian. 'To see if you and your team can handle things to my expectations.'

'I'm sure we could arrange that,' said Dani. 'Cheryl will be able to tell you everything The Majestic has to offer.'

'Yes,' Ian nodded. 'I think this is the perfect place for the reception, Sheena. Only the best for our girl. I just hope her new fiancé is up to scratch. You've got to wonder what took him so long to get round to settling down.'

'He just hadn't met our Lola,' Sheena suggested.

'There is that . . .'

Ian and Sheena seemed to be seguing into a conversation to which Dani really didn't think she should be contributing.

'I should leave you,' she said. 'Service isn't quite finished for me. But congratulations. On your daughter's engagement, I mean. You must be very happy.'

'I'm the happiest man alive,' said Ian. 'I can't wait to walk my girl down the aisle.'

For all sorts of reasons, Dani couldn't wait for her shift to be over that day. When it was time for her break, she sat outside by the wheelie bins feeling thoroughly sorry for herself. Lola's father was clearly a man who liked to get his way and Dani wouldn't have wanted to be Lola, battling to get what she wanted in a wedding, but Ian's obvious pride in his daughter was touching. He couldn't wait to walk her down the aisle.

It was one of Dani's greatest regrets that her father had not been able to do the same for her. She felt her throat constrict at the thought of it. Oh, it was a silly thing. A tradition that should probably have long since been consigned to the annals of history. Women didn't need to be 'given away' as though they belonged to their fathers and then to their husbands. But Dani sometimes wondered whether she had ever given her father a chance to be obviously proud of her. Regret made her heart sore. Even if she did manage to find a man worth marrying, the idea that he might be someone her father had never met just made her sad.

'Pull yourself together,' Dani muttered to herself. She knew that her hangover was not helping her to see things optimistically. She'd never wanted to be married. Definitely not to Flossie's father. She had no doubt that relationship would not have lasted, and then what? How proud would Dani's dad have been to see her go through a divorce?

As for Nat? Well, prior to Lloyd, Nat was the last man she'd seen with any serious intent. They'd shared losing their virginity together. But if Dani hadn't got pregnant by Lloyd, there would have been others, she was sure.

Given their history, it was certainly strange to have watched Nat get engaged in real time thanks to the power of the Internet. But if anyone had asked Dani what she thought had become of Nat, before he came back to Newbay, she would have assumed that he was already married with a couple of kids. Why wouldn't he be? By forty, most people were. Until she saw Nat standing in the restaurant in The Majestic, the shape she imagined his life must have taken would not have bothered her at all. Would it?

'Hair of the dog?' Dave suggested, when he joined Dani by the bins.

'Seriously?' They were still on duty. Of course, they

weren't meant to be drinking but . . . Dani accepted a swig from Dave's hip flask.

'Feel better?' he asked.

Dani spluttered. 'Blimey! What is this? No.'

'My own special recipe,' he said. 'I've set up a still in my shed. I'm not sure if it's legal.'

'It shouldn't be,' Dani said. 'Let me have a bit more.'

Chapter Thirty

As she'd told Dani she would, that afternoon Jane took Jezza for a walk. Sarah, who was eager to ramp up the number of steps she had taken that week, joined them. A step counter was another of the apps she'd had loaded onto her phone. She was obsessed with her numbers.

'Got to keep young and beautiful if you want to be loved,' she suggested to Jane, appearing in the kitchen dressed in walking shorts and carrying Alpine poles.

'We're only going to the beach.'

Sarah discarded the poles.

The two women took a similar walk to the one Dani had taken with Jezza on the day that he ate Lola's engagement ring. The sun was shining and the road to the beach was busy with tourists and locals all hoping to find their private patch of Devon sand. Looking like a walking pompom, thanks to his poodle genes, Jezza attracted plenty of attention that Sarah was only too happy to lap up.

'Having a dog is a great way to meet people,' she observed.

'Had any more dates off that Cinder thing?' Jane asked.

'Tinder? Yes. I mean, I've had offers but I'm not sure it's really working for me any more.'

'What do you mean?'

Jane knew that the retired dentist from Paignton had turned out to be another disappointment. His teeth were great but he suffered from uncontrollable flatulence and Sarah had spent most of their date pressing her handkerchief to her nose like a Victorian heroine in need of smelling salts.

Now she told Jane, 'It's just that the men whose profiles I keep seeing leave more than a little to be desired. Either they are lifelong bachelors, who are flat-out strange. Or they are divorcees, who are secretly out for revenge. Or they are widowers desperately looking for someone to wash their socks. And they are all usually looking for someone much younger anyway.'

'I didn't want to say but I thought that might be the case.'

'I didn't believe all the horror stories in my magazines, of fifty-something women who had to content themselves with fishing in a pond of seventy-something men because the fifty-something men all want to be with women in their thirties. Turns out its true. Meanwhile the sixty-something men won't look at any woman over forty. And the "seventy-something" men are lying about their ages, posting photographs that are decades old to hide the fact they're really in their eighties! The way it seems to me is that women like me should be setting our sights on the ninety-year-olds and considering ourselves lucky if they aren't actually reanimated corpses.'

Jane laughed.

'It's not funny. Those men who do bother to get in touch are on-line for one thing only. I mean, it's not as though I'm really on there for anything different but one would least appreciate a romantic preamble before receiving a wrinkly old dick pic.'

'A what?'

'You heard me,' said Sarah. 'I've had three so far today.'

'Taken this morning?'

'I hope not. It's Sunday.' Sarah cackled. 'Oh, will I ever meet a nice man again? Perhaps I should be more like you.'

'Give up, you mean?'

'Be content with my memories,' said Sarah. She sighed.

'I think I've got different kinds of memories,' Jane said kindly. 'Shall we get an ice cream?' she suggested. 'Ice cream never lets you down.'

They stopped by the famous ice-cream stall and Jezza had another carton of dog-friendly vanilla. He was starting to get quite a taste for it and it was fun to watch him dive in and get it all over his whiskers before chasing the empty carton around the legs of the picnic table in search of one last drop.

The ice-cream stall was doing a roaring trade that afternoon as Newbay's walkers, their children and their dogs all tucked in. Jane had a strawberry swirl. Sarah chose dark chocolate.

'Not for you,' she told Jezza.

But Jezza had other things on his mind in any case. While the women ate their ice creams, he was distracted by a beautiful slate-blue greyhound, which was pulling a small boy in his direction. The boy, who couldn't have been much older than seven, might as well have been trying to control a shire horse.

'Sapphire!' he exclaimed. 'Stop pulling!'

Fortunately, Sapphire stopped to investigate Jezza, giving the boy time to catch up.

'Granddad!' he shouted, while he had the chance. 'Help me.'

Then suddenly there was Mr Hunter.

'Hold on, Seb,' he said. 'I'm coming.'

Mr Hunter took hold of the greyhound's lead.

'She's still a bit too strong for you,' he told Seb. Then he noticed Jezza. And Jane.

'Well, hello,' said Mr Hunter.

'Well, *hello*,' said Sarah in an embarrassingly saucy way. She sucked the end of her spoon.

Jane blushed and swallowed the last of her ice cream a little too quickly. It made her cough. Sarah gave her a whack on the back that only made her splutter.

'Sorry,' said Mr Hunter. 'Didn't mean to surprise you.'

Jane recovered herself. 'Oh no. I'm fine. It's . . . isn't it a lovely day?'

'Yes,' said Mr Hunter. 'I'm looking after my grandson Seb. I promised I'd take him rock-pooling.'

'After we've had an ice cream,' Seb reminded him.

'After we've had an ice cream,' Mr Hunter agreed. 'So this is the famous dog who ate a diamond?'

'It is indeed. Jezza is his name. And I shall be keeping him on a lead while we're on the beach today. Don't want any more mishaps.'

'Quite right too. You know I felt awful just putting you on the bus the other day. I should have insisted on dropping it off that evening. I hope you didn't really have far to go at the other end.' He explained to Sarah. 'Mrs Parker came into my shop – Newbay Pets – and bought a great big bag of kibble only to reveal that she didn't have a car to take it home in.'

'Mr Hunter kindly walked me to the bus stop.'

'Bill,' he said.

'Sorry,' said Jane. 'Did I forget to pay?'

'No,' said Bill Hunter. 'That's my name. Bill. Short for William. All this surname stuff makes it sound like we're in a Jane Austen novel.'

'That's not a bad thing,' said Sarah.

'Granddad,' Seb piped up. 'The queue's gone down.'

Bill looked up. 'So it has. We'd better get over there before they run out of mint choc chip.'

'You better had,' said Jane.

'I'll see you soon, I hope. Lovely to meet you . . .'

'Sarah,' she said with a coquettish smile.

He shook Sarah's hand.

'Until next time, Mrs Parker.'

'Jane,' she said. And blushed. Crimson.

'Who was *that*?' Sarah asked, making it sound as though they'd just had a chat with a film star. Her tone was horribly lascivious. Jane half expected her to say 'hubba hubba'.

'He's the man from the pet shop.'

'Why haven't you told me about him?'

'Why would I? I just went in to buy some kibble.'

'And he carried it to the bus stop for you?'

'I expect he does that for everybody.'

'Everybody? My arse,' said Sarah. 'You had a flirtation with the man in the pet shop and you didn't even tell me. I thought we told each other *everything*.'

'No,' said Jane. 'You tell me *everything* and luckily,

you're always talking so you don't notice when I don't tell you anything in return.'

Sarah took Jane's observation for the tease it was meant to be.

'Well, no wonder you kept quiet about him.'

'What do you mean?'

'Jane! He's really rather lovely. And he clearly fancies you.'

'He does not.'

'Oh come on. If you decide you're not interested, then please do let me know. I might be suddenly interested in buying a hamster!'

The shriek of laughter Sarah made attracted Bill's attention. He turned from the ice-cream counter to see what was so funny. Jane gave him a self-conscious wave before she pulled Sarah away by the arm.

'Come on, you. Let's get some more steps on your app.'

The two women walked the length of the beach, making slow progress as Jezza stopped to investigate *everything*. The beach was full of fantastic smells. Most of them slightly off. Jezza was especially keen on rotten seaweed. The more unspeakable something smelled, the more he wanted to roll in it.

The walk took much longer with Jezza on the lead but at last Jane and Sarah persuaded him it was time to go home. They climbed up the stairs to the car park. While Jane was brushing sand off her feet, so she could put her shoes back on, Sarah's attention was attracted by a fracas near the car park exit onto the main road where a crowd was gathering around a police van. Somebody was shouting.

'Isn't that Flossie?' asked Sarah, putting on her glasses to get a better look.

'Hmm?' Jane was busy tying her laces.

'Yes,' Sarah confirmed. 'Yes it is. It's our Flossie. And Jed.'

'What's going on?' Jane asked.

Sarah hurried in their direction.

'Jane, come quickly for heaven's sake. I think Flossie's being arrested!'

Chapter Thirty-One

By the time Jane and Sarah reached them, Jed and Flossie were already in handcuffs.

'That's my granddaughter!' said Jane. 'What's going on? You can't put her in handcuffs! She's a minor. Where on earth do you think you're taking her? Let her go at once.'

The female police officer who had cuffed Flossie merely shook her head at Jane and gestured that she should move right back.

'You can see your granddaughter at the station,' said the male officer who was tackling Jed.

'What? No! What has she done?'

'It's OK, Grandma,' said Flossie. 'I'm fine. Jed's dad is a lawyer. He's going to get us out. We're innocent. This is a travesty of justice. You pigs are going to pay for this cock-up big time!'

'I'd advise you not to call them pigs,' said Sarah.

'Good advice,' said the female police officer.

'If we don't get no justice, you don't get no peace!' Jed suddenly shouted at the gathering crowd, waving his cuffed hands in the air. 'No justice, no peace. No justice, no peace. No justice . . .'

Jed tried to start a chant but nobody except Flossie seemed particularly interested in joining in.

'Oh, please shut up,' said the female officer.

The crowd just stared and licked their ice creams as

though they were watching the incident unfold on a television screen.

'Don't worry, Flossie,' Jane yelled as Flossie was put into the back of the patrol car. 'Whatever you've done, we're right behind you. We'll come straight to the station. We're going to get you out.'

'Hey hey hey! Ho ho ho! Police brutality got to go!' Jed tried another chant. Still no one joined in.

'Come on, mate,' said the male police officer, who was handling Jed especially gently considering. 'Don't embarrass yourself.'

'No justice, no peace!' Jed yelled one more time before he added. 'My dad is going to hear about this, you know.'

'And I'm sure he'll be able to explain the law to you when he does,' said the police officer.

'No justice! No peace!' Jed shouted.

'No kidding,' said someone in the crowd.

The police car drove away, with Flossie and Jed in the back, leaving Jane and Sarah open-mouthed in the car park.

'They've taken Flossie. I can't believe it.' Jane was on the verge of tears.

'Come on,' said Sarah, taking control. 'We need to get down to the police station and phone Dani on the way.'

'But Flossie!'

'She'll be all right,' said Sarah. 'Though I can't imagine what she's done.'

'They had an illegal cake stall,' said one of the women who had watched the whole incident unfold. She was a Brummie, who had spent too much time in the sun that afternoon. Her face was as pink as her swimming costume. 'They were selling cupcakes and stuff. The police asked if they had a licence to be trading and obviously they didn't so the police told them to move along. And that's when your granddaughter's mate got a bit mouthy. I reckon the police would have let them go with a warning before that idiot crusty started ranting about being free to make a living and called the female one the "bastard capitalist bitch daughter of Maggie T". Or something like that.'

'For heaven's sake,' said Sarah.

'And your granddaughter stood up for him.'

'Well, they are in love,' said Jane.

'I hope for your sake she gets over it,' said the Brummie woman.

'Oh, you're not the only one,' said Jane. 'Believe me.'

Though she had always tried to see what Flossie saw in him, Jane's true feelings about Jed were coming out at last. The arrogance she had seen when he held forth around the kitchen table had got her granddaughter into trouble with the police!

While Jane talked to the woman from Birmingham, Sarah quickly called a taxi. When the driver arrived he said he didn't want to take Jezza, who smelled as though he had rolled across a fishmonger's stall, but Sarah waved a tenner and the problem magically disappeared.

Jane called Dani on the way to the station.

Dani was there less than fifteen minutes after they were. She arrived on her bicycle. Red-faced and still sweating wine from the day before.

'What on earth has happened now?' she asked.

The Brummie woman on the beach was right. Jed

and Flossie had been selling illegal cupcakes. Remembering how Flossie had said that she and Jed were planning a cupcake stall, Dani sighed. Hadn't she told them this would happen? All the same, they probably would have got away with a warning if Jed hadn't started shooting his mouth off. It had gone from being a matter of the police having a quiet word and giving Jed and Flossie the option to pack up and leave, to being a matter of a breach of the peace. And assaulting a police officer. Flossie had knocked the hat off the female officer's head.

It did not look good. Dani asked if she and Flossie could contact a lawyer. The officer on the front desk assured her that one was on his way. Jed's dad.

When he arrived, he did not look happy.

'I had to interrupt a family barbecue for this,' he said.

And when he was introduced to Flossie's family, he greeted them so frostily that Dani wouldn't have been surprised if he'd turned her to ice just by shaking her hand. He was the polar opposite of Jed when it came to appearance – he might have been at a family barbecue, but he still looked ready to stride into court – however, Dani, Jane and Sarah quickly saw where Jed got his arrogance from.

'This had better not be a waste of my time,' Jed's dad said when the attending officer came to take him through to the cells. 'If you were paying for this,' he added as an aside to Dani, 'it would be costing you five hundred an hour plus VAT.'

'Hang on!' said Dani. 'It was your son who . . .'

Jane held Dani back.

* * *

It took an hour for Jed's father to persuade the police that Flossie at least should be allowed to go home. Even then, she couldn't resist shouting out, fist raised in the air as she was led to where her mother and grandmother waited. Sarah had already taken Jezza home.

'Solidarity, Jed! We'll get justice! I promise! I love you!'

Dani pulled her daughter's fist down. 'And I love you but this time, Florence Parker, you've really gone too far.'

'She certainly has,' said Jed's father. 'Selling cupcakes without a licence. A ridiculously hare-brained scheme your daughter came up with.'

'What? My daughter?' Dani just about managed not to point out that it was Jed who'd come up with the idea and Jed who'd upped the ante with his wrong-headed chants. Instead she thanked Jed's father – perfunctorily – and bundled Flossie into a cab.

The drive back to Schooner Crescent was silent and deeply uncomfortable.

Dani had generally resisted grounding her daughter but following that afternoon's events, she really had no choice.

'You're not seeing Jed any more,' she told Flossie when they got home. 'I don't care how much you love him, he's not a good influence. You nearly got yourself a criminal record today, Floss. You haven't even finished school.'

'This is a police state,' said Flossie. 'We weren't doing anything wrong. We were just selling cakes to make some money for the summer.'

'And insulting a policeman? And knocking off another one's cap?'

'They deserved it.'

'You are out of control. And I'm not having it. Tomorrow I'm going to phone Xanthe and Camilla's parents and tell them what happened so that they can be aware of the sort of people you've been hanging out with too.'

'Mum!' Flossie covered her eyes. 'Don't embarrass me.'

'When you stop embarrassing me . . . You're still only sixteen,' said Dani. 'You're my responsibility.'

'I thought you said that people learn by their mistakes.'

'I was thinking about bad outfits and hair colour,' said Dani. 'Not mistakes that could define the rest of your life. You got *arrested* today, Florence Parker. That's no small thing. If Jed's father hadn't been there to talk the police out of pressing charges, you might have been had up for assault! Now, I'm going to need your phone,' she added. It was the ultimate sanction.

Flossie's mouth dropped open in horror.

'Mum! No way!'

'Yes way.'

'But what if I need it? What if you need to know where I am?'

'I will know exactly where you are,' said Dani. 'Because from this moment on, you're not going anywhere or staying with anyone I haven't already approved. And Jed will not be one of those people.'

'You trying to keep me from Jed isn't going to stop me loving him,' Flossie cried. 'I love him and I always will! You can't keep us apart.'

'Watch me,' said Dani. She turned Flossie's phone to 'off'.

As Dani crawled into bed that night, her happy afternoon at the pub with Will seemed a very long time ago. Indeed, the whole day had been one long exercise in mortification, she thought. She'd woken up with a headache and she was going to bed with a bigger one. She was grateful when Jezza climbed up on the bed for a cuddle. He was getting big enough to get onto the mattress without needing to be lifted up now. He pressed his wet nose against her face to let her know how much he loved her.

It was only then that she noticed just how bad he smelled.

'Oh Jezza. What on earth have you been rolling in?'

She heaved him off the duvet but it was already too late. The scent of dead fish lingered around her all night. It really was the perfect ending to a red-letter sort of day.

Chapter Thirty-Two

The whole debacle had been terribly upsetting for Jane too. Her granddaughter being arrested was not something she had ever expected to see. It had frightened and unnerved her. Waiting in the police station for Flossie to be released had aged Jane by ten years, she was sure. And then the arguing when they got home.

Jane knew that Dani was right. Flossie had to be punished for what had happened. It was not something that could be laughed off, though she knew it might be in some households. Jane had been raised to be law-abiding. She'd instilled the same ethics in Dani. And she thought that Flossie felt the same way. It was quite a shock to hear about the level of disrespect she'd shown the police officers, who were only doing their job after all. They were pointing out a rule that protected the public. You couldn't just sell food on the beach. There were hygiene issues. Jane was frankly surprised that anyone would want to buy food from Jed anyway.

Jane thought it was a very good idea that Flossie and Jed be kept apart for at least a while. He was arrogant and hotheaded. What if he'd acted that way in more dangerous circumstances?

All the same, Jane was not happy to see Flossie's tears when Dani told her that she couldn't see Jed again. She never could bear it when Flossie turned on the waterworks. It hurt Jane's heart to hear her grand-daughter still crying at ten in the evening, two hours after she'd stormed upstairs when Dani took her phone.

Jane paused on the landing on her way to bed and heard Flossie let out a choking sob. It was no good. She had to make sure Floss was OK.

'Grandma!' Flossie sat in her bed, dabbing at her red eyes. She looked so small and young.

'Oh sweetheart,' said Jane. 'I hate to see you crying.'

'What am I going to do, Grandma?'

'Everything your mother asked,' Jane said firmly.

'But she doesn't understand. She can't keep me from Jed. She can't! I'm going to die without him, Grandma. I really am.'

'No, you're not,' said Jane. 'Don't be silly.'

'He's my everything.'

Jane patted Flossie's hand.

'Look, I know we made some mistakes today . . .' Flossie began.

'I'll say,' Jane agreed.

'But I'm sure that Jed understands what we did wrong and he would never do it again. He's a good person, Grandma. He just gets carried away when he sees injustice going on. This punishment is just too cruel. Talk to Mum for me, Grandma, please.'

Jane shook her head.

'I can't ask your mum to change her mind about this, Flossie, and honestly, I think she's right. You're too young to be in such a serious relationship. Especially with someone who seems a little immature.'

'But you were sixteen when you met Granddad! You know sixteen's not too early to fall in love for good.'

'The world was a different place. We didn't get to spend time together in the way you and Jed have. And believe me, if your granddad had got me into trouble with the police, my own father would have given us both a good hiding.'

'I can't be without Jed,' Flossie insisted.

'Well, how about you look at it this way?' said Jane. 'If you and Jed are meant for each other, then a little bit of time apart won't matter.'

Flossie looked unconvinced.

'The fact is, Flossie, when I met your granddad, my parents weren't happy at all. They said we were too young and I respected my parents so when they told me I wasn't allowed to go dancing with your granddad, I didn't even think about it. But your Granddad Tom kept coming into the shop where I worked on a Saturday and kept letting me know that I was on his mind. And when I turned eighteen, he came round to our house and asked my father if he could take me out that very night. That was the real beginning of our story. He waited two whole years before we were able to be together properly. If Jed truly loves you, he won't be put off by not being able to see you for a while. He'll hold on for you the way your granddad held on for me. True love conquers all.'

Jane didn't add that she rather hoped Jed failed this test. For now, all she wanted to do was see Flossie smile again. Or at least stop the tears from falling quite so fast.

'You're worth the wait, aren't you? Think of this as a way to make your relationship stronger.'

'Thank you, Grandma,' Flossie said. 'I'll try.'

'Now get some sleep,' said Jane, arranging the covers

around Flossie's shoulders. 'Everything will look better in the morning.'

So Flossie went to sleep. Jane got into bed, but at two in the morning she was still awake. Still thinking about the day. About Flossie and Jed. About young love. About her Tom.

If she had gone first, what would Jane have wanted for Tom in her absence? He would have been hopeless on his own. Like Jane, he hadn't lived anywhere except with his parents before they were married. His mother was old-fashioned. She didn't see the need to teach her son to be self-sufficient. He had never boiled an egg or ironed a shirt. It was a wonder he could dress himself, Jane said with exasperation when they had their first marital row. But though she had talked the good feminist talk about dividing household chores, there was no doubt that the new Mr and Mrs Parker divided those chores along fairly traditional lines too. Jane's domain was the house. Tom's domain was the garden and the car. And, once Dani was born, bringing home all the bacon.

Had Jane gone first, Tom wouldn't have had a clue how to look after himself. Of course, Jane would have wanted him to find someone who could step into her shoes. Perhaps not take her place, entirely, but keep him from being hungry, or lonely, or just too sad. There wouldn't have been any shortage of contenders. Tom was always so popular. At the NEWTS – Newbay's theatre society – he was always in demand for the romantic roles.

She wouldn't have minded if those romantic roles crossed over into real life if she'd gone first. She only ever wanted him to be happy.

But for herself? It was much harder to imagine the other way around. She didn't need a man to provide for her. Or even to take the bins out. She'd been doing that for years. She had the company of her daughter, her granddaughter and her best friend on the other side of the garden fence. A man couldn't make her life more complete. Could he?

There was no way that someone like Mr Hunter from the pet shop could really be interested. He had carried her kibble because he was closing the shop for lunch anyway and he wanted to foster Jane's customer loyalty. He mentioned the opera to make small talk. He acknowledged her on the beach because he was polite. That was all.

Jane traced a finger across her husband's face in the photograph that lived on her bedside table.

'I wish you were here,' she said.

Once in a lifetime was more than enough for her.

Chapter Thirty-Three

Flossie was confined to barracks all week. It was almost as unbearable for Jane and Dani as it was for her. When she was feeling hard done by, Flossie could sigh heavily enough to shake the house to its foundations. Her miserable face, when she sat at the kitchen table pushing food around her plate, was enough to turn most living beings to stone. Dani was almost glad when she had to go to work so that she could have a break from Flossie's loudly and frequently articulated pain.

'You could come to Best Behaviour Boot Camp,' Dani suggested, when Flossie complained that she hadn't been out of the house for five days.

Funnily enough, that didn't seem to appeal. Dani didn't push it. She was pretty sure she'd have a better time without Flossie moping along beside her. She wondered how much longer she could hold out on the phone ban, though she knew very well that the first person Flossie contacted would be Jed. Ugh. Was there any way to stop it?

Though she was almost certain that Will would not be at boot camp that Saturday, this time Dani decided to make an effort. She changed out of her pyjamas into her most flattering jeans and a T-shirt that showed off her best assets.

Several of the male dog owners pretended they hadn't

noticed, Dani thought, as she joined them in the semi-circle. Nurse Van Niekerk did notice.

'White jeans. Never a good idea.'

Will wasn't there. The original Mr Princess, Nat, was back in his place.

Dani found she was glad. That last meeting in the car park, when she handed back the ring, had left Dani feeling unmoored in a strange, intangible way. Here was her chance to get things back on an even keel. To have another of those disturbingly normal conversations which set the tone for their relationship as old lovers and new friends. When they were allowed to talk, that is.

'Puppies, ready? Owners, ready? Three times around the football pitch! Run!'

'How are you?' Dani asked, after Nurse Van Niekerk had delivered that week's closing speech and sent them on their way. 'How was Paris?'

'It was great,' said Nat.

'It certainly looked wonderful. Congratulations on your engagement. Will showed me the pictures on Lola's Instagram.'

'So he made it to Best Behaviour Boot Camp?'

'He certainly did. Nurse Van Niekerk was unimpressed by your lack of commitment, of course, but Will managed to charm her in the end.'

'He's a pretty charming guy.'

'He is,' said Dani. 'But tell me more about Paris? Did you eat lots of good food? Drink lots of lovely wine?'

'Yes. How was your weekend?' Nat quickly changed the subject.

'Nice. Will and I actually had a rather jolly lunch at The Pirate Ship toasting your future happiness.'

'You did?'

'Yes. He's a good laugh, Will.'

She tried not to be disappointed that Nat hadn't seen the Instagram photo of Will, Dani and the dogs. Though Lola must have.

'Nat,' Dani said. 'I've decided that to make up for the hassle of the lost engagement ring, I'd like to make a cake for your engagement party.'

'You really don't have to,' said Nat.

'No. I'd like to. Consider it my engagement gift to you.'

'Only if you come to the party,' said Nat.

'If I'm invited.'

'You are.'

'Thank you.'

'Next Friday at my parents' place.'

'I think I remember the address. Look, Nat, it's nosy of me to ask but I was surprised you didn't use the ring after all. The one that Jezza ate.'

'No. Lola decided that given where the ring had been, she'd rather have a new one.'

'But it wasn't damaged. And I disinfected it. And you disinfected it again.'

'I know,' said Nat. 'But Lola said she was worried that every time she looked at the ring, she would think of dog shit. And that's really the last thing a man wants when his fiancée looks at her engagement ring, right?'

'I suppose it is,' said Dani. 'I hope you were at least able to swap it for the new one.'

'They were only too happy when I asked to upgrade it to a carat and a half,' said Nat.

'Wow.'

'That size looks better on Lola's finger. And quality gem stones are always a good investment.'

'Wow again,' said Dani. 'Is this really Nat the Che Guevara fan I'm talking to?'

Nat groaned. 'Don't. I really was clueless back then.'

'But passionate with it. About equality and alleviating poverty and things like that.'

Nat shrugged. 'It's easy to be passionate until you realise how much there is to be done.'

'Never lose your passion, Nat. Isn't that what you once said to me?'

'Probably,' Nat laughed. 'I really was full of crap.'

'I would have called it heart.'

'You always thought the best of me,' Nat said.

When he asked, Dani said she didn't have time for a coffee.

Dani got back from Best Behaviour Boot Camp to find Flossie sitting in the garden with Jane. They were winding wool. Flossie had a perfectly hangdog expression, as she let Jane wrap four-ply around her hands.

'Oh all right then,' said Dani, without needing even a word from her daughter. 'You can have your phone. But promise me you won't see Jed again, Flossie. The first time I hear you've seen that boy, I'll take your phone away again and send you to boarding school.'

'I won't see him,' Flossie promised. 'I know you're right, Mum. He could have got me into serious trouble. He can't love me very much if he was willing to put me in such a bad position, can he?'

Dani nodded. 'I'm glad you can see it like that now.'

'I do see it like that. Mum, I know I've been silly

and I'm sorry if I've hurt or embarrassed you along the way. Grandma, I need to apologise to you too.'

Jane patted Flossie on the hand.

'And me!' Sarah shouted as she let herself into the garden through the gate. 'I always stuck up for Jed. More fool me.'

'Sorry, Auntie Sarah,' said Flossie.

Sarah wrapped Flossie in her arms. 'Darling, there will be many more men to fall in love with and some of them may even be worth it.'

'Thank you. Could you take over for me?'

Flossie handed the wool to Sarah and fired up her phone. It immediately started beeping and chirping and ringing itself into a frenzy.

'Someone's popular,' said Jane.

'Not full of messages from Jed, I hope,' said Dani. 'Remember you're not answering them.'

'I know. I'm just going to send Camilla a WhatsApp,' she said. 'Mum, is it OK if I go and stay at hers tonight? Only it's her birthday and Xanthe is going to be there too. I swear we won't do anything we shouldn't.'

Dani looked to the two older women for back-up. She hadn't intended to let Flossie have all her privileges back so quickly but . . .

'You've learned your lesson, haven't you, Floss?' Sarah asked.

'Yes,' said Flossie. 'I really have.'

'All right then,' said Dani. 'I'll call Camilla's mum and check that it's ok.'

'Thanks, Mum.' Flossie grinned. After a week of frowns and thunder it was like the sun coming out. Everyone was happy again.

Chapter Thirty-Four

For the rest of the weekend, Dani had work to do. She was determined that Lola and Nat's engagement cake should be even more special than the birthday cake she'd made for Lola's thirtieth. This time, she had more information about Lola's likes and dislikes. She knew that Lola preferred lemon to chocolate, thanks to the cupcake disaster. So, a lemon sponge it was, sandwiched together with a delicious lemon cream that Dani would have happily eaten by the spoonful. In fact, she did eat it by the spoonful and had to make a second batch.

For decoration, Dani decided she would make a couple of figurines as a cake topper. Dani loved making sugar figurines. It took her right back to childhood, when Plasticine and Play-Doh were among her favourite toys. Flossie had been a big Play-Doh fan too. It wasn't until then that Dani realised what a pain in the arse all types of modelling clay are if you're the parent who has to clean the carpet. It was fun, though. Dani enjoyed making the three little figures. Especially the dog.

Of course, Princess hadn't actually been at the Paris proposal but, with a bow in her hair, she made the perfect finishing touch as far as Dani was concerned. Now that she had Jeremy Corbyn, she couldn't imagine creating her own family tableau without putting Jezza in the middle of it.

Dani introduced Jezza to the sugar model of Princess. That did not go well.

'Nurse Van Niekerk? It's Mrs Jezza.'

'What's he eaten now?' Nurse Van Niekerk asked.

'Fondant icing. Not chocolate. About a marble's worth.'

'Watch with care. Expect diarrhoea.'

'*Plus ça change.*'

Dani kept her second attempt at modelling Princess well out of Jezza's reach.

The engagement party was being held at Nat's family home. Nat and Lola had a small town house in one of Newbay's new developments, which they were renting while the Victorian villa Nat had bought was comprehensively renovated. However, the town house was too small for a really good party, so Nat's parents had offered their place instead.

Dani remembered the house well, though it was twenty-two years since she'd last been to a party there – Nat's unofficial eighteenth – a week after his birthday. His parents were away at the time. Mr and Mrs Hayward thought that now their son was eighteen and about to head off to university, they could probably risk leaving him and his big sister Kate home alone while they went to Majorca for a week.

Kate took advantage of her parents' absence to go and stay with her boyfriend in his caravan. Kate's boyfriend was a 'crusty' called Damian who made his living by whittling woodland animals, which he sold at local craft fairs. Like Jed, he eschewed the use of all chemical products including soap. It was safe to say, Mr and Mrs Hayward were underwhelmed by their daughter's choice of beau. But Kate loved him. She loved his caravan.

So Nat had the house to himself.

'You've got to have a party.' It was Dave the chef who suggested it. Dani eagerly awaited Nat's reaction. A party sounded like a great idea to her. It would be an opportunity to meet Nat outside the kitchen and hopefully make him see her as something more than a colleague. She was already planning her outfit in her head.

'I dunno,' said Nat. 'I don't think my parents would want me to.'

'You got no choice,' said Dave. 'We're coming over. All of us. Saturday night, after service. We'll bring along the leftovers.'

Though it was strictly forbidden by health and safety and all manner of other rules, Dave the chef was not above finishing what guests had left on their plates. Or in their wine bottles. Dave was legendary for decanting the nightly dregs into a plastic bottle, which he would then take home to drink over the rest of the weekend. His underlings called it the 'Devil's Urine'. Legend had it that if anyone except Dave tried to drink a whole glass of the stuff, they would go blind on the spot.

On the night of Nat's unofficial eighteenth birthday party, Dave brought along five two-litre bottles of mixed alcoholic leftovers.

'I've been saving this for a special occasion,' he said, as he plonked the bottles full of cloudy purplish liquid on the Hayward family's kitchen table. 'There's Chateau Margaux in one of these.'

There was no guessing which one.

'Wow. Thanks, Dave,' said Nat.

'My pleasure. You can have first taste.' He poured out a pint and dared Nat to drink it. Nat took a sip and winced.

'Come on, Nat,' said Dave. 'You're a man now. Show us what you're made of.'

Nat downed the rest of the pint in one.

It all started to go badly wrong after that.

After Nat had downed his pint, he dared one of his mates from school to do the same. Then another. And another. Before long, everyone was lining up to prove that they were just as hard as Nat was.

'Ladies can do half a pint,' Dave suggested.

'No way,' said Dani, when it came to her turn. 'That's just sexist.'

So Dani too had a pint of her own.

It didn't taste as bad as she expected.

'That'll be the one with the Margaux then,' said Dave.

But it still didn't taste that good.

Everyone who dared to drink from the Devil's Urine had to wash it down with something else. The bath upstairs was being used as a cooler for beer and alcopops. Someone – probably Dave again – mixed an enormous cocktail in a bucket, using up every single bottle in the Haywards' drinks cabinet. There was a hint of floor cleaner too, thanks to the bucket.

And of course, it being a teenage party, there was no food to soak up any of the alcohol, unless you counted crisps. By nine in the evening, there was vomit everywhere and Nat was conked out on the sofa. So much for Dani's seduction fantasies.

* * *

At the end of the party, Dani was the only one of Nat's friends to remain. She did her best to help him get the house cleaned up but even once they'd filled ten bin-bags with empties, washed down every surface and put all of Nat's bed linen (including the pillows) in the washing machine, the smell of vomit remained.

And then they found the graffiti in Kate's bedroom. Someone had drawn a gigantic penis on the wall above Kate's headboard.

They'd used indelible pen.

Dani and Nat desperately painted over the offending picture. With gloss.

'You are in so much trouble, little bro,' was all Kate said, when she saw it.

If Nat hadn't been going off to university, he would have been grounded for a year. As it was, he promised his parents that he would get a job in Bristol and pay off the damages at a rate of ten pounds a month.

'For the rest of my life,' Nat wailed when he told Dani.

Dave the chef, accepting for once that the calamity was largely his responsibility, arranged a whip-round from all the staff who'd attended the bash. Between them, they gathered a hundred quid – fifty of which came from the hotel management (Dave told them he was collecting for a cancer charity and made them honour their pledge to match whatever their employees had raised themselves). He handed Nat the money in a plain brown envelope.

'That's nearly a year off your sentence,' he said.

Now, here Dani was, back at the scene of the crime.

Chapter Thirty-Five

Nat's sister Kate answered the door.

The blue and green dreadlocks that had so upset her parents were long gone, replaced by a neat blonde 'mum' bob. Her outfit was pure Boden. All jolly patterns and A-line.

'Oh my god! Dani Parker!' she exclaimed when she saw Dani on the doorstep. 'Nat told me you were coming. How the hell are you? You haven't changed a bit.'

Dani opened her mouth.

'I know. You wish you could say the same for me, right?' Kate pre-empted her. 'What happened to the free spirit with the blue hair? A job, a marriage, two boys . . . that's what happened. And you?'

'A job, a daughter, no marriage.'

'I think you might have the better deal,' said Kate. She helped Dani carry the cake through.

'It is so nice to see you. Though I have to say, I didn't expect you of all people to stay in this dump of a town.'

'Life has a funny way of working out. Who did you marry?' Dani asked, to move the spotlight.

'Damian, of course,' said Kate, jerking her head towards a bald-headed, rather portly chap standing over by the buffet table.

'That's not . . .'

'I'm afraid it is. The dreadlocks had to go when he

got his job in marketing. Likewise the piercings. Needless to say, Mum and Dad like him much better these days. And those are my kids over there.'

Kate indicated a pair of twins, around fifteen years old, who were absorbed in their phones.

'Gandalf and Merlin,' Kate said. 'Though for some reason, they insist we call them by their second names. Eddie and Mike.'

Mike like Nat's dad, Dani observed.

Mike was in the kitchen when Dani brought in the cake.

'Dani! Nat said you were coming. Jill!' he called for his wife. 'Jill. Dani Parker's here.'

Jill Hayward came in from the sitting room.

'Oh Dani! How are you doing, sweetheart?'

She kissed Dani on both cheeks, enveloping her in Miss Dior, which had always been her perfume.

'Isn't this funny? Here we all are again. I couldn't believe it when Nat said you were at The Majestic.'

Dani found herself a little overwhelmed by all the attention they were paying her. The first time she'd met Nat's parents was a couple of days after the party, when Jill Hayward made it very clear that she viewed Dani as being partially responsible for her son's fall from grace. Dani never really felt she recovered from that inauspicious beginning. Now, it was as though Dani was the prodigal daughter. Or prodigal potential-daughter-in-law, at least.

'How long has it been since we last saw you properly?' Jill asked.

'Twenty-two years, I think. Since Nat's eighteenth birthday party.'

Jill grimaced. 'Ah yes. The eighteenth! Well, I

sincerely hope today's party won't end up like the last time Nat entertained.'

'Gloss paint.' Mike Hayward shook his head. 'I never understood how that boy managed to get into university. He's still paying us off for the damage, you know. Ten quid a month.'

'I am so, so sorry,' Dani began to apologise.

'Oh don't take any notice of Mike,' said Jill. 'It's just a funny anecdote now. The sort of thing we bring up when we want to embarrass Nat in front of his future in-laws.'

Who must be around somewhere, Dani thought.

'Haven't they turned up yet?' Mike asked. 'The Taylors?'

'No. I expect they'll be here in half an hour or so.' Jill leaned in close to Dani to tell her, 'Lola's mother believes in making an entrance. I think that's where Lola gets it from.'

Dani realised then that she hadn't yet seen Lola either. Though, of course she was going to be there. It was her special day. Before her *really* special day.

'You must be really pleased,' said Dani to Jill.

'What about, dear?' Jill asked.

'Er, the engagement?' Dani prompted her.

'Oh that. Well, yes, I suppose we are.'

That 'suppose' hung in the air like a noxious fart.

'But tell me what you're up to these days, Dani. Are you married? Have a family of your own?'

'Not married,' said Dani. 'But I have one daughter. Flossie. She's just turned sixteen.'

'Worrying you silly by going out all night with her friends, is she?' Mike Hayward asked.

'And the rest,' Dani said.

'And you're working at The Majestic, making beautiful cakes. Oh, I do hope Lola will be happy with this one . . .'

Dani tried not to interpret that as meaning Lola hadn't been happy with her birthday cake.

'Where's Nat?' Dani asked.

'He's gone to fetch Lola from the spa,' said Kate. 'Apparently there was a problem with her manicure. She had to go and get the colour changed.' Kate punctuated that with an eye-roll. 'Here, have a drink.'

Dani gratefully took a glass of champagne.

Apart from Nat's family, there weren't many people Dani recognised among the party guests. All the same, she supposed she ought to make an effort to circulate. Even though more than two decades had passed, she was wary of being seen as the sad ex-girlfriend, clinging to the family, so she took her glass of champagne into the living room and positioned herself by the mantelpiece, pretending to look at the photographs upon it, while she surreptitiously checked out the other people in the room in the mirror above.

Spotting no one she knew, her eyes were drawn back to the photos. A photograph that must have been taken on the engagement weekend had pride of place. Lola flashed her ring at the camera. It sent off a flare of light.

To the left and right of that photograph were pictures taken over the years since Dani had last been there. Here were Kate's children as infants. Kate's wedding photograph. Nat's graduation. He still had his floppy hair in that one. Was still recognisably the boy she'd once known. Had been in love with. Madly in love.

'Hey, Dani.'

It was Will.

'I didn't expect to see you here,' said Dani.

'I didn't expect to see you here either.'

They pondered which of them had less reason to be at the engagement celebration of Nat Hayward and Lola Taylor.

'It's good to see you, though,' said Will.

'Yes,' said Dani. 'I'm sorry if . . . well, the last time we met, I think I might have had a bit too much to drink.'

'You're not the only one. That was one crazy afternoon. I spent the entire next day in bed sleeping it off.'

'I had to go to work,' said Dani.

'Ouch. Sorry about that. So, have you been here before?'

'Yes. This is where Nat grew up. It's a bit weird being back here if I'm honest. The first time I ever came to this house was for Nat's eighteenth birthday party.'

'Good party?' Will asked.

'Sort of,' said Dani. 'In that it went down in the annals of Newbay history. Everyone between the ages of fourteen and forty who was living in the town at the time claimed to have been there. Most of them probably were. Suffice to say, it got a bit out of hand. A bit noisy. A bit raucous. The police were called. Someone drew a penis on the wall above Nat's sister's bed.'

'Ah. It was that kind of party. I wish I'd been there.'

'I wish some of the people who were there had stayed for the cleaning up afterwards,' Dani mused. 'So, tell me, Will, who do you know here? Apart from the bride-to-be.'

'Well, I know her family, obviously. Her mother and father over there. Not that I imagine they're pleased to see me. And that's her brother.'

Will pointed out a bruiser who'd joined Kate's husband at the buffet table. They were comparing designer watches, which made Dani smile as she remembered a time when Damian had refused to wear a watch because time was an artificial construct used by the global lizard elite to keep the common man down or something like that.

'That's Lola's sister, Francesca.' Will indicated a woman standing by the French windows. 'Her big sister.'

She couldn't have looked less like Lola if she'd tried. She was wearing the sort of trouser suit favoured by lady corporate lawyers.

'I don't imagine she's too excited about the wedding. Especially if Lola's asked her to be a bridesmaid. Lots of tension between those two.'

Dani watched Francesca watching Lola make a circuit of the room to show off her ring. Francesca's eyes were hard and narrowed. Definitely no love lost between those siblings.

'And that's Lola's little sister, Ivana.'

Will gave Ivana – who looked about twenty – a little wave. She giggled as she waved back at him. Dani suggested that someone had a crush on her big sister's ex.

'Oh no. Not Ivana.'

'I'd put money on it,' Dani said.

'I prefer a more mature woman,' said Will. Which was nice to hear.

Lola came in their direction next. She air-kissed Will before putting her hand out to Dani.

'It's Dani, isn't it? The dog lady. Thank you for making the cake.'

'It's the least I could do under the circumstances,' Dani said. After all, the last time she'd seen Lola was on the day of the unfortunate picnic.

'I suppose it is,' said Lola.

'But you got a bigger ring out of it, as I understand.'

'Yes!' Lola fluttered her fingers. 'It suits me much better. And I got a better proposal too. I mean, Paris or Duckpool Bay? Which would you choose? I know which one looks better on Instagram.'

Dani thought she knew too. She wasn't sure they had the same opinion.

Chapter Thirty-Six

Will was soon spirited away by Lola who wanted to introduce him to some of her new friends. He made his excuses to Dani, who went back to looking at the photographs on the mantelpiece. She wasn't alone for long.

'I saw you talking to Lola's ex-boyfriend, Will,' said Kate as she sidled up beside her. 'How hot is that man? I swear, every time I see him, I feel like I'm thirteen years old all over again. I mean, I love my brother, but to think she's chosen to marry him over that . . . that ridiculous hunk of lovable hotness.'

Dani thought it was best not to comment.

'I'm sorry. I think it might be my hormones. Do you find that you're suddenly absolutely gagging for it all of the time? I thought the peri-menopause was when your sex drive was supposed to drop off a cliff but apparently some women get this sudden late surge of testosterone that makes them absolutely mad for it. That's definitely been my experience.'

'Damian must be happy with that,' said Dani.

'If only. These days he has the sex drive of a bowl of blancmange. In fact, a bowl of blancmange would turn him on far more than I do. Look at him. He thinks about nothing but food all day long.'

Kate curled her top lip as she looked towards her husband, who was leaning against the buffet table, cradling a plate full of sausage rolls. He was mechanically posting them into his mouth, reminding Dani of a Victorian automaton in the museum on the pier.

'It's enough to make a woman want to have an affair. Don't you think? If he doesn't want to come anywhere near me, I should be allowed to look elsewhere. Like at Mr Hippety Hotness over there.'

Will – the Mr Hippety Hotness to whom Kate referred – was now standing by the French windows. He was talking to Nat's godmother, who, despite being in her late seventies, was flirting up a storm. Will seemed to have that effect on everyone. She was fiddling with her pearl necklace, twisting it around her manicured fingers until suddenly the string snapped and pearls scattered all over the floor, like stars shooting out at the creation of the universe.

'Oh!' Nat's godmother gasped.

Immediately, Will was on his hands and knees, chasing after the escapees. The children and some of the other adults followed suit, including Dani. Dani followed one of the escaping pearls under the buffet table. It was a good excuse to get away from Kate if nothing else. Will followed one in from another direction. The two friends met beneath the tablecloth when they almost banged heads.

'Fancy seeing you here,' said Dani.

'Having a good time?' Will asked. Before Dani had a chance to answer, he said, 'Me neither. Shall we get out of here, you and I?'

A man who looked like Aidan Turner was asking if she would join him in escaping from her ex-boyfriend's engagement party? Dani didn't need to be asked twice.

'OK. I suppose we ought to wait for the cake but as soon as that's done . . .'

'The signal is an owl's hoot,' Will said.

It wasn't long before Nat's godmother's pearls had all been retrieved. After that, Lola, thankfully, announced that it was time to cut the engagement cake. While the party guests crowded around the table to see Lola stick a knife in Dani's creation – accidentally slicing off the sugar model of Nat's head as she did so – Will and Dani hung back. Will necked a couple of glasses of champagne. The cake was cut. Dani gave a soft 'twit-twoo'.

Without taking their leave of the host and hostess, Dani and Will crept out into the hallway, retrieved their jackets from the pile hanging from the banister and made a break for it, tumbling out of the front door like greyhounds out of a trap.

Once they were on the other side of the hedge that edged the Haywards' long front garden, Will and Dani stopped running and burst into giggles. Dani had somehow managed to get a stitch. She doubled over and did her best to breathe through great snorting laughs that made Will laugh even harder.

'That was rude, wasn't it? Going off without saying goodbye?' Will asked, when they both recovered their breath.

'They won't miss us,' said Dani. 'I can't think of anyone who'll even notice I've gone. Though maybe someone will miss you.'

'Who?' Will asked. A little over-eager perhaps.

'Well, there's Ivana for a start. And you know Nat's sister, Kate?' Dani asked.

Will squinted.

'Tall. Looks like Nat in a blonde wig? Well, I think she was rather hoping to get to know you better.'

'Oh,' said Will. He didn't seem excited by either of those options.

'I think you had a lucky escape,' said Dani, making a playful growl. 'Shall we go to a pub?' she asked.

Will agreed that it sounded like a great idea but Newbay was not London and their choices were distinctly limited. There were no pubs in the Hayward family's smart residential area. A local hotel said it could only serve residents.

Will and Dani ended up in a rather grotty bar near the train station, where they shared a bottle of red. And then another one. As the landlord announced last orders, Dani, worried that the next stage was for Will to say, 'I guess that's it, then. I'll get a taxi home,' racked her brain for further options. She could come up with only one.

Flossie was having a sleepover at Xanthe's birthday. Jane too was away from home, visiting a pal from her own childhood. Meanwhile Jezza could not be left alone for too much longer. Even with Sarah looking in on him from time to time.

'We'll have to go back to my place,' Dani told Will. To her delight he said, 'That sounds perfect.'

And then he kissed her.

'What are you doing . . .'

He squashed the words back into her mouth. When she realised that he wasn't joking, she flung her arms around his neck and kissed him back. Forget Nat Hayward.

'Wow,' she said when they came up for air. 'Just wow.'

'Still want me to come back to yours?'

'More than ever!' Dani said.

Chapter Thirty-Seven

'I have to tell you I was not expecting this,' Dani warned Will as they sat in the back of the cab they'd picked up in the town centre. 'So the house is a tip and my bedroom is a tip and underneath these clothes . . .'

'Ssssh,' said Will, suddenly pulling Dani towards him again and kissing her so passionately that all thoughts of her untidy bikini line were banished. At least for the minute. Will was enjoying the moment. She just had to do the same. She'd once read a magazine article that insisted men didn't really notice whether you'd had your bikini line done or whether your toenails were painted to match your skirt. They were simply happy to jump into bed with a real live female who wanted them as much as they wanted her.

'Live for the moment,' Dani breathed as Will buried his face in her cleavage.

'Huh?' Will asked.

'Nothing,' Dani said. 'Keep kissing me.'

'This where you want to be dropped off, then?' the cabbie asked, interrupting the moment with a cough.

'Er, yes,' said Dani.

She scrambled upright. Her bra was undone.

Will paid the taxi fare. Then they ran up the garden path hand in hand. Dani found it difficult to find her keys at the bottom of her handbag while Will was so intent on kissing her face, her neck, her arms, her hands. She hadn't been ravished like this in a very, very, very long time.

The house *was* a tip. Not least because Jezza had taken great umbrage at being left for longer than he thought was acceptable since Sarah had last looked in on him at eleven. The angry puppy had shredded Flossie's second-favourite puffa coat. That was going to cause an issue when Flossie came home but for now, Dani gave a total of *no fucks whatsoever*. She opened the back door so that Jezza could go out for a wee. He was still wary of the dog flap. Meanwhile Will was asking if he could carry her upstairs.

'I don't know,' Dani quipped. 'How much can you bench press?'

Will laughed. 'You're such a funny girl, Dani Parker. I like that about you.' Then he swept Dani off her feet. To his credit, if she was heavier than he thought she would be, he quickly rearranged his face to suggest nothing of the sort.

'Which is your bedroom?' Will asked, as he staggered from wall to wall on the landing, finding first the door to Jane's room, then Flossie's aka the Pig Sty, then the spare room, aka the Other Pig Sty, before happening on Dani's own.

He threw Dani down onto the mattress. She almost bounced straight off.

'Whoops,' she said.

Will helped her back into the centre of the bed and went back to the work of kissing her. Until Dani tapped him on the shoulder and said, 'Er, Will, I just need to go to . . .'

Dani pointed coyly towards the bathroom.

'Of course,' he said. 'I'll be right here.'

She left him sitting on what she thought of as 'her side' of the bed, checking his reflection in the mirror on the dressing table.

'Whoah!' Dani greeted her own reflection in the bathroom mirror. Then 'Rawr!' she gave herself a little growl and made a clawing gesture at herself.

Not too bad. Not too bad at all. Certainly not as bad as she'd imagined when they were in the dark taxi. All that kissing had brought colour to her cheeks.

All the same, she would just do a little tidying up before she went back into the bedroom. First things first, she scrubbed her teeth, which were stained slightly lilac from all the red wine she'd downed at the pub. She scrubbed her lips too, which were black with tannins. Then she hopped into the shower and gave herself a very quick (and cold) douche.

She dried herself off and stood on the loo seat so she could see her nether regions in the mirror above the basin. There was no time to do a DIY bikini wax but she decided she should deal with the really long bits. She hunted through the bathroom cabinet until she found the nail scissors.

Just a little trim.

The first attempt was wonky.

It was like the day she tried to cut Flossie's fringe. When she was small, Flossie was absolutely terrified of going to the hairdresser. At the same time, she hated wearing her hair too long because getting knots out was pure torture. So Dani did the only thing she could. She kept Flossie's hair tidy herself. Until Flossie decided she wanted a fringe like her favourite television character, Dora the Explorer. She would not sit still and as Dani attempted to even the fringe out, it got shorter and shorter until Flossie looked less like her favourite cartoon girl and more like a mad medieval monk.

Desperate was how Dani felt as she examined her newest handiwork in the mirror. She looked as though she was going through some weird sort of moult.

Still, there was nothing she could do about it now. She'd kept Will waiting for long enough. She flushed the hair she'd cut down the loo – it took three flushes for it all to go – gave herself one more spritz of Acqua Di Parma and stepped back out onto the landing.

Then stepped straight back into the bathroom to see if just a couple more judicious snips might make all the difference.

Not really, it turned out.

It was a full fifteen minutes later when Dani flung open the door to the bedroom again.

'Ta-daaa!'

Will was still there. He was still on the bed. But he wasn't awake.

'Oh, bum,' said Dani.

She climbed into bed alongside her sleeping friend. At least she wouldn't have to spend the night alone. It was a delicious novelty to have another body beneath the duvet beside her. Such a lovely body to boot. Never mind that he was dead to the world.

As she lifted the duvet, Will stirred. Dani arranged herself on the edge of the mattress in faux sleep so that when Will woke, he would find her looking serene and beautiful. But Will didn't wake. He just rolled over and once he was on his back in a starfish position, he began to snore. Snores that sounded like pneumatic drilling, like jet planes landing, like nothing Dani had ever before heard in her life.

There was something rather endearing about it. Finding out that someone so insanely attractive had a fatal flaw.

Dani decided she wouldn't let it spoil things between them, the snoring issue. She'd get earplugs. Or he could get surgery. He could even wear one of those huge things that looks like an iron lung overnight. Whatever they had to to, they'd live happily ever after.

After daydreaming for a while about life as Mrs Hippety Hotness, Dani too finally fell asleep.

Chapter Thirty-Eight

Jezza provided Dani's wake-up call. Drunk as she had been on her way up to the bedroom the previous evening, Dani had failed to Jezza-proof the house before bed. She left the kitchen door open and thus, unknown to her, he had eschewed the basket they'd recently bought for him, to instead spend the evening sleeping on the armchair in the corner of Dani's bedroom, on a pile of newly washed towels.

Now, however, he needed to go out. Dani hadn't opened the dog flap before going to bed and Jezza was absolutely desperate.

So Dani's first shock was opening her eyes to find that Jezza was staring deep into hers. Her second shock was remembering that she had not gone to bed alone.

Will was there. Will was in her bed with her. Will with his top off.

Dani sat up suddenly and looked down at Will with disbelief and something approaching wonder. He was even more gorgeous than she recalled.

Jezza's whining woke Will too.

'Where am I?' Will asked.

'You're with me,' Dani said, while Jezza gave him a slobbery 'good morning' kiss. It was fortunate that he liked dogs. 'With Dani?' she added, before he could inadvertently reveal that he didn't have a clue who she was.

'Oh god,' said Will.

He put his hand over his eyes.

'It's OK,' said Dani, feeling her self-esteem plummet. 'We didn't do anything . . .'

'Oh no,' said Will, seeming to sense at once that Dani thought he was embarrassed. 'I didn't mean that. Not at all. I'm happy to be here. With you and . . . I just mean . . . How much did I have to drink last night? My head feels like someone's clog-dancing inside it.'

'We did have quite a bit,' Dani admitted. 'And that red wine at the engagement party was rough.'

Will sat up against the headboard.

'It's all coming back to me now,' he said. 'That wine really was rough, wasn't it? Lola's father was always a cheapskate when it came to booze.'

'I think Nat's parents did the wine.'

'Oh. Well, whoever bought it, it was crap. How did we get here?' Will asked.

'Taxi. You paid. So I probably owe you a fiver or something. A tenner?'

'Don't be ridiculous,' said Will.

Dani tried to believe it was a good thing that he didn't want to be paid back.

'Do you want to have a shower or something? While I let Jezza out? I'll get you a clean towel.'

Will shook his head. 'I'll just put my clothes on and get going if it's OK with you. Have a shower back at my place.'

'Oh. OK. I'll just . . .'

Dani made to get out of bed. Noticing perhaps for the first time that she was naked, Will made a big deal of turning his face away.

'To give you some privacy.'

Dani grabbed her ratty old dressing gown from the back of the door. Her brief fantasy of life as Mrs Hippety Hotness was absolutely over now.

Dani stood at the kitchen table and watched as Jezza made his first garden inspection of the day. He sniffed delicately around the borders, stopping to make a deeper investigation of the patch of ground at the bottom of the old apple tree, which was where next door's cat sometimes liked to lay in the shade, taunting Jezza as he watched helplessly from inside the house.

Dani was so envious of Jezza right then. His life was so simple. Eat, walk, sniff and poo. Not for Jezza the endless humiliations of human life. The misunderstandings and the awful embarrassments. How could Dani ever have thought that Will really wanted to spend the night with her?

As Dani was watching her dog, Will walked into the kitchen.

'Breakfast?' Dani offered. 'I can offer you fresh orange juice?'

'I'm not really a breakfast person,' said Will.

Dani wasn't convinced by that answer but she didn't question it.

'I'd better get going. I'll see you soon,' he said, as he headed for the front door. With haste.

Later, as Dani sipped coffee at the kitchen table, she decided it was for the best that she'd spent too long in the bathroom. She'd always previously avoided one-night stands for good reason. Will was probably glad they hadn't done anything either. It would make it a bit less awkward if they ever had occasion to bump into each other again. Though she would never see him again. Dani was pretty damn sure of that.

When she got into the bathroom, Dani did not look quite so good as she remembered. There were still a couple of pubic hairs floating in the toilet bowl. The scissors were in the sink. She hoped that Will wouldn't have noticed them but she was pretty sure that he must have.

Worst of all, Dani still had to go to Best Behaviour Boot Camp.

Chapter Thirty-Nine

Nat was already at boot camp with Princess. Dani shuffled into the semi-circle of puppies and owners beside him. She would have preferred to hide her hangover on the other side of the circle, but alas, there was to be no moving around at this point in the term. Nurse Van Niekerk was there too, however, so there was no chance for anything more than a cursory nod 'hello'.

'Puppies ready?'

Jezza yipped his agreement.

'Owners ready?'

Dani groaned.

As the class progressed, Dani felt very ill indeed. She was sure she must be sweating wine again. She could follow hardly any of Nurse Van Niekerk's instructions and Jezza seemed to pick up on her incapacity. He ran riot. Whichever command Dani tried, Jezza did pretty much the opposite.

'Sit!'

He jumped up at her, tongue lolling.

'Stay!'

He ran for the other end of the field and refused to come back until she went to fetch him.

'Drop it!'

Jezza did drop the ball he was carrying, only to snatch one of Dani's shoelaces and start tugging that instead.

'Discipline!' Nurse Van Niekerk shouted. 'Mrs Jezza, where is your authority today? Find it in your body! In your voice! Stand up straight and make commands like you mean them.'

'I can barely stand at all,' was what Dani wanted to say.

'Drop it!' she tried again. 'Drop my shoelace.'

Jezza pulled the lace so hard it snapped.

'Pathetic, Mrs Jezza,' Nurse Van Niekerk scolded. 'Like this.'

Of course, Jezza behaved for her.

Dani was relieved when Terry the chihuahua started humping Bluebell the hapless Labrador and Nurse Van Niekerk's attention was drawn away.

The final whistle took forever to come that morning and when it did, Dani was sure she had never felt so relieved in her life.

'Water,' she said to no one in particular. 'I need water. I'm going to the shop.'

'I'll come with you,' said Nat.

'Sure.'

They began to walk towards the gates together.

'That was a rough class,' said Nat.

'At least Princess did as she was told. Of course, now Jezza is walking to heel like a proper Crufts champion,' Dani observed. Having burned off plenty of energy in the class, he was finally settling down.

'I like his style,' said Nat. 'He doesn't believe in performing for "the man". Not that I'm suggesting Nurse Van Niekerk isn't one hundred per cent female.'

Dani chuckled.

'Tough night?' Nat asked.

'Your fault,' said Dani. 'Thank you for having me to your party. Did you have a good evening?'

'Yes,' said Nat. 'It was full on.'

'Your family is so lovely. But then they always were. I can't believe your sister married Damian. Who would have guessed how he'd turn out? Is one of their sons really called Merlin?'

'Yep,' Nat nodded.

'Far out,' Dani joked.

'I think Gandalf came off worse. Fortunately, both my nephews have a great sense of humour. They need it.'

As they got to the gate Nat said, 'I didn't see you leave last night. You didn't say goodbye when you went.'

Dani had been rumbled. She tried to style it out. 'Well you were rather busy and I didn't think it was right to pull you away from your guests. I knew I'd see you today after all.'

'But you must have left quite early. I didn't even really get a chance to say hello.'

'It was Flossie,' Dani lied. 'I got a call from Flossie saying she didn't feel like she wanted to spend the night at her friend's house after all. She wanted me to go and fetch her.'

Nat seemed to believe it. Though then he said, 'Will left quite early too.'

'He did?' Dani feigned ignorance.

'Yes. I thought perhaps you left together,' Nat persisted.

'Oh, yeah.' Dani caved in. She didn't have the energy to deny it altogether. 'Now you come to mention it, we did walk in the same direction for a while. I showed Will where the taxi rank is.'

Nat nodded. 'I would have thought he'd have known where it is by now.'

'You know, I feel rough as a bag of spanners,' Dani said then. 'You don't seem too worse for wear, though, considering it was your party.'

'That's because I knew I would have to get up early to drive Lola to a wedding fayre in Torquay.'

'She's started planning already?'

'Well, yes. You see, we've brought the wedding forward,' said Nat.

'Gosh,' said Dani. What else could she say? 'Gosh.'

'The church Lola wants has got a vacancy for the first Saturday of September. We decided to go for it. It is a bit quick but . . .'

'It's not . . . er, shotgun is it?'

'Of course not,' said Nat.

'I'm sorry,' said Dani. 'That was rude.'

'You're excused. No, it's just . . . why wait? We know we want to spend the rest of our lives together. I'm forty next week. I'm not exactly too young. And neither's Lola.'

'No,' said Dani. 'Well, a September wedding. How lovely. Look, I'd better get going.' She really needed to be away from him again. Before she said anything that could be construed as negative.

'I thought you wanted to get some water,' Nat said.

'I'll get some at home. I think the best thing for me right now is to go straight back to bed. See you next Saturday!'

A September wedding. Lola would be Mrs Hayward in a matter of weeks.

Back at home, unable to settle down to anything much, Dani logged onto Instagram. She wasn't following many people so there wasn't much to see, but she had a new message. She'd never had a message on Instagram before and it took her a while to work out how to find it. When she did, her jaw dropped in surprise.

It was from Will.

'Hey,' he'd written. 'Sorry I dashed off this morning. I forgot I had someone coming to fix the boiler. And I'm sorry to contact you via Instagram but you neglected to give me your number, gorgeous girl. I hope that wasn't deliberate! Can we try again on Thursday?'

Dani was absolutely gobsmacked.

'Gorgeous girl?'

Thank goodness for social media. She typed a message in response. And then retyped it. And then retyped it again. She settled on, 'That'd be nice. Thanks.' And her number.

Then she went back through all her own Instagram photos to try to see them through a potential date's eyes. Thank goodness they were mostly pictures of cakes and only one selfie, taken on a day when Flossie had done her make-up. She had a full green face. It was Halloween.

And then she went through Will's pictures, which were in an altogether different class. It was easy to see why he'd been a model. He didn't have a bad angle. Which made it all the more fantastic that he was interested in Dani. But he must be genuinely interested. It would have been very easy for him to simply never see her again.

And now he was messaging her back.

'Brilliant,' he said. 'So glad you're still talking to me. How about The Lonely Elephant. Seven o'clock. Come hungry!'

Who cared if Nat Hayward was getting married now?

Chapter Forty

When Dani asked her on the morning of the date, Jane was most unhelpful as to what she should wear.

'A nice frock?'

Meanwhile Flossie was of the opinion that women should not dress for men.

'Just be yourself.'

That was all very well for a sixteen-year-old to say. The fact is, though most sixteen-year-olds don't believe it, any woman under thirty can get away with going on a date wearing dungarees and Doc Martens because they're naturally, ineffably lovely and a little red dress and a face full of make-up would only be gilding the lily.

A woman facing forty, on the other hand, needs all the help she can get. At least that's what Dani was thinking. Never mind that Will had already seen her in her ratty dressing gown. She was treating this date as a complete do-over. A chance to wow him all over again. Or wow him for the first time. Whatever.

Sarah agreed. 'Darling, you're going to have to make a shopping trip.'

Dani had noticed Lola's boutique, of course, on her ride into work, but it was absolutely not the kind of place she ever expected to shop. Once, and only once, she'd slowed down to look at the window display but upon seeing that the cardigan she thought would make a nice alternative to the one she wore for gardening was priced at £250, Dani accepted she was not the sort of client Lola was after.

But by the time her shift at the hotel ended on date day, Dani wasn't sure she'd be able to get into the town centre before everything closed. And if she was honest, she was curious. She'd met Lola on three occasions, but she'd never really had a chance to chat to her and find out exactly what it was about her that had captured Nat Hayward's heart. And Will's before that. Perhaps seeing her in a business context – in her own professional world – would give Dani a different perspective. So Dani diverted via Lola's eponymous boutique on her way home.

The old Victorian shop front was painted hot pink with highlights in gold. The window display that day featured three mannequins in glittering mini-dresses like the one Lola had worn for her birthday party. The dresses were priced at three hundred pounds each, which made Dani increasingly sure there would be nothing for her inside. Her eyes almost popped out of her head when she saw the handbag with which one of the dresses was accessorised cost more than Dani's bicycle. She was about to turn away. There would be something in her wardrobe she could make work. But it was too late. She'd been spotted.

Lola herself was standing at the counter, flicking through a fashion magazine. When she saw she had a potential customer on the doorstep, she looked up and smiled a smile that was presumably supposed to be welcoming. She had a lot of teeth.

'I've just come from work,' Dani said as she stepped through the door, heading off any criticism of what she was wearing right away. Not that she was much more glamorous when she wasn't at work.

'Dani,' said Lola, coming out into the middle of the store.

'Thank you so much for inviting me to your engagement party.'

'It was the least we could do. You did make the cake after all.'

'I hope people enjoyed it.'

'They left most of it,' said Lola. 'Lots of people watching their sugar. I know I am now I've got to get into a wedding dress.'

It was hard to imagine Lola could lose much more weight without disappearing altogether. She was tiny. Dani suddenly felt distinctly lumpen in her presence.

'So, how can I help you? Just coming in for a nose?'

'Actually,' said Dani. 'I've got a date.'

Lola's eyes widened as if that was improbable. 'Tell me more.'

And because of the way Lola had looked so surprised, it was on Dani's lips to tell Lola exactly who her date was. Instead she said, 'He's someone I met through having a dog.'

'Of course, you take your dog to the same training class as Princess, don't you? I swear I had no idea having a dog would be so much trouble.'

'They're like children,' Dani observed.

'Only you don't have to wreck your figure to have one.'

Dani was sure Lola looked straight at her stomach when she said that. She sucked her belly in.

'So, what are you looking for?' Lola asked.

'I thought perhaps you might be able to suggest something.'

'I can try,' said Lola, in a way that made Dani hear the rest of the sentence in her head as 'but it will be a challenge.'

'Take off your jacket so I can see your shape.'

Dani placed her old denim jacket on the counter, folding it to hide the stains.

'Pear,' Lola said. 'Now, I know people don't like to hear that but trust me I don't mean it badly.'

'Might as well be honest,' said Dani.

'That's what I think. I did a personal styling course in London,' Lola explained. 'Body shape is really important. There's no point trying to flatter someone by telling them they're hourglass only for them to go away wondering why the sheath dress they bought looks so bad. You've got quite long arms too,' Lola continued.

'I thought they were perfectly normal.'

'No.' Lola put her hand on Dani's shoulder and shuffled her in the direction of the mirror. 'You see, your legs should be slightly longer than your upper limbs but I think your proportions are the other way round.'

'Like a chimpanzee,' said Dani.

'Exactly. But we can balance it with a bracelet-length sleeve or actual bangles to cut the line of your forearms – which is where the extra length is – and then we can lengthen your legs with some classic Kates.'

'Kates?'

'Nude court shoes,' Lola explained. 'Like Kate Middleton's.'

'I don't have a duchess-style budget,' said Dani,

feeling she ought to get that message out there before Lola started going nuts. She was already prancing around the store, pulling things off the rails. She held a green dress up against Dani's face and frowned in disapproval.

'I never wear green.'

'Good job,' said Lola.

It was ironic, Dani thought, that she was being dressed for a date with Will by his ex-girlfriend. The ex-girlfriend who was marrying her own ex-boyfriend. But Dani at least supposed it might mean Lola knew what the sort of man Dani went for would like. And Lola certainly seemed to be taking her new mission seriously.

'That looks really good,' she said, holding a purple-blue wrap dress beneath Dani's chin.

Dani looked at the price tag before she looked at the fabric. It was way more than she wanted to spend.

'Mate's rates,' Lola said conspiratorially. 'I can give you three per cent off. Try it on.'

Dani should have told Lola that she wouldn't be taking it. The dress would blow Dani's budget for the month. And that was before she even thought about the shoes. Did she have anything at home that would save her taking the 'Kates'? Alas, she didn't think so. Dani hadn't bought a pair of going out shoes in years, accessorising everything remotely dressy with a pair of black leather stilettoes that were supposed to be 'classic' but which were really best described as 'dull'.

'These shoes are an investment,' said Lola as she handed Dani the nude patent courts. 'You will wear them with everything.'

Lola didn't know that 'everything' in the context of

Dani's wardrobe consisted of three black dresses gone grey and an awful lot of jeans.

But being in Lola's shop and trying on that blue dress made Dani realise perhaps just how much she'd been missing out.

All at once, it was as if her mind had been replaced by an Instagram meme generator. The dress *was* lovely. She would never be any younger, thinner or prettier than she was right then. This might be her last chance at a date, let alone a date with a former model. This was a once-in-a-lifetime moment . . .

'I'll take the dress and the shoes,' she said, surprising herself.

'And the bangles?' Lola suggested. 'To make your arms look a bit less . . . noodly?'

'Well, the last thing I want is for my date to think I've got noodly arms,' said Dani. 'I'll take them too.'

Lola rang up the total amount and Dani did her best not to look shocked. Still she felt hot and cold as she handed over her card and inputted her PIN. She couldn't remember the last time she'd picked up an item of clothing that couldn't be bought contactless. But this was an investment in a future she hadn't dared think she deserved until Will showed up in town. She imagined his face as she walked in dressed to the nines. She felt excited in a way she hadn't for years.

'There you are. You're all set,' said Lola. 'Just that dress, those shoes and the bangles and a blow-dry.'

Dani put her hand to her hair, conscious that she hadn't been to a salon in six months.

'And a mani. And a pedi.'

'The shoes will cover my toes,' Dani pointed out.

'But what about when you want to slip one of them off, so you can stroke his leg underneath the table?' Lola asked. 'You should always be ready for seduction, Dani.'

This was why Nat was in love with her.

Chapter Forty-One

With her seductive new outfit ready to go, Dani started to feel quite excited. The night stretched ahead, full of promise. She might not have had time to get her hair done properly but it didn't look bad after she'd washed it and dried it upside down to give it some oomph. She'd sort of done a manicure too. After she wiped the excess polish off her cuticles with a cotton bud, it would pass muster.

Even Flossie gave Dani a thumbs-up when she saw her all dressed up.

'Lovely,' said Jane.

'Go get him,' said Sarah.

Will had bagged a table at The Lonely Elephant, Newbay's smartest new restaurant. Actually, it wasn't that new. And Dani had been there before, with Dave the chef. Dave made a point of visiting every new opening in the town, to see how it might impact on The Majestic's share of local business.

Dani hoped the proprietor wouldn't remember her from that night, when Dave had dissed The Lonely Elephant so comprehensively and loudly that they were eventually asked to leave. Three years had passed since then. Hopefully, that was long enough for everyone on the restaurant's staff to have forgotten the two idiots from The Majestic who sent back four half-finished bottles of wine, claiming they were all corked.

Dani didn't recognise the girl on the restaurant's reception desk. That was a good start.

'I'm here to meet Will . . .' she began.

The girl's eyes lit up and she examined Dani with open curiosity.

'He's already here,' she said.

'And are you *really* the woman he's been waiting for?' her expression seemed to ask.

'Follow me.' The receptionist clipped ahead of Dani into the dining room. She was much more confident in her heels than Dani was. Those 'Kates' might have made her legs look long but they also made her walk like a newborn tapir.

Will stood up and kissed Dani on both cheeks. He then rushed around the table to pull out her chair in a gentlemanly fashion.

'I'm assuming you'd like to face into the room,' said Will. 'See all the comings and goings. And I took the liberty of ordering you a glass of champagne to get things started. You look beautiful, by the way. What a lovely dress. Let me guess, the designer is . . . Cherry Blossom Days.'

'You got it in one.'

'Lola was mad about that company's designs,' Will said.

Hmmm, thought Dani. That was an awfully quick mention of his ex. But it didn't matter. Will was just making conversation. Dani was happy that he had paid her a compliment. The dress was working.

A waitress arrived with two glasses of fizz on a tray. She placed one in front of each of them. And a small dish of cheesy cracker things too. They smelled delicious.

'Well, here's to you,' said Will, raising a toast.

'And to you,' said Dani, chinking her glass against his.

'To both of us.'

Dani took a sip of the champagne but it was Will's words that made her feel giddy. To both of us. To us. It was going to be a wonderful night.

As he made her laugh again and again, Dani was thrilled to find out how much they had in common. From both loving champagne to both thinking lobster was overrated. From both secretly liking *Strictly Come Dancing* to both being nuts about *Game Of Thrones*.

Will was full of fascinating stories about his time on the modelling scene. Dani was impressed to hear he'd done lots of adverts.

'That guy on the sofa in DFS? That was me.'

And he had great gossip about lots of names Dani recognised from the *Daily Mail*'s sidebar of shame.

'Not that I ever read the *Mail Online*,' she insisted.

'Of course,' said Will. 'Me neither. But did you see that piece about Kylie today . . .'

They were so engrossed in their conversation that the waitress had to cough to get their attention so she could take their order.

For a starter, Dani ordered the goat's cheese salad. Will ordered smoked salmon. He insisted they each had a glass of white wine to go with this first course and made Dani choose it.

'You're the expert,' he said.

As she chugged her way through the Chablis she'd

chosen, Dani found herself feeling happier and happier and more and more relaxed in Will's company. By the time he offered her a piece of salmon – which he insisted on feeding her straight from his fork – Dani had forgotten she'd ever been nervous at all.

An hour in, it was all still going remarkably well. The waitress had just set their main courses on the table – chicken for Dani and a steak for Will – when the tinkling of the bell on the door announced that some new customers had arrived.

Dani looked up from admiring her plate to see who was walking through the restaurant door.

Chapter Forty-Two

'Lola!'

Will actually stood up when he saw who had walked in. 'Fancy seeing you here.'

'Well, fancy seeing you here too,' Lola replied. 'And you, Dani.'

Her expression as she looked at Dani was somewhere between surprise and horror.

'You wore the dress, I see,' she commented.

And now Dani noticed that Lola was wearing a dress of the exact same design but in a different colour. A dark pink. A colour that might have been more flattering to Dani than the blue. Yes, definitely more flattering. And somehow the pink made the dress look even more expensive than it was.

Lola was also wearing a pair of 'Kate' shoes except hers were not 'the sort of pale beige that makes me think of false legs' as Flossie had put it. They were a subtle burnished pinky-bronze that had a similar leg-lengthening effect but did not look as though they could double as office shoes. Instead, they oh-so-subtly suggested that Lola was the kind of woman who had a pair of shoes for each and every outfit and an outfit for every occasion.

Dani had felt pretty good in the clothes that Lola had chosen for her, but now she could see that her ensemble was just a beginner's version of the chic Lola had claimed for her own. Dani felt like a backing singer on tour with a proper diva, dressed in a watered-down version of the main star's style.

The wrap-over front of her dress felt all wrong now. Whenever she moved from a bolt upright position, it gaped open to show her bra. And while it was a pretty bra, Dani knew she didn't fill it out in anything like the same way as Lola filled out hers. Lola's cleavage was like two scoops of ice cream. How could she possibly compete? Her perfect evening was already dissolving like a dream.

While Will and Lola were swapping pleasantries and compliments, Nat was still standing at the restaurant's reception desk. He looked increasingly uncomfortable as the receptionist tapped at her keyboard and occasionally shook her head.

'I wonder what's holding him up?' Lola asked. 'Nat?'

Nat and the receptionist eventually walked over.

'This is terribly embarrassing,' said the receptionist. 'But I'm afraid we have no record of your reservation . . .'

'But I called and spoke to someone not an hour ago,' Lola insisted. 'Tell her, Nat.'

'I did,' he said.

'Well, as you can see,' the receptionist continued. 'All our tables are currently filled. We can offer you a spot at half past nine if you and your fiancé don't mind waiting in the bar area until then. With a glass of champagne on the house, of course.'

A frown darkened Lola's brow.

'Half past nine?' she said. 'That's ages away.'

'I know. I'm terribly sorry. Thursdays are one of our busiest evenings.'

'Come on,' said Nat. 'We can go somewhere else.'

'I don't want to go somewhere else,' said Lola. 'I called and booked a table here. And I'm hungry.'

'I don't know what happened,' said the receptionist. 'We've no record of your call at all. I can only apologise.'

Lola looked as though she was about to let rip.

'It's my fiancé's birthday,' she said.

Nat shrugged. Dani couldn't believe she'd forgotten.

'Actually, it's tomorrow,' Nat said.

'Still . . .' Lola insisted.

'Well, this is silly,' said Will then. 'Dani and I are sitting here at a huge table and you're being sent off to the bar.' He turned to the receptionist. 'Could you not make this table up for four instead of two? Make it a proper birthday party.'

'It's certainly possible but . . .'

The receptionist looked to Dani. She understood, if Will hadn't, that it was only polite to find out whether Dani was happy to share the table as well. But though the receptionist was offering Dani a courteous veto, Dani knew there was no way she could activate it. Lola and Will had already made their minds up.

'What a great idea!' Lola exclaimed. 'Would you swap with me, Dani, so that I can sit with my back to the wall? I hate not being able to see who's coming in.'

Without a word, Dani folded her napkin and placed it on the table next to her untouched chicken.

Now Dani and Nat were standing in the middle of the room like a pair of lemons while two waiters reset the table and whisked away the food which had already been served to be kept warm and brought back once Lola and Nat's choices were ready.

'I'm sorry,' Nat whispered to Dani while Lola and Will conferred over the wine menu.

'It's fine,' said Dani.

'But you were on a date. With Will,' he added with what seemed like a hint of disbelief.

'Oh, it wasn't a date date,' Dani said, thinking she had best play it down.

'I'm sorry all the same. This seems rude but . . . When Lola sets her mind on something . . .'

'It's fine,' Dani insisted again. 'And we get to celebrate you turning forty.'

'Not until midnight,' said Nat.

When at last the table was ready, Dani and Nat sat down with their backs to the room. Nat at least pulled Dani's chair out for her, as Will had done, before he forgot that she existed. Nat also hurried Lola along with her menu choices.

'We don't want Dani and Will's food to get dried out,' he reminded her.

'All right, bossy boots. I'll have the chicken too.'

Lola snapped her menu shut and turned straight back to Will.

'You snuck off from our engagement party early, you naughty boy,' she said to him. 'Wherever did you go? My sister was distraught. You know what a big crush she's got on you. And Nat's sister wasn't too pleased either.' Lola tapped Will on the arm. 'You must try harder not to be such a terrible heart-breaker.'

'Well, that's rich coming from you,' Will replied.

'More wine?' Nat asked Dani.

'Please.'

Ignoring the waiter, who looked horrified that Nat would pull the bottle out of the ice bucket himself, Nat topped Dani up. When he got to within an inch of the top of the glass, Dani said, 'Might as well fill the glass right up, to save having to do it again. Hang on.' She took a swig to make more space first.

While Lola and Will continued to swap news and gossip that meant nothing to the other two, who didn't know the people they were talking about, Dani and Nat were left trying to make small talk. It wasn't that they didn't have news and gossip of their own, or reminiscences they might have shared, but both Nat and Dani had been brought up to understand it wasn't polite to inflict it on your tablemates.

So Dani finished her fresh glass of wine quickly. Nat asked for another bottle. Lola broke off her private conversation briefly to insist that Nat order champagne.

'Anything else gives me a headache,' she explained. 'Don't you find the same?' she asked Dani.

'Oh, yes. All the time,' Dani lied.

Nat and Lola's main courses arrived. Along with the plates that had been kept warm. Dani was more than a little fed up to see that her chicken was looking considerably less succulent for half an hour under a heat lamp. She would have complained but it wasn't the restaurant's fault. It was Will who had insisted that the plates be taken away, after all.

'Much nicer if we all eat at once.'

At least the arrival of the food had forced Lola and Will to pause in their chat, allowing Dani to initiate a conversation that might involve all four of the people at the table. Or at least remind Lola who she'd actually come out to dinner with.

'So, how did you two meet again?' Dani asked Lola.

'Oh, we were on a photo shoot—' she began.

'I meant you and Nat,' Dani interrupted.

'Oh, us! It was very sweet. Nat's father was on the same hospital ward as my granddad. We got chatting by the coffee machine and then he asked me out. I have to admit I wasn't sure I wanted to go – Nat's a lot different from my usual type.' She glanced at Will, as if for emphasis. 'But you shouldn't judge anyone by appearances, right? Nat may have looked really stuffy but underneath he might have a great sense of humour. And he was obviously successful.'

Dani nodded. Nat looked as though he was waiting to hear something more.

'Anyway, we had our first date and the rest is history.'

'Yes,' said Nat. A muscle flickered in his cheek. Dani at once recognised a sign of annoyance.

'Do you remember our first date?' Lola asked Will.

'How could I forget?'

'Perhaps it's not the right time to bring it up,' Nat suggested.

'Oh no. Dani won't mind. It's really funny . . .'

As she told the story, Lola kept touching Will on the arm. Nat kept his hands firmly to himself. Soon Dani was sitting with her arms crossed, hugging herself for comfort against the growing awkwardness. Dani zoned out until Lola came to the punchline.

'I wouldn't even have said yes to the party but I heard that my ex was going to be there with his new girlfriend so I thought sod it, I will go along with this prat Will and make the stupid idiot jealous. Next thing you know, we're an item and we were together for the next year and a half.'

'Good times,' said Will.

'And now we're just really good friends. Isn't that right, Will?'

'Right. It's always sad when a relationship doesn't work out but I consider myself very lucky to still have Lola in my life. At the heart of it all, we've got a very strong friendship.'

Lola cuddled up to him for a moment. Nat twisted his napkin as though he was twisting someone's neck.

Chapter Forty-Three

Though she felt pretty full after the goat's cheese and the chicken, Dani decided that she would order dessert. If this date was not going to end in wild passionate sex (and it was increasingly looking as though that was well off the cards) then it should at least end in sticky toffee pudding. And Dani would not be sharing her portion either. Unlike Lola, who was negotiating with Nat that he should get the toffee pudding and two spoons.

'And you should get the cheesecake,' Lola told Will.

'She always knows what I like,' said Will. 'And what she wants to try.'

Dani shovelled her pudding into her face while Lola took incy-wincy bites of both the men's desserts. It got so irritating and seemed to take so long that Dani was tempted to snatch Lola's spoon from her hand and shovel down Nat and Will's puddings as well, just to get it over with.

When the waitress came over again to ask if anybody wanted coffee, Dani and Nat both almost jumped down her throat.

'No!'

Two bills were summoned with haste.

'Well,' said Lola, when at last the dreadful dinner was over and the bills had been paid. 'Thank you for letting us boring old engaged people crash your little date.'

'It was our pleasure,' said Will.

Dani wished she could at least enjoy the fact that Will had used 'our' instead of 'my', but Lola was still in full control of the evening. Will couldn't seem to take his eyes off her.

'Yes. Thank you. Now we should go,' said Nat. 'Early start.'

'Such an old killjoy. Can you believe it's his birthday tomorrow? Is this what happens when you turn forty? I hope this isn't a taste of married life to come!' Lola laughed.

Will laughed too.

'You lucky single people can stay out for as long as you like,' Lola continued.

'Yes,' said Will, suddenly linking his arm through Dani's. 'And that's exactly what we're going to do. Come on, Dani. The night is still young. Take me to Newbay's best dancing establishment.'

'You mean a club?' Dani asked. This was a turn of events she had not expected.

'Yes. Of course I mean a club. We're going to dance the night away.'

Dani watched Lola's smile stiffen just a little.

'Oh, Nat!' Lola said then, grabbing her fiancé's arm in a mirror image of Will's gesture. 'We should go dancing as well! You know, we're going to have to get up on the dance floor at our wedding. Might as well start practising now.'

'I don't know,' said Nat. 'We really do have to get up early.'

'We won't stay late, late,' said Lola. 'But how often do we get the chance to go clubbing with two great friends?'

Now she linked arms with Dani too. As though they were new BFFs.

'Dani wants us to be there.'

'I know what it's like when you've got to get up early.' Dani tried to wade in on Nat's side. Nat nodded gratefully.

'Don't encourage him!' Lola exclaimed. 'Nat, you're turning forty, not fifty. Don't make me feel like our age gap is bigger than ever.'

That comment hit Nat right in the heart, Dani could tell. He looked visibly pained.

'OK,' he said. 'I'll come dancing but only if you promise that we will be out of there at midnight.'

'Like Cinderella,' Lola agreed.

It was Cinderella's that they visited next. The vast cavernous space beneath the multi-storey car park had always been a nightclub, though it had many incarnations and names in the time that Dani had known it. It was Cinderella's in the nineties. Right now it was called 'Dirty Dixie' and had a Southern US theme with stuffed alligators on the walls and cocktails called things like 'Moonshine' and 'Hooch'.

That night, however, the music at Dixie's was pure nineteen eighties and nineties. Thursdays were the big night out for Newbay's thirty- and forty-something singletons, who liked to hear the music that defined their glory years.

Will paid for all four of them to get into the club, causing Lola to grab him and kiss him on the cheek.

'You lovely man.'

He blushed.

Nat tried to pay him back. Will wouldn't have it.

'Think of it as an early birthday gift,' he said.

The unlikely foursome left their coats in the cloakroom and headed for the bar. The club was still quite empty and they quickly found a table. Will fetched drinks for everyone. Dani had a gin and tonic. Nat said he only wanted water.

'Oh, Nat,' Lola complained. 'Don't be so dull!'

But even with more alcohol, Dani could feel the party spirit slipping away from her too. What she really wanted was to go home. Maybe they could get away with having just one drink. Nat met Dani's eyes. It was clear he felt the same way.

The DJ put on Ricky Martin's 'Living La Vida Loca'.

'Oh, I love this song. Do you like it? We should do a routine together,' said Lola to Dani, nodding towards the dance floor.

Dani thought once again about how she'd ended up in the backing singer's outfit. She did not want to be on the dance floor, providing some sort of complimentary shadow to Lola's glittering fabulousness.

'I'm not mad about it,' said Dani.

'But we only came here to dance,' Lola said. 'Nat? Will?'

'I'm ready,' Will said. He got up and gave a *Strictly* shimmy. Lola stood up next to him.

'I'll get up there if you will,' Dani told Nat.

'OK,' he said. 'I suppose I ought to see my thirties out in style.'

She touched his hand. 'It will be painless, I promise.'

* * *

Will and Lola shimmied on ahead. They were neither of them worried about being under the spotlight. There was to be no hugging the edge of the floor for them. They headed straight for the centre, drawing both admiring and jealous glances from the punters who were already up and jigging.

It was obvious that Will and Lola had often danced together before. They put on a routine that was worthy of a pair of ballroom professionals while Dani and Nat jigged up and down like a couple of embarrassed teenagers watching their parents get down like disco wasn't dead. Except, of course, Will and Lola were not 'dad dancing'. They were properly setting the floor on fire.

Nat pleaded with his eyes to be allowed to sit down.

'Another drink?' Dani suggested as the song ended.

'Good idea,' said Nat as he gratefully followed her off the floor. Will and Lola didn't even seem to notice the other two had gone. They stayed on the floor as one dance classic segued into another. Totally lost in music. And each other.

This time, Nat had a gin and tonic too. The table they'd been sitting at earlier had been commandeered by another group of people, so Dani and Nat leaned on the balustrade that surrounded the dance floor.

'Thank you,' Nat said. 'For rescuing me.'

'I wasn't exactly having the time of my life out there either,' Dani replied.

They chinked glasses.

'I'm sorry we hijacked your evening.'

'It probably would have ended long before now if we hadn't bumped into you and Lola.'

'The last thing I expected was to end up clubbing tonight.'

'Same here. Though I'm always saying how much I miss going dancing. Now I know I've got no need to miss it any more. This is terrible.'

'Yep,' said Nat.

'Music's too loud.'

'Lights are too bright.'

'Drinks are too expensive. Place is full of young people showing off.'

As Dani said that, Will attempted to lift Lola above his head *Dirty Dancing* style.

'That's the standard you've got to beat for your wedding dance.'

'Just watching has put my back out,' said Nat.

'You'll make me snort my gin.' Dani laughed.

'Fancy another?'

'I thought you were leaving after one?'

'Doesn't look as though that's going to happen.'

'I'm sorry.'

'No need for you to apologise. Anyway, I'm very happy to stay here with you.'

Dani chinked her glass against Nat's again.

'I second that.'

'And it is nearly my birthday.'

'Better get a couple of doubles, then.'

When Nat came back from the bar, Will and Lola were still tripping the light fantastic. 'It's great, the way that Lola and Will have stayed friends. And the fact that you're happy to let her hang out with him,' Dani observed.

'It's not a matter of *letting* Lola do anything,' said

Nat. 'Anyway, they're just friends. Jealousy isn't part of my repertoire.'

'That's a good way to be,' said Dani.

'We're all adults,' said Nat. 'We both have pasts.'

'Does she know about ours?' Dani wanted to ask. She didn't.

'So, you're going to have to get Will to show you how it's done before the big day,' said Dani instead. 'The dancing thing.'

Now Will was sliding across the dance floor on his knees while Lola recreated the flamenco scene from the finale of *Strictly Ballroom*, swishing her skirt about her knees.

'I was planning something a little more low key,' Nat admitted. 'You know I always hated dancing.'

'I remember.'

'You still rank as the only woman who has ever persuaded me to take to the floor willingly,' he added.

'Is that true?' The direct reference to their shared past took her by surprise.

'Yes. I do believe that the last time I went dancing was in 1996 . . .'

Chapter Forty-Four

1996

Julie's twenty-first birthday fell on a Saturday in the wedding season when, as usual, it was all hands on deck at The Majestic. But as soon as the shift was finished, the whole gang hit the town. It didn't matter that half the waiting staff was underage. Dave knew everyone on the door at Cinderella's. He also knew pretty much everyone who worked at the local police station and was thus able to assure the younger members of the group that they would have no problem should the police raid the club and ask to see ID. They wouldn't bother Dave's mates.

Nat didn't have to worry, of course. He'd already turned eighteen. And Dani had a fake student ID card that she'd bought for twenty quid from one of the druggies who hung out beneath the Newbay pier. It looked quite realistic in the dark. The bloke on the cash desk seemed happy enough anyway.

Still, Cinderella's was a deeply cheesy nightspot. It was the kind of place that Nat dissed on a regular basis. It was where people with no imagination spent a Friday evening, he thought. It was no secret that Julie didn't have much of an imagination. But it was her birthday and for that reason, she got to choose where everyone would be spending the early hours of the morning.

'I can't believe I've got to go to a club where they might play Whitney Houston,' Nat complained.

'Oh you'll love it,' said Dani, as she tucked her arm through his. He immediately felt more optimistic.

Dave, being the oldest and the most senior member of the Majestic squad, got the first round in. Everyone knew he was keen to impress Julie apart from anything else. She squealed with delight when he ordered her a pina colada that was topped with whipped cream and studded with real sparklers.

'He's trying to get me drunk,' Nat heard Julie say to Dani, before adding in an aside, 'He doesn't need to. I've always fancied Dave.'

Julie beckoned Dave onto the dance-floor and soon they were getting down to Peter Andre's 'Mysterious Girl'. It was quite something to watch Dave – who was built like a rhino – attempting to replicate Andre's snake-hipped moves.

'I can't watch,' said Nat, covering his eyes.

It was the Spice Girls next. '2 Become 1'. Now Nat covered his ears. He then grimaced his way through the opening bars of Livin' Joy's 'Don't Stop Movin''. Still Nat was determined not to dance.

Dani wasn't having it.

'This is a good tune,' she insisted. 'Come on.'

Standing up, Dani took both of Nat's hands and pulled him to his feet.

'I can't dance.'

'Of course you can. It's easy. Everyone can dance. You just have to let go and feel the music.'

'I can't feel the music.'

'Rubbish. You're a musician,' Dani reminded him.

'Don't get a lot of dance tunes for oboe.'

'I'm not taking no for an answer.'

And because it was Dani who was asking, Nat let himself be dragged onto the floor. If only to keep holding her hands. Dave the chef was already in the middle. He was definitely feeling the music, now playing air drums in a manner that looked almost masturbatory. Dani jerked her thumb at their sort-of boss.

'You can't possibly look a bigger idiot than that,' Dani commented.

'Try me,' said Nat.

He felt painfully shy right there under the flashing lights.

Dani leaned close and shouted into his ear. 'Just go for it. No one here is actually watching to see what you're doing. They're all too busy worrying how stupid they look themselves. You stand out more if you don't get down. Don't stop moving . . .' she sang along.

Dani was a natural. She used Nat like a kind of maypole, taking one of his hands and using his long arm as a ribbon, snaking under and around it, but somehow making it look as though Nat was turning her.

It was easy to dance with Dani. All Nat had to do was look into her eyes and he could forget there were other people around them. She made him feel incredible, invincible. It was as though when they were together, he suddenly had superpowers.

Dani even made it easy for Nat to stay on the dance floor when the DJ started playing the 'Macarena', the runaway hit from three summers before and Julie's favourite song of all-time (so far).

'You have to do this,' Dani said, taking him through the steps.

'I'll look like an idiot.'

'The Macarena makes everyone look like an idiot,' Dani yelled back.

With Dani by his side, Nat could overcome his shyness and his doubts.

When she smiled at him, it was as though he was standing in bright warm sunshine. Her laugh was the best sound he'd ever heard. The feeling of her hand in his was pure heaven. He had to make her more than a friend.

When Dave the chef bounced into their little twosome and bumped hips with Dani, Nat did the only thing he could to stay in the game. He moved to the other side of Dani and bumped hips with her too, so that the three work colleagues looked like some daft kind of executive toy, bumping backwards and forwards.

'You having fun, Frank?' Dave the chef asked.

Nat even managed a thumbs-up.

That night was the very first time they kissed.

At the end of the evening, the DJ announced the last dance. Nat and Dani had left the dance floor by that time but she wouldn't let him get away with sitting out the final tune.

'Come on,' she said.

'I can't do slow dances,' Nat said.

'It's not a *very* slow one,' said Dani as the record began to play.

'I love you always forever' by Donna Lewis was not a song that Nat imagined holding close to his heart, but forever after it would be the song that had been playing when he first kissed Dani Parker and for that reason alone it was the best song in the world.

'. . . always together . . .'

She murmured the words against his lips.

Chapter Forty-Five

Fast-forward twenty-two years to the double date from hell.

'Yes,' said Nat. 'You're the only woman who ever made me feel comfortable on the dance floor.'

Dani rattled the ice cubes in the bottom of her glass as she searched for something to say in response.

'I'm sorry if I stepped on your feet,' was all she could come up with.

'I wouldn't have cared.'

'Another g and t?' Dani asked, though they'd probably both had too many.

That night, the last song was not one that Nat or Dani knew. As the DJ announced the evening's imminent end, Will and Lola were still twirling in the middle of the floor and Dani suspected they would have stayed there had she not caught Will's eye and given him a bright but questioning smile. When she did that, Will dutifully escorted Lola to the bar and exchanged her hand for Dani's.

'Come on,' he said. 'We've hardly danced at all.'

'All right.'

Dani let herself be led away. If only to spare Nat the spectacle of seeing his fiancée smooch with her ex.

Once they were on the floor, Will held her in a close but slightly formal hold. His eyes were fixed on the

distance over her shoulder and Dani noticed that he
didn't ever turn her around, as most of the other
couples were. Will's attention was all on the exit.

By the time the music finished, Lola and Nat had
gone.

'They didn't even say goodbye,' Will complained.

Dani found she was glad to have avoided that
awkwardness.

'Thank you for a lovely evening,' she said as she and
Will got their coats. Dani felt very sober now.

'Let's do it again some time, yes?' Will asked.

'That'd be great,' Dani told him, though she
wondered why he was bothering to pretend the evening
might be worth repeating.

Will walked her to the taxi rank, where they took
two cars going in different directions.

Dani didn't know who to feel more sorry for. Herself
– for having looked forward to the evening so much
only to have it turn out so weirdly. Or Will – being so
obviously lovelorn for Lola.

At least Jezza was pleased to see Dani when she got
in. Ecstatic, in fact. He greeted her as though she had
just come back from the front of a distant war. As
though she'd been away for years on end. As though
he hadn't dared believe she would ever come back to
him. He wagged himself into a frenzy, squeaking his
excitement. Though he'd often spend the evening with
Jane, Flossie and Sarah, Jezza only really had eyes for
Dani now.

'Come on, then,' she invited Jezza to join her on the
sofa, not caring that she was wearing an expensive
dress that was almost certainly 'dry clean only'. 'This

is the closest I'm going to get to anything like physical affection today.'

Jezza arranged himself across Dani's lap and let her rub his soft warm belly. If she dared to stop, even for a couple of seconds, he would gently remind her of her duties with an insistent paw pat to her wrist. With his comforting bulk across her knees (Eric the organic veg man had recently revealed that Jezza's father was an enormous standard poodle, the size of a small horse) it was hard for Dani to imagine that there had ever been a time when Jezza wasn't part of the family.

'I'm glad you chose us,' Dani whispered to the top of his head.

Eventually, Jezza dozed off and Dani was able to stop tickling him. Though she wasn't able to move. She picked up her phone and opened up the Internet icon. She entered 'I love you always forever' into Google's search bar. The sound, when she played a video of the song on YouTube, was so much more fresh and raw than she remembered. It was a sound from another life.

In a modern town house on the other side of Newbay, Nat Hayward typed the same search term and listened to half the song while Lola was in the bathroom. Only to see if he'd been thinking of the right song, he told himself. That was all.

Chapter Forty-Six

'So how was your date?' Jane asked over breakfast.

'Busy.' Dani described the foursome.

'Oh,' Jane said. 'How strange.'

'You're telling me.'

'Still, I suppose it was rather nice of Will to offer them the space at your table so that Nat and Lola didn't have to wait for ages at the bar.'

'Yes. I suppose it was.'

Flossie joined them at the breakfast table. Now that her exams were over, she was getting up later and later. She too wanted to know how the date had gone.

'They joined you for dinner? That is so rude,' was her opinion. 'Are you going to see him again?'

'I don't think so,' Dani said.

But Will texted while Dani was cycling down the hill to The Majestic. She checked her phone as soon as she came to a stop. He thanked her for a 'fabulous' evening and reiterated his hope that she was up for another one soon. Dani decided she would wait a while before she responded.

As she was walking into the hotel, Dani bumped into Cheryl.

'How was your date?' Cheryl wanted to know. It seemed that everyone had been waiting on tenterhooks to find out. Dave the chef had spread the news far and wide that Dani had the chance of a shag.

'It ended up being a foursome with Nat Hayward and his fiancée,' said Dani. Cheryl blanched. 'Not that kind of foursome,' Dani assured her.

'Well, that's good news,' said Cheryl. 'Since they're coming in this afternoon to talk about having their wedding reception here.'

'What?'

Why hadn't Nat said anything the previous evening? Why hadn't Lola?

'I'll need you to be on hand to talk about the menus.'

'Can't Dave do it?' Dani asked.

'You know I'm not going to ask him,' said Cheryl. 'Though you can try.'

But when Dani asked him, he said no.

So at three thirty, Dani had to come out of the kitchen – in the cleanest apron she could find – to talk to Nat and Lola about their big day. They weren't alone. Lola's parents were with them.

'Eh, it's the Queen of Cakes!' said Ian. 'I told Nat and Lola how impressed we were with your work at Lola's birthday and the engagement party and that they have to have their party here.'

'Thank you,' Dani said, pressing down the thought that she wished she hadn't been so impressive.

'So,' Cheryl was straight into action. 'I believe you've already had a chance to look at our brochures regarding our typical wedding packages.'

'They'll want the most expensive one,' said Ian.

'Actually, Ian—' Nat began.

'No, don't you worry about it, Nat. Sheena and I

have been saving for this day since Lola was born. We've put money aside for all our girls,' Ian told Cheryl. 'We've got three. Lola's the middle one but she's the first to get married. We're starting to think Francesca might never need her share of the wedding cash. Perhaps we can get a new patio instead.'

'Oh, I'm sure that can't be right,' said Cheryl. 'She'll find her perfect man soon.'

'You haven't met our Francesca,' said Ian. He guffawed.

'Anyway,' said Cheryl. 'The package outlines in our guide are exactly that. Just a guide. They can all be customised and made perfect for you. Table settings et cetera can all be matched to your personal colour scheme. We're well used to dying tablecloths to order, that sort of thing. We dyed some duck-egg blue just the other week. Have you chosen your colour scheme yet?'

Lola launched into a long soliloquy about her vision for the ideal day. She was going to have five bridesmaids – her sisters, a cousin, and her brother's two small girls. She was wavering between a daffodil yellow and dusty mink for their dresses. It was so hard to find a colour that would suit all five of her attendants. On the other hand, since the wedding would be in September, then maybe she should go with an autumn theme . . .

Dani suddenly felt the need for a long drink of water. She reached for the jug that Cheryl had placed on the table, just as Nat reached for it too. Their fingers brushed. Their eyes met. Dani withdraw her hand so abruptly that she knocked the sugar bowl over, drawing everyone's attention. Exactly what she didn't want.

Dani said, 'Look I'm really sorry to interrupt you, Lola, but I'm afraid I need to go back into the kitchen for a moment. I left a tray of biscuits in the oven and I would hate for them to burn. Perhaps Cheryl can come and get me to talk menus when you've sorted everything else out.'

Cheryl looked as though she was about to protest but Dani couldn't sit at that table for a moment longer. Not after she and Nat and touched hands and she'd seen a look of pure despair in his eyes. Had he seen the same look in hers?

There were no burning biscuits, of course. Dani's assistant Joe had everything under control. He always did. Dani got herself a glass of water then went outside to the comfort of the wheelie bin bay.

Nat wasn't in despair. At least, not for the reasons that had briefly flitted through Dani's mind. He was just bored by the wedding preparations and perhaps embarrassed by his blow-hard future father-in-law. Maybe he was a little hung over as well. Or feeling odd about turning forty. He was not thinking what Dani had been thinking. Not at all.

'Dave,' she said to her friend and sort-of boss. 'I can't do the rest of that meeting with Nat and his fiancée.'

'Eh?'

'You'll have to do it for me.'

'With Cheryl?'

'Yes, with Cheryl.'

'I vowed I would never do anything to make that woman's life easier ever again.'

'Not even if it means making my life easier in the process?' said Dani. 'Me? Your oldest friend in this hotel?'

'Why can't you just talk to them? You know what to say.'

'And so do you. Look, Dave. I just to need to go home, OK.'

'You gotta give me a reason,' he said.

'All right,' said Dani, pulling out the big guns. 'I think I've got my period. It's early and I wasn't prepared.'

Dave recoiled and the matter was settled. He would finish the meeting.

Dani didn't wait around for Dave to change his mind. She slipped out through the kitchen's back door, got on her bike and got out of there. But she didn't go home. Instead, she cycled down to the sea front and kept heading west with the sea by her side. The further she got from the hotel, the better she hoped she would feel. She ran out of energy before she got far enough.

She stopped and leaned her bike against the sea wall, looking out at the horizon. And as if to taunt her, into her head popped the memory of another time she'd stopped to look at this view. Her first proper date with Nat Hayward, after their first proper kiss at the nightclub. They were both on their bicycles. He'd made them a picnic. They'd laid out a rug on the sand and kissed all afternoon, until Dani's lips were raw. They were so excited to be together at last. Not having to pretend to be casual about their feelings for each other any more. All their pent-up desire for each other had come tumbling out.

It was so long ago and yet, as the cliché went, Dani could remember it like it was yesterday.

Chapter Forty-Seven

Jane had not been to the pet shop since the afternoon she'd seen Bill Hunter at Duckpool Bay. The afternoon when she hoped he hadn't seen her trying to persuade two police officers not to arrest her granddaughter. What an embarrassing episode.

Today, Flossie was at Xanthe's and Dani was at work so Jane took Jezza with her on her errands.

'If you're good, you can choose a new toy at the pet shop,' she told him, as she attached the lead to his harness. She was talking to Jezza exactly as she used to talk to Flossie and getting similar results with her bribes. Flossie could never be bribed and neither, it seemed, could Jezza. The promise of a new toy did not stop him from pulling Jane to and fro across the pavement as though he were a runaway plough horse.

By the time they got to the pet shop, Jane was quite out of breath.

'Don't show me up in here,' she begged him.

Jane pushed open the door. The bell announced her arrival. Bill looked up from the paperwork he had been going through while the shop was quiet and beamed when he saw who'd walked in.

'Hello stranger,' he said. 'And, it's Jezza, isn't it?'

Jezza wagged his tail, knocking over a pile of cat toys as he did so. Sapphire, Bill's greyhound, had been snoozing on her beanbag behind the counter. She slowly got up and sauntered round to give Jezza a quick sniff. He tried to engage her in a game but Sapphire was far too cool for that. Having established that Jezza wasn't worth worrying about, she padded straight back to her bed.

'Now, what can I do for you?' Bill asked Jane.

'We're looking for a treat,' said Jane.

'Then you've come to the right place. If your idea of a treat is a smelly cow's hoof.'

'Luckily that is exactly what Jezza had in mind. Will it stop him eating shoes?'

'Depends on the shoes.'

Bill picked a good hoof out.

'A properly smelly one,' he said.

'Thank you. How much do I owe you?' Jane asked.

'Nothing,' he said. 'It's on the house.'

'No. I couldn't possibly,' said Jane.

'Then put a quid in there,' said Bill, nodding towards the collection box on the counter. 'It's for the dog shelter. Actually, I'm doing a fund-raiser for them at the weekend.'

'What have you got to do?' Jane asked.

'A sponsored dog walk. From The Majestic to The Driftwood on the other side of town. Do you know it?'

'That's a long way.'

'Only two and a half miles. But there will be plenty of stops en route,' he said. He paused for a moment as though considering. 'Lots of my customers will be there. Perhaps you and Jezza would like to join us? He's only young, I know, so he doesn't have to do the whole route if it's too much for him.'

'Oh, it's me I don't think could make the whole route,' Jane laughed. 'With my old legs.'

'Old legs? You don't look a day over twenty-five.'

'Oh, don't.' Jane waved the compliment away.

'It's true!'

'Well, thank you.'

Jane felt the colour rising in her cheeks. Lately she'd been blushing all the time. It was like a second menopause. Or adolescence.

'So, will you join us?' Bill asked. 'It's always good fun. Give or take the odd dog fight. It's a great way to get to know other doggy people. They're a very welcoming crowd.'

'I'll give it some thought,' said Jane.

'Good. If you do decide to come . . .' Bill scribbled his number on a Post-it note. 'Give me a call. If you decide not to come . . . call me anyway.'

Jane didn't have to give it much thought. By the time she got back to the house she had convinced herself that it was a very good idea. The local dog shelter was an excellent cause. She wanted to give something back to the community. She needed the exercise. She was not, repeat not, merely excited by the idea of an afternoon with Bill Hunter.

Chapter Forty-Eight

It had been three weeks now since Flossie and Jed were arrested for illegally selling cupcakes on the beach. Flossie's exams were long over. The atmosphere in the house was more relaxed than it had been for a while. Particularly since it seemed that Flossie had taken everything Dani said to her on board. Whereas perviously Jed and his opinions had been Flossie's only topic of conversation, now she didn't mention him at all.

Dani was delighted.

She was in the kitchen, making meat-free chilli for supper – Flossie was still a vegan – when Flossie came downstairs at a skip.

'Mum, I forgot to say. I need my passport.'

'What for?' Dani asked.

'For sixth form college? To finish some of the registration stuff I've got to do?'

Those rising endings again. They drove Dani nuts.

'For sixth form college? To finish the registration stuff?' Dani mimicked her to make a point.

'Mum,' Flossie groaned. 'Stop it. I just need my passport as soon as possible. OK?'

'They want the original?'

'Just a copy. But if you let me have the original, I can get it scanned round at Xanthe's. Her mum's got one of those printer–stroke–scanner things. I need a digital file version of it so I can send it as an email attachment.'

'I can do it at the hotel, if you like.'

'Oh no, Mum,' said Flossie. 'I didn't mean to make more work for you. I'll get it done at Xanthe's.'

'That's very thoughtful. But you won't lose it, will you? Passports cost a fortune these days.'

'Of course I won't lose it. Honestly, Mum. I'm not a complete incompetent.'

'OK.'

'And I need my birth certificate too.'

'Really? I thought all this registration stuff was sorted out before you went on study leave.'

'Yeah. Me too. I guess there was some sort of computer glitch and the info didn't go through the first time or something. Anyway, it doesn't matter because I can sort it all out round at Xanthe's. She's having to do it again too. We all are.'

'OK.'

Dani went upstairs into her bedroom and unlocked the safe at the bottom of her wardrobe. Flossie stood behind her, watching as she put in the pin number.

'My birthday,' Flossie observed.

'Yes. So now you know the secret code you can get into the safe and steal everything in it,' Dani joked. 'Or maybe leave some money in there out of sympathy.'

There was nothing exactly valuable in Dani's safe. Just a lot of things that would be a complete pain in the proverbial to have to replace if they were lost in a burglary or fire. Like Flossie's birth certificate and passport. Not that any of the Parker women's passports were getting that much use.

'As soon as you've finished scanning these documents,

put them straight back in your bag and make sure you give them to me the minute you walk through the door. Understood?'

'Understood. But it'll be OK if I lose them after they're scanned because we'll have copies.'

'Not the point,' said Dani, handing over the birth certificate with the blank space where the name of Flossie's father should have been. Lloyd had changed his mind about going with Dani to register Flossie's birth and Dani wasn't allowed to fill out the form on his behalf.

It made Dani a little bit sad, seeing that blank space again. Reliving the moment when Lloyd decided he wouldn't even give Flossie his name. Ah well. At least it meant she didn't have to battle about what Flossie's first name would be. Or her middle name. Which was Rosamund. Rose of the world. She was certainly the Rose of Dani's world, even when she was a small, squally newborn who never seemed to sleep. Even as a sixteen-year-old prone to stupid choices.

'Don't leave this anywhere silly,' Dani said one more time as Flossie tucked the brown envelope containing her passport and her birth certificate into her bag.

'I'll take these over to Xanthe's first thing tomorrow.'

'And give them back to me right away.'

'Right away,' Flossie gave a little salute. She turned to go to her room.

'Flossie.' Dani made her pause in the doorway. 'Flossie, I'm really proud of the way you've been handling the Jed thing. I know it can't have been easy for you to tell him you couldn't see him any more.'

'It wasn't,' Flossie admitted. She'd done it in a text. She showed it to Dani before she sent it.

'Has he been in touch since?' Dani gently probed.

'No, Mum.'

'Not even to see how you're getting on? Or to apologise for what happened?'

'No. Not at all.'

'Well, at least that means you can be quite clear as to how much he really cared.'

'Not much, eh? I'm better off without him.' Flossie's smile faded into a grim line.

'I know it hurts, my love, but you really are.'

Flossie let Dani give her a quick hug.

'Now, promise me one more time you won't lose that passport? Not least because maybe, just maybe, we might have enough money left at the end of the month to do a weekend in France before you go back to school. If we can get the dog's passport sorted out.'

'Excellent.' Flossie gave her mum the thumbs-up.

Chapter Forty-Nine

On Sunday morning, the sponsored walkers, plus Jane and Jezza, gathered in the car park outside The Majestic Hotel. It was the perfect day for a walk along the coast. Dry and sunny but not too hot. A few clouds like cotton-wool sheep added a touch of prettiness to the horizon.

The walk took place every year but this was a record turnout. There were dogs of all sizes, from a couple of enormous Irish wolfhounds down to a trio of chihuahuas, who were making a noise that belied their tiny size. As Jezza and Jane got close by, he began to pull hard on his lead, eager to see who he could find.

'Talk to your dog!' someone shouted, in Jane's direction. 'Don't let him get ahead of you.'

'Are you talking to me?' Jane turned to see the young woman yelling instructions.

'Absolutely. I think you need this.' Nurse Van Niekerk handed Jane a flyer about Best Behaviour Boot Camp, before she and Jezza recognised each other.

'Oh Jeremy Corbyn,' Nurse Van Niekerk tutted. 'This is not how one of my students should behave and you know it. Best Behaviour Boot Camp boys always walk to heel.' She held her hand out to Jane. 'You must be Grandma Jezza,' she said.

'Well, yes,' said Jane. 'I suppose I am.' Jane had

heard all about Nurse Van Niekerk's refusal to bother with human names.

'I heard you were coming today. Now, Grandma Jezza, as Jezza is one of my students, I don't mind giving you a quick crash course about how you can keep him on his very best behaviour today. You seem like an intelligent sort of woman . . .'

At that moment, Dani's friend Liz intervened, linking her arm through Jane's and leading her away.

'You mustn't take any notice of Nurse Van Niekerk. She can be a little abrasive but she does get results. Hello, Jezza.' Liz bent down to scratch the pup between the ears. 'Dani told me to look out for the pair of you. You're walking with us. Evan's over there, surrounded by his clients.'

One of whom was Bill.

'Jane, this is Bill Hunter,' Liz introduced them.

'We've already met,' he said.

'Lots of times,' said Jane.

Liz raised an eyebrow.

'At the pet shop. Best in Devon,' Jane added.

Sapphire was lazing at Bill's feet. The elegant greyhound raised an eyebrow in a bored sort of way as Jezza tried to attract her attention again. As he adopted the 'play' position, bowing to Sapphire with his bottom high in the air, tail flapping from side to side like a windscreen wiper in a hurricane, Sapphire merely closed her eyes.

'Never mind, Jezza,' said Liz. 'There will be other girls.'

'I hope you will be having him done before *that* becomes an issue,' said Nurse Van Niekerk, who'd caught up with them again.

'Done?' Bill grimaced. 'Don't say that in front of the poor lad,' he joked. Jezza continued to court Sapphire while she continued to ignore him.

'Sapphire's very cool,' said Bill. 'But she likes him really.'

'There's no way we'll be able to keep up with you two,' said Jane.

'Sapphire's also very lazy. Greyhounds may be good over sprints but there's nothing they like better than sleeping. She sleeps for twenty-three hours a day, I reckon.'

While Jezza pranced about in front of her, Sapphire closed her eyes again.

When the dogs and owners had reached critical mass, with latecomers spilling out onto the road, it was time to get things underway.

Evan the vet, who had organised the event this year, climbed onto the platform and welcomed that afternoon's walkers.

'We've got almost two hundred dogs here this afternoon,' he said. 'And we're grateful to see every single one of you. Your support is invaluable when it comes to keeping our sanctuary open. Several of our sanctuary dogs are going to be walking with us today. So, if you feel like there's room in your home for another set of paws, please don't hesitate to talk to me or one of my colleagues. A home isn't complete without a dog, in my opinion.'

A shout of 'hear hear' went up from several of the walkers.

'Now let's get going, shall we? There's a barbecue at the other end!'

The walkers, and their dogs, needed no more encouragement.

Still the walk started off slowly as everyone trickled out of the hotel car park through the bottleneck of the gates. The staff of The Majestic had come to wave the walkers off. Jane waved to Dani, who was on the balcony of the restaurant in her kitchen whites.

'Make her proud,' Jane told Jezza. 'Walk to heel.'

Jezza pulled on his lead. 'What did your nurse mean about talking to him?' Jane asked Evan.

'She meant, you just have to keep looking down at him from time to time, making eye contact and reminding him that he's taking his cues from you,' said Evan. 'Like this.'

He took Jezza's lead and by chatting to him had the pup walking sensibly in under a minute.

'Seems like hard work,' said Jane.

'Everything worth doing is hard work,' said Evan, looking across at his wife.

Liz's own dog Ted was not walking to heel at all. He was bustling ahead of the crowd, pulling so hard he was panting.

'He likes to lead the way,' Liz explained.

'There's no doubt who's top dog in our house,' Evan agreed.

'Should have come to boot camp,' Nurse Van Niekerk muttered.

That morning, getting ready for the walk, Jane had been a little nervous. She'd worried that she wouldn't find enough to talk about with Bill if they did the whole walk together so she was relieved that there were plenty of other walkers to pick up the slack.

About a mile into the walk they were joined by a very smartly dressed woman with a jet black French bulldog.

'Mrs Coco!' Evan called, when he saw her.

'Coco is the dog's name, right?' Jane asked Liz for confirmation. 'And her name is?'

'You know, after two years of knowing her, I still have absolutely no idea.'

'We shan't be walking with you very far,' said Mrs Coco. 'On account of Coco's bad legs. But we wanted to show our support.'

'Of course,' said Evan. 'How is Coco doing today?'

'Oh she's . . .'

. . . already sitting down and refusing to move.

'I might just pop back into the house and get her wheels,' Mrs Coco said. 'We'll never keep up with you otherwise.'

While Mrs Coco went inside and returned with a pram, Evan took a closer look at little Coco.

'I think you should bring her in on Monday,' he said. 'See if we can't persuade her to perk up a little.'

'Right you are, Dr Thomas.'

Mrs Coco loaded Coco into the pram and the walk continued. Coco seemed very happy to sit back and let the wind blow past her ears.

The atmosphere on the walk was wonderful. The weather and the company made the day perfect. As the dog walkers made their way up onto the headland, well-wishers, who leaned out of their windows with speakers playing uplifting tunes, played them through the streets. Everyone was glad to see them. At the front of the procession were two people dressed in giant dog-suits – Dalmatians – who carried buckets to collect spare change.

One of them fell back so that he was level with Jane and Bill for a while.

'This bucket's getting heavy,' he said, showing them how much change he'd collected so far. 'And I'm sweating like the proverbial pig in this dog-suit.'

'Keep up the good work,' said Evan. 'This is on target to be a bumper year for the shelter.'

'It's a very good cause,' said Mrs Coco.

At the halfway point, a stall manned by volunteers was distributing water to the walkers and the dogs. Jane gratefully took the bottle Bill picked up for her and shared it with Jezza. Though the pup did not usually walk so far, he was showing no sign of flagging. He was determined to keep up with Sapphire who, with her long legs, was probably taking only half so many steps. She was a truly elegant creature.

'Is Sapphire the first dog you've had?' Jane asked Bill.

'Heavens no. I've always had dogs,' he said. 'Since I was a kid. Can't imagine life without them. When I was growing up, we spent the summer with my grandparents on their farm. That's where I chose my first pup, from a litter by one of the sheepdogs. She was called Dancer. Wonderful dog. She was a bit too clever for me, I think, looking back. Lately, I've had three rescue greyhounds. They make great pets. Really calm in temperament. Don't need much walking. I can take Sapphire into the shop without worrying that she'll get into trouble. And Jezza?'

'He's my first. Well, he's my granddaughter's dog officially, but I feel like he belongs to all of us. Dani

– that's my daughter – wasn't at all sure that we should keep him. Flossie, my granddaughter, well her old boyfriend bought her Jezza without asking whether it was OK. But I'm so glad Dani decided we should keep him. He's such good company. He makes us laugh all the time.'

'And like I said, it's good to know that when you get into the house, someone will be there who's pleased to see you, isn't it?' said Bill.

'Oh yes.'

'That's been a life-changer for me. I don't do well being on my own.'

'You mean since you lost your wife?' Jane asked.

Bill nodded.

'I know how you feel.'

'Though for a long time, I wasn't exactly great company if I did have people around. I hope that might be changing at last, though. I certainly feel like I want to be part of the world again. How about you?'

'Snack, anybody?' Mrs Coco pulled a paper bag out of her handbag and waggled it between Jane and Bill.

Jane was grateful for the distraction from her conversation, until she saw that Mrs Coco was offering her kibble.

'Oh, for Jezza?' Jane asked.

'If he's allowed.'

Jane took one for her dog. As did Bill. They were both astonished when Mrs Coco popped one into her own mouth.

'It's really very tasty,' she said, not looking in the least bit embarrassed. 'I got into it while Coco was on one of her diets. The thing is, she won't eat anything unless she's seen me eat it first. That was part of the problem. She was getting too much rich human food. So it was me who had to make the change.'

'To dog food?'

'Lots of the premium brands are probably better for you than anything you could buy in the ready meal cabinet at the supermarket,' Evan chipped in.

'Exactly,' said Mrs Coco.

'Well done, Mrs Coco. I'm really pleased to see you're both sticking to the Waggy Weight Loss regime. Healthy owner, healthy dog. And vice versa too.'

'It's true. I've lost six pounds since I substituted kibble for Pringles,' Mrs Coco confirmed. 'You just can't eat so much of it, you know.'

No kidding, Jane thought.

Jane could easily see how owning a dog could make people fitter but she hoped she would always draw the line at kibble. These dog people were bonkers, though they were certainly a friendly lot.

Other owners passed human snacks along the chain of walkers. Because so many people knew Evan from his surgery and volunteer work at the shelter and Bill from the pet shop, Jane found herself being introduced to what seemed like hundreds of people. Every one of them stopped to admire Jezza and compliment Jane on his manners. She felt extremely proud. Even if Nurse Van Niekerk was forever tutting in despair when Jezza jumped up to greet new pals.

'Keep him down, Grandma Jezza!' she shouted. 'More authority in your commands, please.'

When Jane looked down into Jezza's eyes, she was sure she saw him wink.

It was quite the loveliest way to spend a Sunday

afternoon. Even though she lived with her daughter and granddaughter, Jane often found herself at a loose end on a Sunday. Dani was sometimes at work over the weekend and now that Flossie was a teenager, she had her own things to do. Since Sarah had put herself on Tinder, she was out more often than in. Walking with Newbay's dog community was so much nicer than sitting at home reading the *Mail On Sunday*.

And it was fascinating to see that the old adage about dogs being like their owners held true. Mrs Coco and her French bulldog were like peas in a pod. The owner of the two Irish wolfhounds Jane had seen in the car park was similarly long of limb and hairy. Though Bill didn't immediately seem to have much in common with his greyhound looks-wise – he was solidly built, reassuringly so – temperamentally they shared a laid-back attitude to life. They were a calming sort of presence. After a while, even Jezza stopped springing about like a newborn lamb and fell into step alongside Sapphire.

'Are you glad you came along?' Bill asked.

Jane confirmed that she was.

Almost two hours after the walkers set off from The Majestic, they reached their destination. The Driftwood. A pub that overlooked the water. It had a huge garden, perfect for canine visitors, and the landlords were ready for them. While the human beings queued for their pints, another team of volunteers distributed water and treats for the dogs. Sausages and burgers were being cooked on a very smoky barbecue. The smell was sending all the dogs a little bit bonkers. Coco strained to get out of her pram.

'No, you certainly can't have a burger,' Mrs Coco told her dog. 'What would Nurse Van Niekerk say?'

'You're staying for lunch, aren't you?' Liz asked Jane. 'You must.'

'You sit here,' said Bill. 'And I'll go and fetch something for you. What would you like, Jane? A burger? A hot dog?'

'A hot dog seems appropriate,' said Jane. She glanced down at Jezza, who quickly found himself a spot in the shade beneath the table. Sapphire settled down beside him, though she was still pretending he wasn't there.

Lunch was a long one. And Jane was in no hurry to leave. She enjoyed sitting among her new friends, listening as they swapped stories of the funny things their dogs had done. Bill talked about a collie cross he'd once had.

'Absolutely hated cats. Chased a Persian up a tree and actually managed to catch it by the tail. Came in with a great clump of fur in his mouth. The cat's tail was completely bald. Well, you can imagine how that went down with his owner . . .'

'The cat was in your dog's garden,' said Mrs Coco, searching for mitigating circumstances. 'When Coco was younger, she almost caught a squirrel. Chased it into the house. It ran straight up my back and into my hair. You can't imagine the mess.'

'Oh, I can.' Jane shivered at the thought.

Nurse Van Niekerk reminisced about her own dogs. Most recently, she'd had a lurcher called Berkeley. Her eyes glistened with tears as she talked about Berkeley's loyalty.

'He was always there for me. It was like he could read my mind.'

'No mean feat,' Liz whispered to Jane.

'I don't know what I would have done without Ted,' Liz told the crowd at the picnic table. 'When I was going through my divorce, sometimes his was the only friendly face I saw all day. He's so much more than a pet.'

'When Berkeley died my heart was broken,' said Nurse Van Niekerk.

'Dogs teach us the real meaning of love,' Evan said. All the assembled dog owners agreed loudly.

'They also teach us that the heart can expand exponentially. Every time I've have to say goodbye to a dog, I've told myself that I will never put myself through it again. The cost of that love is just too high. But then you meet the next one and realise that it's worth it. It's worth the goodbye. And you bring that new puppy home and love with all your heart again. You never forget the ones who went before, of course, but you realise that love isn't finite and the more you give, the more you have to give. The heart is a muscle after all.'

'Oh you're so right, Dr Thomas,' said Mrs Coco.

'Spot on,' said Nurse Van Niekerk, sneakily wiping away a tear.

'I think I know what you mean,' said Bill.

'Good,' said Evan. 'Because my wife sometimes says I talk a load of old whatsit.'

'Not about dogs,' Liz interrupted him. 'Never about dogs, you don't. Or about love.' She pressed a kiss to his cheek and Evan blushed.

Jane blushed too, when she looked up to see that Bill was looking right at her.

'It's time I was getting home,' Jane said shortly after that. 'My granddaughter will be back soon and she'll be wondering who's going to make her tea.'

'Tell her to make her own tea,' said Liz, whose daughter was Flossie's age.

'Oh, Liz,' said Jane. 'I can't do that. I've got to go.'

'I'll see you again soon, I hope,' said Bill.

'As soon as this one needs another toy,' said Jane, nodding at Jezza.

Jane persuaded Jezza to stop pestering Sapphire and got up from the table. As she said a final goodbye and started to leave, she felt shy in a way she hadn't felt for ages. Perhaps it was because she knew Bill was watching her go and with a flash of vanity, she hoped that her back view was as good as the front. It was while she was thinking about this that Jezza – who was not walking to heel now that Nurse Van Niekerk wasn't looking – spotted something that interested him on the right of the path. Unfortunately, he was on Jane's left at the time. He cut across right in front of her, causing her to trip on his lead.

Jane went down with a thump.

Chapter Fifty

It was a nasty fall. Jane already knew that. But she didn't know just *how* nasty until she attempted to stand up again. Still hanging on to Jezza's lead – the puppy merely seemed amused that she was down at his level – Jane tried to pull herself back onto her feet by holding on to the low wall that bordered the pub's garden. But the pain was too excruciating. As soon as she tried to put any weight on it, her left ankle gave way.

'I think I need some help!' she managed, in a voice that came out far more faintly than she hoped. The pain was that intense.

When they realised what was going on, Evan, Liz, Nurse Van Niekerk, Mrs Coco and Bill were all with her in seconds. Evan and Nurse Van Niekerk lifted Jane so that she was sitting on a bench. Liz went into the pub to fetch a glass of water. Mrs Coco bustled after her in search of ice. Meanwhile Bill watched with concern as Evan set about examining the ankle Jane had twisted.

Evan gently moved her foot.

'Does this hurt?' he asked.

'Yes,' Jane squeaked.

'And this?'

'Yes!'

'Oh dear.' Evan sat back on his heels. 'Nurse Van Niekerk, what do you think?'

'It doesn't look good,' she agreed. 'If Grandma Jezza were a dog I'd suggest an anti-inflammatory shot and a splint but obviously . . .'

'She's not a dog,' Liz filled in the gaps.

'I think you need to go to the accident unit,' Evan said at last.

Mrs Coco had fetched a bag of ice from inside the pub. Liz held it to Jane's ankle in an attempt to ward off too much swelling.

'Don't worry. We'll get you to the hospital,' said Liz. 'Evan. Call a cab.'

Evan and Nurse Van Niekerk carried Jane between them to a taxi. Bill tried to take the nurse's place but a single look from her told him not to be so sexist. She was more than capable of taking half Jane's weight.

'I've lifted cows,' she said.

'Now this is what I call being swept off my feet,' Jane tried to joke, though the pain was making it very hard to smile.

'I'll come with you to the accident unit,' said Bill.

'Good idea. Liz and I will take the dogs back to our house,' said Evan.

'It's OK,' said Jane to both men. 'I mean it would be great if you could take Jezza home but I'll be fine on my own at the hospital.'

'No,' said Bill. 'I know what these places are like. If you're too quiet and polite – as I imagine you might well be – they can forget all about you. I'll make sure you get seen and get home again afterwards.'

'I can call my daughter.'

'She's at work. There's no need,' Bill insisted.

'Bill's right,' said Liz. 'Just let him help you. We'll take Sapphire and Jezza.'

Bill got into the back seat beside her. Nurse Van Niekerk scooped Jezza up and made him 'wave bye bye to Grandma'.

The Newbay Hospital accident unit was busy, as it always was, particularly during high season. Jane joined a long queue of people waiting to be seen for foot and ankle injuries, which were especially common in the summer when people swapped their sensible trainers for flimsy flip-flops or went barefoot over broken glass on the beach.

It was three hours before Jane was seen, by which time her ankle looked well and truly damaged. The ice Liz had packed around the twisted joint had not managed to stop the bruising. When she dared to take a peep, Jane thought it looked as though she had got her foot trapped in some kind of snare.

Though she had told Bill she didn't need him to be there, she had to admit that it was nice to have someone to talk to. And someone to fetch cups of tea from the vending machine. Even if after just one cup, tasting more like plastic than tea, Bill announced that they were not going to drink any more. The next time Jane wanted something, he went out of the hospital to a nearby café, returning with some proper tea in an actual china mug – 'I said it was an emergency' – and a plate of sandwiches, which Jane shared with the scared small boy who was sitting beside her and his grateful parents. He'd fallen off a playground swing and was waiting to have his arm put in plaster.

'Will you need plaster too?' he asked Jane.

'I'm not sure,' she said.

As it turned out, she wouldn't need a plaster cast.

'It's not broken,' said the young doctor, when Jane was finally seen. 'But you're going to need to keep your weight off it for a while. Now, how are you going to get home?'

'I'm taking her,' said Bill.

But Dani arrived at the hospital just as Jane was being discharged.

'Mum, I left as soon as I got your text. What happened?'

'I fell over Jezza.'

'He was pulling on his lead,' explained Bill. 'He saw something off to the side and . . .' Bill mimed Jezza shooting across in front. 'Oh. We haven't met. I'm Bill Hunter. I own the pet shop by the station.'

'I know it,' said Dani. 'I used to love going in there when I was a girl.'

'Well, you should come in and see us again. I'm sure things have changed since you were last there.'

'Bill was doing the sponsored walk,' said Jane. 'With Evan and Liz. They've got all the dogs. Bill insisted on coming here with me.'

'Why didn't you let me know what was going on sooner?'

'I didn't want to disturb you,' said Jane.

'Mum, you should always call me in an emergency.'

'I was being well looked after.' Jane looked at Bill.

'Thank you,' Dani said to him. 'I'm very grateful.'

'It was my pleasure. I wouldn't have wanted to be anywhere else.'

Dani could tell that he meant it. So could Jane.

* * *

The following morning, just as Dani was leaving the house to go to work, a girl from the local florist's shop arrived with an enormous bouquet.

'Ms Parker?' the girl asked.

'That's me,' said Dani, eagerly accepting the blooms. She felt as if she was certainly owed some after the last few crappy weeks. Perhaps Will had woken up to how disappointed Dani might have been by the way he focussed so much attention on Lola. If that was the case, then Dani might consider another date with him. She still hadn't responded to his last text. But when Dani got the flowers into the kitchen and opened the little card that accompanied them, she discovered that they were not for her after all.

'They're very pretty,' said Jane, as she hobbled into the kitchen.

'They are. And they're for you! Mum, you've got an admirer.'

Jane read the card, which revealed that the flowers were from Bill.

'Bill from the pet shop. He must really like you.'

'Nonsense,' Jane said. 'They're just a nice gesture to wish me a swift recovery.'

'Mum. He could have sent you a text. Bill is obviously infatuated with you. I could tell that the minute I met him. He's such a nice man. And the way he looked into your eyes . . .'

'Well, I mustn't encourage him,' said Jane, tucking the note back into its envelope with brusque efficiency. 'When I said he could take me to the hospital, I certainly didn't intend for him to get the wrong idea.'

'Oh Mum,' said Dani. 'You're allowed to admit you like him.'

Jane bristled. 'Of course I like him but I don't want to like any man like *that*.'

It was an odd reaction, thought Dani.

Jane hobbled to the sink and tried to juggle her crutches while filling a vase with water.

'I'll do that,' Dani took over.

'Just put them in the vase as they are, please,' said Jane.

Dani did as Jane asked. She placed the vase in the middle of the kitchen table and Jane affected not to be that impressed. But with her daughter gone and only Jezza left in the house to see what she was up to, Jane pulled out one of the kitchen table chairs and sat down. From there, she was able to subtly rearrange the flowers in the vase, trimming some of the longer stems and taking off the leaves that would only go soggy in the water.

They really were beautiful flowers. Expensive, Jane had no doubt. But also, if Bill had actually specified anything more than the budget, very well chosen. The roses were the orange of a perfect seaside sunset. They were studded with bright pink gerberas, like flowers drawn by a child. She'd always loved gerberas. They seemed so very optimistic.

It was a long time since Jane had received flowers from anyone other than her daughter or granddaughter.

She read the card again and thought about Bill's friendly smile.

Of course, she had to say 'thank you' but the question was 'how'?

Then she thought about the careful way Bill had wrapped his arm around her waist for support as he led her to and from the car. She thought about his kind eyes. His genuine concern. His easy affection.

She had his number. She should call and thank him right away. She was about to . . .

But some things only happen once in a lifetime. Jane was a firm believer that her 'once in a lifetime' happened when she met the man who would become her husband. Tom.

That he had died so young was just bad luck and she had to live with it.

Sure, Jane had friends who had found love again but she could never quite understand how they could do it. How they could even think about being with someone else? The love she'd had for her husband was so great that it kept her warm even now he was gone.

And yet. That wasn't to say that she didn't get lonely. Of course she did. Even though she lived with Dani and Flossie. It was a godsend for Jane that around the time Tom died, Dani had needed Jane as much as vice versa. Dani always made sure to let Jane know how much she appreciated everything she'd done for her since Flossie was born, but the truth was that being able to be such a big part of Dani and Flossie's life had almost certainly saved Jane from deep depression.

Now things were changing. Flossie was sixteen. She didn't need Jane in the way she had done even as a thirteen- or fourteen-year-old. She was hardly ever at home. And maybe Jane was cramping Dani's style now. It wasn't too late for Dani to find someone great and perhaps even add to her family. It would be hard for her to get a man to accept that she came with her mum as a permanent plus one.

Jane was not yet quite seventy. Sarah was always

reminding her that in the twenty-first century, seventy was 'young old'. They weren't ageing in the same way their parents had. Jane had friends who were still active and living independently well into their eighties. Who were still living their lives as though they were worth living well. If not with new spouses, then at least with new companions.

No. Jane pushed the thought from her mind. She couldn't get involved.

She got out her best stationery and wrote Bill a little note, thanking him for his generosity. Best wishes. No kisses. She would ask Flossie to drop it into the pet shop next time she was out with the dog.

Opening Jane's note two days later, Bill couldn't help but be disappointed. He'd hoped for a phone call at least. He'd been gearing up all week to ask her if he could take her to the opera. He'd thought perhaps she liked him. Obviously he was wrong.

Chapter Fifty-One

Soon it was the middle of August. Newbay's beautiful beaches played host to holidaymakers from all over the country, keen to make the most of an unexpectedly beautiful summer. The temperatures hovered in the high twenties all month. It was picnic weather every day. It was all distinctly un-British.

Jane's ankle continued to heal. She was soon pretty nifty on her crutches. Flossie spent her days on the beach with Xanthe and Camilla, working on their tans and dreading the results of their GCSEs.

Dani was busier than ever at The Majestic as wedding season reached its peak. She still found time to take Jezza to boot camp, though Nat hadn't been for a while. Not since he and Lola came to plan their wedding reception at the hotel. He was probably busy with that. Weddings take over. Dani saw it happen all the time. On the one hand she was disappointed but on the other, at least she didn't have to hear about the wedding prep. Meanwhile, she'd heard nothing more from Will, after finally sending him a text suggesting that perhaps his heart wasn't quite as free as he pretended. He didn't protest.

Another Friday evening came round. Over breakfast, Flossie announced that she was going to stay over at Xanthe's.

'I thought Xanthe and her family were going on holiday,' Dani said.

'That's next week,' Flossie told her. 'Over the bank holiday.'

'Oh. Give Xanthe's mum my love, won't you?'

'I always do.'

'All right. Be good. I'll see you tomorrow.'

Flossie picked up her rucksack and hung it over one shoulder – as usual, defeating the back-saving objective of having a rucksack in the first place. She stood in the kitchen doorway. Dani had gone back to the recipe she was reading but gradually she became aware that her daughter hadn't moved.

'You OK?' she asked. 'Forgotten something?'

'No,' said Flossie. 'It's just . . . Mum . . .'

Flossie suddenly dropped her rucksack on the floor. She rushed up to Dani and threw her arms around her.

'What's this for?' Dani asked. Spontaneous displays of affection were increasingly rare now that Flossie was almost an adult.

'I just want you to know how much I love you,' said Flossie. 'And that you're the best mum in the world and I'm sorry for all the ways I've disappointed you over the years. Especially lately.'

'Disappointed me? What are you on about, my silly little thing? You've never disappointed me.'

'Not even when I got arrested?'

'No, because you soon learned your lesson. Flossie, you're great. I'm very proud you're my girl.'

Dani touched the end of Flossie's nose with the tip of her finger, like she used to do when Flossie was small. Flossie sniffed, as though she was trying to stop a tear from rolling down her cheek.

'Are you sure you're OK?' Dani asked, looking deep into her daughter's eyes. She didn't look quite OK. 'What's brought all this on?'

'Oh, I'm fine,' said Flossie. 'I'm just feeling a bit sentimental, that's all. And I'm allowed to tell my mum I love her, aren't I?'

'You can tell her as often as you like,' said Dani. 'And I love you too. And so does Jezza.'

Who was even now trying to insinuate himself into the hug.

'Group hug, Jezza,' said Dani, as Jezza got onto his hind legs and buried himself between the two women. When there was affection on offer, Jezza always liked to be involved.

'Be good, Jezza,' Flossie told him, as she extricated herself from the embrace. 'Don't give Mum any trouble. Do everything she asks you to do. No playing up. I'll see you soon.'

'See you tomorrow,' said Dani.

'Yeah,' said Flossie, absently. She looked at her phone. 'I better go, Mum. Xanthe's wondering where I am.'

'Well,' said Dani to Jezza, as Flossie left the room. 'That spontaneous PDA was strange. But rather wonderful.' Jezza wagged his tail in agreement.

Dani went back to reading the recipe book with a warm glow around her heart. There were moments in her life as a parent that made it all worth it. This was one of them. All the crying, arguing, the sleepless nights were as nothing when weighed against this. Her daughter had just told her that she loved her. Dani must have done something right.

While Dani was reading, Jane limped into the kitchen. The doctor had told her just that afternoon that she'd be on crutches for another two weeks.

'Flossie's gone to Xanthe's,' Dani said.

'I know. She just came into my room to say goodbye,' said Jane. 'Gave me a lovely big hug.'

'That's nice,' said Dani.

'Isn't it? It's good that she has such a nice friend like Xanthe. I mean, I know she looks a bit dodgy with all those strange piercings, but it's clear the girls can't do enough for one another. I'm so glad Flossie's got good pals like her and Camilla.'

'Yes,' said Dani. 'Me too. They seem to be keeping her mind off terrible Jed, at least.'

'Yes. I wonder what's become of him?' Jane asked.

'I really don't care, so long as he's not getting our little girl into trouble any more.'

'Hear hear. What are you doing this weekend?' Jane asked. 'You're not working, are you?'

'No. I've got the whole weekend off and nothing to do but doggy boot camp.'

Which wasn't half so much fun as it once had been, Dani thought. When Nat was there too.

Chapter Fifty-Two

Dani was disappointed that she had nothing to do on Friday night except watch TV with her mother, but at the same time, she was grateful that when she woke up on Saturday morning, she was not nursing a hangover. It did not do to be hung over at Best Behaviour Boot Camp.

She was minding her own business, going through the 'drop' command with Jezza – who would happily drop anything in return for a big enough piece of sausage – when Nat arrived with Princess. He was unexpected, late and very flustered. He apologised profusely to Nurse Van Niekerk, who sent him and Princess off on a circuit of the field to get rid of some of the puppy's excess energy. By now, so many weeks into the course, the run was not as daunting as it had been at first. The boot camp was working its magic on the humans as well as the dogs.

Still, Nat was flushed when he took his place next to Dani again. He ran his hand through his hair in a gesture she remembered from years before. Nervous? Anxious?

'I didn't think you were coming to boot camp any more,' she said.

'Yes, well . . .' Nat began but Nurse Van Niekerk caught up with them. There would be no talking except to issue puppy commands until the end of the class. But Nat's obvious distraction was distracting to Dani in turn. She wondered what might be on his mind.

Nurse Van Niekerk blew the final whistle.

'Good work today, puppy parents,' she said. 'It's great to see how well your dogs are coming along. They're going to make wonderful canine citizens.'

'Praise indeed,' said Dani as Nurse Van Niekerk jogged on to the surgery where her Waggy Weight Loss group was gathering, leaving the boot campers to tidy up their kit. 'Do you want a coffee?'

'Yes. Definitely. Let's go to Daffodil's,' suggested Nat.

'You seem a bit, er, stressed. Too much wedmin?'

'I don't really seem to be needed,' Nat said.

'Just have to turn up on the day?'

'Something like that.'

As they walked, Dani could feel her phone vibrating in her pocket.

She pulled it out just far enough to see who was calling. It was Flossie. She probably wanted to ask if she could stay at Xanthe's for another night. Dani didn't answer the call because she sensed that Nat might be about to say something important. He was definitely building up to something, she thought. Flossie would text if she didn't pick up and then, if it was with a question or request that required some thought – or the making-up of a good reason why Flossie couldn't have another sleepover with her friends – Dani didn't have to answer at once.

Nat suddenly stopped on the pavement. He closed his eyes tightly and pinched the bridge of his nose. Then at last he began to talk.

'The thing is, Dani, ever since that afternoon in the hotel restaurant, I can't stop thinking about . . .'

Then Flossie *did* text.

Dani glanced at the screen automatically.

'Mum will you flippin' answer the phone. This is serious. I'm in trouble!!!!'

Trouble?

'Nat, I'm sorry. I've got to ring my daughter,' Dani said.

Dani phoned Flossie back at once. Flossie picked up on one ring.

'Where are you?' Dani asked. 'What's going on?'

Nat watched, his face growing concerned, while Dani fired questions at her daughter.

'I'm OK, Mum. At least, I haven't had an accident or anything but . . . Oh Mum! Something terrible's happened.'

Flossie burst into loud, anguished sobs.

'Flossie,' Dani tried to cut through the crying. 'What is it? Where are you?'

In between sobs Flossie managed to choke out. 'Jed's broken up with me.'

'What? But I thought you broke up after the arrest?'

'Not exactly. Not really. And now I'm stuck in Gretna Green.'

Dani covered her mouth. She felt nauseous. Those two words had more power to move her than Flossie could possibly know. When at last she could speak again she said, 'Are you serious? But what are you doing there, love?'

What did Dani think she was doing there? Flossie asked.

'Were you and Jed going to get married?'

Flossie choked out a 'yes'. 'Yes, Mum, we were.'

But evidently – thankfully – Jed had changed his mind. They'd had a huge row outside the wedding chapel where their ceremony was supposed to take place and Jed had walked off with their shared rucksack.

'And he's got my purse and passport and my wash-bag and my charger. The only thing I've got with me is my phone and I'm running out of . . .'

The line went dead.

'Flossie!'

Dani tried calling back but was put straight through to Flossie's voicemail. Dani listened in agony to the oh-so-familiar message.

'Hi, this is Flossie! Leave me a message!'

'Flossie? Flossie? It's Mum. Listen, darling, please don't worry. Stay calm and stay exactly where you are. We're going to sort this out. Everything will be fine. I'm on my way.'

Though how she would be on her way she had yet to work out.

Dani stood in the middle of the pavement, with her phone in her hand, just staring at the screen.

'What's going on?' Nat asked.

'She's only in bloody Gretna.'

'What's she doing there?' Nat asked.

Dani covered her eyes at the thought.

'Stupid question,' said Nat. 'Is she OK?'

'I don't know. She sounded terrible and now her phone's out of battery. I don't know what to do.'

'Is she on her own?'

'Since Jed's walked off, she is.'

'Has she got money for a train?'

'Jed's got her purse and her bloody charger. I swear I'm going to kill him. How on earth did she end up falling for such an idiot? If only her phone was working, I could get her to go somewhere safe like a B and B and call them with my credit card details so they could look after her but god knows where she is.'

'Should you phone the police?'

'Good idea.'

But the local police station didn't want to get involved. The subtext was that they got a lot of sixteen-year-olds up in Scotland without their parents' knowledge. And once someone gets to sixteen, they're no longer considered vulnerable. Not vulnerable enough for a search in any case.

'Of course she's vulnerable!' Dani insisted. But she got no joy from the woman at the end of the line, who said she would take Flossie's name and ask her team to look out for her in passing but could promise nothing more.

'You just spoke to her,' the woman said. 'You know she's OK really.'

'We should go there,' said Nat, when Dani threw her phone onto the grass in despair. 'That's the only solution I can come up with.'

'To Scotland? How? A train will take all day.'

'I'll drive you,' said Nat.

'But . . .'

'I've got time.'

'It's the weekend. I can't take you away from Lola.'

'Lola's on her hen do. I dropped her off at the airport first thing this morning. She's in Majorca with her friends. I was going to spend the weekend reading back issues of the *Economist*.'

'You still can, Nat. This doesn't have to involve you.'

'Dani, you don't have a car, right?'

That was true.

'Heaven knows how long it would take to get there by public transport. Not to mention how expensive it would be at short notice. I can drive you to Gretna Green. You'll get there faster and you'll have company. It's a no-brainer.'

'You'd really do that for me? Drive me to Gretna Green? After . . .' she didn't finish the sentence.

Nat nodded. 'Isn't that what friends are for?'

They walked quickly back to the house Nat shared with Lola so that he could pick up his car. The dogs were going to have to come with them. Jane wasn't at home to look after Jezza – she and Sarah had gone to Exeter for the day, despite Jane's crutches – and likewise Nat had no one with whom he could leave Princess. They'd tried Will but he wasn't picking up his phone.

'Sounds like a foreign dial tone,' said Dani. 'He must have gone away.'

So they put the dogs into the back of the car with everything they'd need for the journey. Kibble. Water. Bowls. Blankets. Toys.

'Jezza's never been in a car,' said Dani, when she saw that the upholstery in Nat's beautiful BMW was a deeply impractical light grey. 'What if he gets travel sick? Your car is so new and clean.'

'It's just a car,' said Nat matter-of-factly. 'It can be cleaned. Some things are much more important than that new car smell. Like your daughter. Come on, we need to get on the road.'

'But what if Flossie starts to head south without telling us?'

Nat had an answer for that too. 'She's not going to beat us back here, is she? As soon as we hear from her, we can adjust our plan accordingly. We can meet her halfway. Or we can turn back and see her when she gets home. Let's just get started. If she's in Scotland, the closer we are when we hear from her the better.'

Dani agreed. She buckled herself into the passenger seat, which was as deep and luxurious as an expensive armchair. If she hadn't been so stressed she'd have been impressed. She might even have looked forward to eight hours cocooned in such aerodynamic splendour.

'Nat, I'm so sorry about this,' she said.

'Dani, stop apologising. I'm just glad I can help.'

As Nat navigated Newbay's one-way system, Dani sent Flossie a text outlining the plan. The best-case scenario was that before Nat and Dani could get very far Jed – stupid bloody selfish Jed – would reappear with the rucksack so that Flossie had her cash card and her phone charger again. At least then Dani would know her daughter was OK and had the funds to get a train perhaps as far as the Midlands. They could meet her there. On the other hand, Dani sort-of hoped that Jed really had done a runner and would keep on running. The last thing she wanted was to rock up in Gretna and discover she had a new son-in-law. Though that, thank goodness, was unlikely. A quick Google search showed that you needed to send in paperwork at least twenty-nine days ahead of any ceremony. Would Jed and Flossie have been that organised?

Dani suddenly remembered how Flossie had asked

for her passport and birth certificate out of the blue that afternoon. Dani thought it was odd that the sixth form college needed them again. Why hadn't she asked more questions? And when was it Flossie had asked for her ID? Six weeks ago, Dani calculated.

'Oh please no!' Dani explained the timeline to Nat.

'Don't panic. Jed's walked off, remember? She doesn't have a groom.'

'I can't believe she was actually going to marry him,' she wailed.

'Young love,' said Nat, with a half-smile.

'Total idiocy,' said Dani.

'Stupid things make perfect sense when you're sixteen.'

Chapter Fifty-Three

Nat drove as swiftly as he could but there was terrible traffic on the A-road towards the M5 and progress was difficult. It was the very height of the summer season and thousands of people were on the move to and from their holidays in Devon and Cornwall. Dani hated every single one of them.

'Who are all these people?' she asked. 'And why can't they just stay home?'

Two hours had passed since Flossie's anguished phone call and Nat and Dani were still only fifty miles from their starting point, trundling along so slowly they might have been in a funeral procession. Meanwhile, Dani checked her phone roughly every thirty seconds, hoping that Flossie would have somehow found someone to lend her a charger. Surely people in Gretna Green had phones like hers?

'She's going to be OK,' Nat insisted from time to time. 'She's an intelligent girl.'

'You haven't met her,' said Dani.

'But she's your daughter.'

'You're very kind. She may be clever but she hasn't got the common sense she was born with. Hence Jed.'

'She might surprise you,' said Nat. 'Once she's calmed down a bit, she'll come up with a plan. I'm sure she knows you'll be on your way. I bet she's already found herself a place where she can sit tight and wait in comfort.'

Dani wasn't convinced.

'Do you think it's cold up there?' Dani asked. She checked the weather app on her phone. 'I bet she hasn't got a proper coat. She never dresses appropriately for the weather.'

'It may be Scotland but it is the middle of summer,' Nat pointed out. 'She won't freeze to death. Or starve.'

'She hasn't got any money on her. How can she get any food?'

'We'll be there in . . .' Nat checked the sat nav. 'Seven hours max. She won't fade away before we get there even if she doesn't get to have lunch. Besides, I bet someone has already seen how upset she is and taken her under their wing. Most people are good, Dani. You know that. We'll probably arrive to find she's spent the day watching telly in a kindly Scot's front room, while being plied with lots of lovely food. Talking of which . . .'

Nat's stomach gurgled.

'I'd rather we kept going,' said Dani, answering the unasked question. 'Your kindly Scot might turn out to be some kind of human trafficker, planning to send Flossie to Russia.'

'Trafficking generally happens the other way round,' said Nat.

All the way up the M5, Nat tried to move the conversation onto a happier track but Dani wasn't to be distracted. She could hardly breathe with worry for her little girl – for Flossie would *always* be her little girl – on her own all the way up there in Scotland, with no money, and a dead phone. Jed hadn't even left her with a toothbrush.

'How could he do this to her!' Dani exclaimed.

'You really didn't have any inkling they were planning to run away together?' Nat asked.

'None at all. After the arrest . . .'

'The arrest?'

Dani had neglected to tell Nat about that.

'Yes. Jed got them both arrested. They were only selling cupcakes on the beach but he insulted a policeman who tried to move them on . . .'

'Never a clever move.'

'Exactly. And the whole thing ended with them both being taken to the station. After which, I grounded Flossie for a week and told her she couldn't see Jed any more at all. Not if she wanted to be let out of the house again. She promised me – promised me to my face, Nat – that she wouldn't go anywhere near him. She said she understood he wasn't right for her. I believed her. She hadn't mentioned him in the best part of a month.'

'So where did she pretend to be last night?'

'She told me she was going to stay over at her friend Xanthe's. She goes there almost every Friday night. They have a takeaway and watch a DVD and then on Saturday morning, they work on their school course-work together.' Dani paused. 'Oh god. She's never been at Xanthe's house, has she? Every time she's told me she's stayed over at Xanthe's, she's been with that awful waster underneath the pier.'

'He lives there?'

'No, his parents have got a very nice house at the good end of town – his mum's a doctor and his dad's a solicitor – but that's where he hangs out when he's not at the Arts café. And my daughter's been there with him! Drinking and taking drugs and doing god knows what else. I'm going to kill him!'

'Sounds like you won't need to if Flossie gets hold of him first.'

'I never trusted him. He comes across as this big-hearted eco dude but I knew he was a waste of space the first time I met him. He's full of hot air and entitlement. I should have put my foot down right at the start. Oh god, Nat. You don't think they decided to get married because . . .'

Dani suddenly imagined her darling Flossie cradling a baby bump.

'It's not the only reason people decide to get married,' Nat reminded her, without needing to hear the rest of the sentence.

'But . . .' Dani was about to say something else but her phone rang. She leapt on it. It wasn't Flossie. It was Jane.

'I'm sorry, Mum. I'm going to have to cut you short. Nat and I are on our way to Gretna Green.'

'What? But he's getting married to that Lola girl!' Even Nat could hear Jane's exclamation.

'I'm not going to Gretna *with* Nat. At least, not like that.'

Nat's mouth twitched at the corners.

'Mum, Flossie wasn't at Xanthe's last night. She ran away to Scotland with Jed. And yes, I know she wasn't supposed to be with him any more. Clearly, she's been seeing him behind our backs.'

Jane asked if she needed to worry.

'There's no need to worry,' Dani said, in her own most worried voice. There was no point getting Jane all worked up too. 'But perhaps if you could get back home as soon as you can and check the answering machine. And of course, if she calls you on your mobile, please let her know we're on our way and then call me right back.'

Jane said she would go straight home to make sure she was on hand should Flossie somehow turn up there.

'But you're out with Sarah?'

'This is a great excuse to leave. She's tracked down another date on Tinder. Now, darling, are you sure you're OK? You sound anxious.'

Jane repeated many of the arguments Nat had as to why Flossie would be OK and Dani listened to her mother's soothing words but didn't feel soothed in the least.

Once Jane had hung up, Dani tried Flossie again. She went straight through to voicemail.

'Flossie, sweetheart. It's Mum. We're getting close to Manchester. We'll be in Scotland before you know it. Just hang on, my love. Hang on.'

'I really am going to have to stop at the next service station,' Nat said.

'I don't need to,' said Dani.

'No,' said Nat. 'But we need to get some petrol. And the dogs might want to pee.'

Dani turned to look at the two puppies on the back seat. The darkening patch in the middle of the blanket they'd been sitting on suggested it was already too late for a comfort stop as far as the dogs were concerned.

'Nat,' said Dani again. 'I am really, really sorry.'

While Dani aired out the wet blanket, Nat bought a couple of sandwiches in the service station and two bottles of water. Dani took the one he'd bought for her – a Cheddar ploughman's, which was the most edible-looking of the choices on offer – but she couldn't eat it.

'How can I eat when anything might be happening to Flossie?'

'Fair enough.'

Nat had given up trying to persuade Dani that it really would work out fine. He concentrated instead on getting them to Gretna as fast as he could so that she would *know* for sure everything actually *was* fine.

From time to time, Dani ranted about Jed. She couldn't understand how her daughter had been so stupid. How had they even got up to Scotland? When did they set off?

It all made sense now. Flossie asking for her passport and birth certificate. She didn't need them for college. She needed them to get married. She'd given them back after supposedly getting them scanned but of course she knew the code to the safe.

And all that business before she left the house on Friday night. All that hugging. Flossie told Jane and Dani and Jezza that she loved them because she wasn't sure when she would see them again! Dani felt slightly sick as she remembered how she'd spent the previous evening, scrolling through the *Daily Mail*'s sidebar of shame with one eye on the telly, having no inkling that her sixteen-year-old daughter was running away.

Had Flossie told her friends what she was planning? Dani found it hard to believe that Xanthe and Camilla didn't know what was going on. Why didn't they sound the alarm? They were so irresponsible. Underage tattoos were one thing. But a marriage!

All the same, Dani couldn't help but chastise herself

for not having guessed. The long goodbye was such a giveaway in retrospect. The way Flossie had paused at the door and looked back. There was so much quiet drama in the way she'd left that night. Dani should have known that something was going on.

'Why would you have known?' Nat asked her. 'Teenagers are very good at keeping secrets, as I recall.'

'I should at least have checked with Xanthe's mother every time she said she was going over there.'

'Would your mum have done that to you? You have to show kids you trust them at some point. You can't watch them twenty four seven. You have to let them go and hope for the best.'

Nat paused.

'I'm sorry. I shouldn't be telling you how to parent when I don't have any kids myself.'

'But you'll be a good dad when you do,' Dani said.

'If I do,' said Nat.

Maybe this was all just karma, thought Dani then.

'Put some music on,' said Nat. 'It might make you feel less jumpy.'

'I don't know how to work your music system,' said Dani.

Nat's car was a seriously fancy BMW.

'It's a touch screen. Like an iPhone. You just turn it on and follow the menus until you get what you want.'

Dani turned the system on. It started playing the song that had been on when it was last used.

'*Say you love me . . .*' it began. Dani recognised the song in two beats. She stopped it.

'Maybe we should listen to the radio instead,' she said. 'For the traffic news.'

Nat agreed.

Chapter Fifty-Four

Once they were beyond Carlisle, the road finally seemed clearer. It was hard to believe they were still on the same island. The landscape was so very different from that which they'd left behind in Devon. The hills were higher. The valleys were deeper. The light had an entirely different quality. This was a part of Britain that Dani had always wanted to see. Now, however, she couldn't wait to get through it.

If Nat was tired – and he must be – he wasn't complaining about it. Dani had allowed him a half-hour nap in a service station car park in the middle of the afternoon, followed by two strong coffees. He had been up since six, after all, when he drove Lola to Exeter airport for her flight to the Balearics.

When Dani asked what Lola would think of him driving to Scotland on a mercy mission, Nat said he hadn't yet told Lola what he was doing. She was busy Instagramming photos of her pedicured toes in the Spanish sand. There was no need to worry her.

'I don't think she'd be that bothered anyway,' Nat said.

'Are you having a stag do?' Now that they were almost in Scotland, Dani made an effort to turn the conversation from her worries for a second.

'Not my style,' said Nat.

Nat was never a 'lad', that was true. Even when they

were teenagers. His friends were like him. Quiet, clever, funny. Deep thinkers who didn't need to prove themselves by downing pints and getting rowdy (unless you counted his eighteenth birthday debacle).

'Maybe I'll go for a pint with Dad and my brother-in-law,' he said.

'You'll have to watch they don't tie you to a lamppost at the end of the night,' Dani joked feebly.

While Nat drove, a knight in a silver BMW, and the dogs intermittently snoozed and scrapped on the back seat, Dani continued to check her phone obsessively. Every time her phoned pinged to tell her she had a text, her heart soared, only to sink straight back down when she saw that the text was from her mum, who asked every half hour or so whether Dani had heard anything more from their beloved Floss.

Nothing. It seemed impossible. Nothing at all since that call as they left puppy boot camp. Was there really no one in the whole of Gretna who could provide Flossie with a bit of juice for her phone? Dani began to wonder if Flossie had even tried asking. Was she just too shocked and upset by Jed's sudden departure?

Flossie had never really had a boyfriend before Jed. There were boys in her class that she'd had crushes on but those only ever lasted a week or two. So this was her first proper break-up. Dani understood now that what happened after the arrest was not a break-up at all. No wonder Flossie had been so sanguine about it. How would she be handling the real ending of a relationship that had meant so much to her? Remembering her own first heartbreak could still make Dani draw breath.

Dani squeezed her eyes shut and tried to send her daughter a virtual hug.

'Hang on, Flossie. Hang on.'

At last the road signs announced that they were crossing the border. They were upon Gretna Green, where the anvil priests had been marrying starry-eyed young couples without their parents' approval since the 1770s.

They arrived in Gretna at eight in the evening. Because it was high summer and they'd driven so far north, it was as light there as it would have been an hour earlier in Devon. The place didn't look quite as Dani had expected. Not so cute. The low buildings looked functional rather than quaint for the most part but it still seemed like a friendly town. Not the kind of place where bad things happened.

'Where should we start?' Nat asked.

The little town was busy with tourists and wedding-goers. As they drove through the centre, Dani scanned the crowds for any sign of her precious girl. Her look was, at least, pretty distinctive, with her dirty blonde locks and her big Russian combat boots.

Nat found a place to park, before he and Dani set out in opposite directions, with one dog each, to search the town on foot. Dani had texted Nat a recent picture of Flossie so that he could show it to hoteliers and bar staff on his phone. Dani did the same, her heart fluttering with optimism and then sinking every time someone seemed to recognise her girl then said, 'No. I don't think I have seen her after all.'

It was such a small town. Flossie stood out even in

Newbay, which was far larger. How was it possible that she could have disappeared?

An hour later, after they'd covered every street in a half-mile radius, Nat and Dani met up again in the town's centre, in front of the famous white-walled Old Blacksmith's Shop where weddings were forged on an anvil. Princess and Jezza greeted each other rapturously, as though they had been apart for months. Their owners were less excited. While a gang of delighted Italians posed for wedding photographs beneath a sculpture of interlocking hands, Nat and Dani shared their bad news.

'No luck,' Nat confirmed.

'Where is she?' Dani asked. 'This isn't exactly a huge teeming city. Somebody must have seen her.'

'Perhaps she left right after talking to us,' Nat suggested.

'But she didn't have any money.'

'Maybe she thought she would hitch back.'

Dani pinched the bridge of her nose at the awful thought. It really was the last thing she wanted to hear.

'Hitch back! Anyone might have picked her up! Oh Nat, what am I going to do?'

Dani sank down on a bench and buried her face in her hands for a good old cry, ruining the scene for all the tourists who just wanted to take a pretty picture and Instagram it. But Dani didn't care. Nat sat down next to her and laid his arm around her shoulders. Jezza and Princess both sat at Dani's feet, gazing up into her face. Anyone who didn't think that dogs could read emotion had never seen puppies looking as concerned as Jezza and Princess did.

'I should have taken her feelings for him more seriously. I should have told her she could keep seeing Jed so long as he stayed out of trouble. I should have agreed they could go to a festival. I should have hired a car and driven her there. She never would have felt the need to run away then. I did everything I did because I just wanted to keep her safe and now I don't even know where she is. She could be halfway to Aberdeen in the back of a serial killer's lorry.'

'She's not in a serial killer's lorry,' said Nat.

'How do you know?'

Nat had to admit he didn't really know. 'But there is such a low probability of that having been what's happened, Dani. You know that. That's crazy.'

'I thought there was a really low probability of my daughter running away to get married.'

'Why?' Nat asked.

'Because I didn't think she could be so like . . .'

Dani didn't finish her sentence. The tears she had been fighting to hold back all day finally breached her defences.

'Here. Come here,' said Nat. He held out his arms to her. Dani shuffled closer so that he could wrap her inside them. He held her tightly as she cried out her distress. He leaned his chin on the top of her head and from time to time planted a kiss on her parting as he tried to soothe her.

'It will be OK, Dani. I promise you. We're not going home until we find your daughter. If we have to stay up here for weeks, I promise we will not go back to Devon without her. I'm with you in this. I'm with you every step of the way.'

The words were familiar. An echo. Dani sank against

Nat's chest. She was tired and more scared than she had ever been but something about his arms around her kindled another tiny spark of hope.

'Let's go back to the car,' Nat said. 'We can cover more ground by driving. If we don't find her here in the next hour, we'll try to work out which route she's most likely to have taken out of town. We will find her. I swear.'

But just as Dani was texting Jane with the new plan, her phone chimed.

'Mum where the hell are you?' the text from Flossie asked.

'It's her!'

'Thank god,' said Nat.

Dani called her daughter right away.

'I'm in Gretna. Right in the middle of town.' Dani stood up on a bench and scanned the people around them. 'Are you still here? Where are you? We're in front of the Old Blacksmith's Shop. The white place? Do you see the big hands?'

'Stay where you are!' said Flossie. 'I can see you. That's amazing. You got here. And Jezza! But who's the strange bloke you're both with?'

Chapter Fifty-Five

All thoughts of giving her daughter a piece of her mind vanished as soon as Dani saw Flossie running up the road towards them in her big ungainly boots. Dani felt nothing but relief and pure happiness to see her baby girl again. Recriminations could wait for another day.

'Mum! You got here. You really got here,' Flossie cried.

Dani folded Flossie into her arms and squeezed her until she squeaked. Jezza did his best to join in.

'You silly, silly girl! Of course I'm here. I came as quickly as I could. Are you OK? Let me look at you.'

Dani held Flossie at arm's length for a moment and checked her for obvious signs of mistreatment. Flossie's face was alarmingly pink – a combination of too much crying and having spent the day in the sunshine without any sunblock – and she looked grubby (so what was new) but she didn't look as though she'd come to any permanent ill harm.

'I was a bit scared,' Flossie said. 'But I knew you'd come and find me.'

'I was so worried. I've been feeling sick all day. Why did it take you so long to charge your phone?'

'I asked lots of people to help me, Mum, but most of them waved me away. I think they thought I was begging because of the way I dress. I said I wasn't but one bloke told me "that's what all the beggars say" and he wasn't going to give me the chance to nick his phone.'

Dani clenched her fists at the thought of anyone being so unkind.

'In the end, a Japanese couple helped me. They wanted a picture of me for their Instagram so I made a deal. They had one of those booster pack things.'

'Oh thank goodness for them. And thank goodness we've found you,' said Dani. 'How do you feel?'

'Hungry,' Flossie said bluntly.

'Me too. I'll take you both for something to eat,' said Nat.

'You will not,' said Dani. 'After the favour you've done for us today? *We're* taking *you*.'

'Aren't you going to introduce me first?' Flossie asked.

'Nat, this is my daughter, Flossie. Flossie, this is Nat.'

'Nat, your old boyfriend? The one who really changed? Who got all square?'

Nat raised an eyebrow.

'I was wrong about that,' said Dani.

They found a pub where they could take the dogs and ordered dinner. Flossie was ravenous. She said she hadn't eaten since first thing that morning when she and Jed shared an apple in a lay-by near Carlisle. They had hitched all the way from Devon, spending the night in a service station café just past Liverpool. It was Dani's worst nightmare.

'When did you start planning it?' Dani asked.

'As soon as I got my phone back after the police thing. Jed researched it. You can still get married in Scotland when you're sixteen without parental permission and we thought if we got married, you'd have to believe we were seriously in love and let us be together properly. We were going to find jobs and stay up here until you and his parents calmed down about it and we could come back to Devon without you going berserk. Jed said there was bound to be lots of bar and hotel work. But then we got here and we went from place to place asking for jobs. And some people just flat out laughed at us. One bloke said we should come back once Jed had been to the barber.'

Dani could understand that.

'I said that maybe Jed should get his hair cut. Maybe we both should. Especially since we were going to be living undercover until we could get married. But he went ballistic. He said that he wasn't cutting his hair for anyone. If the pub owners couldn't see beyond his looks, then he didn't want to work for them anyway. And if I was going to start suggesting he made compromises to his way of life and his beliefs before I even had a ring on my finger, then perhaps we shouldn't get married after all. And then it just turned into this great big argument about everything we've ever disagreed about and he walked off and left me. I stayed put because I really thought he'd come back when he'd calmed down. He's done it before. But he always came back.'

'He's left you in the lurch before?'

Jed was sounding less and less charming by the minute.

'Have you heard anything from him?' Dani asked. Now your phone is working again?'

'Nothing,' Flossie confirmed.

Good, Dani thought.

'He went off with all my money, Mum. The money that Xanthe and Camilla gave me for my birthday tattoo. The money I got out of the building society. All the savings I had. He knew I didn't have anything else with me.'

'We'll get that back,' Dani promised. 'We know where his parents live after all.'

'I can't believe he turned out to be like this. I really, really loved him.'

Past tense already, thought Dani. Better and better.

After they'd eaten, while Dani and Flossie chatted and hugged as though they hadn't seen each other in months, Nat walked the dogs again and tried to get some of the tightness out of his shoulders. It was too late to drive back to Devon. Particularly since Nat was the only one insured to drive his BMW. He'd already spent far too long on the road for one day.

Nat definitely needed a good night's rest ahead of the long drive home. He fantasised about having a nice warm bath before climbing into a big clean double bed and spreading out like a starfish. But the little border town was packed that summer weekend. Though Dani and Nat tried calling every bed and breakfast and hotel in town, they were out of luck. There was just one room available for miles around, in the last place they would have chosen to stay – a sticky-floored pub called The Sgian-Dubh, which was out near the retail centre.

The room was the hotel's best wedding suite – complete with a four-poster bed – which had become suddenly available after a cancelled marriage ceremony.

'Cold feet. Happens all the time.'

Flossie's bottom lip trembled.

Then the hotel manageress said it wasn't possible to put a third bed in the room.

'It's not something we're often asked for,' she said.

And in any case, she definitely wouldn't take the dogs.

'I'll stay with the dogs,' said Nat.

'But where?' Dani asked. A Google search of dog-friendly hotels in the area with availability had drawn a blank.

'In the car,' said Nat.

'You can't sleep in the car!'

'I'd be happy to. The seats recline pretty well and right now, I feel like I could fall asleep standing up, like a horse.'

Nat's kindness made Dani feel ashamed. But there was no other way that made sense. Nat couldn't share with Flossie. The hotel owner was adamant that she couldn't accommodate Nat or the puppies. The best she could do was lend Nat a couple of blankets and a pillow for a night in the car park.

'But if they get dog hair on them, there will be a laundry charge,' she said.

'They don't look that clean as it is,' Dani observed as she helped Nat take them down to the car.

The landlady overheard. 'They're cleaner than your daughter looks,' she said. 'You'll have to bring the car round the back as well. I can't have people thinking I've got a down and out in my car park.'

'A down and out in a brand new BMW,' Dani observed.

Chapter Fifty-Six

Once Nat was settled in the car, Flossie and Dani went up to the room. The bedroom was as miserable and down-at-heel as the rest of the hotel. It didn't look like the kind of place you would want to spend your honeymoon, though a guest book on the dressing table was full of messages from people who had done exactly that. Perhaps love made you blind to such things as dust and decay. Dani flicked through their glowing reviews while Flossie was in the bathroom, washing off the dirt of a very long couple of days.

Eventually, Flossie came out of the bathroom, wrapped in a threadbare white dressing gown that had long since gone grey. All the same, to Dani, Flossie looked like an old-fashioned angel. She offered to brush out the tangles in her daughter's freshly washed hair, just like she used to when Flossie was small.

'OK,' Flossie said in a tiny voice.

Flossie sniffed as Dani brushed away the knots. It was clear that she was trying to hold back tears. Eventually, she turned round and buried her face in Dani's jumper.

'Mum, I'm really sorry. You were absolutely right about Jed. I should have listened to you. Are you ever going to be able to forgive me?'

'I already have,' said Dani, as she stroked Flossie's hair back from her face and kissed her forehead. 'You're my daughter and I love you. I'm just happy that you're safe. Besides, everyone's allowed to make mistakes when they're sixteen.'

'I bet you didn't.'

'I just made them so that nobody found out,' said Dani.

One day, perhaps, she would tell her.

After they got into the bed – which was horribly soft and saggy – Flossie fell asleep quickly, leaving Dani staring at the ceiling, trying to process everything that had happened since she left the house to go to dog training class that morning, oblivious of what lay ahead. Her head ached with the thought of what might have happened had Jed not got cold feet.

After a while, Dani got up and went to the window. The wedding suite at The Sgian-Dubh had a view of the wheelie bins and, that night, of Nat's car. Looking down, Dani could see that Nat was also still awake. Probably too uncomfortable to sleep. The light of his smartphone illuminated the windscreen. She could see a slice of Nat's face, lit from below. He looked even more tired in the unflattering blue light and Dani felt another rush of guilt for putting him through all this fuss. No matter how much he had insisted that he would be perfectly fine for one night, Dani found it hard to believe. He was too tall to sleep in a car. And he was sharing with Princess and Jezza. As Dani watched, Jezza was trying to get onto Nat's lap. Nat moved so that Jezza could cuddle up more easily. He lazily stroked the dog's fur while continuing to look at his phone.

Dani wondered what he was reading. News?

Facebook? Emails? He started typing. Texting Lola, probably. What was he going to tell her about this weekend's adventure? Would he tell her at all? She didn't actually need to know, away as she was on her Balearic hen do. What would she think if she found out? Would she be jealous? Thinking back to the double date from hell, Lola hadn't seemed to think that Dani was any kind of threat. Not any kind of competition. At least not for Nat.

And yet . . . There was a moment when Nat had folded his arms around her outside the Old Blacksmith's Shop when Dani thought she felt something more than friendly concern. Even though he was just trying to comfort her, his embrace had felt so right. The familiar smell of his skin. Even his chin resting on her head. He always used to do that because he was so much taller. It had driven sixteen-year-old Dani mad but mostly, whenever he held her, she simply felt safe. And loved. Why had she felt that again? Was it just some kind of weird muscle memory?

Looking down on the car, Dani imagined Nat finishing his text to Lola with kisses. Kisses and 'miss you's. 'Love you forever's. She wished she had someone to text her at night.

Dani's own phone buzzed.

'Just wanted to say night night. Xxx'

From Nat to her. She felt her cheeks grow warm.

Dani held her phone close to her heart for a moment. Kisses good night.

But perhaps they weren't really meant for her, she started thinking then. Perhaps he meant to text Lola.

'Did you mean to text me?' Dani responded.

'Nutter,' Nat replied. 'Of course I did. Jezza says night night too. Sleep tight. Xxx'

More kisses.

She looked down at the car. At the same time Nat leaned forward so that he could look up at her through his windscreen. He grinned and made Jezza wave a paw.

She texted him back.

'Watch the bugs don't bite. Xxx.'

Chapter Fifty-Seven

The next morning, Dani woke to find that the bed beside her was empty. For a moment, she wasn't even sure where she was. When it came back to her, she scrambled upright. Had Flossie snuck off again? Had Jed turned up and whisked her away from under her nose? No, Flossie was coming out of the bathroom, looking pink and clean and perfect again. Her little girl.

'I'm so sorry, Mum,' Flossie said again, as she wrapped her arms around Dani and peppered her face with kisses.

'Stop it. It's worse than being woken up by Jezza,' Dani joked.

'I'm going down to check on Jezza now,' said Flossie. 'And I need some breakfast. I'll see if Nat wants some too, shall I?'

'I'll be right behind you,' Dani said.

In the bathroom, Dani inspected her own face in the mirror. She hadn't slept well and it showed. The bed was one of the least comfortable she had ever known. It didn't help that she didn't have any clean clothes to change into. Or any of her usual toiletries. She washed her face with the overly scented pink soap the hotel provided. It left her cheeks feeling stretched too tight. The complimentary toothpaste tasted terrible. The complimentary toothbrush snapped when Dani brushed too hard. There was no hairbrush so she had to make do with trying to persuade her hair into place with her fingers. She looked a mess. She felt guilty, tired and confused. And even though they'd spent the whole of the previous day together, the thought that Nat was downstairs made her feel strangely nervous. What would he be thinking this morning? After a night in the car? Would he still be feeling so generous towards her?

Nat didn't look too bad considering he'd spent a night in the back seat of his Beemer. He said the landlady had allowed him to use the utility room on the ground floor to wash and brush up.

'I felt like I should clean the room first,' he whispered.

The dogs were already walked.

'I woke up pretty early. When the local council came to fetch the wheelie bins. The dogs wouldn't stop barking so I took them round the block.'

The landlady was also kind enough to allow Nat to join Dani and Flossie in the dining room for breakfast. At an exorbitant fee. When breakfast arrived, Nat speared a sausage.

'Worth more than its weight in gold. Quite literally.'

Flossie sniggered. She seemed to be hitting it off with Nat. She didn't even give him a lecture about the evils of eating meat.

As soon as they'd finished breakfast, it was time to get back on the road. Flossie had never been a very good passenger so Dani had to concede the front seat.

Fortunately, the back of Nat's BMW was as comfortable as any limo and Dani sank into the leather embrace. Jezza and Princess were on the back seat beside her. Far from being difficult passengers, they seemed quite happy in a furry heap of tangled legs and tails as the car motored back down south. They were both fast asleep by Carlisle.

The atmosphere of the journey back to Devon was always going to be slightly different from the ride up. Then, Dani just wanted to get where she was going. Now there was no hurry, she was happy to watch the world go by. And listen to Nat talking to her daughter.

'So, like, Mum said you were like really big into Che Guevara?' Flossie said.

'I don't think I had a clue what he really stood for,' Nat said. 'I just liked that iconic portrait.'

'It's really cool,' Flossie agreed.

They talked about music. Dani was surprised to hear that Nat had heard of, and liked, lots of the bands that Flossie and her friends claimed to be into.

'How old were you when you went to your first festival?' Flossie asked.

'Thirty seven,' Nat deadpanned.

'No way.'

'OK. Thirty-five. And I hated every minute of it. We were staying in one of those "glamping" tents with all mod cons and it was still bloody awful. It rained non-stop. The mud was up to your knees. I thought I had trench foot by the end of the weekend. You couldn't pay me to go to a festival again. I would rather sit in a bath full of warm sick.'

Flossie laughed.

It was a sound that lifted Dani's heart.

'After hiking up to Gretna,' said Flossie. 'And washing in a service station bathroom, I think I'd feel the same.'

About two hours into the journey, Dani closed her eyes and drifted off.

When a bump in the road jolted her into a state of semi-alertness, she found that Nat and Flossie were still talking. But they'd moved on from music and folk heroes. Flossie was dabbing at her eyes with a tissue. It could only be because of Jed.

'I've never been able to trust any of the men in my life,' she said. 'Right from the very beginning. I guess I threw myself into things with Jed because I thought he might be able to fill the space in my heart that was always meant for my dad. The first man who let me down.'

'Was he never there for you?'

'Never.'

'Do you have a relationship with him?' Nat asked.

'No. Not any more. When I was born, he told Mum he didn't even believe I was his. Then, when he decided I was his after all, he sent me a couple of birthday cards. Then Mum says he met someone new and decided to have a family with her. He forgot all about me after that. It's like I never existed.'

'That's not good,' said Nat.

'I guess I wasn't worth hanging on to. Now Jed doesn't want me either. That proves it.'

'Don't say that,' said Nat. 'Don't even think that. The way your dad behaved towards you has absolutely nothing to do with you or anything you've done. How could it be? You were a baby, Flossie. Never ever blame yourself for the neglect of people who should have known better. As for Jed . . . He's just a kid. He got scared. Nothing to do with you. You're a beautiful, funny young woman and way out of his league.'

'You don't know Jed.'

'I don't think I need to. You've got so much life ahead of you, Flossie. So many things to do. So many people to meet. You've already grown into a fabulous person without the input of your father. You don't need a man to validate you.'

Flossie nodded. 'I know you're right but it's hard.'

'I get it.'

'Mum's always been great but she's a bit over-protective.'

'I expect she feels she has to do the parenting for two.'

'And after this weekend, I guess I've shown her that I don't deserve to be trusted at all.'

'I think she'll understand what happened better than you think,' said Nat. 'I know I do. I really understand what you're going through. And you probably feel as though nothing will ever make you happy again but I promise you it will. And there will also come a time when you look at Jed and feel grateful that he made the decision he did. The right thing doesn't always look like the right thing at the time.'

Flossie agreed.

'Put some music on?' Nat suggested. 'I know you've got good taste.'

As she searched through the tunes on Nat's iPhone, Flossie asked, 'Tell me about Mum when she was my age, Nat. What was she like?'

'What do you want to know?'

'Was she always as square as she is now?'

Nat laughed. 'Is she square?'

'Oh, you know.'

'No. She wasn't square. I thought she was really out there, in fact. She gave me my first cigarette.'

'What? Mum doesn't smoke.'

'Perhaps I shouldn't have told you that.'

Flossie shook her head.

'She's so hypocritical! She told me I'd be grounded for life if she ever so much as caught a whiff of smoke on me. And yet she smoked too.'

'Parent's prerogative. Do as I say, not as I do.'

'What else, Nat? What did she dress like?'

'She dressed like she was in the All Saints. Combat trousers. Logo T-shirts. I fancied her like crazy.'

Flossie grimaced.

'It's not that hard to believe. She's a beautiful woman. She was my first love.'

'Was she really?'

'Yes. More importantly, she was my best friend.'

Dani couldn't listen to any more. Not in this secretive, eavesdropping way. She sat upright and made a big show of yawning and stretching, to draw their attention to the back of the car and convince them that she'd only just woken up.

'Sleeping beauty stirs,' said Nat.

'Have I been asleep long?' Dani asked.

'You've been snoring since Carlisle,' said Nat.

'Stop it.'

'You do snore, Mum,' said Flossie.

They stopped for lunch in the Midlands. Dani would have been happy with a service station but Nat said that since they were on an adventure, they should go somewhere decent. He had Flossie look up a dog-friendly gastro-pub that wasn't too far from their route. She found a great place in a pretty village, where the dogs were treated as stars.

What did they look like? Dani wondered, as they sat at a table in the pub garden. Did they look like a little family? A couple with a daughter and two dogs? Best friends who'd made their lives together? Was this how it might have been?

Chapter Fifty-Eight

It was around six in the evening when they crossed the county border into Devon again. Soon they were in the centre of Newbay.

'You can drop us here,' said Dani as they passed the bus station. 'We're completely on the other side of town from your place.'

'No way, I'm driving you right to the door,' said Nat.

He was already heading in the direction of their place.

He found the house without needing to be told how to get there. When he pulled into the drive, Jane was at the front window with Sarah, eager to see who'd arrived.

'I remember this house,' said Nat. 'Is that the hedge your dad had just put in all those years ago?'

The beech hedge was five feet tall now.

'He always said that a true gardener plants for the generations who will come after him.'

'He was a great man.'

'Yeah,' said Dani. 'He was. He liked you too.'

While they were unloading, Jane rushed out of the front door and grabbed Flossie in a bear hug the moment she stepped out of the car.

'Flossie! We were all so worried,' she said. 'Whatever were you thinking?'

Dani subtly shook her head to let Jane know that there were to be no recriminations.

'Nat,' Jane changed tack. 'I'm so grateful to you for looking after my girls. Would you like to come inside for some tea?'

'Yes. I made a cake,' said Sarah.

'I'd better get home,' he said. But first he wanted to say goodbye properly.

'All right, Flossie. If you do hear from that loser, Jed, tell him he can drop off your money and your charger when you're not in and then take a hike, OK? And next time you take someone up on a marriage proposal, make sure he's not a total flake.'

Flossie gave Nat the thumbs-up.

'I promise I will never get married without running my potential fiancé past you first, Nat. You're my relationship guru from now on.'

Flossie threw her arms around him. 'Thank you, thank you, thank you. You really are the best.'

Nat looked over the top of Flossie's head at Dani.

'You are pretty bloody special,' Dani agreed.

Escaping Flossie's embrace, Nat leaned forward to kiss Dani on the cheek. She quickly wrapped her arms around him.

'You're a star.'

'That one is a keeper,' said Sarah as Nat drove off. 'That Lola woman has really lucked out.'

After Nat had gone back to his house, the three Parker women and Sarah were soon settled in for the night.

Flossie curled up on the sofa with Jane. Jezza squeezed himself in between them.

'You've always got to be at the centre of everything!' Flossie tutted.

Jezza responded by stretching out his legs and shoving Flossie into the armrest so that he had more space.

'Jezza!'

He got his way.

Flossie looked so young, thought Dani as she carried in a tray of tea and biscuits. Way too young to have been on such a crazy adventure. It was a total blessing that it hadn't worked out. The idea that Jed might have been her son-in-law by now!

But Dani was beginning to come round to the idea that she couldn't be too angry with Jed. The adventure had sprung from a romantic notion. They were still children really. Both of them. Jed wasn't much older than Nat had been, back in 1996.

On the sofa, Jane stroked Flossie's hair. 'Don't you worry about anything, my darling,' said Jane. 'You've got me, you've got your mum, you've got Auntie Sarah and you've got Jezza. We'll look after you. You can always rely on grandmas, mums, aunties and dogs.'

And Nat, thought Dani. She could always rely on him.

While the others chilled out in the sitting room, Dani went up to her bedroom. She found a text on her phone from Nat.

'I hope Flossie's feeling a bit better now. I'm getting an early night. Got to pick Lola up at the airport again tomorrow.'

Dani almost texted him back but decided instead to call. There was still so much to say. She had to do it while she was feeling brave.

'Hello.' He sounded tentative when he picked up.

'Hello,' said Dani. It was strange that they'd been together for the last twenty-four hours and yet now, on the phone, Dani felt suddenly shy again.

'Is everything OK?' Nat asked.

'We're all fine,' said Dani. 'Flossie's watching telly with my mum and Sarah and Jezza. I've had a much-needed bath.'

'Me too. So . . .'

'So, I wanted to call you to say thank you again. You drove all the way to Gretna Green and back for my daughter and me. You had to sleep in the car. With the dogs.'

'They were very good at keeping me warm. Jezza's the equivalent of a ten tog duvet.'

'But you must have been so uncomfortable. At least let me give you some money for petrol to make up for it.'

'No, really. It's no big deal.'

'It's a huge deal,' said Dani. 'Especially . . . You know . . . It being what it was.'

The elephant got up and walked to the centre of the room, where it waited for Dani to keep talking.

'Nat,' she continued. 'Before all this happened . . . Yesterday morning, before I got the call from Flossie to say she was in Scotland, it seemed like you were going to tell me something important.'

'Was I?' asked Nat, ushering the elephant straight back to its corner. 'I don't remember.'

'You said that you'd been thinking about something . . .'

'Did I?'

'Maybe I got the wrong end of the stick.'

'I was probably just going to ask your advice about wedding stuff.'

'Oh. Well, if you remember what it was you wanted to know,' Dani tried to recover. 'Then I'm always at the end of the phone.'

'Thank you.'

'No. Thank *you*, again, for everything.'

'I would have done the same for anyone.'

There was something about that sentence that Dani didn't like.

'I know you would,' she said.

'And I know you would have done the same for me. It's called being a friend, isn't it?'

'Yes. I'm glad you're my friend.'

'And me vice versa.'

'Look, there's one more thing,' Dani said.

'What?'

'You know when I fell asleep in the car?'

'Yes.'

'I wasn't really asleep the whole time. I heard you talking to Flossie about her father. I'm really grateful for what you said.'

'She deserved better. I don't know how any man could walk away from his responsibilities like that. Why he wouldn't have been excited to have a baby girl?'

'I know,' said Dani. 'I picked a wrong 'un.'

Should she say she'd heard the rest of the conversation or pretend she'd dropped off again?

'I've got to go to bed,' said Nat, while she was plucking up the courage. 'I can't be late for Lola in the morning.'

Lola. Of course.

'I'm sorry we hijacked your weekend.'

'You and Flossie *made* my weekend.'

'Good night,' said Dani.

'Good night.' Nat put the phone down. Dani held on to her handset long after he'd gone, listening to the silence.

Chapter Fifty-Nine

Dani had to wait until the following Saturday at boot camp to see Nat again.

'Well, that was Princess's last class,' said Nat as they left the playing field.

'You're not coming next week?'

'Er, we've got something else on.' Nat grimaced.

'Oh, of course. Yes.' Dani blushed. 'The wedding.'

'I can't believe it's come round so quickly.'

'Neither can I. I hope it goes well. I'll do my best to make sure the cake's suitably wonderful.'

'I know you will.'

'I probably won't see you on the day, though,' Dani said. 'I'm not due to be working. My assistant will make sure everything's up to scratch.'

Nat nodded.

'I'm looking forward to seeing the wedding photos,' Dani continued brightly. 'You in a penguin suit.'

Nat tugged at his shirt collar as though he was already wearing tails.

'You never told me what the colour scheme is.'

'I don't know myself. Lola is sorting out the cravats and buttonholes and sending them over, so I'll find out on the day.'

'Always good to have some surprises,' Dani said.

'I suppose.'

'Have you written your speech?' Dani asked, forcing yet more brightness into her tone.

Nat nodded. 'I haven't practised it, though.'

'I hear you shouldn't over-practise these things,' said Dani. 'Or you'll squash all the emotion out of it. You've got to let some of the excitement of the day come through.'

'Yes.'

'And don't worry if that excitement takes over and you end up in tears. Everybody loves a sobbing groom.'

Dani thought Nat might laugh at that but he didn't.

'And then you must be off on honeymoon?'

'Two weeks on the Amalfi coast.'

'That sounds great.'

'I hope so. Then hopefully we should be able to move into the house. The builders should have been finished weeks ago. If they're not done by the time we're back from honeymoon, Lola won't be happy.'

'Of course not. It's been taking a long time, that renovation.'

'So,' said Nat.

'So,' said Dani.

'I'm not sure when we'll see each other again.'

'Newbay's a small town,' said Dani. 'I'm sure we'll bump into each other all the time.'

But things would be different when they did, was the unspoken message between them.

It was time to say goodbye. If not to each other, then at least to something like a dream.

Chapter Sixty

Two days later, Dani was in the kitchen, working on Nat and Lola's wedding cake.

'You've got a visitor,' said Dave the chef. 'It's Frank's fiancée.'

'You mean Nat's fiancée.'

'Yeah, whatever. Maybe she's coming to tell you that the wedding's off. She's realised she needs a real man in her life. Like me.'

'In your dreams,' said Dani. She washed her hands and went out into the restaurant.

Lola was standing by the window. In almost exactly the same spot as Nat on the day he came to talk about Lola's birthday party. The first time Dani had seen him in twenty-two years.

Lola was dressed all in pale camel. The luxurious kind of pale camel favoured by Italian women and sold in places like Max Mara. Though it wasn't exactly cold outside, she had a thin fur collarette around her neck. It made her look a little bit like a toy dog in human form, Dani thought.

Lola didn't immediately notice that Dani was in the room with her. She stayed looking out of the window. She lifted a hand to her face and delicately touched the skin below her eye as though checking her make-up wasn't running. It was a gesture that gave Lola a vulnerability Dani wouldn't have expected.

'Lola,' she said warmly. 'How are you? Just a few days to go. You must be getting excited.'

'I've come to look at the cake,' Lola said.

'It's going well,' said Dani. 'I think you're going to like it.'

'Sure.'

'Follow me.' Dani took Lola into the kitchen and showed her the three tiers with their perfectly flat white icing, waiting to be decorated with Dani's magic touch.

'It looks nice,' said Lola.

'The cake topper is done, of course. Would you like to see it? You know the sort of style we're going for. It'll be the same as your engagement cake. A continuation of the story, in a way. You, Nat and Princess, heading into the next stage of your life together.'

'Great,' said Lola.

She didn't sound particularly enthused. Lola chewed her lip and Dani felt a small jolt of adrenalin. She looked strangely shifty. Perhaps Dave the chef was right and Lola really had come in to tell Dani that there was no need to finish the cake after all. The wedding was actually off.

'Are you OK?' Dani asked Lola. 'Would you like a glass of water?'

Lola nodded. She perched on the stool where Dani sat to do her most complicated icing work. Dani placed a glass of water in front of her. Lola took a handkerchief out of her handbag and twisted it between her hands. She was clearly plucking up the courage to start speaking and Dani decided not to prompt.

'Do you understand Nat?' Lola asked suddenly. 'I mean, I can't get my head around him sometimes. He goes quiet. Like he's thinking about something. When I ask him what's going on he says nothing. But I know it's not nothing. I can tell.'

'I don't know,' said Dani. 'In my experience, men are quite often thinking about nothing in particular when they go all quiet like that. Or maybe they're thinking about something totally mundane – like who played in the 'ninety-six FA cup final – and they're embarrassed to admit it so they say "nothing" instead. It's when we try to winkle an answer out of them that things get messy.'

Lola nodded but she seemed unconvinced.

'You've known Nat for a long time, haven't you?'

'I suppose. We met when we were teenagers. When we worked here.'

'And you went out?'

'For a short while.'

So Nat *had* told her.

'But it was serious, wasn't it?'

'I don't think you can call it that in retrospect. We were only together for a month or so all told. He was eighteen and I was only sixteen. It was just full-on in that teenage way.'

'He must have told you lots of stuff, though.'

'Well, yes.'

'So you know him really well?'

'At the time, perhaps you could have said. But there have been a lot of years since, when we weren't in contact, Lola. So I'm not sure that I can say I really *know* him now.'

'I certainly don't feel like I do,' said Lola.

'He takes a while to open up,' Dani suggested.

'But we're supposed to be getting married in less

than a week. And if I didn't know better, I'd say that you still know him much better than I do. Like that night at The Lonely Elephant. He talked to you all the time.'

'If that was the case, it was only because you were talking to Will,' Dani said.

'Will's one of my oldest friends,' Lola protested. 'And how about in the nightclub? I could never have made Nat dance.'

You didn't give him a chance, Dani said to herself.

'He often has a coffee with you after Best Behaviour Boot Camp and he drove you all the way to Scotland to pick up your daughter.'

'It was a very kind thing to do.'

'Not over the top?'

'No. Just a friendly gesture.'

Dani didn't like the direction in which this conversation was heading.

'Just friendly?' Lola asked.

'Yes. Just friendly.'

Lola narrowed her eyes.

'Lola, what are you trying to say?' Dani asked. 'What do you really want to know? If you want to know whether anything is going on between me and Nat then I can tell you unequivocally that there isn't. I'm sorry if you got a different impression. Nat can't wait to get married, I'm sure.' Dani forced the last words out.

Lola took a sip of water.

'OK. Thanks. I just . . .' She glanced over towards the cake. 'It's going to be wonderful. Thank you.'

Then she got up and left without even seeing the little models Dani had made for the top of the cake.

Chapter Sixty-One

The first Saturday of September marked the end of that term of Best Behaviour Boot Camp.

In the run-up to the last class, Flossie, Jane and Dani had all been working hard to implement Nurse Van Niekerk's training tips and there were moments when it seemed as though it had all sunk in.

Well, there was no doubt that Jeremy knew what he was supposed to do. It was more a matter of whether or not he felt like doing it on the day.

He did. As the puppies were put through their paces one last time, Jezza did the Parker family proud. He sat, stayed and dropped when he was told to. He walked to heel as though the only thing that existed in his world was Dani's face. Nothing could distract him. He was truly on his best behaviour. Until . . .

'And this term's award for "Most Improved Puppy" goes to Jeremy Corbyn!' Nurse Van Niekerk announced.

At which point, Jezza immediately let himself down. Rushing to Nurse Van Niekerk and jumping up and down in an attempt to get at the bag of treats she was holding.

'Now, that's not the sort of behaviour I expect from you,' Nurse Van Niekerk told him.

Jezza duly sat down at her feet and looked up at her winningly.

'Paw?'

He offered his paw to be shaken.

'Good boy.'

He playfully bit Nurse Van Niekerk on the knee.

After all the excitement of the prize-giving, Dani didn't give her walk back home from Best Behaviour Boot Camp much thought. Had she considered it at all, she would have chosen a different route, because her usual one took her right by St Mark's Church. The venue for Nat and Lola's wedding.

As though she had sleepwalked there, she suddenly found herself at the top of St Mark's Street. Dani thought about turning round and going home the long way but it was as if something was drawing her closer. She glanced at her watch. It was almost eleven. A few wedding guests were still dashing in through the lych-gate, keen to be inside before the arrival of the star of the show. The blushing bride.

Dani walked a little nearer. Despite having won 'most improved' at BB Boot Camp, Jezza was pulling a little on his lead again, as though he'd caught a particularly interesting scent.

'Heel,' Dani reminded him. Jezza took no notice. He wanted to be closer to the church.

'Heel.'

Jezza yanked Dani forwards.

There was a small crowd outside the church gates. People who weren't invited to the wedding – perhaps didn't even know the bride and groom – but who still wanted to see the moment when the bride and her father got out of the bridal car. As they stood and watched, the bridesmaids arrived in an enormous Bentley.

A couple of ushers – young men Dani recognised from the engagement party – helped the bridesmaids out of the car. They were stuffed in like sardines in taffeta sauce. Five tumbled out altogether. Three adults and two heartbreakingly cute flower girls. The adult bridesmaids wore dresses with sequinned bodices and ballerina skirts in a pale lemon yellow, which was a lovely colour and flattering enough if you were covered in fake tan, as all three of the adult bridesmaids were. The flower girls were in cream with a yellow sash around the waist.

The bride's attendants arranged themselves in a little huddle so that the photographer could snap them. They pouted and posed – even the little ones – for a full five minutes while they waited for the bride to arrive, at which point the photographer turned his lens on the main event.

Lola and her father were being driven to the wedding in a Roller. The silver car gleamed in the early autumn sunlight. Its bonnet was adorned with yellow and cream ribbons to match the bridesmaids' colour scheme. After the car pulled up to the lychgate, a liveried driver sprang out to help Lola and her father from the back. The driver stood, holding the door open, while Lola posed for the traditional 'getting out of the car' photograph, which took another five minutes, as she insisted on seeing each shot on the camera's digital screen so she could be sure that the photographer was getting the angle she wanted.

But finally, finally, Lola climbed out of the car. The three adult bridesmaids immediately clustered around her like worker bees welcoming the queen back to the hive. They fluffed up her full skirt – the voluminous likes of which Newbay hadn't seen since the nineteen eighties, and made sure the pavement was as clean as possible before they spread out her train. The chief bridesmaid helped Lola to arrange her veil. Lola gave her best 'demure' pose for the photographer through the clouds of lace. Dani couldn't help finding it funny that Lola had chosen to cover her face though the dress itself was strapless, sleeveless and showcased her breasts like a pair of blancmanges.

The church warden came out to see what was going on.

'Are you ready yet?' he asked. 'We can't wait for much longer.'

It was twenty past eleven. It may have been traditional for the bride to be a little late, but St Mark's was the prettiest church in Newbay and doubtless Nat and Lola's wasn't the only wedding it would be hosting that day.

'I'm ready,' said Lola, taking her father's arm.

The bridesmaids fell into formation behind her and the bridal party began its slow, stately progress towards the church door.

At which point, Dani looked up at her fellow onlookers and saw that one of them was Will. He was holding Princess.

'Will?' Dani tried to attract his attention but Will was utterly focussed on the bride heading for her happy ever after. Poor Will's eyes were red and bloodshot. He had never looked less like a former cover star of *Men's Health*. It was clear he'd been crying. But what was he doing with Princess?

'Will?' As the crowd of onlookers dispersed, Dani

drew closer to him. 'Are you OK? How come you've got Princess?'

'She asked me to look after Princess during the wedding and while they go on honeymoon. Princess is surplus to requirements. Just like me.'

'Oh, Will.'

Dani put her arm around Will's shoulders. 'Some things just aren't meant to be.'

Princess was wriggling in Will's arms. As Will turned to cry – quite literally – on Dani's shoulder, Princess managed to free herself from his grasp.

'Princess!'

The little pup slipped to the floor and made a run for the church door and her mistress. With a dog's devotion, Princess didn't care that she wasn't invited to the wedding. Jezza, with his devotion to Princess, was determined to follow her. He gave a tug on the lead that took Dani by surprise, jerking the chain from her hand. Before Will and Dani even knew what was happening, the two dogs had legged it down the church path and slipped through the door, which the church warden was closing in a particularly ponderous ceremonial sort of way.

'Balls!'

Dani abandoned Will to his crying and set off in hot pursuit.

Chapter Sixty-Two

Lola was halfway down the aisle when the dogs got to her. The organist was still playing 'The Arrival of the Queen of Sheba'. Badly. Soon the aisle was a flurry of taffeta and dogs. Bridesmaids were shrieking, guests were laughing, Dani was using every piece of kitchen language she knew. She chased Princess and Jezza up and down several pews. It was a great game to them. Even better when the humans were joining in.

Though they were both nearly eight months old, Jezza and Princess were still small and fast enough to easily evade capture. Even with the whole church trying to get hold of them, they somehow managed to escape time and time again.

Meanwhile, Lola and her father stood as though frozen halfway down the aisle. The organist continued to massacre the Handel. The vicar stood open-mouthed at the altar. Nat and his best man – his brother-in-law Damian – didn't know where to put themselves.

'Just grab them!' Dani shouted.

Eventually, Princess was captured by one of the ushers. Jezza continued his rampage alone. He shot up one of the side aisles so fast he looked like a flying wig.

'I'm sorry, I'm sorry,' Dani muttered between swear words, as Jezza shot back down the side aisle again.

'Someone just grab him, please. He won't bite you. He's really soft.'

But Jezza was on fire. Perhaps it was a morning spent being on his best behaviour that had wound him up to such a state of excitement. His eyes were wide and delighted. His tongue hung out of the side of his mouth like a bright pink pennant. He was Jeremy the Wonderdog. The fastest Staffy-poodle in the world.

'Jeremy Corbyn!' Dani's voice had taken on a tone of sheer desperation. She stood at the back of the church with her head in her hands, while Jezza did another circuit with the speed of a champion greyhound. The laughter of the congregation only spurred him on. They were loving it. Loving him. Even the vicar was seeing the funny side. Nat, who was now holding Princess in his arms, shrugged to his side of the church as if to say, 'This will make a great story later on.'

Emboldened by the reaction of the crowd, Jezza decided to finish his rampage with a bolt straight up the aisle to Dani and freedom. Only one thing was in his way.

Lola and her father had almost reached the altar.

The congregation gasped as Jezza leapt at the bride, landing with all four muddy paws on her skirt. For Dani the world went into slow motion as Jezza leapt up at Lola again and again and again until the front of her skirt looked as though it was fashioned from chiffon deliberately printed with muddy brown camouflage. He might have thought he was being friendly but Lola was unlikely to see it like that at all.

Lola dropped her bouquet and stood staring down in silent horror until, 'This is not how my wedding is supposed to be!' she shouted at the top of her voice.

'This is not how anything is supposed to be! Please, somebody, help me! Help me!!!'

'I think perhaps we need to take a moment,' said the vicar, taking both Nat and Lola by the hand and leading them out of sight.

Chapter Sixty-Three

Dani had been happy with her little Newbay life, until Nat Hayward walked back into it. When she saw him standing there in the restaurant, just the sight of his familiar broad shoulders and the shape of his body made her want to sigh with relief. He was back. He was home. He was *her* home.

Except that he wasn't back for her. He'd come back for his parents and he was staying only for Lola.

Dani and Nat shouldn't have tried to rekindle even so much as a friendship. They should have marvelled briefly at all the years that had passed since they last saw each other and moved straight onto nodding terms. They shouldn't have started going for the occasional coffee after the dog-training course. Dani shouldn't have started looking forward to those moments, making them the high spot of her week.

She could only imagine how much Nat must be regretting reacquainting himself with her now. It was because of Dani that the wedding ceremony descended into chaos. Lola would probably be within her rights to sue her for not having had Jezza under control. How much was it going to cost her for having let Jezza ruin the delicate white lace skirt?

Hiding from the chaos back at home, Dani didn't know what to do with herself. Her phone was buzzing with messages but she couldn't bear to check them.

She wanted to know what was going on and yet at the same time, she didn't think she would be able to live through hearing what had happened after she left the church. Would anyone believe she hadn't let Jezza off the lead on purpose, to deliberately ruin the wedding of the man she had once loved – perhaps still loved – to someone else?

Meanwhile, Jezza was oblivious to the trouble he'd caused. He was still a pup. Still spending more of the day asleep than awake. Dani might be unable to sit still for a moment, jangling as she was with nerves, but Jezza was tucked up in his basket, his paws twitching as he dreamed of running. Perhaps he was reliving his mad dash around the church.

Dani shook her head as she watched him. What would Nat and Lola expect her to do with Jezza? Could they ask her to have him put down? She offered up a little prayer.

'Please let them be finding this funny.'

Later, holding her phone at arm's length, as though the distance might help, Dani checked her texts. None from Nat. That was a good sign. Sort of. But here was one from Dave the chef.

'Frank's wedding reception called off. WTF?'

Chapter Sixty-Four

Flossie heard about the debacle from Camilla, whose mother had been in the church choir booked to sing while Nat and Lola signed the register.

Flossie buried her face in Jezza's fur.

'What did you do, you silly dog?'

'What did everyone think?' Dani asked.

'They thought it was really funny.'

'But what happened? After Jezza and I ran away.'

'The bride and groom went into the vestry with the vicar. They were in there for ages. The choirmaster had the choir sing a medley of tunes to keep everyone occupied while they were waiting. And to drown out the sound of shouting from the bride's father.'

'Oh no.'

'Then, after about forty-five minutes, the vicar came back out and told everyone that they could all go home. The wedding wouldn't be happening that day. Camilla's mum and the choir had to stay, though, because there was another wedding due at midday.'

'And she didn't see Nat and Lola go out.'

'They went out through the back door,' Flossie said. 'If you ask me, that doesn't sound like a good sign.' There was an unseemly amount of glee in Flossie's telling of the tale.

Hearing all this, Jane did her best to reassure Dani.

'A couple of paw prints on a wedding dress is not enough to stop a wedding,' she said. 'When your grandparents got married, people didn't bother with special wedding clothes at all. Grandma wore her Sunday best, but that was all.'

When Sarah came over that afternoon, she agreed, 'There's so much ridiculousness around weddings these days. The idea that if it isn't perfect, it isn't worth doing. It's about the marriage. Not about the day.'

'Thanks,' said Dani. But it didn't make her feel any better.

By late evening, Dani's phone had stopped fizzing with messages from people who wanted to know what was going on. That was a relief. But there was still one person she wanted to hear from.

She checked her bank accounts to see how much cash she had to hand. She went on-line to the church's website to see if there were any details there regarding the cost of a ceremony.

She already knew what the reception at The Majestic was going to cost, of course. Did they have insurance? Would it pay out for a disruptive dog?

Dani typed out a text to Nat.

'I'm so sorry,' she wrote. 'Please let me know how I can make it up to you both.'

No reply.

She imagined Nat and Lola at their executive home. She imagined Lola's fierce father demanding that someone be held accountable. She imagined Lola's mother crying. Nat's parents. Nat's sister. His nephews.

The way Dani saw it, the only person who could possibly be pleased about that day's turn of events was Will.

Will! He might be able to tell Dani what was really going on. She snatched up her phone, only to remember that she had deleted his number after the date that had turned into a foursome. The night when Dani and Nat might as well not have been there.

Dani did know how to get hold of him, though. She would send him a message on Instagram.

Will's account was still in Dani's search history. She brought up his feed. He'd posted an awful lot of pictures since she last looked and Dani couldn't help but look through them. There were at least fifty new shots. Including a whole sequence taken on the beach at Palma, Majorca.

Dani sat back in the kitchen chair and examined the photographs more closely. When was Will in Majorca? She checked the dates. He was there the weekend that Dani and Nat had to drive to Gretna (which explained the foreign dialling tone). He was there when Lola was on her hen weekend.

Had Will flown out there to stalk his ex-girlfriend?

Lola's Instagram and Will's Instagram contained almost identical pictures. They'd both posted photographs from the same beachside restaurant in Portixol. The same large lady in an orange sarong was walking through the background of both shots. Which meant that Lola and Will must have been there on the same day. At the same time? How was it possible that Lola hadn't noticed her ex-boyfriend was on the very same terrace? Unless?

The penny dropped.

Will hadn't followed Lola to Majorca stalker-style. She knew he was going to be there. He'd met her there.

If there had ever been any point getting Will's take on the whole disaster, Dani changed her mind about it now. She thought back to Lola's visit to the kitchen. Lola wasn't warning Dani off. She wanted Dani and Nat to be having an affair. She was looking for an excuse.

Though she really didn't want to, Dani had to go back to work the Monday after the wedding-that-never-was. She tried to keep a low profile as she walked into the hotel, but everybody wanted to talk to her. It wasn't often that someone cancelled a wedding reception at The Majestic.

'I can only remember it happening once before,' said Dave the chef. 'Because the bride's sister stood up and said she'd slept with the groom when they did that "anybody know of any reason" bit. Was Frank having it away with one of his bridesmaids?' Dave wanted to know now.

Dani didn't explain her theory.

She was going through the motions. Fortunately, she could do her job with her eyes closed these days. There was nothing out of the ordinary about today's service.

When she went into the pantry, however, she couldn't fail to see the wedding cake.

'We should box it up,' she said. 'And ask where the bride wants it sent.'

Dani held the two little icing sugar people in her hands. The red colouring of the bride's smile had bled into the surrounding icing over the course of the weekend, leaving her looking as though she'd necked a bottle of red wine. The figurine that was supposed to be Nat wasn't looking that perky either. His long legs had bowed, leaving him looking as though he was halfway through a curtsey.

Dani placed the figurines side by side in a box lined with shredded tissue.

Poor Lola. Poor Nat. Poor Will.

When Dani got home that night, Flossie was crying at the kitchen table. In front of her she had a box.

'Jed dropped my things off,' she said.

'Were you here when he did?'

'No. Gran spoke to him.'

'What did he say?'

'He said he was sorry. He said he really did love me but sometimes things just don't work out.'

'It's true,' said Dani. 'Sometimes they don't.'

'I thought what we had was once in a lifetime!' Flossie sobbed.

Dani lay her hands over her daughter's. 'Flossie, love, I've got something I need to tell you. It's something I should have told you ages ago. I don't know why I didn't. I suppose I was embarrassed.'

'About what?'

'Having to admit that you're not the first sixteen-year-old to have made a big mistake when it came to love . . .'

Chapter Sixty-Five

1996.

Dani's summer had been all about Nat. From the
moment they shared their first kiss at Cinderella's nightclub, they spent every second they could together. Dave
the chef started to call them 'Tweedledum and
Tweedledee'.

They didn't care. Nothing mattered but their blos-
soming love. Every minute they could snatch with each
other was precious. Especially once they lost their
virginity to one another.

But towards the end of August, Dani started to feel
a little strange. And not in a good way.

On the last Saturday of the month, she grabbed Nat
by the arm as they passed in The Majestic's kitchen.

'Nat, I need to talk to you. As soon as service is
finished.'

'You look worried,' he said. 'Do you want to talk to
me now?'

Dani shook her head. Julie was within hearing
distance and Dani could tell she was all ears.

'Later will be fine. You'll probably need some time
to yourself after we've spoken anyway.'

'What is it?' Nat pulled Dani towards the door into
the car park. 'You can't just say that to me then leave
me hanging for the rest of the night.'

'I can't tell you now,' said Dani.

'Why not?'

'Because I'll cry.'

'Are you going to break up with me?' Nat asked. His face was suddenly drained of colour.

'No,' said Dani. 'But you might decide to break up with me.'

'Why? What is it?' He grasped both her hands and held them tightly.

There was no way she was going to get away without telling him now. What a stupid thing to have done, tell him that she needed to talk to him after service. She should have sat on her news for just a couple more hours, rather than flagged up that she was desperate to have a conversation. If she didn't tell him everything now, then he would only spend the whole of service worrying – if he went back into the restaurant at all after hearing what she had to say.

'I can't work while I'm worrying about what you've got to tell me,' he said.

'OK,' said Dani. 'But you probably won't be able to work when I tell you what it is either.'

'Try me.'

Dani pulled Nat further behind the wheelie bins. It wasn't exactly where she'd expected to be having the conversation but perhaps it was appropriate, given how shitty she was feeling.

Nat's face was pale and anxious as Dani struggled to find the words, even though she had played the conversation through her head a thousand times already. What she would say. How he would react. What he would say back to her. Spinning his answers every possible way. Good. Bad. Ugly. She felt as though she

was underwater. Everything seemed muted and shim-
mering.

'Spit it out,' Nat said at last, pulling her back to the
surface.

'Nat, I think I'm pregnant,' she said.

Nat's face was immediately and strangely, thought
Dani, relieved. As though it was good news and not
the worst possible thing that could have happened to
two kids on their way to university.

'What do you mean by "think"?' Nat asked. 'Have
you done a test?'

'No. Not yet. I don't think they work until your
period is two weeks late.'

'How late is yours?'

'Three days.'

'Is that soon enough to worry?'

'I dunno, but I sort of feel different. I feel as though
something is happening inside me. Mum always said
she could tell straight away when she got pregnant with
me.'

'Have you spoken to your mum about it?' Nat asked.

'No way! She's going to go crazy. And as for Dad.'

Dani felt suddenly quite weak at the knees. She
leaned into Nat's side and was relieved when he
wrapped his arms around her, holding her upright and
strong.

'It will be OK,' he said. 'It will be fine. We'll be fine.
Your mum will be fine. Your dad will be fine. I'll make
sure everything goes smoothly. Whatever you decide to
do,' he added. 'Just know that I'm behind you whatever
you choose.'

Which Dani was already assuming should be an
abortion. Until Nat said, 'If you feel as though you

could keep the baby, I would be right there with you, you know. I'd be the best father I could.'

'Would you?'

'It would be an honour.'

'Oh Nat.'

'Are you two finished smoking?' Julie shouted from the door. 'Only the restaurant is filling up out there and I can't be expected to do everything on my own.'

'Coming,' said Nat.

He gently brushed his thumbs across Dani's cheeks to wipe her tears away.

'Remember,' he said. 'We're in this together. You and me. Always forever.'

Those Donna Lewis lyrics again.

Dani nodded.

The day after Dani told Nat she thought she might be pregnant, they went for a walk on the cliffs. They held hands, as they always did, though their mood was slightly subdued.

'I didn't think I'd ever meet someone like you. Someone who really understands me.'

'I felt the same way,' said Dani. 'Though it took you long enough to notice me!'

'I noticed you the first time you came to rehearsal,' said Nat. 'I just didn't think you could possibly be interested. You were really cool and beautiful and I was the class geek.'

'You were different.'

'I feel like you're my reward.'

Dani lay back on the grass. High above them, so high they couldn't even see it, a skylark sang its triumphant song as it tumbled in the air.

Nat lay beside her. She reached for his hand.

'You're the best thing in my life,' she said.

'You're the best thing in mine. Whatever happens about you being pregnant, let's stay together forever. I am never going to leave you,' said Nat. 'I want to be with you for the rest of my life. You *are* my life.'

Nat raised himself up onto his elbow and looked down into Dani's face. She tried to look up at him but the sun was too bright and she had to squint. But even squinting wasn't ideal so instead she closed her eyes.

'Dani.' Nat cleared his throat. She could tell it was a portentous moment. 'Dani, will you marry me?'

Dani kept her eyes closed as she told Nat, 'Yes.'

Nat made a ring from three blades of grass plaited together and tied it around Dani's finger.

'With this ring,' he said.

'It's perfect.'

'I'm going to get you a massive diamond. Just you see.'

'I don't need a massive diamond. I only need you.'

'You've got me. You'll never get rid of me now. So, when are we going to do it?' Nat asked.

'What?'

'Actually get married.'

'Shouldn't we find out if I'm pregnant for sure?'

'We could do it right away.'

'How? I'm not eighteen yet, Nat. Mum and Dad won't let it happen.'

'That wouldn't matter if we went to Scotland.'

'Why would we go to Scotland?'

'Gretna Green.'

'Are you serious?'

'I want you to be my wife as soon as possible,' Nat said. 'Nothing has ever felt so right! Let's do it, Dani. Let's elope. It will be an adventure. And then nothing and no one can come between us. Even if we have to be miles apart for our courses, we'll know that what we have is real. You'll be Mrs Hayward and I'll be the happiest man on earth.'

He took both of Dani's hands in his and made her stop and look at him.

'And I'd be the happiest woman,' she said.

'Then I'll sort it out,' said Nat.

She loved Nat. She loved him more than she had ever loved anyone. More than she ever imagined she could love anyone. When Nat was sad, she was sad. When he was happy, she was walking on air.

Her parents would come round to the idea. Their getting married wasn't going to change anything. Not really. They were still both going to go to university. But it meant that when they were at home during the holidays, they could be properly together – either at Nat's family home or hers – without their parents feeling weird about letting them stay in the same room.

Dani was not the sort of girl who had spent her childhood dreaming of a perfect princess wedding. If she thought about getting married at all, she imagined something like the elopement Nat was suggesting. Though to a desert island rather than a cold Scottish border town. And yet . . .

She thought she felt something flip inside her like a small tadpole. She was definitely pregnant. She didn't need a test to know.

They agreed to go to Scotland in two days.

Nat withdrew five hundred pounds of the money he had been saving for university. He bought Dani a dress for the ceremony. It was the dress she had admired in the window of The Rainbow Shop. The one that looked as though it had been made from an actual rainbow, plucked out of the sky and turned into a skein of chiffon. He spent two hundred pounds on an engagement ring, which he presented to her when they met at the train station on Saturday morning.

'It's just a chip of a diamond,' he said. 'And you're worth a diamond as big as the Ritz. I will buy you one. When we're rich.'

Dani nodded.

'You're really quiet,' said Nat.

'It's a big moment,' Dani told him. 'I want to savour every minute.'

'Good.'

In reality, Dani was feeling oddly homesick, as though she really was running away for good and would never, ever see her hometown or her parents again. Her stomach churned and rumbled. Her head ached. Her eyes pricked and burned with tears. She wanted to say, 'I can't do this.' But maybe the nausea was because she was carrying his baby.

They got as far as Wolverhampton, where they had to change trains. Nat studied the departures board to find out which platform they wanted next. Dani told him she needed the loo. She didn't. What she needed was to be alone.

But Dani was in the cubicle for such a long time that eventually she decided she did want to pee after all.

A red spot swirled in the water.

The tears came again but this time there was no doubt. What she felt was relief.

Back in the ladies' room, the tension of the journey so far finally broke through. Dani leaned against the tampax machine and cried. A woman in her thirties asked if she was OK.

Dani shook her head.

'I need some help,' she said.

The tale came tumbling out. 'Everything is just happening too fast. I love Nat but I really don't want to get married. Not yet.'

'Then you mustn't,' said her new friend. 'What does your boyfriend look like? I'll go and talk to him if you like.'

'Would you?'

'Of course. He sounds like a nice guy. I'm sure he'll understand. You'll work it out. You can always get married when you finish university. Sounds like a much better idea to me. You stay here. I'll go and have a chat with him and when he's got his head around it, I'll come and fetch you and the two of you can work out what to do next.'

Dani watched her guardian angel head out to the concourse. She waited for three minutes then followed her through the exit and tried to see what was going on.

She could see her with Nat. He was where she had left him, only now he was sitting on the floor with his rucksack between his knees. He had his head in his hands. Dani knew at once that he would be crying and every cell in her body wanted to rush to his side and comfort him, tell him that she was just having a moment of madness. Of course she wanted to be with him. Of course she wanted to marry him.

But it wasn't true and perhaps this was her one chance to make her escape.

So instead of going to comfort Nat or even trying to explain in person, she slipped past and got on the next train south. It was the wrong train and she had to change three times to get back to Exeter but her relief grew with every mile that passed.

Dani was back home before eight in the evening. Her parents, assuming that she'd been at work all day, barely even looked up from the television when she walked into the sitting room.

'There's lasagne in the fridge,' said Jane. 'Warm some up for yourself. There's salad too.'

'Thanks.'

It was the most surreal moment in Dani's life. That morning, she had left the house with a rucksack, thinking that she was pregnant and that she might not be back for months. Yet here she was. Her parents hadn't noticed anything. Nat hadn't even called to find out where she'd gone.

Dani saw Nat just one more time after that.

She didn't tell her parents where she'd been and neither did Nat. They met up in The Sailor's Trousers – the pub they would unwittingly visit with their dogs years later – neutral ground to go over what hadn't happened and whether anything could ever happen again.

As Dani walked up to the table, Nat could hardly look at her. He stared into his pint.

'I thought you loved me,' he said.

'I did. I do!' Dani added emphatically.

'Then why . . .'

'I don't know. Because I was scared.'

'Why were you scared?'

'We're so young . . .'

'You didn't trust my feelings for you.'

'People change.'

'And you thought I would?'

'We don't know, do we? Where was the harm in waiting? If we're meant to be together for the rest of our lives, a couple more years won't make any difference.'

Dani was pleading for a second chance. That they need not break up just because they hadn't made it to Gretna. But Nat still wouldn't look at her. He picked up a beer mat and started to shred it, just as he had done the first time they went out together alone. On the night they first made love.

This was different.

'Dani, if you don't know me by now, you will never know me.'

'Isn't that a song?' Dani tried to lighten the mood.

Nat wasn't having it.

'I was willing to give you everything. You had my body, my heart, my soul.'

'You've still got mine.'

'No, I haven't. Not really. And you know it. I can't keep seeing you, Dani, because every time I do, I'll be reminded of the difference between what I feel for you and what you feel for me.'

'Oh Nat. Come on. Don't be so dramatic.'

'I'm telling the truth. What we had can never be the

same. You don't get a second chance at once in a life-time.'

'Well, if that's the way you feel.'

'It is.'

'I think you're being ridiculous.'

'I'm protecting my heart.'

Dani snorted. She slid the engagement ring Nat had bought with his savings across the table.

'I'll pay you back for this and the dress,' she said.

'Good luck,' Nat said, looking straight at her at last. Dani could no longer see any love in his eyes. He walked out, leaving her sitting alone. She thought she would never see him again.

' . . . so you see,' she told Flossie, 'I was once every bit as young and crazy as you were. And I didn't back out of the wedding for any lack of love. Not at all. I backed out because my feelings for Nat were so strong. I was confused. It was all happening so quickly. I've spent the past twenty-two years wanting to make it right. Wanting Nat to know that I did love him. Those feelings were absolutely real.'

Flossie wiped her eyes with the back of her sleeve.

'Thank you, Mum. Thank you. Are you going to tell Nat how you really felt now?'

'I don't think I'll ever have the chance to speak to him again.'

'You could call him right now.'

'I've done enough damage as it is.'

Chapter Sixty-Six

Dani didn't text Nat again. Not after the apology she'd sent on the night of the wedding-that-wasn't. She knew that single text had been delivered but it was still showing as unread. She pictured Nat seeing the message come in and deciding to ignore it. Perhaps he had deleted it without reading. Who would have blamed him for that?

The only window Dani had into Nat's world was via Lola's social media. But Lola hadn't posted anything much. No photographs that would really give Dani any insight into her state of mind. Just one thing on the day of the wedding itself. A sunset with a quote overlaid. 'What doesn't kill us makes us stronger.'

What did that mean? It mentioned 'us'. Not 'me'. Dani took it to mean that Nat and Lola were working things out. The cancelled wedding was not going to be the end of them. They were going to work through their difficulties and emerge on the other side as a happier couple. Strengthened by their ordeal. They were going to make it. Together.

She checked Will's Instagram too. Not much useful info there. A couple of sunsets taken from the sea front. Were they melancholy sea-scapes?

'Mum,' said Flossie, when she caught Dani on-line.

'You've got to stop stalking them. You've got to do what I've done with Jed. Stop looking.'

'Sometimes,' said Dani. 'You're incredibly wise.'

Life went on. Jezza still needed walking. Dani and Flossie usually took him out together on Sundays.

'Duckpool Bay?' Dani suggested, one Sunday in late October.

Flossie shook her head. 'I've got coursework, Mum.' She was enjoying her first term at sixth form college. But Jezza had to be walked. Dani pulled out her puffa jacket. She hated that moment in every year when she had to get out her winter coat. She knew she would be wearing it until April at the earliest. Maybe even beyond.

Fortunately, Jezza was excited to be out whatever the weather. Evan was right about Jezza's poodle heritage. He couldn't resist a puddle. Though strangely he was still fiercely resistant to having a bath.

It was the time of year when dogs were allowed on the main beach. The one dominated by the pier. Dani and Jezza made the most of it. He needed a run. She needed to breathe in the sea air and let it fill her lungs, taking her sadness with it when she breathed out again.

When they got onto the sand, she unclipped Jezza's lead. He was soon off, chasing after a seagull that had dared to come to rest. It was a wild sort of day. No point yelling after him, Dani soon realised as the wind whipped the words right out of her mouth and tossed them away.

Jezza ran, his tongue lolling out the side of his mouth

as he chased after the birds he would never catch. The braver ones let him get close before they lifted into the air and out of reach, coming to land again just a few metres away, unruffled and unperturbed.

There was no point trying to put up an umbrella in such terrible weather.

Dani watched a couple a little further down the beach, battling against the wind. The woman tucked herself into the man's side, using him as a windbreak. Dani felt a twinge in her heart as she watched them make their unsteady way across the sand. She put up the hood of her coat and pulled the drawstring tight around her face.

There was a lone figure by the pier. He stood with his hands in his pockets, watching the kite-surfers jousting with the waves.

Dani didn't need to see his face to know who he was. She didn't need to see his dog, who was digging a hole in the sand.

And Jezza was heading in their direction.

'Jezza,' Dani hissed, hoping that Jezza's bat senses would pick up her call against the wind. 'Jezza!' she tried again.

But he was running on. His ears streaming behind him like banners. He would not come back for anyone. Even if he could hear them call.

As Jezza skidded to a halt beside him, Nat leaned down to stroke the dog's ears.

'Shall we go to The Sailor's Trousers?' Nat asked Dani when she caught up with him.

Dani felt relief flood her body.

'Yeah.'

Chapter Sixty-Seven

At last, Dani found out what really happened the day of the wedding-that-wasn't.

'I knew that Lola was upset about more than paw prints on her dress,' Nat said. 'She was hysterical.'

'I'm not surprised. We ruined your wedding.'

'No. It was more than that.'

Nat's story echoed Jane's opinion. 'If what had really mattered was getting married and being with me, then a bit of dirt on the front of her dress wouldn't have mattered. It would have been something to laugh about. A crazy anecdote to relive with our friends and families in years to come. She could have brushed the skirt down, gone out through the back door of the church and come in through the front again. But she didn't want that.'

'Some brides get very worked up about having the whole day perfect,' Dani said.

'Of course. But Lola didn't really want to get married. Not to me, anyway.'

'How did you feel?' Dani asked.

Nat looked down into his terrible coffee. 'Honestly? I felt completely calm. I heard her saying the words and everyone was looking at me like they expected me to go berserk but all I could think was "that's that then". Her father went crazy, of course. I understand the choir had to sing the Hallelujah chorus to cover the shouting – but eventually the vicar got him to calm down and

373

the verger ushered us all out of the back while the vicar let the congregation know what was happening.

'That was the last time I saw Lola. We agreed that she would stay in the house and I would move back in with Mum and Dad while everything was sorted out. Will was there to help her, of course. He was there all along. Even on her hen do.

'Lola and I met when we were both at a low ebb. I was worried about my father. She'd just seen her grandfather die. We both needed comfort. We shouldn't have been anything more to each other than a flirtation but there was a sense that we should make it something more because we both needed to know that life wasn't just about endings.

'She should have been with Will all along. They're made for each other, those two. I only hope Lola's father can come round to the idea.'

'He loves her, doesn't he?'

'Yes. And she loves him.'

'Two jiltings in one lifetime has to be something of a record,' said Nat then. 'But I can tell you now that it definitely didn't feel so bad the second time around. Nowhere near.'

'I suppose everything gets easier with practice,' Dani tried to joke.

'Or maybe it's just that this time I knew for sure that it was for the best. More than anything, when Lola said she wanted to call the wedding off for good, I felt a sense of enormous relief. Whereas the first time . . . The first time I knew I'd lost something really special.'

Dani felt tears prick at her eyes.

'Don't say that,' she said.

'But it's true. For years I told myself that I'd been wrong about you and that your decision not to get married was a lucky break for both of us. We were young and we were stupid and we were bound to have grown apart as we got older. But then I met you again and saw that you hadn't really changed at all. And you spoke to the part of me that hadn't changed either. When I was with you, all that youthful enthusiasm I once had for life came rushing back. I felt alive again after years of living my life with the volume down. I realised that no matter what I had achieved, something was always missing, unless you were there too.'

Dani twisted in her chair. She could hardly bear to hear what Nat was saying.

'This grotty old pub. This is where we said goodbye all those years ago, isn't it?'

Dani nodded.

'That day when you asked me for a second chance and I refused to give it.'

Dani nodded again.

'I was wrong. I was so wrong to be so hard on you and give you no choice but to walk away. I should have opened my arms to you and told you that no matter what we'd said and done in the past, I couldn't see my future without you. I should have pushed through any notion of being humiliated by what had happened and found the love inside.'

'I don't blame you,' said Dani.

'So this is where we said goodbye. Can it be where we say "hello" again?'

Nat reached for Dani's hands across the table.

The landlord swept up their glasses.

'We do have rooms upstairs,' he said.

Chapter Sixty-Eight

By Christmas, Flossie had forgotten all about Jed. She had a new boyfriend. Dani was pleased to hear that Luke was in Flossie's class at sixth form college. He was serious about his studies and he was no stranger to deodorant and soap.

'Is it love?' Dani asked her daughter.

'Mum,' said Flossie. 'I'm too young to know that.'

Auntie Sarah had come off Tinder because she'd met her match. Or rather, re-met her match. One afternoon she discovered that her ex-husband Adam had swiped right on her so she swiped him back. And gave up wearing Fracas again.

Over the months since the sponsored dog walk, Jane had thought a great deal about what Evan the vet had to say about dogs and love. About how the heartbreak of losing a pet made you certain you would never be able to go through it again. The love and the loss. But then you realised that you had to.

Perhaps Evan's theory could be applied to human love too.

Bill Hunter's face was a picture when Jane walked back into the pet shop and invited him over for supper.

Acknowledgments

Another year, another book. Did I say that last year? Anyway, as usual, I couldn't have done it without the support of dozens of people.

At Hodder, Emily Kitchin and Madeleine Woodfield worked especially hard to turn this book around at short notice. Thank you both. Thank you Alice Morley, Louise Swannell and Jenni Leech for your sterling PR work. Thank you, copy-editor Helen Parham, for catching all my spelling mistakes. And thank you Jo Myler, for a wonderful new cover look. Thank you also to Laetitia Rutherford and Megan Carroll at Watson Little.

In what has occasionally been a crappy old year chez Manby, I'm especially grateful for the love of my friends. Victoria Routledge, Jane Wright and Alex Potter, thank you for listening, for making me laugh, and for holding my hand through the dark parts. A special mention also has to go to Jane Ayres, Kirsten Hesketh and Moira Please, who lifted my spirits more than they could know with tea, cake and unicorns, while I finished a final edit.

As always, I'd like to thank my family. Mum, Kate, Lee, Harrison and Lukas. You're the best. And Mark. Still there. Still putting up with me. Still making the tea in the morning. Thank you for everything.

April 2018

Do you wish this wasn't the end?

Join us at www.hodder.co.uk, or follow us on
Twitter @hodderbooks to be a part of our community
of people who love the very best in books and reading.

Whether you want to discover more about a book
or an author, watch trailers and interviews, have the
chance to win early limited editions, or simply browse
our expert readers' selection of the very best books,
we think you'll find what you're looking for.

And if you don't,
that's the place to tell us what's missing.

We love what we do, and we'd love you to be part of it.

www.hodder.co.uk

 @hodderbooks

 HodderBooks

 HodderBooks